Praise for Spencer Quinn

"Suspenseful, laugh-out-loud funny in places, and surprisingly tender." —Stephen King on *Of Mutts and Men*

"Delightful . . . Dog lovers won't want to miss this one." —*Publishers Weekly* on *Heart of Barkness*

"A match made in heaven. Would that we all were as infallible in our dogs' eyes as Bernie is in Chet's." —Susan Wilson, *New York Times* bestselling author of *What a Dog Knows*

"Cleverly plotted . . . Chet is a source of wisdom and innate doggie joie de vivre, making this a real pleasure for anyone who has ever looked into a dog's eyes and asked: Who's a good boy?" —*Publishers Weekly* on *Tender Is the Bite*

"A sterling tale of love between a man and his dog . . . Amusing and introspective." —*Kirkus Reviews* on *Of Mutts and Men*

"Even readers unfamiliar with earlier titles will enjoy this quick, engaging tale.... . Most will find the humor and charm to be icing on the smart whodunit cake." —*Library Journal* (starred review) on *Tender Is the Bite*

Other Books in the Chet and Bernie Series

It's a WONDERFUL WOOF

A CHET & BERNIE MYSTERY

Spencer Quinn

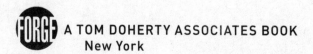
FORGE A TOM DOHERTY ASSOCIATES BOOK
New York

IT'S A WONDERFUL WOOF

Copyright © 2021 by Pas de Deux

A Forge Book
Published by Tom Doherty Associates
120 Broadway
New York, NY 10271

www.tor-forge.com

Forge® is a registered trademark of Macmillan Publishing Group, LLC.

The Library of Congress has cataloged the hardcover edition as follows:

Names: Quinn, Spencer, author.
Title: It's a wonderful woof / Spencer Quinn.
Other titles: It is a wonderful woof
Description: First edition. | New York : Forge, 2021. | Series: A Chet &
    Bernie mystery; book 12 | "A Tom Doherty Associates book."
Identifiers: LCCN 2021028490 (print) | LCCN 2021028491 (ebook) |
    ISBN 9781250770325 (hardcover) | ISBN 9781250770356 (ebook)
Subjects: GSAFD: Mystery fiction. | Suspense fiction.
Classification: LCC PS3617.U584 I77 2021 (print) | LCC PS3617.U584
    (ebook) | DDC 813/.6—dc23
LC record available at https://lccn.loc.gov/2021028490
LC ebook record available at https://lccn.loc.gov/2021028491

ISBN 978-1-250-77036-3 (trade paperback)

Our books may be purchased in bulk for promotional, educational, or
business use. Please contact your local bookseller or the Macmillan Corporate
and Premium Sales Department at 1-800-221-7945, extension 5442, or by
email at MacmillanSpecialMarkets@macmillan.com.

First Forge Paperback Edition: 2022

Printed in the United States of America

0 9 8 7 6 5 4 3 2 1

For Owen

IT'S A WONDERFUL WOOF

One

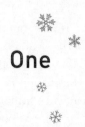

The Muertos throw the best Christmas party in the whole Valley. The Valley's where we live, me and Bernie. It goes on forever in all directions, and is almost certainly in Arizona, based on things I hear from time to time. That's not important. Is it important that the Muertos are the roughest, toughest biker gang around? Maybe to you, but not to us. The Little Detective Agency deals with the roughest and toughest every day. Little is Bernie's last name, I'm Chet, pure and simple, and the agency's just the two of us. Why would we need anyone else? That's the important part.

The Muertos party takes place in their clubhouse and lasts for several days, but we usually leave before dawn on the first night. It gets pretty noisy what with the motorcycle races up and down the big staircase to the second floor, and a sort of dance on motorcycles to a tune called the hora, I believe, which I knew from a bat mitzvah where I'd come upon a forgotten tray of steak tip canapes, our departure following soon after.

Right now, as we made our way to the door, the hora amped down and Junior Ruiz, president of the Muertos, began zooming around in tight circles on his giant Harley with his wife on his shoulders and his mother on her shoulders. He braked to a stop beside us, revved the engine once or twice, and over its roar yelled, "Wanna climb up on Mama, Bernie?"

"Um," said Bernie, "I don't really—"

"Aw come on, Bernie," Mama called down. "Where's your sense of fun?"

"Very nice of you, given the history, but—"

"History? What history?"

"Didn't you end up doing eighteen months at Northern State?"

"Turned out as only three on account of overcrowding. Three months I can do in my sleep."

"Which is actually how it went down, no?" said Junior's wife.

Mama, up on Junior's wife's shoulders, if I haven't made that clear, gave Junior's wife a sort of kick in the sides with the heels of her white cowboy boots, like she was on horseback. Junior's wife did not look like a horse. She actually looked a lot like Mama, except younger and not quite so jiggly.

"Watch your mouth, girl," Mama said. "And besides, Bernie, I'll never forget how nicely you busted me—especially the way Chet grabbed my pant leg, so gently."

Grabbing perps by the pant leg is how we close our cases, me doing the grabbing and Bernie standing by with the cuffs. I checked out Mama's pants and wouldn't you know? They were the exact same pants she'd been wearing that day, red leather with golden leather fringes! I remembered the taste of those golden fringes so well! Have you ever noticed how the taste of something—or even the memory of the taste—makes long-ago happenings suddenly pop up in your mind like they were just yesterday? It all came back to me: Mama lighting the fuse, the door blowing off the safe, Mama reaching inside with a lovely look on her face, so excited and alive, which was when we showed up. There's a lot of fun to be had in this business. A strong breeze started up behind me. In practically no time I figured out it was my tail, feeling tip-top and letting all our Muertos buddies know. I couldn't wait for . . . for whatever was going to happen after now.

A moment or two later we were out in the street, a dark alley, in fact, and in the sketchiest part of South Pedroia, which is the sketchiest part of town. The sky was dim and pinkish, no moon, no stars, a typical Valley night sky. Bernie glanced back at the door to the clubhouse.

"There's your holiday spirit, Chet," Bernie said. "No grudges. Instead—forgiveness. Maybe not standard biker philosophy but isn't that all the more reason to value it?" I had no idea, didn't understand the question. But it was about bikers and I understood them very well, so no worries.

"Is forgiving possible without forgetting?" Bernie went on. He smiled at me, a pinkish smile that was a bit scary. "You're the expert on forgiving. Fill me in."

Forgiving? A new one on me. I was very familiar with forgetting of course, could forget like you wouldn't believe. My takeaway? I was a good, good boy.

We turned the corner, which led to another alley, darker and sketchier than the one we'd been on. Our ride—a Porsche, but not the old one that had gone off a cliff, or the other old one that got blown up, but the oldest one of all, with martini glasses painted on the fenders—sat at the end of the block, in a cone of light shining from a rooftop lamp. In between us and it, we had some sort of commotion going on. We picked up the pace and headed toward the action, our MO when it comes to trouble ahead.

At first it looked like this particular commotion was all about two shadows—one big, one small—dancing a choppy kind of dance, but as we closed in we saw it was a real big dude beating up a real little one. The big dude backhanded the tiny dude across the face and the tiny dude went flying. He landed on his back, snatched up a trash can lid and held it like a shield, closing his eyes. Closing his eyes? How was that going to help? The big dude whisked the trash can lid out of his hands and flung it away. Here's something I've noticed: You may be eager for whatever's coming next, but it's very hard to predict in this life. For example, who would have guessed that the trash can lid would now be spinning through the air just like a Frisbee! Who could blame himself for what followed? Not me, amigo. I charged after that trash can lid, sprang up, actually too high—I love when that happens—and snagged it on my way back down.

After that I trotted over to Bernie as I always do with a freshly caught Frisbee. Only . . . only a trash can lid is not a Frisbee, and Bernie was not waiting to take it, a happy smile on his face, but was turned the other way, trying to haul the big dude off the tiny one. The big dude didn't like that. He jumped to his feet, drew back his fist, got ready to launch an enormous roundhouse punch.

Oh dear. That was my thought at the moment. Not "oh dear" on account of Bernie being in trouble and there I was, his partner, standing by with a trash can lid in my mouth—although let me point out that I quickly dropped the trash can lid and got right back to looking like a total pro. But my "oh dear" was more about disappointment at the big guy's technique. An enormous windup like his meant the fight was already over. Bernie stepped inside and threw that sweet, sweet uppercut. Click! Right on the point of a too-large chin. Not bang or boom, but simply a click, very neat and tidy. Then came the part I love the best, how speedily Bernie's fist gets back to the starting position, just as speedy as the actual punch or even speedier, in case another uppercut was needed—which would still be a first, in my experience. Meanwhile the big guy's eyes were rolling up and he was slumping down, one of those interesting sights you see in our line of work. And all at once I understood what humans meant when they said they were having an up and down kind of day! Wow! You could learn so much in this life just by being there.

I trotted over to the big guy and barked, not loudly, simply sending a message. *I'm here too, buddy boy.* Bernie glanced over at me and now came that happy smile. "Can't believe you caught that thing," he said. "One of your very best."

So I'd done good after all! What a break, just one lucky day after another, starting with the day I'd met Bernie, which was also the same day I'd washed out of K-9 school—and on the very last test, namely leaping, my very best thing! How had that happened? Was a cat somehow involved? I thought so, but the details had grown dim. None of that mattered. We were partners, me and Bernie, case closed. Whoa! Aren't cases closed with me grabbing the perp by the pant leg? For just a second I had the crazy idea of grabbing Bernie's! No way I could let that happen, so in order to direct my teeth into something good and useful, I turned to the big dude. Still in dreamland. Was there any point in grabbing his pant leg? Not that I could see. I was a bit confused. My tail drooped. Oh no! I got it back up there, and in no uncertain terms. At that point, Bernie looked down at the tiny dude and this strange confused interlude went pop like a soap bubble. The fun I've had chasing those around! But no time for that now.

Bernie bent down, looked closer. "Victor?" he said. "Is that you?"

My goodness! Victor Klovsky, for sure. He had an inky smell you didn't run into often with humans, except for old ones, and Victor wasn't old. He had a scruffy beard without a trace of white, a narrow face, now somewhat mashed up, and, behind the thick lenses of his glasses, eyes that were always on the nervous side. Right now the glasses weren't quite in place, but were kind of twisted and hung off one ear. He'd looked a lot better the last time I'd seen him, at the Great Western Private Eye Convention where Bernie had given the keynote speech. Easy to remember since Victor was one of the few remaining in the audience when Bernie's speech came to an end. Wait. I take that back. There was still a big big audience. I just happened to spot Victor in the crowd. The point is that Victor is in the same business as we are! Sort of.

"Bernie?" he said. "What are you doing here?"

"Right back atcha." Bernie removed Victor's glasses, straightened them out, gently replaced them on Victor's face.

Victor blinked a couple of times and then groaned. It hurt him to blink? You didn't see that every day. There are a lot of tough guys and gals in our line of work. Victor wasn't one of them.

"I'm on a case." Victor sounded a little annoyed. "What else would I be doing?"

"I thought your MO was all about working online and then calling in Valley PD for the heavy lift—um, for the mopping up."

"I'm branching out," Victor said. He wiped his nose on the back of his hand, saw a faint reddish smear. His eyes opened wide. "Oh my god—I'm bleeding!"

Bernie peered closer. "It doesn't actually look too—"

Victor grabbed Bernie's wrist. The sight of Victor's small, delicate hand wrapped around—or partly wrapped around—Bernie's mighty wrist said something to me. I didn't know what but at the same time knew I would never forget it. Funny how the mind works.

"Bernie! Am I lacerated? Do I need stiches?"

"Don't know about lacerated," Bernie said. "I'm not even sure of the definition, but—"

"Lacerate, for god's sake, from the Latin laceratio, a tearing, rending, mutilation. Bernie! Am I mutilated? Tell me the truth! I can take it!" Victor's eyes filled with tears.

Bernie glanced around, patted his pockets, ended up ripping off a small strip from the hem of his shirt, the Hawaiian shirt with the surfing cats, my least favorite of Bernie's Hawaiian shirts. He folded the strip in half and pressed it lightly to the side of Victor's nose.

"Ouch!" said Victor.

"Just hold it there like that," Bernie said. "You're going to be fine."

Victor placed his hand on a surfing cat, took over the pressing from Bernie. He winced but didn't say ouch again.

"Who's your friend?" Bernie said, pointing his chin at the big dude, lying in the alley, chest rising and falling peacefully.

"He's no friend," said Victor. "Turns out he's a dangerous criminal."

"Want me to cuff him?"

"Hmm," Victor said. "Hadn't thought of that. Would it be legal?"

Bernie gave Victor a long look. "I'll take responsibility. Got cuffs on you?"

"On me? You mean on my person in the here and now? Afraid not. I don't actually own any. Should I?"

"The plastic kind works fine," Bernie said. He took a pair of cuffs from his back pocket, flipped the big guy over on his front, got him nice and cuffed in no time. Then he sat down beside Victor, resting his back against the brick wall. I sat, too, but much closer to the big guy.

"Is there a warrant out for him?" Bernie said.

"Oh, definitely. Although I didn't know that at the time.

Meaning when I took the case. He's an email scammer, preys mostly on little old ladies. A lot of my business is about tracking down guys like that."

"So most of your clients are little old ladies?"

"They feel humiliated. It's an eye-opener for some of them, brings out a sort of hidden ferocity. I'm on eggshells twenty-four seven. But with this guy it turned out the scamming was more of a fill in between jobs. He's a truck hijacker, liquor trucks especially."

Bernie shot Victor a sideways glance. "So what are you doing in a place like this with a guy like that?"

"Like I said, I'm branching out. I was planning on bringing him in. There's a ten-thousand-dollar reward from the state Longhauler's Association. Nothing to sneeze at."

And sure enough neither of them sneezed. It turned out I was following this back and forth rather well, a bit of a surprise.

"You were planning to bring him in without cuffs?"

"I confess it slipped my mind." Victor lowered his voice. "But I'm armed, Bernie."

"Oh?"

Victor shifted slightly, a movement that made him groan. "Stupid thing got stuck in my back pocket. That's when the situation began to deteriorate."

"You have a firearm stuck in your back pocket?"

"Duly licensed."

"Is the safety on?"

"You push it forward for that? Or is it the other way?"

"How did you get into this business?" Bernie said.

"I'm a researcher par excellence," said Victor. "It seemed like a logical extension."

"Roll over," Bernie told him. "Slow and easy."

"Huh? What are you trying to do?"

"Clear that weapon from your pocket without killing anyone," Bernie said.

No worries. It turned out that Victor's gun was loaded backward, so no one could have gotten killed anyway. Next Victor discovered his phone had no service in this part of town, so Bernie lent him ours to call in. As soon as we heard the sirens, Bernie rose. I rose with him.

"Where are you going?" Victor said.

"Home," said Bernie. "It's late."

"But . . . but don't you want to stay for the denouement?"

Whatever that was about delighted Bernie. A real big laugh just burst out of him. I jumped right up and got my paws on his chest, pretty delighted myself for no reason I could have explained.

"It's your case," Bernie said. "Merry Christmas and . . . and . . ."

"Get back to doing what I do best?" said Victor.

"Something like that."

"Good advice," Victor said. "Taking it a little further, have you ever considered hiring anyone, especially of the information-era type?"

Bernie shook his head.

"Doesn't it get a bit lonely, working all by yourself?"

"All by myself?" Bernie said. He didn't get it. Neither did I. The big guy's eyes fluttered open, checked things out, fluttered closed. Bernie went over to him, crouched down, and spoke quietly in his ear, an ear of what I believe is called the cauliflower type. "Don't even consider getting up."

Not long after that we were in the Porsche and headed into what remained of the night, just one of the many things *we* do best. The sound of the sirens faded down to nothing, but then popped up in another part of town. There's lots of danger in this world, which was exactly what Bernie had told Ms. Pernick, our accountant, when she asked him to describe our business plan. Ms. Pernick had opened her eyes wide and shook her head, a human combo that comes before they say, "Wow!" Although in this case Ms. Pernick had left it unsaid.

Two

"Ten days till Christmas," Bernie said. "Anything special you want?"

"Teach me how to drive," said Charlie.

"How old are you again?"

"Dad!"

"Not yet seven, I believe?"

"Almost."

"And what's the driving age in this state?"

"I don't want a license. I just want to drive."

"Why?" said Bernie.

"Why I want to drive?" Charlie said. "Come on, Dad." He raised his hands like they were on a steering wheel and said, "Vroom vroom."

Some humans are easier to understand than others, in my experience. Of all the humans I've met, Charlie is the very easiest to understand, which makes the fact that we only have him some weekends, and either Thanksgiving or Christmas depending on something or other, even harder. But right then it came to me that since Thanksgiving was over—how could I ever forget the gravy . . . what would you call it? Incident, perhaps? Good enough. The point being that Thanksgiving was over—and the incident would be soon forgotten and that antique tureen or whatever it was replaced—but Christmas had not yet come, so this had to be a weekend. Wow! Had I done a so-therefore, usually Bernie's department, me bringing other things to the table? I kind of thought I had. What would it be like to . . . to be human? My goodness. What an amazing idea! I just stood where I was—which happened to be out on the patio, and for some reason facing the side fence and rather close to it—possibly with my mouth hanging open. From what seemed like far away, I heard Bernie say, "We'll have to think about it."

"Who's we?" said Charlie.

"That's the first thing we'll have to think about," Bernie said.

"You and Mom?"

"That's one possibility."

"Why?"

"She's your mom."

"But you're divorced."

"That doesn't change anything when it comes to decisions about you."

"What about Daddy Malcolm?"

"What about him?"

"Is he in on it, too?"

"Maybe."

"He can't have kids."

"No?"

"He got tied off."

"Tied off?"

"That's when they make a knot in your pee-pee. Then you can't have kids."

Bernie said nothing.

"It must hurt but he never says ow," Charlie said.

"The, um, truth of the matter," Bernie began, but before he could go on, Charlie said, "Hey, Dad. How come Chet stands like that sometimes, facing the fence?"

I turned my head and looked at them over my shoulder. They were both watching me.

"I've wondered about that," Bernie said. "It's a mystery. I suppose it could be—"

That sounded so promising. But just then I heard a car out front, pulling into the driveway. I trotted through the back doorway and into the house, so I never found out why I was doing that standing-in-front-of-a-fence thing. Don't forget security is my job at our place, which is on the canyon side of Mesquite Road, by the way, nicest street in the Valley. I should also point out that even if the back door had been closed, I could have gotten in. The handle is the kind humans open with their thumb. Bernie and I have been working on doors, and it turns out that paws can be as good as thumbs, or even better. No offense.

Meanwhile I was in the front hall just before the doorbell rang. I barked a special bark I have for this situation, a combo of letting Bernie know we've got company and letting the company know what's what. Bernie and Charlie came up behind me and Bernie opened the door.

A small man stood outside. He smelled very interesting, partly from the flower in the lapel of his dark suit, partly from something he'd used to slick back his hair, partly from whatever he'd sprayed—and sprayed heavily—in his armpits.

"Bernie Little, private investigator?" he said.

"That's me," said Bernie.

The small man's eyes—very big and very bright, went to me, then Charlie, and back to me. I knew right away that he was not comfortable with me and my kind. A real smelly guy? That was good. Not a fan of the nation within the nation, as Bernie calls us? That was bad. We were off to a middle-of-the-road type start.

"Perhaps this is not your place of doing business?" the small man said.

"It is," Bernie said.

"Well, then," said the small man, rubbing his hands together, soft hands with a big purple ring on one finger, "since I have business to discuss, may I enter? I am Lauritz Vogner, at your service."

Bernie hesitated. Why? Didn't we need the business? The Little Detective Agency is very successful, especially if we leave out the finances part. And that would have been off the charts, except for the Hawaiian pants issue. We'd invented the product! Unless I was missing something. But now all the Hawaiian pants in the world were in our self-storage in South Pedroia, actually not far from where we'd run into Victor Klovsky. "Why," Bernie often says after a bourbon or two or more, "Hawaiian shirts but not Hawaiian pants? It makes no sense." And there you have an example of Bernie's brilliance. *It makes no sense.* Presto, and everything murky is clear. But that's Bernie. Just when you think he's done amazing you, he amazes you again. For example, he almost got us out of the Hawaiian pants hole in one fell swoop, whatever that is, exactly, namely with the Bolivian tin futures play. If only that earthquake hadn't happened! Or the earthquake that hadn't happened had. Or maybe both. But the point was we'd come so close!

"Ah," Lauritz Vogner was saying, "is it that you do not work on weekends?"

"Ha," Bernie said.

"'Ha' is meaning . . . ?"

"We work weekends." Bernie glanced at Charlie, then turned back to Lauritz. "Mind waiting here for a moment?"

"Here before the door?" said Lauritz.

"Um," Bernie said, and closed the door in Lauritz's face, but very slowly and softly. "Charlie?" he said. "How about playing in your room for a bit?"

"Playing what?"

"You've got toys in there."

"I've outgrown them."

Bernie gazed down at Charlie. Charlie gazed up at him. That gaze! It was a Bernie gaze, but just littler. For an instant—a very scary instant—I felt like I was about to see the future. But before that could happen, Bernie said, "You could read a book."

"What book?"

"You like the pirate one."

"I'm bored of it."

"Bored of pirates?"

"Dad! I've read it a billion times. I know it by heart."

"Oh? Then what's Davy Jones's locker?"

"Where sailors drown at the bottom of the sea," said Charlie. "Dad?"

"Yeah?"

Charlie lowered his voice. "Think that guy has a gun on him?"

Bernie put his hand on Charlie's shoulder. "Here's what I need you to do right now—take Chet out on the patio and play the wall ball game. He loves that."

True. I love the wall ball game. The way it works is someone—namely Bernie but sometimes Charlie—throws a ball. Tennis balls work best but lacrosse balls do the job, the only problem with lacrosse balls being their wonderful mouthfeel which makes them hard to give up, as you may or may not know. The thrower flings the ball so it bounces on the patio floor and then caroms off the tall gate at the back, where it spins high in the air and I, Chet, leap even higher and snatch it on the way down, sometimes twisting right around before landing. Then I drop the ball at the feet of the thrower—especially if it's a tennis ball—and we do it again and again until the cows come home, as humans say. But they never do since we have no cows at our place on Mesquite Road. A very good thing, cows being almost as stubborn as mules, in my experience. You think to yourself, *Come on, ladies, shake a leg, let's get a move on,* but they never do. Back to the wall ball game, which I love. I did not want to play wall ball at the moment. We had a possible customer waiting at the door. Work comes before play. That's one of our rules at the Little Detective Agency. I got ready to sit down and make myself unbudgeable, one of my slickest moves.

But I didn't have to use it, because Charlie shrugged Bernie's hand off his shoulder and said, "I don't want to play wall ball."

Bernie's hand hung motionless in the air, like it was confused. He stuck it in his pocket.

"What do you want to do?"

"Daddy Malcolm took me to take your kid to work day."

"What was that like?"

"He has all these screens and he sits in front of them. But you have a real person. So can I watch?"

"Out of the question."

"Why?"

"Go play wall ball. I'll explain later."

"It's because of the gun, huh?"

"What gun?"

"You think he has a gun in his pocket."

"I do not. And that's not the point, which is that this is not take your kid to work day. So out you go, and pronto."

Charlie shrugged. "Have it your way."

"Thank you."

"Come on, Chet," Charlie said. He headed for the kitchen. The kitchen leads to the back door. The back door leads to the patio.

"Chet?" Bernie said.

And I headed to the kitchen, too. Even though I knew it was the wrong play, I followed. I just couldn't help myself. A moment later, we were on the patio, me, Bernie, and Charlie. Bernie picked up a tennis ball and tossed it to Charlie. Charlie made no attempt to catch it. The ball rolled into the far corner of the patio. I let it.

"Know what Esmé says?" said Charlie. "The smartest kid in the class?"

"No."

"She has the same IQ as the bagel guy."

"Bagel guy?"

"Einstein. And Esmé says it's always a bunch of blah blah blah that means because I said so."

Bernie's eyes got an inward look. Charlie paid no attention. He went over to the ball, picked it up, threw it real hard against the gate. It flew back our way, smacked off a wing of the stone swan in the fountain, and soared high above. There are times for not thinking—a strength of mine, as it happens—and this was one of them. The next thing I knew I was doing some soaring myself, snagging that tennis ball right out of the big blue sky. Bernie had gone inside the house and closed the door before I landed.

Charlie and I just stood there, both of us facing the stone swan.

"Want to play wall ball?" he said after a while.

I stayed where I was.

"Me neither," Charlie said. From inside the house came the sound of Bernie's voice, a slow sort of rumble. Then came the voice of the smelly dude—Lauritz, was it?—quick and higher pitched. Charlie glanced at the back door. I realized something important, maybe a little late in the game. Charlie was somewhat like a puppy, and I understood puppies very well. I wasn't always a hundred-plus pounder with a gator-skin collar around my neck—and different-colored ears, one black and one white, as I'd heard humans endlessly comment upon in my presence, if you want a full description. I'd been a puppy at one time. So it made perfect sense to head for the back door, press my paw against the little thumby thing, and give the door a gentle shoulder shove. The next thing I knew we were in the kitchen, me and Charlie, once again standing side by side, but in much better moods.

Lauritz's voice came flowing down the hall from the living room like a stream, the way voices do, a thin and narrow stream in his case.

"No," he said, "not German, although there is German in me. My ancestors are a sort of Mittel European goulash. You can think of me as simply a modern European man."

The stream of Bernie's voice was thicker, if that makes any sense. "Fine with me," he said.

"'Fine with me!'" Lauritz said. "Ha ha! You of course are an instantly identifiable American."

"'Fine with me' is American?" Bernie said.

"The tone, the cadence, the freshness. Ah, the freshness of America, somehow still retained even though your history is no longer so short. In fact, that is what I am here to discuss."

"American history?" Bernie said.

"In a way," said Lauritz.

"I'm no expert on American history," Bernie said.

"Nevertheless you are recommended highly."

"By who?"

"Ha ha. I hope you don't mind if that remains confidential for the moment. But certain of your exploits are matters of the public record, after all. The case of the country music singer was of particular interest, most especially the Mexican aspect."

"Oh?" said Bernie.

"You speak Spanish, I assume?" Lauritz said.

"Badly."

"Oh, I cannot believe that. Such an easy language after all. I speak eleven myself."

"Is Spanish important to—to whatever it is you're proposing?" Bernie said.

"Relevant but not essential," said Lauritz. "And what I am proposing"—now came a grunt and some papery sounds—"is to pay you five thousand dollars to begin—please feel free to count the money—followed by ten times that, meaning fifty thousand dollars at the successful conclusion of your work. There may even be a supplemental bonus."

"And if the conclusion is unsuccessful?" Bernie said.

"I can't even imagine such an outcome," said Lauritz. "I don't say it will be easy. Much research will be necessary. But there is no danger involved, and in the end I'm sure a man of your capacities will—what is the expression? Sail through?"

"Research but no danger?" Bernie said.

"Exactly," said Lauritz. "What do you know of the Baroque, Bernie?"

"Nothing."

"Your taste in art runs more to the contemporary?"

"I don't have a taste in art."

"Ha ha." Lauritz laughed for what seemed like a long time. Human laughter is usually one of their best sounds, but this particular laugh seemed a bit unpleasant, and maybe even unfriendly, like Lauritz was not actually liking Bernie. How could anyone not like Bernie? It made no sense.

The laughter died away at last. There was a silence. Then Bernie said, "Thank you for the offer but the answer is no."

"Begging pardon?" Lauritz said.

"But I can put you on to an investigator who will be perfect for the job. His name's Victor Klovsky."

"You are wanting more money, is that it?" said Lauritz.

"It's not the money," Bernie said. "It just doesn't sound like the kind of work we're good at."

"Who is this 'we' you keep referencing?"

"Chet and I," said Bernie.

"The dog?"

"Yes, sir."

"I had imagined that the role of the dog was nothing but typical journalistic coloration."

"Nope," Bernie said. I heard the kind of thing you might not have, namely the sound of a pen tip moving on paper. "Here's Victor's number. He's a very smart guy. You won't be disappointed."

Another silence. Then in an icy voice, Lauritz said, "Very well."

Two sets of footsteps moved away. The front door opened and closed. One set of footsteps returned, Bernie's of course. He walks like no other, so smooth, except when his old leg wound bothers him. He came into the kitchen, saw us, and stopped.

"You said not to watch and we didn't," Charlie said.

Bernie's face was blank for a moment. Then he smiled.

"What did that guy want?" Charlie said.

"Nothing that I was interested in."

"But what about the money, Dad?"

"You know the answer."

"Money's not everything?"

"Bingo."

I went into the front hall. Even though I'd heard Lauritz leave, I like to make sure about things like that. I did some careful sniffing, corner to corner, and picked up something I'd missed. Lauritz did have a gun on him after all, a gun that had been fired, although not recently. I went to the window and gazed at the empty street.

Three

"Rui?" said Nixon Panero. "What's the matter with you? More butt!"

Rui raised his visor, paint gun dangling in his hand, and said, "Huh?"

We were getting an oil change in the yard out back of Nixon's Championship Autobody, best autobody shop on the whole autobody strip, which goes on and on to the edge of the desert in both directions. There's a surprising amount of oil that has to be changed now and then for reasons that aren't clear to me, and last time Bernie had jacked the Porsche up in our driveway and done it himself, all part of a tweak to our business plan called budgeting. Now we were back to getting it done at Nixon's, but I'd learned from the experience, mostly about oil in surprising amounts.

Nixon spat out a thin stream of tobacco juice—not spitting, exactly, more like spraying it through the gap in his front teeth—and pointed to the van Rui was working on, a pink van with red writing on the side. "Tell him, Bernie."

"Tell him what?" said Bernie.

Nixon motioned for us to come closer. "What do you see?"

"A woman in bikini," Bernie said.

"What else?" said Nixon.

"She's got her back to us but she's glancing around with a smile."

"That's it?"

Bernie peered more closely. "The neck part looks so natural. That must be hard to do, Rui."

Rui shrugged.

"Neck?" said Nixon. "How is that relevant? Check out her butt, for god's sake."

Bernie lowered his gaze slightly. "It looks too large for those bikini bottoms." He shot Rui a quick glance. "But not much. It's subtle."

"Subtle," Nixon said. "Do me a favor, Bernie. Read the name of the client—it's right there on the side."

"'Girls girls naked dancing girls dot com. We never close.'"

"Is that subtle?" Nixon said.

No one answered.

"More butt, Rui." Nixon sent out another jet of tobacco juice. "If you please." He walked away, entered the office, and closed the door.

We stayed where we were, Bernie watching Rui work and me smelling the paint smells.

"Wow," Bernie said. "Amazing how fast you did that. And you didn't really add—it's more like you highlighted what was already there."

Rui went on spraying. "You know something about art, Bernie?"

"Not a thing. It turns out I have no taste in art. I don't even know what taste in art means."

Rui shut off the gun, raised his visor. He had wide-apart blue eyes and unlined skin, and looked almost like a college kid, except for his mustache, which was mostly gray. "It's whatever moves you, that's all."

"I don't think any art has done that to me," Bernie said.

"No?" said Rui. "What about music?"

"That's different."

Rui shook his head. "The entry point is different. After that it's all the same."

Bernie thought about that. He gave his head a quick little shake, maybe to stir things up in there. "I don't know," he said. "What's your taste in art?"

"If we're talking just painting, it's changed over the years," Rui said. "Like lots of people I was a sucker for the impressionists. Then I got to realize that they were just too easy. Not talking about the work—just the effect. I didn't want to be a sucker so I started educating myself."

"You went to art school?"

"Nope. The service, right out of high school." He took out his phone, tapped once or twice, turned it so Bernie could see. "My taste in art these days," he said.

"What is it?" said Bernie.

"Jackson Pollock's second drip painting. I don't think he ever got any better."

"What's it called?"

"Can't remember, actually. It doesn't matter."

"But what's it about? What's the subject?"

Rui pocketed the phone, lowered the visor, got back to work. "With the impressionists, say, there's a scene, you take it in, and then have an emotional reaction. With the Pollock, you skip all that and go straight to the emotions."

"So what's the emotion you get from that one?"

Rui laughed. "A whole nother question," he said. And maybe would have gone on, but at that moment Nixon returned.

"Now that's more like it," he said. "The female butt—there's no getting around it. Tell him, Bernie."

"He knows."

Rui laughed.

"Everybody knows!" Nixon said. "We're lucky to be here, boys and girls. Merry Christmas!"

Bernie smiled. How happy he can look, especially at times like these, just palling around. He was still looking happy when his phone buzzed.

"Hello?" he said, moving off to the side. I moved with him, goes without saying. On the other end I heard a woman, not young, very worried.

"Is this Bernie Little?"

"Yes."

"Bernie Little, the detective?"

"That's right."

"This is Elise Klovsky, Victor's mother. I—I don't know where he is."

"Um," Bernie said, "he's not with us, if that's what you're asking."

"Do you have any idea where he might be, Mr. Little?"

"I don't," Bernie said. "The last time we saw him was late Friday night. Before that we'd have to go back a year and a half at least. And call me Bernie."

"Thank you, Bernie. I know you're not a close friend. But Victor thinks the world of you. I haven't seen or heard from him in almost two days, not since Sunday."

"Do you live together?" Bernie said.

"Victor moved back in."

"Does he have an office?"

"No longer, except for the room over the garage."

"Maybe he's working a case," Bernie said. "Sometimes you get so involved you can't think about anything else."

"Oh, he is working a case—the one you so kindly . . . how did he put it? Farmed out to him? And he's terribly excited about it. But . . . but maybe this will sound silly to you—we talk every single day, no matter what."

Then came a long silence. Spike, an old buddy of mine who'd been snoozing by a stack of tires, raised his head. He was one huge dude and we'd mixed it up more than once, way way more. But Spike's face had gone white and he wasn't so huge these days. He saw me, gave me a look that said *you're toast,* and went back to sleep. I thought about going over and pawing him, not hard, just to get him going a bit, like in the old days.

Good idea? Not so good? I went back and forth on that.

Meanwhile, Bernie finally spoke. "What's your address, Elise?"

And we were out of there, no decision necessary on my part. Who has all the luck in the world?

We drove down a quiet street in the old part of Pottsdale, not the rich old part but just below that where the foothills begin, and stopped in front of a small house. It had a desert-style yard a lot like ours, and a big shady tree out front. A number of members of the nation within had marked that tree—no surprise—so on the way to the door I paused to lay my mark on top of theirs.

"Must you?" said Bernie.

Which had to be one of his jokes. Of course I must! As he knew perfectly well. Did we enjoy each other's company or what? Perhaps, so pleased with how well things were going, I dillydallied a little. For whatever reason, I hadn't quite wrapped things up when the front door opened and a woman looked out.

She was very small, with a face not unlike Victor's, except a female version, older and softer. A strange thought popped up in my mind—*that kind of face looks better on a woman than a man*—and then quickly vanished before it became bothersome.

"Bernie?" she said.

"That's me," said Bernie. "Nice meeting you, Elise. And this—" By that time I was right beside him, giving myself a quick shake, just clearing the deck before we got going on whatever it was we were here for. "—is Chet."

"Victor told me all about him. Still, I didn't expect him to be so . . . so . . ."

I really wanted to hear what was coming next, but Bernie jumped in before it could.

"Nothing to be alarmed about. When you get to know him, he's just a big—well, I wouldn't say pussycat, but . . . but just nothing to alarmed about."

"I'm afraid I have no treats for him," Elise said. "But please come in."

Whoa! Things were going too fast. Bernie wouldn't say pussycat? Of course not! How could he even think such a thought? And to know there wouldn't be treats right from the get-go? What were we doing here? Was anyone even paying? Pussycat? Sometimes in the heat the human brain gets a little mixed up, but the heat was gone. Wasn't this wintertime? My own brain got a little mixed up, and the next thing I knew we were in the house. I picked up Victor's smell right away, and sort of wrapped into it, a very faint armpit and flower scent that reminded me of . . . of Lauritz. My mind cleared at once. But why? Because I was a pro, and on the job? I could think of no other reason.

We sat in the kitchen. Elise made coffee for her and Bernie, poured me some water in a tiny saucer, the kind you might put cream in for a cat. I didn't go near it. On the table stood a silver candle holder with lots of unlit candles in it. Elise noticed Bernie looking at it and said, "Last night was the first night of Hannukah."

"Oh?" said Bernie.

"When we start lighting the candles. He wouldn't miss that."

"I didn't know Victor was religious."

"He isn't," Elise said. "We're not. Not in any formal sense. But he wouldn't miss lighting the candles."

Bernie sipped his coffee. "Maybe he'll show up to take care of it tonight."

Elise nodded, but in her eyes was a distant look. "Private detective," she said.

"Not quite following you," said Bernie.

Elise put down her mug. A tiny wave of coffee splashed over the lip. "I look at you and I think, sure, private detective. I look at Victor and . . ." She shook her head.

"You don't have to be, um, physically imposing to do the job," Bernie said. "Especially with Victor's method, mostly behind the scenes and then bringing in Valley PD."

"In theory," Elise said.

"What do you mean?"

She shrugged. "In practice it doesn't pay, at least not for Victor, not yet."

"Who's his contact downtown?"

"That's been a problem," Elise said. "He hasn't found anyone reliable. In fact—no naming names—the last one asked for some sort of, quote, incentive."

Bernie's face darkened. I knew right away that he was against incentives, whatever they were, and made what he calls a mental note to watch out for any incentives that came down the pike and chase them off immediately.

"I know some good people down there," Bernie said. "I can give Victor an introduction or two."

"That's kind, Bernie. Meanwhile I want to hire you. Do you go by the day or by the job? I believe Victor has experimented with both."

"We're by the day," Bernie said. "But what is it you want us to do?"

"Why, find Victor, of course."

"Well," Bernie said, "since we can't really consider him missing at this stage, why not—"

"Please," said Elise. "I'll feel better."

Their eyes met. Not all humans are smart—what a lot of time it took me to realize that!—but Elise was. I could see that in her eyes. In fact, she might have been very smart, although of course not the smartest human in the room. Even though it was her room! Was that an interesting thought? Perhaps not.

"Okay," Bernie said, "we'll make a few preliminary . . . we'll see what we can do. No charge."

"I'd feel better with a charge," Elise said. "I don't want charity."

"It's not charity," said Bernie. "It's . . ." He paused, which sometimes happens when he's waiting for his brain—his mighty brain—to kick in. "Call it friendship," he said at last.

Elise bowed her head.

"Usually," Elise said, as we walked across her lawn, headed for the garage, "since Victor moved back in, that is, we have a sit-down breakfast at seven thirty, but his first day on the case he just grabbed a muffin and left. I hadn't seen him that energized in ages. He was so grateful to you."

"What did he say about the case?"

"Nothing, really, except that the client reminded him of a certain actor. Victor can be close-mouthed when it comes to work. But the next afternoon I'm pretty sure I caught a glimpse of the client."

"Oh?"

"I was coming home from the market and he was just driving

off, passing right by me. He had dark hair, slicked back, and prominent eyes—very like the actor Victor mentioned."

"Which one?" Bernie said.

"From long ago," said Elise. "You're probably not familiar with him."

"Try me," said Bernie.

"Peter Lorre."

Bernie smiled. "I'd thought the same thing."

He had? First I'd heard of it. He'd never mentioned anyone by that name. I took a dislike to Peter Lorre, not nice of me, I know. Heads up, Señor Lorre. Bernie and I are a team.

We came to the garage, a big one with some sort of apartment above. "Here's where he lives and works, for the time being," Elise said.

"When did he move back in?" Bernie said.

"July first, when his lease expired," Elise said. "He had a lovely place over one of the Old Town galleries, but the landlord raised the rent and I told Victor to please stay here until he found somewhere new." Elise stopped and turned to Bernie. "He didn't ask."

Bernie nodded. He has a bunch of different nods meaning all sorts of things and sometimes nothing. This one didn't mean nothing but that was as far as I could go on my own.

Elise took out a key fob, pressed a button. The garage door rolled up. Two cars were parked inside.

"The convertible is Victor's," Elise said. "He always wanted a cool car so I . . . so he finally got one."

This boxy little grayish thing was a cool ride? I hadn't realized.

"Does he have another car?" Bernie said.

"No."

"Did he say where he was going on Sunday?"

"No."

"Did someone pick him up?"

"Not that I know of. I wasn't watching through the window or anything like—ah, I see. You're probing for how Victor got to his destination."

"I wouldn't say probing," Bernie said.

Elise pointed to a ceiling hook with nothing hanging from it. "He must have taken his bike. There's an entrance to the bike trail one block south. Victor goes all over the place on his bike, especially at this time of year. He says it helps him think."

"What make of bike?" Bernie said.

Elise opened a door and we started up a narrow staircase. "I couldn't tell you," she said. "It's bright neon green, the same color you see on all those bike shirts—for safety."

At the top of the stairs we came to a small and very tidy office—desk and chair, filing cabinets, white board.

"The bedroom and bathroom are through that door," Elise said.

"Thanks," said Bernie. "Mind if we have a look around?"

"Not at all," Elise said. "I'll show—" She paused and started over. "I'll leave you to it." She went out and down the stairs. Right away I felt—how to put it? More like myself, my full self? Something like that. It's a feeling that often comes the moment we're left alone together, me and Bernie.

He went to the desk. A single sheet of paper lay on it. Bernie picked it up, squinted at the writing. "Is that a B? Blight into . . . nope, must be an F. 'Flight into Egypt.'"

Bernie looked at me. "That rings a faint bell." I gazed back at him, waiting for him to go on. I could wait as long as it took. We did a lot of our best thinking just like this.

"Or maybe it's something else," he said at last. "Did Lauritz mention Egypt? Didn't he describe himself as Mittel European? Can that have anything to do with Egypt? How did he explain it? Goulash, was it? That's a kind of soup? Or is it a stew?" He shook his head, like we were getting nowhere. I myself was much more hopeful. Specifically I was hoping for stew, preferably beef stew, about which I had no complaints. Not only that, but I could almost taste beef stew even though I smelled not a morsel of food of any kind here in Victor's office. I was starting to enjoy this case, if it was a case, and if not I was enjoying whatever it was. Some go through life being hard to please. Others are like me.

Bernie started in on the desk drawers, opening them from bottom to top, rooting around inside. Some cash lay in the top drawer. Bernie counted it. "Five hundred, in fifties." He tapped the little wad against the palm of his hand a few times. "Hmm," he said. I waited for more, but no more came. Bernie dropped the money back in the drawer and closed it softly. Then he turned to the white board. There was one small bit of writing on it. "'Folonari,'" he said.

We went through the open doorway and into a small bedroom, the bed made, nothing on the floor. A baseball cap hung on a wall hook.

"Need a quick refresh?" Bernie took the cap off the hook and held it in front of my nose. Victor's scent came flowing through the air like water from a hose, although it didn't smell watery, more sugary, if anything, and sweaty, of course, coming from a hat and all, this particular sweat being of the anxious kind. But the truth was I needed no quick refresh when it came to Victor's smell and would have turned my head if anyone else had made the suggestion. But it was Bernie. I made myself look interested.

"That's the stuff," Bernie said.

And right away I felt tip-top!

We moved into the bathroom, also neat and tidy. A book lay on the toilet tank. Did you know those things are full of water? It's best not to shoot at them, but I've seen it done more than once. Bernie picked up the book. "'Fundamentals of Logic.'" He opened it, skimmed through, put it down.

"No phone, no computer, no gun," Bernie said. "It's like the dog that didn't bark."

After that he took the sheet of paper off the desk and we headed downstairs. He might have done a few other things, but I was too distracted to notice. The dog that didn't bark? What did that even mean? We bark, period. We can bark all day and all night for any reason or for no reason at all. Was Bernie under some sort of strain? I gave him a close look.

"Chet? Okay if I squeeze by?"

Squeeze by? I had no idea what he was talking about. Then

I noticed that I seemed to be at the bottom of the stairs, facing them and even possibly blocking the way.

"Chet? Some problem?"

A bark—perhaps quite loud, even a bit on the savage side—burst out of me, all on its own.

"My god! Are you all right?"

Never better. I turned and trotted out of the garage and onto Elise's lawn. The first thing I saw was the big tree. I knew right away no one had laid their mark on mine so . . . I did it, just taking care of business for the nation within. We bark. We pee. And lots more there may be time to go into later.

Four

Elise came out of the house as I was lowering my leg. Did she give me a funny look? If so, I couldn't think why.

She turned to Bernie. "Did you find anything helpful?"

"Can't say yet. Does the word 'Folonari' mean anything to you?"

"Isn't it a kind of wine?" said Elise.

"I don't know." Bernie showed her the sheet of paper. "Is this Victor's writing?"

Elise nodded.

"Did he say anything about Egypt in the last few days?" Bernie said.

She shook her head. "But isn't the Flight into Egypt a Christmas thing?"

Bernie thought for a bit. "After the manger, maybe?" he said.

Elise raised both hands, palms up.

"Um, which reminds me," Bernie said. "I wished Victor Merry Christmas."

"So?"

"Before I knew he . . . that is, you and he were, um, Hannukah fans. Well, not fans, more like—"

Elise interrupted. "Anything with 'merry' in it can't be bad," she said.

Bernie smiled a little smile. Elise took his hand and held it between both of hers. His little smile went away.

We can work outdoors and we can work indoors, but outdoors is our favorite. Once on a salt flat near Dismal Springs, Bernie took a deep breath and said, "Ah, the great outdoors. No one ever says 'the great indoors,' do they, big guy?" That's the kind of thing you don't forget.

We drove down Elise's street, made a turn, and came to a small empty parking lot. Bernie and I hopped out of the car, me actually hopping, and started along a hard packed dirt trail, houses on one side and open country on the other. Soon the houses got farther away and we pretty much had open country on both sides.

"This was a dirt path going way back in prehistory," Bernie said. "Then they thought they'd found another Comstock Lode— where the North Pottsdale mall is now—and laid down tracks. And here we are back to a dirt path." His face brightened. "You can't turn the clock back, but what if there are many clocks and you can turn some of them back?"

A tough one. I'd seen clocks, of course, often hanging on walls, and once a drunken perp name of Shifty Ifterman had fired a round or two at the clock behind the bar at the Deep Six and yelled at us when we collared him that he'd been "just killin' time," but other than that I was at a loss.

We walked along side by side. A woman on a bike had been by recently—bike smells being hard to miss—plus a woman on foot, a man on foot, a man on a bike, two women drinking lattes, a turtle, a fox, a coyote, two toads, another toad, and another! Were all bike trails this toady? Did toads like them for some reason? As for Victor, there were traces of his scent, too, but faint and scattered in ways that made no sense. A leaf blower had been on the scene some time after Victor. I won't go on about leaf blowers.

From up ahead came some interesting sounds, whooshing and crumbly. Then I heard the voice of a kid: "Whee-ooo!" And another kid: "Ooo-whee!" Kids having fun? For sure. I moved on, slightly ahead of Bernie.

Or perhaps more than slightly. By the time Bernie caught up, I was around a bend up ahead, where we had a sudden steep drop-off on one side of the path. Far below, two skinny long-haired kids were zigzagging down a narrow, rocky trail on skateboards with big rubber wheels.

"Wow," said Bernie, gazing down. "Mountain skateboards—what a great invention! Wonder if—"

I always love to hear what Bernie wonders, but this time I didn't get to find out. Way down there, where the zigzagging trail straightened and flattened out, something glinted by a big red rock. Bernie went still, and so did I. We often move together and also often are together when we don't move. What I'm trying to get at is that we're together, moving and not, but I don't know how to put it.

We started down the steep trail. This kind of thing isn't always easy for Bernie, depending on how his wounded leg is doing. All I know about his wound is that it happened in a far-off war; everyone we run into who knew him back then thanks him, pats him on the back, and buys him drinks; and he doesn't wear shorts. Once or twice at home when he's in his boxers, I've given that poor wound a quick lick, but he doesn't like that so it won't happen again, not if I can help it.

Meanwhile I'd already overtaken the kids on their mountain skateboards—the looks on their faces as I flashed by! Especially on the face of the kid I flew right over!—and had reached the bottom in no time. Beside the big red rock lay a bicycle, almost certainly neon green, although Bernie says I can't be trusted when it comes to colors. This bicycle was all bent and twisted and broken. The smells that rose from it were a mix of the oily and leathery smells you get from bikes, as well as typical human male smell with hints of sugar and anxious sweat. In short, this was Victor's bike, unless I was missing something.

The skateboarders were standing by their boards at the last zigzag up the trail, watching Bernie make his way down. A breeze rose up, blew their long hair in their eyes. Their faces were covered in red dust and they looked kind of wild. I liked these kids.

Bernie came to the last zigzag, looked down at the kids.

"We thought it was teacher training day," said one.

"Huh?" said Bernie.

"Like no school," said the other.

"So?" said Bernie.

The kids both brushed their hair out of their eyes. "You're not the truant officer?" one said.

"There are still truant officers?" said Bernie.

The kids nodded.

"Those boards look amazing," Bernie said.

"Wanna try mine?" said one of the kids.

"Next time." Bernie walked down the rest of the way, came over to the red rock, stood beside me. We both gazed at the bike. The kids picked up their boards and followed, stopping nearby.

Bernie and I walked around the red rock. He gazed out over the flat ground, which ended in another rise, with some houses on a distant ridge. I picked up an oily scent at once. It seemed to lead toward a fat barrel cactus, not far away. But so what? There's nothing unusual about oily scents, not in these parts.

Bernie took surgical gloves from his back pocket, put them on, lifted the bike. One of the pedals fell off.

"You a cop?" said one of the kids.

"The plain-clothing kind?" said the other.

"Sort of," Bernie said.

"Is your dog a K-nine?"

"Sort of," Bernie said.

"He jumped right over my head."

Bernie nodded.

"Did you teach him that?"

"He's a natural," Bernie said. "Were you guys here yesterday?"

They shook their heads.

"Ever seen this bike before?"

They nodded.

"Where?"

They pointed up to the bike path.

"A guy with a scruffy beard rides it."

"But he's not good enough for this."

"What do you mean?" Bernie said.

"For riding it down this trail."

"You'd have to be great on a bike like this. It's a hybrid."

"Hybrid?" said Bernie.

"Not a road bike but not a mountain bike neither. No suspension. You'd have to be great to ride it down here."

"How do you know the guy's not good enough?" Bernie said.

"Seen him ride."

"Does he fall a lot?"

The kids shook their heads. "But he holds on too tight. Can't squeeze and be good."

"Gotta be, you know, loose."

"Yet here we are." Bernie leaned the bike against the red rock.

"So what happened?" The kids stood there, their bodies very loose for sure, their smooth-skinned faces upturned toward Bernie, waiting for an answer.

We hauled the wrecked bike all the way to the top, Bernie doing the hauling and me running around him in circles. Everybody needs a little encouragement from time to time and I . . . I like encouraging folks! Is that what it means to be a natural? Wow! It was like I was suddenly getting a peek inside myself! Chet the Jet! But that was enough inside peeking for now.

Bernie bungee corded the bike to the back end of the Porsche and called Rick Torres, our buddy downtown who was now heading up Missing Persons, or maybe heading it up till the actual head returned from rehab.

"Ever heard of a PI named Victor Klovsky?" Bernie said.

"Nope," said Rick.

"He might have taken a fall off the North Pottsville rail trail yesterday, around mile seventeen. I'd like to know if anyone got a call."

"Anyone like who?"

"The usual—you guys, the sheriff, EMTs."

"So you want me to do your work for you?"

"Call it a Christmas present."

"Do I look like Santa Claus?"

Bernie didn't answer.

After a long pause, Rick said, "Are you suggesting I'm putting on weight?"

"I didn't say a word."

"It's how you didn't say it, as you very well know." Click.

I was glad that conversation, impossible to follow, was over. Bernie got out my portable bowl, filled it from a water bottle under my seat—meaning the shotgun seat, in case you need reminding on that little detail—and we both had a nice refreshing drink. Bernie smacked his lips. So did I. He gave me a funny look.

The phone buzzed. "Nope on Victor Klovsky," Rick said. "Want to file a report?"

"Yes."

"Anyone in particular you want to work with? Sergeant Wauneka, maybe?"

"That's not my call."

"Word is you and the sergeant are a thing."

Bernie didn't answer.

"Sergeant Wauneka it is," Rick said. "Say thank you."

Bernie said nothing.

"Ho ho ho," said Rick, and hung up.

We drove back to Elise's house. Her door opened before we'd stopped the car. I liked Elise—I liked pretty much all the humans I'd ever met, even some of the perps and gangbangers—but she was starting to make me nervous. She came toward the car, walking at first and then running, a jerky sort of movement you see from a lot of older humans, not really what you'd call running at all. Do they forget how to run as they grow older? That doesn't happen in the nation within. We don't forget. We just slow down. Although not me, personally. Bernie says I'm getting faster. It's nice to be fast. I won't deny it.

Elise saw the twisted-up bike, now kind of hanging off the back of the car. Her hands—thin and very pale—rose to her face and she held them there, one to each cheek. For a moment, she was all pale hands and dark liquid eyes. My mood changed. I went over and sat next to her, not quite touching.

Bernie raised his hand. "Don't be alarmed," he said.

Her voice rose and cracked. "Don't be alarmed?"

"Not yet," he said. His voice was calm and not very friendly. Elise lowered her hands, took a breath.

"If you say so," she said, her voice closer to normal.

"The bike's not in good shape, but that doesn't mean he isn't." Bernie gestured toward the bike. "This could have happened in a number of ways."

And he started in on the zigzag trail and how we'd found the bike. Elise nodded along like she was following the story no problem, something you want to see in a client but often don't. I almost forgot she wasn't paying, and then did totally forget, my mind suddenly taken by the notion to mark her big tree one more time. I didn't have to go or anything like that, but I'm the type who always saves a spurt or two for marking purposes. Good idea? Not so good? Before I could decide, Elise said, "There's something I'd like you to do before you go."

We went into the house, followed Elise to the kitchen. She stood before the silver candle holder. "You're supposed to wait for sunset," she said, "but you're here now."

"And you want us to watch?" Bernie said.

Elise handed Bernie a book of matches. "I want you to light them."

"Me?" said Bernie. "I don't know how."

"You don't know how to light a candle?"

"It's not that," Bernie said. "It's the ritual. Do you do them all? Is there some order? A special prayer?"

"This is the second night," Elise said. She shook her head the way people do when they're not happy with themselves. "Last night I didn't light the first one. When Victor didn't come and didn't come I . . ." She went silent.

"So I should light two?" Bernie said.

Elise took a deep breath. "Just light 'em all up, Bernie. And say whatever you want."

Bernie struck a match and began lighting the candles one by one. You might have thought that with so many candles one single match couldn't do the job, but you'd have been wrong. That match hardly burned down at all, and at the end it was still plenty long, maybe as long as it had been before Bernie lit it, or . . . or even longer, which was kind of crazy. He blew out the match flame—not so easy since it didn't seem to want to go out—and looked a little surprised.

His gaze went to Elise, then to me, and finally to the burning candles. "We'll do our very best to find Victor," he said. "But if there's such a thing as . . ." He paused for what seemed like a longish time, candle flames flickering in his eyes. ". . . such a thing as outside help, that would be nice, too."

Five

The phone buzzed as we pulled into the Donut Heaven lot.

"Bernie?"

Oh, good. It was Suzie. There are many kinds of human voices. In fact, no two are the same! If I've heard you once, all you have to do is make one tiny sound and I'll know it's you. That's been a big help in my line of work. Also, there's my nose, of course. And my teeth are something else. Have I mentioned my leaping ability? But enough about me, and back to human voices. I'm afraid that many are quite disappointing—too scratchy, too screechy, too breathy, not breathy enough like they're starving for air, and worst of all those human voices that have a kind of emptiness at the bottom of them. But don't get me wrong: most human voices are very pleasant and a few are off the charts. Bernie's is the best, like it's actually coming from inside my head and I have some beautiful instrument in there. Suzie's voice has some of that music, too—and how nice it was just to hear them talking even if I had no clue about what, back in the days when they were together—although her voice never came from inside my head. And they're not together anymore. It's a long story with details fading away or getting jumbled, the way details do in long stories, but things started to go wrong when she got hired away from the *Valley Tribune* by the *Washington Post*—which I believe from things I've heard is a lot like the *Valley Tribune* except bigger and less fun—who then sent her to London, and London turns out to be very far away and the kind of place where, according to what Bernie said late one night after several or more bourbons, he'd be "a fish out of water." I understood at once and completely, having witnessed a fish out of water—a brightly colored little fella name of Montego, if memory serves—whose tank had somehow fallen off a very high shelf. Bernie flip-flopping all over the floor? Not on my watch, amigo.

Now Suzie was no longer in London or with the *Washington Post,* but back in the Valley and working on some news business type start-up with her partner Jacques Smallian who like Bernie had played college baseball, but at Cal Tech, not West Point. "Cal Tech has a team?" Bernie had said more than once, and Jacques had laughed more than once, and now they were kind of buddies, a little bit. Also Jacques and Suzie got married, maybe should have mentioned that off the top. We'd even been to the wedding, me and Bernie, but hadn't stayed long.

"Hi, Suzie," Bernie said. "How're things?"

"No complaints," she said. "How's Chet? I miss him."

Bernie went still just for the tiniest time—you wouldn't have noticed. Then he glanced over at me. "He caught a trash can lid the other day."

"A trash can lid was flying through the air?"

"Yup."

"On purpose?"

"Not following you."

"I mean did you throw it for him—like a Frisbee?"

"*I* didn't throw it," Bernie said.

"Ah," said Suzie. "Working on anything that might be of interest to a wider audience?"

"I don't think so," Bernie said.

"Well, keep me in mind," said Suzie. Bernie went still again, for slightly longer this time—this stillness you'd have noticed, if you're the alert type I think you are. "One of the things we're learning is how our readership, across all demographics, loves crime stories."

"Why?" Bernie said.

Suzie laughed a soft little laugh. I missed her, too. "We were discussing it just the other day. There's the frisson, of course, but it goes deeper than that—crime's like one of those temblors that hints at huge stresses down deep."

"What's frisson?" Bernie said.

"French for shiver—the 'there but for fortune' feeling."

Bernie thought about that. I did not. Impossible to follow, but also I was wondering when they'd get back to me and the trash can lid.

"Baroque is also a French word?" Bernie said.

"Correct," said Suzie.

"What's it mean, exactly?"

"I'm no expert, Bernie, but wasn't it the artistic period after the Renaissance, say from sixteen hundred to seventeen fifty?"

"You tell me," Bernie said.

"I just did," said Suzie.

Bernie laughed, this lovely surprised laugh he has, really one of his very best things. "So it's a style of painting?"

"Plus sculpture, architecture, even music."

"This was in Europe?"

"Originally. But the Spanish brought it to Mexico, and here as well."

"Here in the Valley?"

"There aren't many examples, but Nuestra Señora mission is one."

"The church with the crooked bell tower?" Bernie said.

"Right," said Suzie. "Muted and scaled way down, but basically Baroque, what's left of it. Why are you asking?"

"Baroque came up the other day."

"You're working an art world case?"

"Me? No way."

"Why not? You've got a good eye."

"Oh?"

"You see what others miss."

"First time I've heard that."

"Come to our Christmas party and I'll repeat it in person," Suzie said. "The party's why I called. We're renting a bubble where they lower the temperature and make snow. A white Christmas guaranteed—Ling found out about it."

"Who's Ling?"

"Our first hire—best researcher I've ever seen," Suzie said. "And bring a plus-one if, um, if there is one. Plus Chet, of course. So it's really a plus-plus."

Suzie laughed. So did Bernie, laughing again and so soon. They laughed a lot when they were together, Bernie and Suzie, but then a squad car entered the Donut Heaven lot and Bernie's laughter trailed off. Sergeant Wauneka was at the wheel.

"Uh, thanks, Suzie," Bernie said. "I'll get back to you."

Sergeant Wauneka parked next to us cop style, driver's side door to driver's side door. There's a lot I should tell you about Sergeant Wauneka but I don't know where to start. Just stay with me and maybe it will end up making sense.

"Hi, there," Bernie said. I felt a change in him and thought at once of a case we'd worked down Mexico way where late one night I'd heard some she-barking, not far away—in fact, rather close by as it had turned out. Funny how the mind works.

"I noticed on Thanksgiving your fondness for pecan pie," Sergeant Wauneka said.

"I'm not denying it," said Bernie.

"See what you think of this." Sergeant Wauneka held out a little cardboard box. Their hands touched and stayed touching for an extra moment or two. Bernie's hands are the most beautiful you'll ever see, big, strong, perfectly shaped, and somehow the one finger that's a bit twisted and the odd swollen knuckle make them even lovelier. But Sergeant Wauneka's hands were very nice, too, smaller and not as strong, of course, and showing no signs of any dustups.

"What is it?" Bernie said.

Somehow or other he didn't know! Just because it was in a cardboard box? Humans—even the very best of them—have to do a lot of slogging through life. I feel for them. Maybe you knew that already.

"A pecan and pinon tart," said the sergeant, bringing no news to me.

"Where'd you get it?" Bernie asked.

"I found it in my oven," she said.

Maybe I should have described Sergeant Wauneka before

this, perhaps starting with her thick, glossy hair, now worn in a tight bun but I'd seen it untied and free, hanging down her back, or what about her eyes, deep and dark and often with an inward look, although hardly ever when Bernie and I were around, or then there's her smile, so quick and white and huge when it comes, like a powerful light going on. Do me a favor and pick one of those. Her name's Weatherly, by the way, some story about her dad being in the merchant marine, whatever that may be. Or it might have been her mom.

"I didn't know you baked," Bernie said.

"Did you want me to fire all my guns at once?" she said.

Whoa! What a sharp and sudden turn! Were there any targets nearby? That was my first thought. But also, what did she mean by guns? She had only one with her in the squad car, out of sight but of course not out of smell, if I can put it that way. Still, a lot of fun can be had with just one gun. They could take turns shooting dimes out of the air. And that's just one example, and possibly a bad one since I had no idea if Weatherly could even do it. Bernie never misses.

But no gunplay happened, maybe because Bernie said, "I'm not sure I'd survive." Which I didn't get at all. And then Weatherly said, "One day let's try it and see."

They looked at each other, a long look that seemed kind of . . . urgent to me.

About what exactly? My takeaway was that spinning dimes were in my future, and quite soon.

"But in the meantime," Weatherly went on, "we've got work to do."

"Oh?" said Bernie, opening the cardboard box.

"This missing PI, Victor Klovsky," Weatherly said. "Didn't Rick loop you in?"

"My god!" Bernie said, or something like that—hard to tell with his mouth so full.

"He didn't?"

"Oh no, he did. But this is fabulous!" He gestured with what was left of the tart. I'm the restrained type but I can only be pushed so far. The aroma of pinons happens to be a big favorite of mine. In short, I snapped that tart right out of Bernie's hand and downed it in a flash.

"Hey!" said Bernie.

Weatherly gazed at us like we were . . . unusual in some way. Unusual? Me and Bernie? I tried and tried to think how.

"What I'd like to do, since I'm on the case," Weatherly said, "is check out where you found the bike."

"Sure," said Bernie. "Now?"

"I'm off in ten minutes. How about I swing by my place, pick up Trixie, and meet you at the mile ten lot? She could use some exercise."

"See you there," Bernie said.

Trixie? Trixie was suddenly in the picture? We drove across town, toward the sun, getting lower, fatter, and more reddish as it did at the end of every day. Once Bernie had explained the whole thing to Charlie. Did you know, for example, that . . . I waited for one of the facts Bernie had told Charlie to pop into my mind, but none did, maybe because my mind was already busy, specifically thinking, *Trixie?* Trixie was suddenly in the picture? Weren't we working a case at the moment? Was Trixie a trained professional? Certainly not. Who was the trained professional around here? I believe you know the answer.

We parked in a small empty lot by the side of the bike path, now reddish gold in the early evening light. Weatherly drove in soon after, no longer in the squad car but in her dinged-up old Wrangler, a dinged-up old Wrangler that Bernie loved, by the way. Why was that? I myself did not love Weatherly's dinged-up old Wrangler. I loved the Porsche, end of story.

Weatherly, now out of uniform and wearing jeans and a cream-colored cowboy-type shirt, stepped out of the Wrangler. Bernie gave her a look, and then a smile. She did the same to him. Was Bernie wearing jeans and a cream-colored cowboy-type shirt? No he was not, except for the jeans part. His shirt was Hawaiian. Not the one with the surfing cats, which seemed to have disappeared. Had someone—just an ordinary someone doing an ordinary thing such as sniffing through the laundry pile—somehow come upon that surfing catty shirt and . . . and done whatever? Someone, somehow, whatever: that had to be the answer. But the truth was my eyes weren't really on Bernie and Weatherly. They were on Trixie.

Was she riding in the shotgun seat of the Wrangler, as I would have done? Oh no, not her. Trixie liked to sit in the back. I hadn't known her long, but more than long enough to know she could be bothersome. We'd rescued Trixie from a cave or abandoned mine—the details growing dim—and it had turned out she'd been kidnapped from Weatherly. Was that how Weatherly came into our life? Kind of. Things can get complicated, even for an expert in keeping them simple. But here are two big takeaways, and two will be all, since that's the edge of my comfort zone when it comes to numbers.

First, Weatherly loved us for finding Trixie. Second, Trixie and I—this is from what I've heard, not really seeing it myself—looked alike. Why would anyone think such a thing? Just because our coats were the same—shiny black except for one white ear? Didn't my being so much—or at least somewhat—bigger count for anything? One little irritation was another fact, namely that aside from the she-ness of her scent and he-ness of mine, they were rather similar. But who knew that, other than Trixie and me and every single member of the nation within? Certainly not Bernie or Weatherly. Just the same they'd come up with this strange idea that Trixie and I must have been puppies together and couldn't let it go.

Weatherly and Bernie came together and hugged, almost like they were getting pulled by something.

"Nice shirt," Bernie said.

"This gal can rope and ride," said Weatherly.

"Why am I just finding that out now?"

Weatherly laughed a low kind of laugh, possibly called a chuckle, but didn't answer. Instead she kissed him and he kissed her back. How long were they planning on doing that? I never found out, because at that moment Trixie hopped out of the

Wrangler in a casual and annoying way, landing lightly and silently in a way that was also annoying. And then she trotted right over to Bernie and straight out held her head up for some patting. For some reason Bernie and Weatherly thought there was something amusing about this. Oh, how they laughed! Would they still be laughing when they saw what I was about to—

"Okay to give Chet a bacon bit or two?" Weatherly said. "The lady at the diner always saves me some."

The next thing I remember we were at the foot of the steep slope where we'd met the skateboarding kids and found the bashed-up bike. Who was in the lead? You know.

We gathered around the big red rock.

"The bike was right here," Bernie said.

Weatherly checked out the spot, then glanced up the slope. It glowed red in the sunset light, and the switchback trail was gold.

"The kids skateboarded down?" Weatherly said.

"And made it look easy."

"Would you let Charlie do that?"

Bernie took a long look at the trail, following the golden switchbacks from top to bottom with his eyes. "I'd be of two minds," he said. "But it won't be my call."

"It'll be Leda's?" said Weatherly.

"Charlie's," Bernie said. "And he'll be ready to do it by the time he wants to, if we've raised him right."

Weatherly kicked at a little stone. Trixie watched it. I watched her watching it. Was she about to retrieve that little stone? The first twitch I saw from her I'd be in motion. But instead of going for the stone, she slowly turned my way and yawned. Can you beat that?

"Ever think of having another kid?" Weatherly's gaze was on the little stone when she began that question, but it was on Bernie's face when she finished.

"Yes," Bernie said, not loud but very clear.

I felt a little shift of some kind in Weatherly. Hard to explain, really—just a feeling.

We circled the big red rock. Trixie sniffed here and there. What was there to sniff? Faint bike smells and faint Victor smells? I already knew all that. I sniffed anyway, in fact, out-sniffed her, as anyone could plainly see.

"Any chance Victor decided he was ready to take on those switchbacks?" Weatherly said.

"Not the adventurous type," Bernie said. "And even if he took a swing at it, and then wiped out, where is he?"

"What if someone was chasing him?" Weatherly said.

Bernie nodded. "I like it," he said. "But it still doesn't—"

Whatever the thing Bernie liked didn't do remained unknown to me, because at that moment Trixie went trotting over to the fat barrel cactus. Following the oily scent I'd noticed on our first visit, no doubt, of no interest since oily scents were everywhere, but not being a professional Trixie didn't know that. I trotted after her, a rather quick trot that ended with me reaching the fat barrel cactus first. I circled it, searching for a good marking spot, the idea— obvious to you, I'm sure—being to send Trixie a message. But what did we have here? Stuck among the needles was one of those little tool kits you see hanging from bicycle seats. Very carefully— I've had experience with those needles, many more times than once—I got hold of a corner of the tool kit and pulled it free.

Then came a big surprise, and not a good one. Trixie snatched that tool kit right out of my mouth and took off toward Bernie and Weatherly. I sprinted after her, but here's something very bother- some about Trixie that you might as well know. She's fast. Not as fast as me, of course, goes without mentioning, and I would have caught up to her easy peasy if Bernie and Weatherly had been farther away.

But they were not. Could this get any worse? Oh, yes. Because next Trixie presented that tool kit to Bernie. I was the one who presented things to Bernie, me, myself, and I, only I.

"Well, well, Trixie," Bernie said, reaching down and taking the tool kit, "what have we here?"

Six

What can you do when things go wrong? Start over! That's what you can do. Go back to the beginning! Get it right! What did that mean in this case? I had to grab that tool kit, zoom back to the fat barrel cactus, drop the tool kit, pick it up, zoom back here, and present it to Bernie. What an awful lot of work, you may be thinking, but we have no fear of work, one of the many reasons the Little Detective Agency is so successful, except for the finances part.

To get things rolling I leaned in and—

"Chet?"

Bernie has many ways of saying Chet and I love them all, but this longish sort of *Che—et?* is the one I love the least. I paused, and during that pause Bernie shifted the tool kit slightly, away from my mouth. He opened it and took out a very small bottle of oil, leaking a bit from a loose cap, a couple of tools, and a bent postcard. We get postcards from perps at Northern State Correctional. Bernie reads them to me. *Say hi to Chet* is on every one. And just the other day we had one that said, *Hey you guys, Merry Christmas and sure would appreciate a fruitcake with a file inside, if you got one to spare.* But none of the postcards ever has a picture of a church on the front, like this one. I knew it was a church from the bell tower. I'm very aware of bell towers. We have a surprising number in these parts. Those bells all start ringing at about the same time, but each one sounds different, so some amazing sounds wash back and forth across the Valley every day, although humans don't seem to notice.

"What is that?" Weatherly said.

Bernie turned the postcard over. There was nothing on the back except one little line of print. "An artist's rendering of what

Nuestra Señora de los Saguaros mission church looked like in the sixteen hundreds."

Weatherly peered in, her head just touching Bernie's. For an instant, Bernie's eyelids came down the slightest bit, like something peaceful was flowing into him.

"That ruin on the old De Niza highway?" Weatherly said.

"Baroque," said Bernie. "It's a Baroque old ruin."

"How do you mean that?"

"The architecture. Baroque. A kind of style from way back. The Spanish brought it with them. There are lots of examples in Mexico but not many up here."

"Wow," Weatherly said. "I had no idea."

"About the Spanish?" said Bernie.

"No," Weatherly said. "I had no idea you were interested in art."

"Did you want me to fire all my guns at once?" said Bernie.

Weatherly laughed long and loud. Then she wrapped a forearm around the back of his head, pulled him close, and kissed him on the mouth, a kiss that went on and on. There was something fierce about Weatherly.

"Where have you been?" she said.

"Huh?" said Bernie.

"All my life," Weatherly said.

Bernie blushed. Bernie? Had I ever seen that before? Not that I remembered. Were we in some sort of new territory? I was still wondering about that when Trixie squeezed in between them and broke this thing up. The right play, but that was my job. We were in new territory for sure.

We all walked over to the fat barrel cactus, circled around it, seeing nothing but the cactus and pebbly ground. Bernie gazed up at the sky. All sorts of colors were blazing away up there, like Charlie's whole paint pot set had spilled at once, something that had actually happened, unluckily on Leda's couch, the white leather one she'd had shipped over from Paris, wherever that might be.

"Lauritz Vogner mentioned the Baroque," Bernie said.

"The prospective client?"

Bernie nodded.

"What about it?"

"He didn't explain."

"I looked Vogner up, Bernie," Weatherly said. "No hits in our database. There doesn't seem to be anyone of that name in the whole state."

"He's a foreigner."

"From where?"

"He's Mittel European goulash, in his own words."

"'Mittel' meaning middle?"

"I think so. He reminded me a bit of Peter Lorre."

"I loved that movie," Weatherly said.

"*The Maltese Falcon*?" said Bernie.

Weatherly nodded. "At least I did until I learned they had to light Humphrey Bogart from special angles because he spat when he talked. I pictured Ingrid Bergman having to endure that in all those romantic scenes and the whole movie went sour on me."

Bernie gazed at Weatherly like . . . like . . . like I didn't know what. But it was something big.

"Don't start spitting when you talk," Weatherly said. "That's a deal breaker."

"Wish you hadn't put the idea in my head," said Bernie.

"I ruin everything," Weatherly said.

Bernie started to laugh, but then stopped. Was there a tear in Weatherly's eye? I couldn't tell. The light was getting tricky.

Weatherly took the postcard and gave it another look. "Are you operating on the assumption that Victor got together with Lauritz before he disappeared?"

"It's for sure," Bernie said.

"But couldn't this disappearance be about something else?" said Weatherly.

Bernie thought about that. "You're right. Can't keep your nose too close to the ground."

Whoa! How did he know that? Yes, there were times to get

your nose right down in the dirt, but you had to hoist it up in the air as well. Two different scent worlds are going on all the time, on the ground and in the air. But that was Bernie. Just when you think he's done amazing you he amazes you again.

"For example," Weatherly said, "what other cases was Victor working on?"

"I know of one," Bernie said, "but I think it got settled the other night."

"You haven't mentioned your client," said Weatherly. "Maybe he—or she—has some information on this."

"I doubt it."

"You do have a client, Bernie? You're not doing this on your own—out of feeling bad about recommending Victor?"

"Oh no." He smiled. "We're running a business here."

"So who's the client?" Weatherly said.

Bernie gave Weatherly a direct look. Then he shook his head, hardly at all, the barest hint of movement. "We keep the names of our clients confidential."

Weatherly's head went back. "What did you say?"

Bernie said it again, exactly the same as the first time, not loud but very clear.

"You're joking, right?" she said.

Bernie shook his head again, again hardly any movement at all, but it meant no and nothing but.

Weatherly's voice got very quiet, like she didn't want anyone to hear. "This is me," she said.

"I know," said Bernie.

"So what's with all the stuffy bullshit?"

"It's for everyone's protection."

"I'm not asking for protection," Weatherly said.

"It's protection for the client, too," said Bernie.

"Oh?" said Weatherly. "You think I'd blab the name all over town?"

Uh-oh. All of a sudden they didn't seem to be getting along very well, unless I was missing something. But why? I had no clue.

"Of course not," Bernie said. "But you'd do the same thing in my place."

Weatherly's nostrils narrowed slightly, almost sharpening. She came close to looking scary. "I've heard that one before, word for word. It didn't end well."

"What do you mean?" Bernie said.

"I'm not going to talk about it," said Weatherly. "Do you trust me or not?"

"Totally. But the name of the client stays confidential."

"This is me," she said again, although not so quietly this time. "The same me you've been sleeping with."

"I know," Bernie said. "And I, um, appreciate that."

"Oh, really? You appreciate having sex with me? Should I feel honored?"

"You know I didn't mean it that way," Bernie said.

"Now you're telling me what I know and don't know?" said Weatherly.

"No," Bernie said. "My fault. I wasn't clear. By appreciating I meant I take it into consideration, but it doesn't change things when it comes to client confidentiality. It's for everyone, all the people in my life. Even if we were married—"

"Good luck with that," said Weatherly. I'd never seen her so angry. Or—and this is kind of strange—so beautiful looking. Anger turns most humans ugly. "Are you afraid I'll find Victor first? What is it about men?"

Bernie held up his hand. "Whoa!"

"Exactly." Weatherly spun around and walked quickly away, headed toward the base of the steep slope. She whistled, just once—the loudest, most piercing whistle I'd ever heard from a man or a woman—and Trixie took off after her.

"Weatherly!" Bernie called.

But she didn't stop or even look back. Instead she picked up the pace and ran all the way up the steep switchback trail, Trixie beside her. They reached the top and disappeared from sight.

I turned to Bernie. His mouth was open and his face was so pale, like he was sick, and Bernie never gets sick. I went over and pressed against his leg. His hand came down and scratched between my ears—but kind of on its own. Bernie—my Bernie—was somewhere else.

There was very little light left as we made our way up the switchbacks, Bernie going slow and me going slow also, instead of zooming to the top as I would have done normally, because keeping close to Bernie was what we needed right now. A cool breeze sprang up, actually almost cold. When was the last time I'd felt cold air? Well, this morning, when Bernie opened the fridge. But outside-type cold air? I was still trying to think of a time when Bernie spoke, his voice quiet and not happy, "Cold front. Feel that Canadian air?"

I did! I did feel that Canadian air, rather fresh! First I'd heard of Canada. Did they have perps? If so, we'd get there eventually. There's so much to look forward to in life. It never ends.

We got in the car. How strangely Bernie was moving! Not just slowly, which can happen when he's worn out, but like he was just . . . just going through the motions. Wow! I'd heard about going through the motions more than once and never had a clue. And now, out of the blue, I understood it.

Bernie turned the key but then just sat there. The gearshift, Bernie, the gearshift!

He didn't touch it, sat still, gazing into the growing darkness beyond the drop-off. His eyes were dark, too, the darkest I'd ever seen them. I rested my paw on his knee. He didn't seem to notice. I pressed harder, perhaps digging my nails in the slightest bit. He turned to me.

"You're right," he said. "Let's get something to drink."

Something to drink? Where had that come from? But it was nice to be right. All at once I felt thirsty.

We stopped at a place we'd never been, a small bar on not the worst street in Rio Vista. Out front they had a saguaro with flashing Christmas lights, a plastic saguaro, of course, plastic being one of the real easy smells to pick out, and always in the Valley air. We went inside and sat at the bar, which we had to ourselves. Over in one corner some kind of party was going on, guys and gals wearing party hats, plus a Santa or two. On the floor practically beside me was a metal water bowl. I took a little taste test. Ah. Not long out of the tap, not long at all. I liked this place.

The bartender looked over the bar at me and smiled. "Quite the pooch you got there," he said. "What'll it be?"

"Bourbon on the rocks," said Bernie.

"Any special kind?"

Bernie checked out the bottles behind the bar and pointed to the one with the red roses. "Make it a double."

The bartender fixed Bernie's drink, slid it across to him. Bernie picked it up and took a sip—much more than a sip. The bartender shot him a quick sideways glance. Bernie caught that glance and said, "And his name's Chet." Was he mad at the bartender for some reason? That was what it sounded like. But Bernie hardly ever gets mad and never at friendly-type guys like this.

"Nice name," said the bartender. "Short for Chester?"

"No." Bernie downed the rest of his drink, set down the glass. "I'll have another."

"Single or double?"

"Double."

Uh-oh. Were things going south, wherever that was? Usually the short-for-Chester question leads to some easygoing back and forth about names and the nation within, occasionally to nothing at all, but never a double. The bartender got busy making a new drink. A woman in a pointy-red party hat, a rather small red dress, and very high red high-heels came out of the bathroom and passed by on her way to the party in the corner. She gave Bernie a long look, which he didn't notice. I started to get a bit edgy for no reason I could think of.

Bernie shook his head. Just out of the blue, a head shake. I could feel him having thoughts, not good ones. Was it time to go home? Even though the water here was icy cold and the bartender friendly, my answer was yes, time to go home. And the best way to get that ball rolling would be to—

I was closing in on figuring that out when the bartender set Bernie's new double in front of him.

"Start a tab?" The bartender said, but not with any—what would you call it? Enthusiasm? Close enough. It was almost like he didn't want Bernie to start a tab, like he, too, thought it was time for us to go home.

But Bernie said, "Why not?" The bartender nodded and moved down the bar. Bernie took a sip that again turned into much more. The partygoing folks in the corner began singing "Jingle Bells." One even had a little bell he rang, and every time he rang it a very jolly and rather enormous Santa threw back his head and laughed and laughed. Over at the bar we had Bernie drinking and staring straight ahead at the bottles on the shelves with a faraway look, and me watching Bernie and no longer in the least bit thirsty.

The woman wearing the little red dress and the pointy red party hat came over, a big frosty drink with a cherry on top in one hand and another pointy red party hat in the other.

"Hey, there," she said.

Bernie turned slowly toward her. There's a certain kind of woman who has a certain kind of effect on Bernie, and she was one of them. His eyes began to lose the faraway look.

"You don't seem to be in the Christmas spirit," she said.

"Oh?" said Bernie.

"I could drop a dime on you."

Bernie sat back a bit and said, "Oh?" again.

"The law says you gotta get in the Christmas spirit," she said. "It's in the Constitution."

"Which article?" Bernie said.

She pointed a finger at him, a finger with a gleaming red nail. "There you go! Nitpicking!" With a little grunt she got herself hoisted on the stool next to Bernie. "Nitpicking is not in the Christmas spirit. Here—put this on." She handed Bernie the extra party hat.

Bernie took it but didn't put it on.

"Whatsamatta?" she said. "Don't want anything to distract from your good looks?"

Bernie turned to her. His eyes closed and opened again, now somewhat livelier. Was he actually seeing her for the first time? That was one possibility. As for what was going on in her mind, that was clear from her scent.

"Ha!" Bernie said at last, and he put on the party hat.

The woman laughed. "There we go," she said. "Isn't laughter the best medicine?" She gave Bernie what I believe is called a quick up from under look. "Or at least second," she added.

Now a new scent started to come off Bernie. Did I make it clear he's helpless around a certain kind of woman?

This certain kind of woman gestured toward me. "What's the name of this handsome fellow?"

"Chet," said the bartender, busy sticking an umbrella in a drink at the other end of the bar.

The woman gave him a look. It said buzz off. The bartender carried the drink over to the partygoers in the corner.

"Cool name," said the woman. "And what about you?"

"Bernie."

She nodded. There was a silence. Then the woman said, "And now, in the time-honored way, you say, 'And you? What's your name?'"

Bernie laughed and took another drink, not a gulp this time, but nothing you could call a sip.

"Should I tell you or do you want to guess?" the woman said.

"I'll guess," said Bernie. He looked into the distance and thought for a bit. "Samantha."

The woman's eyes widened. "Oh my god! Oh my god!"

"Am I right?" Bernie said.

"Oh my god! How did you do that?"

"A lucky guess."

"Oh my god." She put her hand on Bernie's, resting by his glass on the bar, and squeezed it hard. "But I don't believe in luck."

"No?"

Samantha shook her head. "Fate, maybe, but not luck. Let's see your other hand."

Bernie held up his other hand.

"No ring," she said.

"I'm not married."

"Makes two of us," Samantha said. "Did you know I live quite close by?"

"No," Bernie said.

"I've got a condo just at the edge of downtown. Twelfth floor, Astra Park Tower. Mountain views. Number 1234, easy as pie."

"Sounds nice."

"Do you like mountain views?" Samantha said.

"Very much."

"How about valleys? Like them, too?"

Bernie swallowed. "I do," he said, his voice strangely thick.

"It's Christmas," Samantha said. "Good things can happen at Christmas."

"Going way back," Bernie said.

"Exactly." Samantha finally let go of Bernie's hand and glanced over at the party in the corner. Then she took out a pen, scribbled on a cocktail napkin, and slid it over to Bernie. "Tell you what. I'll freshen up, say my goodbyes, and head home. You let a proper gossip-killing interval go by, then come and . . . and ring my bell."

"You're a very organized person," Bernie said, pocketing the cocktail napkin. "Although I can probably remember one two three four."

Of course he could, going past two not a problem for him.

Samantha laughed. She got off the stool with another little grunt, and walked toward the bathroom. Bernie watched her back, or at least the back of her, all the way. Then he reached for his glass, took a big swallow, and happened to glance in my direction. I was just sitting there beside his stool, doing nothing much. He gave me a long look. I gave him a long look back.

Bernie put down the glass. It wasn't empty but he made a little ch-ch sound with his tongue. That sound meant we were gone.

Bernie laid some money on the bar and we walked out into the night.

We took what seemed to me a longish route home, at one point crossing the Rio Calor bridge—no actual water flowing below in the rio—and turning down a quiet street. Bernie slowed as we passed a small lemon-colored house with a lemon tree in the yard and a nice shady porch, a house I knew. The lights were off, but inside a member of the nation within barked a soft, rumbly bark. That was Trixie.

We drove home. Bernie laid the postcard on the kitchen table and went to bed. That was when he noticed that he was still wearing the red party hat. He tossed it in the wastebasket and pulled up the covers. I paced around and listened to his restless sleep.

Seven

Moments before the first glimmer of daylight comes a special smell, a lovely scent that maybe is simply the aroma of light, although I'm not really aware of it during the rest of the day. There are so many things to figure out in this life! But I'm just way too busy.

So there I was, lying in the front hall where I like to spend most of the night—security being a big part of my job at the Little Detective Agency—and smelling through the crack under the door the coming of day and waiting for light, when I heard Bernie stirring in the bedroom. Was Bernie a smeller of light? If so, this was the first I'd heard about it. I trotted down the hall and into the bedroom.

He was sitting up in bed, rubbing his face. His fingers opened and he looked at me through the gaps.

"Hey, big guy."

Always nice to start the day with a friendly greeting, but I'd never seen Bernie look at me through his fingers before and I suddenly remembered the one time he'd been locked in a cell and I'd been on the outside. We made them pay in the end, of course, whoever they happened to be, but the sight still made me uneasy. I stepped up to the bed and whipped off the covers.

Bernie lowered his hands. "Chet? Is there a problem?"

Or something like that. I was too busy—didn't I just mention the busy-ness of my life?—twisting those covers this way and that, sending them a message, but good. I felt better almost right away, although a bit disappointed that the covers hadn't put up more of a fight. I let them go and sat by the bed, head high, a total pro, ready for action.

Bernie gave me a long look, a look that turned into a smile—a slight smile, here and gone, but nice to see. He got out of bed and went into the bathroom, perhaps a little pale in the face and limping just a bit. Then came different types of splashing sounds, all very interesting, and when Bernie emerged, drying his hair with a towel, he was pretty much back to himself, takin' charge and namin' names. Bernie. Chet. Those are the names.

Bernie was almost all dressed, just tying the laces on his sneakers, laces that came very close to matching, one set black and the other blue, when he noticed the red party hat, its pointy top sticking out of the wastebasket. He went over and plucked it out.

"The name was on her bracelet," he said. "'Samantha,' in big loopy letters. Are all miracles like that, if you only had the facts?" He went still. "I'm going to look up the Flight into Egypt."

Bernie had lost me completely. You can't let that kind of thing bother you, and I never do. Meanwhile we moved into the kitchen, Bernie carrying the party hat. We have some hooks on the wall hear the fridge, where we hang things like a set of car keys and Charlie's baseball glove. Bernie stuck the party hat on an empty hook and turned to me.

"Call it a red flag," he said.

I've come to realize that you can't expect a person who drinks too much bourbon at night to be quite himself the next morning. By the next afternoon, sure, unless the person, whoever it might be, has pretty much polished off the whole bottle, which certainly hadn't happened last night. So I knew that quite soon Bernie would be realizing that the red party hat was not a flag, and toss it back in the wastebasket where it belonged.

He made coffee in the fancy new machine, given to us by Malcolm, who had suddenly found himself the owner of the company that makes them.

"He just can't help making money," Bernie had said at the time. "Sure, he's smart and a hard worker, but so are lots of people who don't have appliance companies thrust upon them. What makes Malcolm different?"

An easy one. Malcolm had the longest toes I'd ever seen on a dude. Bernie's toes are normal size. Did that mean we might not end up being rich after all? My mind refused to believe it. My mind, by the way, is just about always on my side. I've been lucky my whole life.

Bernie sipped his coffee and the light—his normal light—returned to his eyes. I have no interest in drinking coffee myself, but the smell is amazing. Even humans are onto that, no offense. "Wake up and smell the coffee," they often tell one another, even when everybody's awake. Humans can't be completely understood. Maybe I should have mentioned that much earlier. For example, they never say, "Wake up and smell the tea," although the smell of tea is also amazing, in fact more so than the smell of coffee.

But no time to explain right now. Bernie drank a sip or two more, then took a deep breath, reached for the phone and tapped the screen.

"Weatherly? Please pick up."

She did not. Bernie clicked off. The phone buzzed almost right away, but it wasn't Weatherly.

"Bernie?"

"Hi, Elise."

"I'm not disturbing you?"

"Not at all."

"I don't want to be the kind of client who calls every fifteen minutes."

"Don't worry about that," Bernie said.

"But I . . . I just couldn't help it," Elise said. "Is there any news?"

"No."

"Even unfavorable news? Please don't hold back."

"I'm not and I won't," Bernie said. "Did Victor mention anything about Nuestra Señora before he left?"

"Our lady?" said Elise.

"I'm talking about Nuestra Señora de los Saguaros, the mission on the old De Niza highway."

"No," Elise said. "Is it important?"

"I don't know," said Bernie.

There was a silence. Then Elise said, "Do you know a police sergeant named Weatherly Wauneka?"

Bernie's eyes shifted toward me. "I do."

"She called half an hour ago."

"Oh?"

"The police department has opened an investigation, looking for Victor."

"I was aware of that," Bernie said. "Do you want me to continue?"

"Oh, yes. In fact, I was going to ask your advice on whether I should cooperate with her."

"Why wouldn't you?"

"Victor doesn't have a high opinion of Valley PD," Elise said.

"You should cooperate with Sergeant Wauneka. They don't come any better. One more thing—have you got a good photo of Victor?"

"For showing possible witnesses?"

"Exactly. Send it to me."

"Now?"

"Now." Did Bernie's "now" sound kind of urgent? He said it again, this time with less oomph. Then he watched his phone. He held it so I could see. Sometimes I look and sometimes I don't, phones not being a big interest of mine. But how nice of him to think of me! I get it, of course. I think of him all the time.

The phone went ping, and ping again. Two photos appeared on the screen, Victor in both. In the first, he was alone and unsmiling, maybe deep in thought. In the second, he had his arm over the shoulder of a woman with dark, curly hair, and both of them were laughing. Victor looked so happy I almost didn't recognize him.

"You sent two?" Bernie said.

"I know he's not alone in the second one," Elise said, "but it's a much better likeness."

"Who's the woman?"

"A girlfriend. Well, a former girlfriend. She's very nice."

"What's her name?"

"Jada," Elise said. "Jada Brooks. But formerly the girlfriend, as I mentioned."

"Is there a present girlfriend?" Bernie said.

"No. Victor hasn't really had what you'd call a lot of girlfriends. Perhaps that's why I find the photo so affecting."

"When did they break up?"

"A couple of months ago."

"Why?"

"I only asked that once and he got very angry and said it was none of my business. Only more . . . colorfully. It shocked me, to tell the truth. Our relationship has always been so . . ." Her voice trailed off.

"Where do we find Jada Brooks?" Bernie said.

"Are you suggesting Victor's with her? But then why wouldn't he simply pick up—"

Here's something about Bernie. He never interrupts. We've talked to a lot of people, me and Bernie—with him doing the talking and me bringing other things to the table—and he's never interrupted anybody, not once. But now he did.

"Elise?" he said. "You're a very smart person and very astute, but that doesn't mean you can do my job."

Elise was quiet for so long I thought the call was over. Then she said, "Jada owns a little art gallery in Pottsdale—Celare Artem."

"Can you spell it?"

"Spelling isn't part of your job?" Elise said.

Bernie laughed like that was a good joke. And here I'd thought, just from the sound of her voice, that it was an insult. Was he enjoying an insult about himself? That was something to think about. Where to begin?

Before the answer could come to me, Elise spoke again. Her voice had changed, as though she was . . . was hearing Bernie in a new way. As for what she said—possibly about spelling, a mystery to me—I missed it completely. Sort of a double miss, if you see where I'm coming from.

Bernie tapped his fingers on the wheel and began to sing. "It came upon a midnight clear, bum bumpity bumpity bum." Wow! What a great song, and brand-new to me! Bernie has the best singing voice you've ever heard and sometimes accompanies himself on the ukulele, which he can do while he's driving, no problem, although we didn't have the ukulele today. Pretty much the only song he'd been singing recently was "Death Don't Have No Mercy." I liked this midnight clear one better, but anything Bernie wanted to sing was fine with me.

We drove into Pottsdale, the most peaceful part of town, not very interesting from my point of view, although I always enjoyed a visit to Livia's Friendly Coffee and More, where Bernie sometimes bought coffee beans but never entered the back of the establishment where the More part went on, even though Livia had mentioned and mentioned again that it would be on the house. But often when we showed up, Tulip or Autumn—or sometimes both at once!—would appear from the back. "Who's the handsomest guy in the whole Valley?" they'd cry, and then run over and start petting me. I've been petted by some first-rate petters—Bernie at the top of the list, of course—but no one comes close to Tulip and Autumn. If you haven't been petted by one of them, try to make it happen. You won't regret it.

Right now we actually drove past Livia's place, but didn't stop. As we went by the door opened—a door hung with silver bells that tinkled in a way my ears liked a whole lot—and Autumn stepped out, head down so she didn't see us. She was busy counting some money, flicking through it with her red-nailed thumb. We turned a corner, drove down several blocks, and parked in front of a store selling western gear, easy to tell from the boots and saddles in the big window. Here's something about Bernie that will surprise you: He doesn't own a single pair of cowboy boots! Yet he's from here and his family has been here forever and once had a huge spread on both sides of Mesquite Canyon, our place on Mesquite Road being all that remains. The point I'm trying to make is that Bernie wearing cowboy boots isn't like some tourist from back east, wherever that is, clomping around in them. He has every right! And Bernie can ride, by the way. Have I mentioned Mingo? All horses are prima donnas but Mingo was off the charts. You should have seen Bernie on him! And then off! And back on! And—but perhaps a story for another time. The point is I wanted Bernie to have cowboy boots. It just so happens I'm an admirer of fine leather. Was today the day?

Answer: No. We walked right past the western gear place to the next store, much smaller, with a single painting in the window, a painting maybe of a huge lake of ice cream melting under a blue sun or possibly moon, but I couldn't be sure. Bernie read the gold-painted sign hanging out front: "'Celare Artem.'" We went inside.

There was no one around. Paintings hung on the walls, lit by soft light in different shades, shades that made me a bit sleepy. The paintings weren't the kind we like, me and Bernie. Our paintings at home—the biggest one covering the office safe—are all about waterfalls. I once saw a waterfall, on a missing-kid case at a summer camp up in lovely green mountains. The sounds of a waterfall—and there are so many, all at once!—are wonderful, and when I look at our waterfall paintings I can hear them. I couldn't hear any of the paintings in this place.

A door opened at the back and a woman came out. She had dark, curly hair with a tinsel strand caught in one of the curls, and although she wasn't laughing like in the photo I recognized her right away. Victor's girlfriend, for sure! Or possibly former girlfriend? Only her name escaped me.

She gave us a nice smile. "Welcome," she said. "Anything I can help you with?"

"Jada Brooks?" Bernie said.

"Yes," she said, her smile starting to fade.

"I'm Bernie Little and this is Chet. We're friends of Victor Klovsky."

Jada nodded. "He talks about you. Often in fact. But I didn't know you were actually friends."

"Not close friends," Bernie said. "What does he say about us?"

"'Us' meaning?"

"Chet and I."

"Ah. Victor's a big admirer of yours. He's made a study of some of your cases, but it . . . it didn't seem to bring about the improvements he was hoping for. I suggested—this was back when we were together—that he get himself a dog." She looked at me. "But where would he find one like this?"

That was an easy one! Just show up at K-9 school and grab whoever flunks out on the last day! For the first time I got the feeling that this case was going well.

"So you're no longer together," Bernie said.

Didn't we know that already? But sometimes Bernie went over things we knew already. Whoa! Was that one of our techniques at the Little Detective Agency? We were even better than I'd imagined.

"That's right," Jada said.

"Can I ask how come?" said Bernie.

"How come we're not still together?" Jada's eyes sort of hooded a little and I felt a bit of the strength that was inside her. "Is something wrong?"

"Possibly," Bernie said. "Or probably. Victor's gone missing. We're trying to find him."

"Missing? But I spoke to him—when was it?—just the day before yesterday."

"In person?"

"No, he called. We hadn't spoken in weeks. Our breakup was . . . not messy, but a bit ragged. An upside-down take on an old theme, would be one way of putting it."

"I don't understand," Bernie said.

Jada gave Bernie a direct look. "Victor wanted to settle down—get married, have kids, all that. It's not that I'm not ready—that implies it's a necessary step. I'll just say the expression 'to settle down' makes my skin crawl."

"Did he use those words?" Bernie said. "'Settle down'?"

"Verbatim."

"And that was the moment?"

"The moment things changed?" Jada said.

Bernie nodded.

Jada's head tilted slightly. I knew that one, the head tilt of someone seeing Bernie in a new way. "How did you know that?"

Bernie shrugged.

"Sometimes I wish things hadn't changed," Jada said.

"Oh?" said Bernie.

"Victor's a fine person. He's soulful, when you get to know him. And very kind. Those aren't everyday qualities, not in my experience. Something bad has happened to him—I can hear it in your voice."

She was right about that. This was unusual. I took a close look at her ears, normal human ears, on the small side if anything.

"We can't say that yet," Bernie said. "It's possible he had an accident on his bicycle."

"Oh god, that stupid bike. What happened?"

Bernie went over the bike story.

"But then where is he?" Jada said.

"That's the problem," Bernie said. "Tell me about the phone call."

"It was very brief. And not about the two of us or how it ended or any of that. In fact, he seemed happy, even excited."

"About what?"

"He didn't say. He sounded in a hurry. All he wanted to know was whether I'd heard of Caravaggio."

"Who's that?"

Jada smiled. She had a beautiful smile, but like Bernie's eyebrows it had a language of its own. I could see that, although all I understood was the beauty part.

"Funny how someone so important in my world can be completely unknown everywhere else," she said.

"He's a painter?" Bernie said. "Or she?"

Jada's scent changed slightly. Was it because of Bernie? This had happened before with other women, although Bernie never seemed to notice. She patted her hair, felt the tinsel strand, pulled it out, glanced at it in surprise, and stuck it in her pocket.

"He," Jada said. "Caravaggio was an Italian painter, circa sixteen hundred. His reputation wasn't high for centuries but now he's seen as one of the most influential of all artists. The last time one of his paintings came on the market it sold for over one hundred million."

"Yeah?" said Bernie. "Was he Baroque?"

"Ah. So you know something about art after all."

"Nothing," Bernie said. "The word came up recently."

Jada nodded. "Caravaggio couldn't quite be called Baroque. It's more like he led there, although he's far more earthy." She took out the phone, tapped at the screen. Bernie peered in. Their heads almost touched. For a moment, she reminded me of him.

"What's this?" he said.

"David with the head of Goliath." David and Goliath were both new to me, and quite possibly perps, just from the way that sounded, but from where I was I couldn't see the screen, and for some reason didn't even want to. "But what's revolutionary is the dramatic contrast of light and shade."

Bernie took a long look. "Kind of like the movies."

"The very best ones," Jada said. "Times ten. And here's a little trick if you want to separate the good painters from the great— check out the parts of the canvas that don't draw the eye."

Bernie went still. Just for a very quick moment, but I noticed. I'm a great noticer of Bernie.

He took a closer look at the screen on Jada's phone. "I can't find any of those parts."

Jada shot Bernie a speedy glance. I'd seen that one before, the speedy glance of someone getting to know Bernie. "Exactly," she said. "Caravaggio is very controlling. A difficult man—he was a murderer, among other things."

"Was he caught?" said Bernie.

"Caught?"

"Arrested. Tried. Convicted."

"He wriggled out of it somehow," Jada said. "Didn't he disappear somewhere for a while? I don't remember."

Bernie's gaze returned to the screen. "Did you tell all this to Victor?"

"Not in this detail, but yes . . ."

"What was his reaction?"

"He thanked me and said goodbye."

"Nothing about why he wanted to know?"

Jada started to shake her head and then stopped. "At the end he said, 'I love the name of the shop, by the way.' A bit odd, since he'd never mentioned it before, but Victor can be odd, as you might know."

"What shop?" Bernie said.

"This one," said Jada. "Mine."

Bernie glanced at the sign. "Celare Artem?"

"From a Latin expression. *Ars celare artem.*"

"Meaning?"

"'The art is to hide the art.'"

Bernie thought.

"You're thinking it's a crazy name for a business that's supposed to be selling art?" Jada said.

"Actually not," Bernie said. "I was wondering if Victor mentioned a man named Lauritz Vogner."

"No."

"Does the name mean anything to you?"

"No," Jada said. "Is he an artist?"

Bernie started to shake his head and stopped, almost exactly the way she had done it. "Maybe of a kind," he said. "One more thing—mind printing out a copy of that painting?"

"No problem," said Jada. "May I ask why?"

Bernie shrugged. "To educate myself."

"Here's a start," she said. "Goliath's severed head is thought to be a self-portrait of the artist."

"With blood dripping from the neck?"

"Very much so."

A few moments later, Jada handed Bernie one of those small glossy sheets of photo paper. Bernie glanced at it and stuck it in his pocket. Fine with me. Whatever it was, I didn't want to look.

Eight

"Celare artem," Bernie said, as we drove past a bunch of used-tire stores, meaning we'd left Pottsdale. "Can't read too much into things, but reading into things is what we do. See the problem?"

I did not. In fact, I was confused. Reading was what we did? I myself never read. Bernie reads sometimes. When Charlie was little Bernie would read aloud to him. For some reason, the book Charlie liked best was about three little bunnies. Three little bunnies, over and over again. Why? I grew to dislike that book very much, and wasn't at all unhappy when it went missing. Was that the end of the matter? Far from it. You may be thinking, *Oh, Chet, don't tell me you actually got involved in the search?* And you'd be onto something because it turned out Charlie got very upset about his bunny book. Hadn't he toddled over to me and said, "Chet, please please find my bunny book"? Which I'd done without the slightest hesitation. A snap, of course, since the thing was exactly where I'd—

Enough of that. I never read. Bernie no longer reads aloud to Charlie, although he does read to himself from time to time, most recently a book with a picture of a baseball on the cover. But by now my point should be clear. Reading is not what we do. Catching perps and sending them up the river is what we do, regardless if there's water in the river or not. I gave Bernie a careful look. He seemed fine but the bourbon from last night was still messing with him. There was no other explanation.

He glanced at me. "Waiting for me to get on the stick, aren't you, big guy?"

Well, I would have put it more . . . gently? Would that be it? Close enough. I would have put it more gently, but yes, that's what I was doing.

"How about we get the hell out of Dodge?"

We were in Dodge? News to me. Otherwise it sounded like a plan. Bernie stomped on the gas, then stomped on the brake, because we seemed to be in heavy traffic, but not long after that we were rolling through open country, the wind in Bernie's hair and in my fur, and both our moods tip-top.

"The old De Niza highway," Bernie said, as we turned onto a long straight stretch of two-lane blacktop, potholey, bumpy, dusty. We even had a ball of tumbleweed tumbling by. Who could ask for more?

"De Niza was the first European in Arizona," Bernie said.

Ah. Things were starting to come together. De Niza, whoever he was, knew what was what when it came to highways.

"Although," Bernie went on, "there must have been other Europeans with him, names unknown, at least to me. Plus some Aztecs, maybe, some Sonoran locals—no borders then, big guy." Bernie laughed, then fished around here and there for a cigarette and finding none, the fact that he'd quit smoking possibly slipping his mind. He was a champ at quitting smoking, had done it many times. I could tell he was in the mood to do some thinking out loud—I loved when he did that!—and cigarettes got his hands involved in the conversation, meaning we actually had a bit of a crowd: Bernie, his two hands, and me, Chet the Jet. But today, out on this lovely highway, it was just us two.

"Seven cities of gold," Bernie said. "That's what he was searching for. Maybe a strange quest for a monk, which was what he was. Why not something spiritual?" He gazed into the distance. "A material quest in a spiritual land?" He took a deep breath, let it out slowly. "Let's not push it too far. Judge not, right, Chet?"

Judges were in the picture? I knew several, had even once been Exhibit A in Judge Jaramillo's court, Exhibit B being a .44 Magnum I'd dug up out of some perp's flower bed. Judge Jaramillo had invited me up to sit beside him. Down under his big judging desk where no one could see, there'd been a quick handing over of a biscuit. Also, life being full of fun surprises, I'd somehow ended up with that very tasty wooden judging hammer with a special name that might come to me later. We were outside in the courthouse parking lot when Bernie noticed, asked me for it very nicely, as he always does in situations like that, and took it back to Judge Jaramillo. But the point is, if judges were in the picture, things were looking up. And weren't they already pretty high already? Then I happened to think of Victor's smashed-up bicycle and had . . . what was it called? A moment of doubt. A short moment, as it turned out. I'm lucky that way.

A bell tower appeared in the distance. It wobbled and blurred, the way things sometimes do in these parts, almost vanished and suddenly seemed much closer, still and clear: a desert-colored bell tower, a bit crooked, on the roof of a desert-colored building that had the look of a church. I knew churches from funerals I'd been to, funerals coming up from time to time in our line of work.

"Nuestra Señora," Bernie said.

Not long after that, we turned onto a dirt track that curved around a sort of island of saguaros and palo verde trees with their nutty smell, a bit like pistachios, and came to the church. We parked in the shade of a big palo verde, standing all by itself, and got out of the car. Whoa! I'd forgotten to hop out! How could I make a mistake like that? I turned to the car, and was considering hopping back in so I could hop out properly, when Bernie said, "Chet?" in this way he has. We headed toward the church.

No one around and no sound but the faint whine of the wind in the bell tower. This church—Nuestra Señora, if I was following things right—was not in good shape. There was a blue tarp on the roof, scaffolding here and there, broken orange tiles on the ground. The wooden door, scarred and heavy-looking, was padlocked.

Bernie knocked. The knock echoed inside the church and also outside in the open desert. "Hello? Anyone here?"

The wind made its whiny sound in the bell tower. I thought I heard a trace of Bernie's words coming from up there, but metallic, as though the bell was saying "Hello? Anyone here?" I glanced at Bernie. Were we done?

He backed away from the door, but didn't head toward the car.

Instead he started walking around Nuestra Señora, with me soon in the lead. I saw a couple of wheelbarrows, picks and shovels, a sand pile. We came to a pit in the ground, not deep, roped off, and with a few small tools lying in the dirt at the bottom. Beyond the pit was another, also roped off, and then another, and beyond that stood a trailer.

We went up to the trailer door and knocked, Bernie doing the actual knocking. I stood beside him, alert and ready for anything. Have you ever had a situation with a door suddenly opening and a meth-head popping out with a twelve-gauge in his hands? I have, and more than once. You learn from things like that, or else one day . . . But let's not go there.

The door opened. No twelve-gauge, no meth-head, instead a woman dressed in denim, work boots, a bandanna on her head, and a pencil behind her ear. She had a deep tan and bright blue eyes. They went to Bernie, then to me, and back to Bernie, and the brightness got toned down.

"Yes?" she said.

Yes, in my experience, can be spoken in many ways. This one was close to no.

"Hi," Bernie said. "We were hoping to go inside the church."

"Why?" said the woman.

"To have a look," Bernie said.

"For religious purposes?"

"Not really, but it is Christmas."

"The structure is no longer a church," the woman said. "It was deconsecrated last year."

"I'm not sure what that means," Bernie said.

"The church is no longer sacred, in plain English. It doesn't belong to a religious organization."

"Who owns it?"

"A private nonprofit."

"What's its name?"

The woman's eyes narrowed. "Why do you want to know?"

Bernie smiled. "Don't nonprofits encourage contributions from the public?"

"You're a donor?"

"Potentially."

"What's your name?"

"Bernie Little. This is Chet. And you are?"

Was Bernie asking for her name? Maybe not, because she didn't give it. Instead she said, "He's not on a leash."

"No," Bernie said. "You can trust Chet."

"In what sense?"

Bernie looked a bit confused, which hardly ever happens. I was confused myself. Had she mentioned a leash? What would be the point? Weren't we working a case? That meant I'd be right where I was, at Bernie's side. How would a leash help with that? People can get tangled up in leashes, fall down, even end up being dragged around in the dirt. I'd seen it happen.

She gestured with her hand. "This is an ongoing archeological site. Any tampering, intentional or not, interferes with our research."

"You're an archaeologist?" Bernie said.

"Correct."

Bernie glanced at the pencil behind her ear. "I won't waste your time. I'm a private detective looking for a missing man named Victor Klovsky."

"Never heard of him."

"Maybe he came here and didn't mention his name." Bernie took out his phone. "This is Victor."

I caught a glimpse of the photo Bernie showed her, not the one where he and Jada were laughing, but the one with him alone and sad.

The woman shook her head. "Never seen him."

Bernie took out our card, a somewhat bothersome card we were still using, designed by Suzie some time back. Why had she put flowers on it? I'd heard Bernie ask himself that question more than once, but he'd never asked her, and he never said anything about getting new cards.

He handed the card to the woman. "If Victor shows up, or if you hear anything that might help, please get in touch."

"Sure," said the woman, sticking the card in her shirt pocket.

Bernie gave her a little wave goodbye. We turned and headed back the way we'd come, but I got a bit distracted by an interesting scent that came wafting by. Not a particularly strong scent—hardly there at all, really—but it reminded me of Bernie's suit. Bernie has only the one suit, very dark gray, which he wears to funerals and weddings and then takes off as soon as we're back home, hanging it back in the closet. It's made of some sort of light cloth that keeps him cool even in the heat, the name not coming to me. I sometimes linger in the closet just to sniff. I like the smell of that suit! Who knows why?

I followed the smell, which led away from the church and all the digging, across a dirt road and onto hardpacked rocky land sort of fenced off by a broken-down wire fence.

"Chet?" Bernie called. "Need to pee?"

Nice of him to be concerned, but it wasn't that. Bernie paused before a faded sign on a post and read it aloud. "'Eight prime acres. Subdividable. All offers considered.'" In a lower voice he added, "How about just leaving it as is?"

Fine with me. I liked this patch of land, although nothing seemed to be growing on it but a saguaro, a two-armed one, maybe the biggest I'd ever seen, blackened here and there and with some bullet holes, but still standing, those arms outstretched. The linen-type scent—yes, it came to me!—led to a small pile of old stone blocks, not far from the saguaro, stone blocks of the same sandy color as the church. I sniffed around the blocks. No member of the nation within had marked them and neither had any foxes or coyotes. How interesting! I was considering a bit of digging when Bernie said, "If you're going to pee, pee."

I had no intention of peeing but when someone keeps urging you, intentions can fly out the window. In short, I marked those stones.

We headed back across the dirt road toward the car. The woman appeared from around a corner of the trailer. She seemed surprised to see us.

"Still here?" she said.

"Just on our way," said Bernie.

She glanced around, gazed at me, then at Bernie. There was a very long pause before she said, "I've a got a few minutes."

"Oh?" Bernie said.

"If you still want to see inside."

"That would be great."

"I'll get the key."

She popped back into the trailer, disappearing from view.

"What changed her mind?" Bernie said.

Had to be because she'd realized we were nice guys. Didn't folks like doing things for nice guys? I gazed at Bernie's face, checking whether he'd figured it out. He must have, of course. What kind of world would it be where Chet figured things out before Bernie?

The woman came out of the trailer, a large and rusty key in her hand and the bandanna no longer in her hair. She had fair hair cut very short, a tough sort of haircut, if that makes any sense. But I liked it anyway! Tough customers don't bother us. We're pretty tough customers ourselves, me and Bernie.

We walked around the church, me, Bernie, the woman. I felt her gaze on my back. "What do you know about Fray Marcos de Niza?" she said.

"What I learned in school," Bernie said. "Less what I've forgotten."

"Ah," said the woman, as we circled around the church and reached the door. "You have a sense of humor." She stuck the huge old key into the huge old padlock.

"Is that a compliment, Ms., uh . . . ?"

"Just an observation," she said, turning the key. It made a noise like a squeaky groan. "And it's doctor, by the way, Dr. Johanna Borden, but you can call me Johanna."

Bernie nodded. "Is that a PhD type doctorate?"

She looked up, the key half-raised, almost like she was thinking of pointing it at Bernie. "Inferior to an MD doctorate in your mind?"

"Not at all. You said you were an archaeologist and—"

"And you were just nailing it down?"

"I wasn't going to put it that way."

"No problem. I suppose nailing things down is what private detectives do." Johanna, if I'd caught her name, not always so easy on the first try, frowned. "Are you armed?" she said.

"Not at the moment." Which couldn't have been truer, the .38 Special presently all on its lonesome in the glove box of the Porsche, a few steps away.

"I'm not comfortable around guns," she said.

"So you're not from Arizona," said Bernie.

Was that one of Bernie's jokes? He can be quite the jokester, and you can always tell from a certain look in his eye. He had it now but Johanna didn't laugh or even show a hint of a smile. Some humans, by the way, have faces that seem nicely set up for smiling. Johanna's wasn't that kind.

"Correct," she said.

"Where are you from?" Bernie said.

"Back east. But I'm very familiar with the state from multiple angles—historical, geological, anthropological, and of course archaeological. I did a two-year postdoc at Valley College."

She opened the lock, turned the knob, very big and rusty—and gave the door a push. It didn't open. She drove her shoulder into it with a surprising amount of force. The door swung open, a heavy old door that moved slowly and with some groaning, like . . . like a heavy old person! What a thought! Actually a bit tiring, to come up with thoughts like that. With any luck at all another one wouldn't strike me for some time.

But meanwhile we were inside the church, where it was pretty dark, shafts of light—the silvery kind we get at this time of year—coming through the two windows that weren't boarded up, as well as cracks in the walls. The ceiling curved sharply up from all sides, quite high, forming a rounded sort of arch up there, but the church itself was narrow. Here and there lay piles of stone blocks and broken adobe bricks. Other than that, there wasn't much to see.

But smells? That was a different matter! We had smells out the ying-yang. The strongest was the smell of snakes, somewhat fishy, but sharper and more thinned out than the smell of real fish. My gator skin collar has a somewhat similar smell, except it's grown very faint now, and gotten just about completely mixed with my own smell. But not the point, which was that I'd never picked up so much snake scent in one place in my whole career. Snakes loved it here in this church! So therefore—my goodness, here I was doing a so-therefore, usually Bernie's department—I did not love it here. You could say Chet's no fan of snakes, and that would be true. You could also say they scare the hell out of him, and that would also be true. But, and this might surprise you, I actually caught one once, fat and black, on a hike we took in high piney country somewhere. The look on Bernie's face!

His face didn't have that look now. Instead it had the look it gets when he's seeing something new, a calm sort of look although deep inside him things are very busy. I felt them humming away. At the same time, Johanna was off to the side a bit, watching him. Were they both totally unaware of the snake issue? Hard to believe, but why weren't they saying, Yikes! Crawling with snakes! Let's vamoose!?

Bernie gazed up at the ceiling. "So this is Baroque?" he said.

"Of a kind," said Johanna.

Bernie turned to her.

"It's a small-scale example of Mexican Baroque," she went on, "nowhere near as imposing as San Xavier del Bac, to say nothing of what Mexico City has to offer."

"But it must have been more impressive back then," Bernie said. "In De Niza's day."

"It wasn't here in De Niza's day," Johanna said.

"But I thought—"

Johanna interrupted. "In the beginning—possibly around 1550, but we're not sure—the Franciscans built a very small chapel on this spot. What you see here dates from the mid to late eighteenth century. Furthermore, there's no evidence in any records that De Niza was actually ever here, or within a hundred miles. All we know is that the chapel was built fairly early in the Spanish exploration."

"Hmm," said Bernie. He walked around, kicked at broken roof tile.

"Please don't do that," Johanna said.

Did Bernie redden just a bit? Hard to tell in this light. He picked up the roof tile and gently placed it back where it had been. I happened to glance Johanna's way. From the expression on her face, I could see she didn't yet realize what a fine man Bernie was.

He moved toward the end of the church, the dimmest part, where there was another one of those roped-off pits.

"What's going on here?"

Johanna glanced over. "Routine archaeology. This one didn't pan out."

"What were you hoping to find?"

Perhaps a cloud passed over the sun, because the light on her face got dimmer. "Pottery shards, tools, belt buckles—the usual."

Bernie peered down into the pit.

"Looking for something?" she said.

As she spoke I heard a car pulling up outside. I moseyed over to a crack in the wall, Bernie possibly replying, "Not really."

I looked through the crack. A big black SUV was parking outside the church. The front doors opened and two men got out, the driver—a huge dude with a handlebar mustache—and a fattish guy wearing a suit and what I believe is called a Panama hat. He had a curly whitish beard, kind of like Santa's, and he looked like he was in a jolly mood. They took a step or two before the fattish guy noticed the Porsche, sitting on the far side of the big palo verde. His mood changed. He motioned to the huge dude, made some sort of sign. The huge dude went over to the Porsche, leaned in, and rummaged around. Then he straightened and held up a card. Our business card! This was outrageous. I started barking my head off.

"Chet!" Bernie said. "Knock it off!"

I did not knock it off. I ran to him and barked and barked.

"Is something wrong with him?" Johanna said.

I didn't like the sound of that and neither did Bernie. I amped up the barking. He went quickly to the big heavy door, threw it open—me arriving first—and looked out. The fattish man in the Panama hat, the huge dude, the big black SUV: all gone.

"Chet?"

I amped it back down in stages, and had almost reached total silence by the time we returned to the roped-off pit. "Not sure what that was about," Bernie said. "A bit odd."

"One way of putting it," Johanna said. "What even made you think your missing man had been here? Is he an archaeologist?"

"No."

Her eyes narrowed. "An art historian?"

"No," Bernie said. "It was a long shot."

"Does he have anything at all to do with Nuestra Señora?"

"Not that I can see."

"What does he do?" Johanna said.

"He's a private investigator."

"Investigating what?"

"I wish I knew," Bernie said.

Johanna watched him, maybe waiting for Bernie to say more. When he did not, she gestured with her chin toward the pit and said, "Well, he's not in there. I didn't find a thing." Then she laughed, so it must have been a joke of some sort, a bright sounding laugh, high-pitched. I love human laughter, but I prefer the less sharp kind. Johanna had gotten a little nervous. Some smells are unmissable.

Nine

"Here's another way of approaching the problem," Bernie said. "What did Lauritz want us to do? What's the case even about? I screwed up that conversation, Chet, big time."

Bernie screwing something up? He expected me to believe that? Not going to happen. I stuck my head into the breeze—actually the wind, since we were zipping along pretty quick in light traffic. The wind in my face: ah! It blew my ears straight back and made my lips billow every which way, side to side, up and down. There's fun to be had in this life, my friends.

"It's all about where to drill the first hole," Bernie said.

The drill? Please not the drill. Did you know, for example, that certain wires lurk behind the walls in your house, and that if you drill into a wall—say for some purpose, now forgotten, that seems to make sense at the time—you might drill right into one of those wires, and then the driller will be flat on the floor on his back and the whole wall will be in flames? Trust me on this one.

"The logical beginning," Bernie went on, "is to find out who recommended us to Lauritz." He was quiet for a while after that. I could feel his thoughts, slow, heavy, and finally motionless. He took out the postcard of Nuestra Señora. "Less logically, we could try to find out if this is something that matters or just some random scrap." He glanced at me. "What do you think?"

So nice of Bernie to ask, but his timing could have been better. I had no thoughts at the moment. My mind was completely empty of thoughts, like the bright blue sky on a cloudless day. I tried to think of a thought. Nothing came. Why couldn't I have a thought right now when I needed one, say about when I first met him—in the Donut Heaven parking lot, just a passing moment on my last day of K-9 school—and got a whiff of his scent, all about apples, bourbon, salt and pepper, the nicest human scent I'd ever come across, and also got a good look at his face, one of those strong faces you sometimes see on men, often also showing a trace or more than a trace of mean, but not in his case, where there was no mean whatsoever?

But no thoughts came. Maybe some other time.

He took his eyes off the road, checked out the back of the postcard. "What do we know about postcard identification? Nada. I've never even considered the possibility. Do you see how ignorance expands? Suppose all of life is a race between knowledge and ignorance, two expanding universes with speeds governed by factors we may never discover?"

That sounded like a tough one, one of the toughest we'd ever come across. I was at a loss.

He laid the postcard on the dash. "Let's take a swing at it anyway."

Wow! What a brilliant solution! I began to feel very good about the case.

We drove downtown, went by the college, catching a glimpse of the college kids taking a little break outdoors from their books with their beers and their bongs, and parked in front of a building that seemed to be made of the same reddish stone as all the college buildings, but was much smaller. Bernie took the postcard off the dash and we went to the front door. A worker in white overalls was up on a ladder, hanging a sign.

Bernie read it aloud. "'The Western Reporter.' I like it."

The worker, a skinny old dude missing some teeth, glanced down. "Kinda plain, doncha think?"

"In a good way," said Bernie.

The door was open. We moved around the ladder and went inside. It was a big open space, full of light but otherwise mostly empty, except for boxes stacked here and there. The only person around was a strange sort of woman sitting at a glass desk and typing so fast on a laptop that her fingers blurred. She was small and dressed mostly in green, with a pointy green hat—her glossy black hair poking out from under the brim—green jacket with big round red buttons, tight green and red striped pants, and green sneakers with red soles.

"Yes?" she said, not looking up from the screen.

"Uh, is Suzie around?" Bernie said. "Or Jacques?"

Her eyes shifted our way but her fingers didn't stop. "Negative to both," she said. "Can I help you?"

"I don't know," Bernie said. "We weren't expecting an elf."

"No one ever does," said this elf, whatever an elf happened to be. This particular elf smelled and looked exactly like a young woman. That was as far as I could take it on my own. "That's one of our many advantages."

Bernie laughed, a relaxed, full-throated laugh. I realized right then that he had no fear of elves, or at least this particular elf, so I didn't either. We're a team, me and Bernie.

Meanwhile the elf had snapped her laptop shut and was coming over to us. I should mention the floor, made of wide wooden planks, polished and wonderful feeling under my paws. Floor feel is an interest of mine. Maybe I don't get into it enough, but I promise to from now on, if I remember.

"Am I in the presence of Chet and Bernie?" she said.

"In that order," said Bernie.

"I've been looking forward to this," said the elf. "I've heard so many good things about you. I'm Ling." She held out her hand, a nicely shaped little hand, not weak. It got lost in Bernie's.

"I've heard good things about you, too," Bernie said.

"Really?" Ling the elf looked surprised and pleased.

"Just the other day Suzie said you were the finest researcher she'd ever seen."

Ling put her hand to her chest. "Oh my goodness! So far from the truth! Suzie's just the best!"

"True," Bernie said. "Although she failed to mention you were an elf."

Ling laughed. She had a soft, quiet laugh, but somehow lovely just the same.

"Would you believe that three years ago I had no idea what an elf even was? Well, the Tolkien kind, yes, but not the Christmas kind. I couldn't even speak a word of English—as I'm sure you can tell from how bad I am at it."

"Excuse me?" Bernie said.

"And now I'm into Christmas elfhood like you wouldn't believe!"

"I do believe it," Bernie said.

Ling the elf laughed again. "Would Chet like a treat? I don't think we have any yet. I'll add it to my list."

"Thanks," Bernie said. "But he's fine."

What was that? Run it by me one more time. Have you ever noticed that when you need something run by one more time it never happens, but when you don't they come running over and over? Fine, was it? Chet was fine? Well, yes. I felt fine, in fact, tip-top. But would I feel finer—yes, even tip-topper!—with a treat? Please. Who wouldn't? I sat down, made myself unmovable. If a better play had occurred to me I would have made it. But you go with who brung you to the dance, as folks around here often say. Right then I began to feel a bit confused. I got up and gave myself a good shake. Something went flying out of my coat, possibly a dead leaf. I felt much better.

"Jacques's on a flight to Paris at the moment," Ling the elf was saying, "but I can try to reach Suzie, if you like."

"That's all right," Bernie said. "What we really need is a crack researcher."

"Is it crime-related?"

"Not for sure," Bernie said. "But likely."

"How exciting is that! What can I do?"

"I was planning on running that by Suzie," Bernie said. "I wouldn't want to step on anyone's toes—especially hers."

Of course not! And it wasn't going to happen. Bernie's not the least bit clumsy. Here's something you may not know: He's a very good dancer. The truth is no one knows except for me. Bernie hardly ever dances and only at home, and not only that, but only if "If You Were Mine" is playing on one of his music loops. Then he'll stop whatever he's doing, get up, and do this real smooth shuffle around the house, revving things up a bit when Billie Holiday stops singing and hands things off to Roy Eldridge and his trumpet, that trumpet solo still the best sound I've heard on this earth. But my point is that Bernie wasn't about to step on anyone's toes, end of story.

Ling the elf seemed to get that, because she said, "Oh, I'm sure Suzie won't mind—she thinks the world of you."

Bernie's face brightened.

"And so does Jacques," she added.

The brightness faded a bit from his face.

"What is it you'd like me to look into?" Ling went on.

Bernie handed her the postcard. "I'd like to find out where this was purchased."

Ling glanced at it, turned it over, checked the back. "What about when and by whom?"

Bernie smiled. "Why would also be nice. But where would be great for starters."

"Dokey-oke," Ling said. "Sit tightly." She walked quickly to the back of the large open space, through a doorway with hinges but no door, and disappeared. Bernie watched her the whole way. He looked very happy. As for me, I'd never met an elf before. It took a little getting used to, but so do a lot of things, like staying strictly away from porcupines, for example. Bottom line: I was cool with elves.

The walls in this place were white and bare, except for a bit of writing in crayon on the far one. Bernie went closer and read it aloud. "'It is the stories we don't get, the ones we miss, pass over, fail to recognize, don't pick up on, that will send us to hell.— Molly Ivins.'"

He gazed at it in silence. Molly Ivins? A new one on me. A perp of some sort? For some reason I didn't think so.

At that moment, Ling returned, her walk a very fast one, close to running.

"I'm so sorry," she said.

"That's all right," said Bernie. "It was a long shot."

"Oh no, it's not that. I mean I'm sorry for dokey-oke. How stupid! Of course I meant okey-doke."

"I like dokey-oke better," Bernie said.

"You do?" Ling smiled a huge smile. "I love this country," she said. Then she handed Bernie the postcard.

"Thanks for trying," he said.

Ling's forehead wrinkled slightly. "But it's all done," she said. "And so easy. This postcard company—Graphics By Clio—only deals with one outlet in the whole state, and that's the gift shop at the Sonoran Museum of Art. I can write down the address."

"I know where it is," Bernie said. "But you were so fast! How did you do that?"

"Trade secret," said Ling. "Maybe now you'll loop me in again sometime. Oh, and I found this. I'm not sure what it is—one of the workers must have left it behind. But is it an appropriate treat for Chet?"

She reached into a pocket of her elf jacket and took out a Slim Jim.

Sometimes there's just too much all at once. At least for me. Appropriate was what, again? Elves didn't know what Slim Jims were? And those were just for starters. The next thing I knew for sure was that the Slim Jim was in my possession and Bernie was saying, "What do we owe you?"

"Nothing!" Ling said. "I love the crime beat."

She glanced at me and lowered her voice—like that would make it hard for me to hear what she was about to say. Humans can be so entertaining.

"I'm only now getting comfortable around—" Ling glanced my way and lowered her voice even more. "Canines," she said. "We never had one growing up, of course, but not only that, my horrible Uncle Ma . . ." She went silent.

Bernie took a deep breath and let it out slow. He was very quiet after we left. The Slim Jim was one of the best I've ever tasted. Each one is a little different, by the way. For example, this one had shared time in some dude's pocket with a partly smoked stogie. Delish.

First time inside a museum, or at least the gift shop of a museum. Some places have a way of sending a silent message: *Best behavior, buddy boy.* This was one of those places. Here's something maybe a little puzzling about me. When I get a silent message like that, I'm suddenly struck by a powerful urge to do the exact opposite! To even swing all the way to the other side, namely my worst behavior. What would that be, here in the museum gift shop? Well, you could start by prancing over to this display rack of fancy plates with beautiful desert scenes painted on them—and not so long ago, since I could still pick up a whiff of the paint—and sort of allow your tail, especially if it's a big, powerful one like mine to—

"Ch—et?"

We walked over to the counter side by side, me and Bernie, alert, heads up, two total pros ready for action. There was no action whatsoever in the gift shop, not a single customer, and the dude behind the counter had his eyes glued to a screen and hadn't even noticed us.

Bernie laid the postcard on the counter. The movement caught the dude's eye. He glanced at the postcard.

"Three ninety-five," he said, his gaze going right back to the screen like it was on a . . . leash. Uh-oh. What a strange thought! Interesting, maybe, but strange. All and all I hoped it wouldn't come around again.

Meanwhile Bernie said, "It's not for sale."

The dude turned to us. He blinked a few times. "Um?" he said. He sounded like a kid but he looked way too old to be a kid. Had we come across a few others like that recently? I thought so.

Bernie checked out the ID tag around the dude's neck. "Because, Wallace, this postcard is ours. We just walked in with it."

"Yeah?"

"But it was bought here and we'd like your help in identifying the buyer."

"How come?" said Wallace. Then he had a thought. You could tell from the way his eyes narrowed, almost to slits. "Are you a cop?"

Bernie laid our card on the counter, beside the postcard.

Wallace peered at it. "I'm not authorized to . . . to . . ." Whatever it was, he couldn't come up with it. I began to like him.

"No problem," Bernie said. "Do you remember selling this postcard?"

Wallace shook his head.

"The sale might have been recent," Bernie said.

"Recent? I wasn't here recent. I was on vacation till today."

"Where'd you go?" Bernie said.

"Disneyland."

"How was it?"

"Cool."

"Good to hear," Bernie said. "Is your supervisor around?"

"She's not in. Her vacation comes right after mine. That's how we do it. Staggering, it's called. First one person—"

A door behind him opened and a woman appeared, a woman of the no-nonsense kind. I could tell at a glance. One of the many special things about women of the no-nonsense kind is how quick they are on the uptake. She looked right at us, smiled in a friendly way, the mouth part at least, the eyes remaining watchful, and said, "Welcome to our museum. Is Wallace taking care of you?"

Wallace turned to her. "Boss?" he said. "It's, like, a postcard situation."

"Oh?" said the no-nonsense woman.

Bernie held up the postcard. "We're pretty sure this postcard was bought here in the gift shop. We're trying to find out when and by whom."

"And you are?" she said.

Bernie handed her our card. She glanced at it.

"Come with me." She motioned for us to walk around the counter.

"Want me to tag along?" said Wallace.

"And desert your post?" she said.

"Uh," said Wallace, staying where he was.

We followed the woman through the doorway, down a short corridor, and into a nice office with lots of daylight, flowers, and paintings on the walls. She didn't sit down or ask us to sit down. Instead she turned to Bernie and said, "Proceed."

"You want to know why we're asking?" Bernie said.

She nodded.

"We're trying to locate a missing man," Bernie said. "There's not much to go on, other than this postcard."

"What makes you think it was bought here?"

"The maker, Graphics By Clio, doesn't deal with anyone else in the state."

"How did you establish that?"

"Research."

There was a tiny pause. Then she said, "Can anyone vouch for you?"

"Lieutenant Rick Torres at Valley PD."

"Don't know him," the woman said. "I am acquainted with Captain Lou Stine."

"Try him," Bernie said.

The woman got on the phone, right in front of us. She was checking us out, unless I was missing something. We'd been checked out before, but whoever was doing the checking out always went into another room or at least moved off a bit, maybe so we couldn't hear, although I always could. But this woman did it right then and there, her eyes sometimes on Bernie and once or twice on me.

"Captain Stine? Katherine Cornwall over at the Sonoran Museum of Art."

"Hey, there," said Lou Stine. Even though Katherine Cornwall had the phone pressed tight to her ear so sound couldn't leak out, Captain Stine might as well have been standing next to me.

"I've got a private investigator here working on a case of some kind," Katherine Cornwall said. "I wonder if you could vouch for him."

"Name?"

"Bernie Little."

Stine chuckled. The human chuckle is one of their best sounds, although maybe not in Stine's case, his voice having an odd metallic edge. "Is Chet with him?"

"Are you referring to a rather large dog?"

"That's him. I'll vouch for Chet."

"I beg your pardon?" said Katherine Cornwall.

Uh-oh. Begging was a complete no-no. No begging. Stop that begging. Don't beg. You heard it all the time. Yet somehow—out of all possible people!—this no-nonsense woman didn't know that. The case had taken a bad turn.

"A joke," Stine went on. "Although actually not. As for Bernie, I named my kid after him. The middle name, on account of my wife's esthetic preference. Got another call. Nice talking to you, Katherine."

Katherine clicked off, pocketed the phone, held out her hand. Bernie gave her the postcard. She took it to her desk, sat before the screen. "Take a seat," she said.

Bernie sat on a strange chair that looked like it was made of huge sausages all twisted up. It didn't smell of sausages, huge or not. I went over to a bookshelf and snapped up a small potato chip that I'd known was there the moment we'd entered the room.

Katherine looked up. "The postcard was sold at 3:42 P.M. December nine—unfortunately a cash transaction."

"So you won't have the name of the buyer," Bernie said.

"I'm afraid not. But at least we should be able to get a good look at whoever it was."

"Ah," said Bernie.

"Our system is state of the art," Katherine said. "Anything less would be irresponsible in this business." She motioned us over to her desk. We stood beside her, me on one side and Bernie on the other, the way we'd do it with a perp. I was pretty sure Katherine was no perp, but it felt right just the same.

Pictures zoomed by on her screen, way too fast to make sense of. Then they slowed down and down, and there was the gift shop.

"Here we go," Katherine said.

A man—not Wallace, but much older and happier-looking—stood behind the counter. Another man approached, a postcard in his hand. A small man with bright liquid eyes, slicked back hair, and a flower in the lapel of his suit: Lauritz Vogner. I recognized him at once. Katherine touched a key and the image went still.

"I've never seen him before," she said. "Have you?"

"Yes, ma'am."

"Another angle, just to confirm?"

"Sure," Bernie said.

Katherine tapped another key or two. The screen went blank and then the gift shop popped up again, only now we were watching from somewhere over on the side. The same thing happened—Lauritz taking the postcard to the counter, and reaching for his wallet. But right then we saw something that hadn't been in the picture last time, namely another guy coming in through the front door. He took a step or two into the gift shop and then spotted Lauritz at the counter. Lauritz, his back to the door, didn't see the new guy. The new guy looked very surprised, and not the happy kind of surprise. He backed out the door, moving so fast he stumbled a bit. That seemed to get Lauritz's attention. He turned to look, but by that time the new guy was gone.

"Also unknown to me," Katherine said.

"Can we watch it again?" Bernie said.

We watched it again.

"Know him?" Katherine said.

"Nope," said Bernie.

No one asked me, of course. That's just the way things go down in this world. But in another world, I could have told them that I, Chet, had seen the new guy before. He wasn't new to me, amigo. Remember the fattish fellow with the Santa beard and the Panama hat? I sure did. Where had I seen him? Outside Nuestra Señora, accompanied by a huge dude with a handlebar mustache? Something like that. In any case, the guy who'd booked from the gift shop was him. Were we onto the next case? That's what it felt like to me.

Ten

Katherine walked us outside to the Porsche. She saw it and smiled for the first time.

"I had one of these!"

"Yeah?" said Bernie.

"A long time ago." The smile faded. Some people are much stronger than others. I've got a feel for that. Katherine was one of the real strong ones. But that didn't mean she was happy way down deep. Lots of the real strong ones are not, and she was of that kind. Bernie's the other kind of real strong—happy inside. Most of the time. Or at least a lot of it. Certainly some.

"You can take it for a spin if you want," he said.

Whoa! Where had that come from? But before I had even the first notion of how to stop it in its tracks, Katherine said, "No thanks, Bernie. Very nice of you all the same." She shot him a quick sideline glance, a glance that was much younger than she was, if that makes any sense. Bernie missed it.

"I suppose you'd like me to get in touch if I see either of those characters again," she said.

"Please," said Bernie.

"Should I ask questions? Try to detain them?"

"Please don't."

Katherine nodded. "Do you think the subject matter of the postcard—meaning Nuestra Señora de los Saguaros—is important?"

"I'm leaning that way."

"We tried to buy it last year," Katherine said.

"Oh?" said Bernie. I loved hearing that oh! Bernie has this quiet way of saying it that's one of our best techniques at the Little Detective Agency.

"'We' meaning the museum," Katherine said. "It's a fascinating site. De Niza was never there, of course, but the earliest parts do date from the late sixteenth century and there was lots of back and forth between it and Mexico for two hundred years. An Italian in the court of Phillip III—king of Spain but also king of Naples at that time—wrote a very interesting account of a trip from Guaymas and back. It's part of our collection. But we were outbid on the site by another nonprofit."

"Named what?" Bernie said.

"People For Preservation, I believe. I actually hadn't heard of them, but they offered almost a million dollars. We couldn't come close."

"Who was the seller?"

"The Priory of the Valley," Katherine said.

"Never heard of it."

"A dissolved priory, actually, the dissolution leading to the sale. Nuestra Señora passed through a number of ecclesiastic hands in its lifetime, but the priory had it for the last fifty years or so."

"We visited the site," Bernie said. "Do you know an archaeologist named Johanna Borden?"

"No."

"She seems to be doing some digging out there," Bernie said.

"I hope she's being careful," said Katherine.

"Quite a person," Bernie said as we drove away from the museum. "Woman, actually," he added.

After that came a long silence, and then he got on the phone. We were on speaker, so the buzz buzz you hear before someone picks up on the other end was super clear, clear enough to send a strange buzzing down my back all the way to the tip of my tail. I wriggled around a bit, couldn't help myself.

Then came Weatherly's voice. "Leave a message at the beep."

"Pick up," Bernie said. And once more, very quiet. "Pick up."

But Weatherly did not.

Bernie glanced over at me. "I need a plan."

He did? Had that ever happened before? I wanted to help,

goes without mentioning, but I wasn't quite done with wriggling around.

The moment we pulled into the driveway, our neighbor's door opened. I don't mean our neighbor old man Heydrich, who collects Nazi memorabilia, whatever that may be, and turned out to have a big-time video system for watching what was happening up and down the street, including our place—a big-time system, yes, but no longer operating, so no worries. The neighbor I mean is the one on the other side, Mr. Parsons, almost certainly older than Heydrich, as is his wife, Mrs. Parsons, who mostly lives at the hospital these days. And then there's my pal Iggy. The fun we used to have, back before the electric fence guy came around, making a sale at Iggy's place but not at ours, goes without mentioning. The problem was the Parsonses never quite figured out the electric fence and now Iggy didn't get outside much. I mostly saw him through the narrow floor-to-ceiling window in their front hall.

Iggy didn't seem to be there now. Mr. Parsons came out of the house as fast as he could—not fast, what with his walker and all—and closed the door real quick, saying, "Stay, Iggy, stay."

How often have I heard Mr. Parsons say that! He's a very nice man but perhaps not a good learner. "Stay" to Iggy did not mean stay and never would.

Mr. Parsons came stumping over.

"Hi, Bernie. Merry Christmas."

"And to you and Mrs. Parsons," Bernie said. "How's she doing?"

"Just fine, given . . . well, the list is too long." He shook his head. "She's such a . . ." His voice got thick and blocked whatever was coming next, a human thing you sometimes see. "But the good news is she's coming home for Christmas Day, maybe until New Year's. I'm decorating like crazy. Decorating's not so easy, Bernie. It's a skill—even a valuable skill, I'd say. Oh god, I'm rambling, aren't I?"

"Not at all—I'm clueless at decorating," Bernie said.

"Well, skills can be learned to an extent, I'm sure," said

Mr. Parsons. "Oh dear—and now I'm lecturing? Sorry, Bernie. What I'm really here for is very embarrassing."

"I'm sure not," said Bernie.

"But it is," said Mr. Parsons. He licked his lips, old person's lips, thin, cracked, dry. "I'm afraid a letter addressed to you got delivered to us yesterday. When I say addressed to you I mean your name was on the envelope. But the actual address on Mesquite Road—sorry this is sounding so disorganized, Bernie—was ours. And we have a new mailman—actually a very nice woman but she hasn't had time to learn all the names. Herbie retired—don't know if you're aware of that."

"I wasn't."

And neither was I. Herbie gone? Had I heard right? No more biscuits flying out the window of the little mail truck as it came down Mesquite Road? "Woo hoo, Chet! You around, big fella?" I was going to miss Herbie.

"Had thirty years in and his arthritis is getting pretty bad," Mr. Parsons said. "But a bit off topic. The topic is . . . um . . . the letter, which I realized right away was for you, and put on the high-top green table by the front door so I wouldn't forget to bring it over when I saw you were home. The problem, which I didn't foresee . . ."

He paused to catch his breath. In that pause, I happened to glance past him to his house. Through the tall, narrow front hall window I could see the high-top green table he'd mentioned. Iggy was standing on top of it.

". . . was that . . ." He turned back toward his house and saw what I saw. So did Bernie. Mr. Parsons reached into his pocket, took out a very small and rather damp-looking scrap of paper. "This was all I could salvage. I hope the letter wasn't important." He handed the scrap of paper over to Bernie.

"I'm sure it wasn't," Bernie said, taking a quick glance. His eyes told a different story, but only for the briefest moment. You had to really know him to spot it, and of course I did. He smiled at Mr. Parsons and said, "I'm just surprised that Iggy can get himself up so high."

"As am I," said Mr. Parsons. "He seems to be thriving these

days. Edna believes he senses how she and I are going in the other direction, and he's doing what he can to rally us. Do you think there's anything to that?"

"Yes," Bernie said.

"I'll relay that to Edna," Mr. Parsons said. "She'll be pleased." He turned, stumped back to his house, grasped the doorknob.

"Daniel?" Bernie said. "I wouldn't—"

Too late. The door was already open, just the smallest crack, but Iggy doesn't need much in the way of openings. Just like that he was on the loose, with his amazingly long and floppy tongue somehow in the lead, and his eyes as crazy as you'll ever see.

"Oh no!" cried Mr. Parsons, as Iggy tore off down the block, probably lost already.

"Chet?" Bernie said. "Mind rounding him up?"

I lay on the rug in the office. I'm not the type who's easy to tire out. Ask some of the perps I've tracked day and night across the desert, next time you're in the visitor's room up at Northern State Correctional. But Iggy has a way of tiring me out.

My eyes began to close. Through the tiny slits I could see Bernie at the desk, peering through the magnifying glass at the little scrap of paper.

"Is that a D or an O?" he said. "Or could it be . . . kind of looks like 'en' something. Enclose, maybe? Some word ending in 'ong' and then 'enclose another copy, just in case he or they—' And then comes the part Iggy's keeping to himself."

What was that? I tried to concentrate but got distracted by elephant smells. Our rug in the office had an elephant pattern. Once I'd worked a case involving an elephant named Peanut. She and I had come to a sort of understanding in the end, but she'd never been here in the office, or in the house at all. How would she get in? Well, actually quite easily, through the wall, for example. Once she'd stomped on a car and flattened it! I've never been so excited! But that's not the point, which is that although Peanut had never been in the office, I could sometimes pick up her scent rising off the elephant pattern rug. It was very relaxing, although being with Peanut in person was not.

My eyes closed.

"Tired, huh, big guy?"

Ah! Bernie's voice. I could sleep forever and just listen to him talk.

"How about I leave you here for now? Be back soon."

Moments later we were in the Porsche, Bernie behind the wheel and me in the shotgun seat, our usual positions. Once— maybe hard to believe but true—we'd ended up briefly flipping things around, Bernie riding shotgun and me behind the wheel. This was down Mexico way in what you might call a firefight, and Bernie had an actual shotgun at one point.

But no time to go into it now. We parked in front of Elise's little house in the not-rich part of old Pottsdale. Elise was standing by a flower bed with a watering can—a tiny flower bed and the only one on her desert-style lawn. A whiskery old member of the nation within was marking her big shady tree. Elise wasn't happy about it.

"Shoo! Shoo!" she said.

The old guy did not shoo, or pay the slightest attention.

I hopped out of the Porsche.

He shooed.

"Bernie?" Elise said. She set down the watering can with a jerk, as though it had gotten suddenly heavy.

Bernie shook his head. "No news," he said.

We joined her by the flower bed. Only a few flowers grew there, all of them droopy and giving off the heavy smell they do when they're not long for this world. There was only one thing I wanted to do and that was lay my mark on the trunk of the big shady tree. I wanted to do that very, very badly and pronto, yet I knew this was not the time. But how about laying my mark on these poor flowers, as a sort of substitute? Was it a good time for that? I didn't see why not but I could feel the why not, if that makes any sense. I hate when that happens. As a substitute for the substitute, I began digging a very small hole in the flower bed, gently and with only one paw. You wouldn't have noticed.

Bernie took out the scrap of paper. "Another writing sample," he said.

Elise had glasses hanging around her neck. She put them on, peered at the scrap of paper and said, "It's Victor's."

"Are you sure?" Bernie said.

Elise pointed. "See how the T's are crossed? With a little wiggly line like a tilde? That's Victor." Her eyes—like tiny creatures, round and scared, went back and forth. "'Enclose a copy, just in case he or they.' What does it mean?" Elise looked up. "Where's the rest of it?"

"Not recoverable," Bernie said. "This is all we have of a letter written to me. A letter we now know Victor wrote, thanks to you."

Elise gazed again at the scrap of paper. "Did he enclose a copy of something with the letter?"

"It looks that way, but maybe not," Bernie said. "He could be talking about an enclosure in some future letter, even to someone else."

Elise was holding the scrap of paper closer to her eyes now, and didn't seem to hear. "'Just in case he or they' what?" she said. "And who is 'he'? Who is 'they'?" Her voice cracked. "Oh, I don't like the sound of this. I don't like it at all!"

Bernie reached out and touched her arm. She twisted away.

"And did you see what comes before?" she said. "This 'ong'?

"Yes," Bernie said, "but there's no way to—"

"Wrong!" said Elise. "O N G are the last three letters of 'wrong'." She lowered her glasses and looked up again, and this time glared at Bernie. "Victor is saying that if things go wrong and whoever he or they are do . . ." She turned away, bit her lip, lowered her voice. ". . . do whatever it is they're capable of doing, then he's sending you the enclosure in the hope that—"

Tears began to flow from Elise's eyes. She thrust the scrap of paper back to Bernie and covered her face with her hands. Tears leaked out from between her fingers and her whole body shook, but she didn't make a sound. Bernie reached out again to touch her, but stopped himself, his big strong hand frozen for a moment in midair. Then he folded the scrap of paper, put it in his pocket, and in a business-like voice—even a bit hard—said, "Elise? We're not there yet."

Elise went still. She slowly lowered her hands, wiped her eyes on her forearm. "I know that. I know it with my mind, but not my heart."

"Your mind is right," Bernie said. "Try to be patient. Let us work the case."

"But work it how? Don't you need clues?"

"We have some."

"Like what?"

Bernie thought for a moment. "Caravaggio."

"Caravaggio the painter?"

"Victor was asking about him, not long before he disappeared."

"Asking who?"

"Jada."

"That makes sense," Elise said. "She knows a ton about art. How I wish—" She stopped herself, took a breath. Her eyes narrowed. "But what's the relevance of Caravaggio?"

"That's one of the things we need to look into."

"All that takes time. Does Victor have time?"

"I don't know," Bernie said. "But he's not helpless, Elise."

"He is if violence is a possibility. He's always been so . . . so scrawny."

"Don't forget that pocket nine," Bernie said. "An equalizer, especially when loaded right."

"Pocket nine?" said Elise.

"Victor's Ruger."

"That's a gun?"

"Nine millimeter semiautomatic."

"Victor owns a gun?"

Bernie nodded.

Elise closed her eyes and kept them closed for what seemed like a long time. When she opened them she said, "I'm an ignorant old woman. I don't understand a goddamn thing."

On our walk back to the car, I left her big, shady tree unmarked.

Eleven

"With some cases," Bernie said, "you hit a plateau where you think—okay, we have all the pieces we need. Now all we have to do is shift them around a bit, and understanding will dawn. Suppose, for example, you had a box and in that box were all the pieces required for assembling a car. Eventually you'd figure it out."

That sounded pretty amazing. Then I remembered a time when the Porsche—the one that ended up going off a cliff—was in pieces in the driveway. Not the whole car, now that I thought about it, perhaps just the engine. But the point is Bernie had attempted that very thing he'd just mentioned, namely putting all the parts back together—this was all about making the car even faster, so there were no problems with the basic idea—but he actually hadn't been able to—

My mind stopped right there and refused to go on, almost like it had learned my trick of making itself unmovable. Wow! Look at me, teaching my mind a thing or two at last! Did life just keep getting better and better? Why wouldn't it? I went over to my water bowl—this was out on our patio, having an after-dinner drink and watching the stars come out—and slurped it dry.

Bernie sipped his bourbon. "But I'm not getting that feeling with this case. We've got a box with parts in it, except not enough or even the wrong ones. So we literally need to think outside the box, although since the expression's figurative to begin with, then maybe . . ."

His voice trailed off. That can happen when he reaches a certain height of brilliance, kind of like when a bird flies higher and higher till you can't see it anymore. I don't mean that the bird is having brilliant thoughts. I know birds, and brilliant thoughts just aren't them. Mostly they just soar around in the big blue sky and watch what's doing below with their angry little eyes. Now and then they swoop down and snatch up some creature that's not paying attention. In my earlier days I made a play for a bird or two, always without success. Here's a bothersome fact—cats are good at doing the kinds of things I'd had in mind for birds. Why would that be? Is there some plan out there? If so it needed a few tweaks, as humans like to say, starting with—

Bernie banged his glass down on the arm of his chair and sat up straight. "Oh my god!" he said. "What if there was software for thinking outside the box?" He sprang up. "Chet! And it could come in a box! A box called Outside the Box! This is so good! Way better than Hawaiian pants! Or even leveraged puts and calls in the tin market! Chet!"

By that time, as I'm sure you're already imagining, I'd sprung up myself and we were both on the move, kind of dancing around the patio. Better than Hawaiian pants? Was that even possible? But of course, if Bernie said so. At that moment I knew one thing for sure: We were going to be very very rich. And when that happened—maybe not tomorrow but possibly the day after that—we'd get started on doing all the cool things rich folks do, none of which came to mind immediately.

Bernie grabbed his glass and drank it down. "All we need now is someone to write the code. A kid will do. Let's aim for next year's Christmas shopping season. What kids do we know?"

Charlie! Charlie came to mind at once. And what about his friend Esmé, smartest kid in the class! There was only one thing to do: leap over the high gate at the back of the patio—a high gate that no one used to believe I could clear, but they do now, baby!—and get this show on the road! I wheeled around, gathered my strength, and—

"Chet?"

Soon after that we were in the house, back door closed and I believe bolted as well. Bernie got on the phone.

"Prof? Bernie, here."

"Well, well, it's been a while," said Prof. He was our economist buddy, whatever that was—not the buddy part, buddiness being something I think I've got a pretty good grip on—and our expert for money stuff, except for the part about how to get some. "How's the life of action going? Been in any physical confrontations lately?"

"Those are rare, Prof. I wish you wouldn't fixate on that aspect of the job."

"But why not? It's like not fixating on the cherry on top."

"Cherry on top?" Bernie said. "Ever been in a fight?"

"Hell, no."

"Not even as a kid?"

"I was too busy with chess club. And I know what you're going to say, Bernie—nothing's more violent than chess."

"Actually I was going to ask if you'll be in your office tomorrow morning," Bernie said.

"I will be now," Prof said. "Bring your symbolic brass knuckles."

That night I had some trouble falling asleep. It was the thought of brass knuckles that did it. Once we'd been in a bit of a dustup with a pair of hopped-up twins, one or both slipping on the knucks when things started going south for them. They were planning on using those horrible things on Bernie! Just the sight of them made me so mad that things went even souther for those twins, and fast. Now, here on a quiet night in our peaceful house, knucks were making me mad all over again. Did Prof really think we would ever own them ourselves? I realized he needed straightening out on that subject and soon, like the very next time I saw him.

Which turned out to be the very next morning! Too soon for me to have forgotten! As we walked into Prof's office at the college, I knew this was going to be a lucky day.

Prof has a big desk in his office, covered with books and papers, but he seems to spend most of his working time on his couch. He was lying on it when we came in, his glasses pushed up on his forehead. I barked a savage bark.

"Goodness," said Prof. "What's with him?"

Bernie shot me a glance. "Probably just overexcited to see you."

That wasn't it at all! I wasn't overexcited—what did that even mean? When you're excited you're excited, end of story. I was mad, that's what I was, mad on account of . . . of . . . it would come to me. Knucks! Yes, brass knuckles, of which there were none nearby, the smell of brass being unmissable. I sat down and yawned a big yawn.

"Take a seat, Bernie," Prof said, motioning to the swivel chair at the desk.

Bernie cleared away a stack of files and sat.

"I have to give a speech tomorrow," Prof said, "and was just contemplating a little aperçu—if you could use the term coming from someone like him—of Lyndon Johnson's. 'Making a speech on economics is a lot like pissing down your leg. It seems hot to you, but it never does to anyone else.'"

Bernie laughed. What was funny? I had no idea. All I knew was that I wanted very much to meet this Johnson dude.

"I've got something I want to run by you," Bernie said.

"What kind of something?" said Prof.

"A business idea," Bernie said. "A start-up, more or less."

"Please don't," said Prof.

"You'll like it."

"In what sense? I liked the *Titanic* movie. Doesn't mean I'd want to book a stateroom."

"I just want your opinion. It won't cost you a thing."

"It'll cost me psychically—like those tin futures of yours."

"I never took possession of the tin," Bernie said.

"Precisely," said Prof. He folded his arms over his big, round stomach. "Go on."

Bernie started in on the out of the box in the box idea, if that was the way to put it. Impossible to follow. I detected a chewy in one of Prof's desk drawers and sidled over in that direction.

". . . and that's kind of the um, kernel of it," Bernie was saying.

"The kernel," said Prof with a sigh. "For the sake of discussion, let's say I click on the link for your product—"

"Link?" said Bernie. "I was thinking of an actual box."

Prof shifted his glasses down from his forehead, peered through them at Bernie. "When you conceive a baby you're not picturing the baby, or diapers, doctor's visits, college applications. But when you conceive a business idea you have nail it all down from point A, and that includes every single detail of the customer experience."

Bernie gazed at him. "I was hoping you'd know some bright kid who's good with software."

"To do what?"

"The nailing down."

Prof gave him a long look.

"I'll pay whoever it is, of course," Bernie said. "And you, too, for the referral."

Prof sat up, and surprisingly fast. You didn't see that every day. "I would never take money from you under any circumstances, and you should know that—not after what you did for my sister." He lay back down. "And I'll try to find some poor unsuspecting kid for your boxes."

"Thanks," Bernie said.

And maybe there was some more about the boxes, but I was stuck back at the sister part. Prof had a sister? News to me. And Bernie had helped her out—helped her out in that strange time before he and I got together? That was bothersome. I got a grip on the handle of the desk drawer and gave it a little tug. My, my. The door slid right open.

"Anything else I can do for you?" Prof said.

"Maybe," Bernie said. "Ever hear of a priory going out of business?"

"The technical term is dissolution, and yes," said Prof. "And there'll be more and more of that as religion loses its grip. Or should I say as the religions of today lose their grip. Ever think of what religions will be like in two thousand years?"

"No."

"I have, and I've come up with some nightmarish scenarios. In fact—" Prof sat up again. ". . . you'll find a yellow pad on the desk. Jot down 'nightmarish scenarios.' I'll include it in my speech."

Bernie shuffled through papers on the desk. I nosed through the drawer, found the chewy, and moved over to the farthest corner of the room.

"Did you have any specific priory in mind?" Prof said.

"The Priory of the Valley."

"Never heard of it."

"They owned Nuestra Señora de los Saguaros," Bernie said.

"On the old De Niza highway?" said Prof. "I always liked that name. Saguaros are native only to the Sonoran desert, so the juxtaposition sends a nice message."

"Of what?"

"Universality. On the other hand, you tell me the priory's out of business. What happened to the church?"

"They sold it to a nonprofit called People For Preservation," Bernie said.

"Doesn't ring a bell," said Prof. "What do you know about them?"

"Nothing."

"Now I'm curious." Prof sat up and then actually rose to his feet. I noticed he was wearing slippers with a reindeer pattern. The last time I'd seen him stand up he'd gotten dizzy and Bernie had caught him just in time, but now he went with hardly a stumble to a computer on a shelf, sat down with a grunt, and began tap-tapping away. I was hoping he might kick off those slippers, just to give his feet a little fresh air if nothing else, but he did not.

Time passed. That can be boring, but not when you're busy with a chewy, as you may or may not know. After I don't know how long—because chewies have a way of making time disappear, if I haven't yet made that clear—Prof sat back, rubbed his chin, and said, "This is interesting."

"What is?" Bernie crossed the room, gazed over Prof's shoulder at the screen.

"As you can see here—I'll just bring this up—People For Preservation seems to be part of this umbrella group."

Bernie leaned in closer. "Friends of Merisi."

"Also a nonprofit, but registered in Monrovia."

"Where's that?"

"Liberia, Bernie, where things are more . . . relaxed, shall we say. To the point of permitting the executives and board of Friends of Merisi, supposing they exist, to remain anonymous. But that's not the interesting part—which you see over here."

Bernie pointed at the screen.

"No," said Prof. "That's just the law firm representing the priory, in the name of their last business manager, Walter L. Lessig."

Bernie leaned in, took out a pen, wrote something on the base of his thumb. I loved when Bernie did that! But maybe Prof did not.

"What are you doing?" he said.

"Just making a note."

Prof opened his mouth like he was going to say something, then maybe decided to keep it to himself. Instead he tapped the screen. "Here we have the firm representing the Friends of Merisi, also not the interesting part, just below. A third party sent a letter to the county opposing the sale."

"On what grounds?"

"It doesn't say. But I believe we can find out."

"How?"

"I happen to know the gentleman. His name is Marco Folonari."

"Folonari?" Bernie said.

Prof twisted around to look at Bernie. "You know him, too?"

Bernie shook his head. "But his name has come up."

"Would you like to meet him?" said Prof.

"Very much," Bernie said.

"He's a professor in the art department, former head at one time," Prof said. "His office is down the hall."

There's a puffy-faced sort of smile humans have when they're pleased with themselves. Prof was smiling it now, big-time.

We followed Prof down the hall. What a slow walker he was! I considered running circles around him but this was not the time.

We were on the job. Bernie was giving off his on-the-job feeling. That was all I needed to know.

Prof came to a door and knocked on it.

No answer from inside. Kind of strange, since someone was in there. I also knew who.

Prof knocked again. Again no answer. Prof turned to Bernie. "He doesn't seem to be in."

Was this a good moment for my soft, rumbly bark? I thought so, and then realized I'd already barked it. Wow! Chet the Jet!

Bernie glanced down at me. Then he knocked on the door, a knock far more forceful than Prof's.

A woman answered. She sounded pretty annoyed. "Yes?"

"Hi," called Prof. "I'm looking for Professor Folonari. I'm a colleague."

"He's not here."

Bernie reached out, turned the knob, pushed the door open. Inside a woman with some files under her arm stood before a bunch of filing cabinets, all the drawers open. It was Dr. Johanna Borden.

Twelve

"Excuse me?" she said, like we were all strangers to her. Then she recognized me. I've seen that look before, on the faces of perps who think they've gotten away and all of a sudden here we are again! And it's often me first, just before Bernie. Maybe I'm extra recognizable in some way or other. Is it the gator skin collar? That was as far as I could take it on my own, and I'd already gone too far, Johanna Borden not being a perp but some sort of scientist, or perhaps janitor. She wore denim, not dusty as out at Nuestra Señora, but clean and fresh.

By now she'd recognized Bernie. Her face went through some changes, too quick for me to catch, except maybe a trace of confusion and even fear, the kind of fear when, say, one human bumps into another in the dark. That never happens in the nation within because we can smell and hear each other a mile away, however far that is, exactly, and also I have a feeling we see better than you in the dark, no offense.

Her face smoothed itself out. At first, when you get to know men and women a bit, you might think men have stronger faces. But women can have faces that are just as strong. They just keep looking like women at the same time. But forget all that. The point is that Johanna had a strong face. So does Suzie, by the way, and also Weatherly. All strong but in a very different way. If I had to pick a favorite it would be—

But no time for that now.

"Bernie Little, wasn't it?" Johanna said. "What are you doing here?"

Prof's eyebrows—maybe the shaggiest I'd ever seen—rose up over the rim of his glasses. "You two know each other?"

Well, yes, they did, but I knew Johanna, too. Any reason Prof wasn't including me in all this knowing? Maybe it had slipped his mind. Obviously Prof had a fine mind—although not as fine as Bernie's, goes without mentioning—but even the finest mind can slip up at times. I decided to cut him a break, often my go-to move when it comes to dealing with humans.

"Not well, but we've met," Bernie said. "This is Johanna Borden. She's in charge of—I'm not quite sure what to call it? A dig? Down at Nuestra Señora de los Saguaros."

"A dig?" said Prof.

"Not at all," Johanna said. "We're protecting and preserving an archaeological site. It's part of our remit." She turned to Bernie. "But you still haven't answered my question. What are you doing here?"

Before Bernie could reply, Prof spoke up. He sounded annoyed, a bit odd coming from him. Was it because he was the roly-poly type? Roly-poly types—and I'd never met one I didn't like—never sounded annoyed, in my experience.

"I was going to introduce Bernie to my old colleague, Marco Folonari," he said. "Is this not still his office?"

Johanna changed her position slightly, seemed to relax. I realized she'd been giving off a whiff of human fear scent—a sour, pre-sweat aroma, hard to describe—but now it stopped coming.

"Yes, it is, sir," she said to Prof. "But Marco's on sabbatical. He asked me to send along a few files."

Prof nodded his roly-poly head. "Ah," he said, no longer sounding annoyed.

Johanna turned to Bernie with a little smile. "Marco was my advisor when I took my masters. He's really been a mentor to me, although he dislikes the term."

Prof nodded again. "I've discussed that with him several times."

"That's nice," Bernie said. He shot Prof a quick look. I believe it meant zip it. "But—" Bernie began. Prof interrupted.

"Marco and I agreed to disagree."

There was a moment of silence. Bernie waited, maybe so Prof could finish talking about whatever this was, totally beyond me, but Prof seemed to be done. Bernie turned to Johanna.

"So where is Marco?"

"I told you," Johanna said. "On sabbatical."

"Right," Bernie said. "But he must be in some geographical place."

"He's traveling and unavailable."

"Where?" said Bernie. "In outer space?"

Johanna laughed. "Are all private eyes so funny?"

Interesting question. Bernie was quite the jokester, of course, but what about our private eye buddies? All at once it hit me: we didn't have any private eye buddies. Weren't buddies for hanging out with? We hung out with Valley PD types sometimes—and even a perp or two!—but other private eyes? I could only think of once—in the airport hotel bar after Bernie's keynote speech at the Great Western Private Eye Convention where Georgie Mal-houf, president of the Great Western Private Eye Association had offered some big green for . . . for me. How weird, almost like I was for sale. What a thought! And Georgie had ended up regret-ting it, big-time. So I had no answer to Johanna's question. All I could do was wait to find out from Bernie.

He smiled and said, "I'll take that as a compliment." He laid our card on the nearest file cabinet. "Please ask Professor Folonari to get in touch the next time you're speaking to him."

And we were out of there. Johanna looked surprised. I was a bit surprised myself. We walked down the hall.

"Whatever this is about can't be very important," Prof said.

"Oh?" said Bernie.

"You didn't push very hard, if you don't mind my saying so. One obvious step would have been asking her for Marco's phone number. I know Marco. I'm sure he checks his messages no mat-ter where he is."

"You don't say," said Bernie. "Any chance you've got it?"

"Marco's number?" Prof said. "I probably do."

"My lucky day," Bernie said.

Prof gave him a funny sideways look. Bernie missed it but I didn't. I'd seen it before, although never on the face of someone of Prof's brilliance. A very short time later we had the number.

But, maybe somewhat to Prof's disappointment—human eyebrows are good for showing things like that, and those shaggy eyebrows of Prof's hide nada—Bernie didn't make the call until we were back in the car, just the two of us. Bernie tapped the screen a few times. A voice spoke on the other end: "The number you called is not in service."

Bernie nodded, like that was no surprise. We drove away from the college. He was quiet for a long time. Then he said, "Christmas in two thousand years? Or Hannukah? They've already been around that long. So wouldn't the smart money be on . . ." His voice trailed away. I was fine with that. Maybe we didn't have much in the way of money—at least for now—but the money we did have was the smart kind. No way Bernie could ever mess up a detail like that. I wriggled around on the shotgun seat and got even more comfortable.

We came to a red light. Bernie checked the writing on the palm of his hand. "Walter L. Lessig, 9420 East Mesa, Apartment 106. I would have expected a more . . ." Whatever it was, he didn't say. Probably for the best, what with all those numbers right off the jump. I seldom go past two, occasionally getting as far as . . . as far as . . .

The light turned green. Bernie took a look in the rearview mirror, sharp and sudden. We drove on.

"Mesa Road," Bernie said. "One of the longest and most interesting streets in the Valley. Starts on the east side of South Pedroia and ends way up in the West Hills gated communities." He pulled over and parked behind a dented van with a sagging back bumper. A palm tree grew in one of those tiny sidewalk plots we have around here, a stunted little palm tree that wasn't doing too well. "And in between, we have miles and miles of this worn-out middle."

A brown palm leaf broke off the tree and landed with a soft clatter on the roof of the van. We got out of the car and went to the front door of an apartment building—not the brand-new tower kind we have downtown, but the stubby old kind that's everywhere else. Some of the stubby ones are all fixed up and full of hipsters. This one was still waiting for that to happen.

Bernie opened the front door. We entered a very small lobby with mailboxes on one side wall and a row of buzzers on the other. Bernie checked the buzzers. "One oh six," he said. "No name." He raised a finger to press the buzzer, stopped himself, and tried the inner door instead. It opened. We walked inside and down a dim corridor to a door at the end.

Bernie knocked. Footsteps approached on the other side, the footsteps of a woman wearing slippers. *"Quien es?"* she said.

"Is Walter Lessig in?" Bernie said.

"Que?"

"Walter L. Lessig, apartment 106."

"Momentito." She raised her voice. "Carlos!"

More footsteps, this time of a barefoot kid. The kid and the woman had a quick conversation of which I understood zilch. Then the kid called through the door.

"Who is it?"

Bernie's voice changed a little bit. It almost always does when he's talking to kids. How to describe the change? It gets closer to the voice he uses for me. But these changes are tiny. I'm afraid with your ears you wouldn't pick them up.

"My name's Bernie," he said. "I'm here with my partner Chet. We're looking for Walter Lessig."

The woman spoke in a sharp tone. *"No es aqui."*

"But Tia," said the boy, "didn't he live here before?"

The woman raised her voice. "He no here!"

"Listen," Bernie said, "we're not going to harm you. A man's gone missing and we need to talk to Walter Lessig. Did he leave a forwarding address?"

The woman and the kid had another quick back-and-forth I didn't get.

"Are you with ICE?" the kid said.

"No," said Bernie.

"The police?"

"No."

Then we waited. And waited some more. I heard very very soft breezes from the other side, like gestures were going on in there. The door opened.

The woman was small with gray hair. The kid was skinny, much younger than the skateboarding kids, more like Charlie's age. A big and beat-up old baseball glove hung off his little hand. Behind them I could see a small bare room with a tiny metal Christmas tree on a stool.

But meanwhile, we had a little commotion here at the door.

"Oh my god!" said the woman.

"What a huge dog!" said Carlos.

"No worries," Bernie told them. "Chet loves kids." He turned to the woman. "And folks in general."

She didn't look convinced.

Bernie gestured with his chin. "That's some glove—a Fernando Valenzuela model?"

"It was my grandfather's," Carlos said.

"You like playing baseball?"

"A real game? I never played a real game. But I like playing catch."

"Yeah? Step out here and I'll toss you a couple."

"No ball." The kid shot me a quick glance. "A dog took it. Out on the street."

Ah. At last we were making sense.

"Maybe Santa will come through for you," Bernie said.

The woman's eyes—narrow, dark, unhappy—shifted to Bernie and then quickly away. *"Por favor, espero."* She turned and walked away, disappearing into another room.)

"His name's Chet?" Carlos said.

Bernie nodded.

"Is he fast?"

"Like the wind."

"Does he like getting patted?"

"Try it and see."

Carlos hesitated for a moment, then reached out and stroked my shoulder very lightly. The woman returned, said something to Carlos, and handed him a scrap of paper. Carlos gave it to Bernie.

"The man left this in case of . . . que, Tia?"

"Letters," said the woman. *"Los paquetes."*

"Or packages," said Carlos.

Bernie checked the scrap of paper. "Thank you." He reached in his pocket and took out some money.

The woman shook her head.

"But—" said Carlos.

The woman smacked him on the back of the head, not hard, but not soft either.

Out on the street, Bernie fished around under the seats of the Porsche and found a baseball. No surprise. I could smell a couple more down there. He rubbed it on his shirt and then honked the horn. Carlos appeared in a window of the stubby apartment building. Bernie motioned for him to raise the window. Carlos raised the window. Bernie showed him the ball. Carlos's eyes opened wide. Bernie made a little motion, like, hey, let's go. Carlos extended his hand, the huge glove kind of dangling off it. Bernie tossed him the ball. It disappeared inside the huge glove and stayed there.

"Natural born center fielder," he said.

"Walter's come up in the world," Bernie said. "And not just topographically speaking."

I stared straight ahead through the windshield, but my mind wasn't on the view, a very nice one as we climbed a steep, twisting road in the Horseback Hills, one of the nicest parts of the whole

Valley. No, it was on Bernie and that mind of his. Topographically speaking—imagine that! Was it possible he was getting even more brilliant as time went on? Where would that lead? The answer was obvious: somewhere good!

We topped the hill, started winding down the other side. How lovely the air was up here! Some places seem to collect all the desert smells at once—like mesquite, greasewood, sagebrush, palo verde—and this was one of them. Plus plenty of snaky scent. What was with all this snakiness these days? Before I could figure it out or even begin, Bernie pulled onto a small bare patch at the edge of the road and grabbed the binoculars. We got out of the car and peered over the ridge at the view below.

"That has to be his place," Bernie said.

A few switchbacks down, but practically straight beneath us as the crow . . . forget about the crow. The point is that almost right below—how far was hard to tell—a biggish house stood on a sort of pad-shaped property that jutted from the hillside. There was a pool extending to the drop-off, a pool house, a garage, all the buildings with orange-tiled roofs. Was the whole setup in the style that Suzie called "fauxspagnole"? I had no idea but I remembered how she said it, and how Bernie laughed.

Also the air was very still up here, so still I could hear the front door of the house open like it was right beside me. A blondhaired woman stepped out. I heard the click click of her high heels on the paved circle in front of the house. She walked toward a little red convertible.

"Oh no," Bernie said. "Is it . . . ?" He raised the binoculars. "Autumn." The only Autumn we knew was the Autumn who worked at the More part of Livia's Friendly Coffee and More joint in Pottsdale. Hadn't we just seen her a few days ago? And she'd been doing exactly what she was doing now, namely counting money. She opened the car door, kicked off her high heels, kicking them right into the car—a neat trick as far as I was concerned, but Bernie said nothing about it. Autumn drove away barefoot. Red flashed through the treetops as she went down and down.

Bernie lowered the binocs. He looked sad. Why would that be? I shifted over and pressed against his leg. He scratched between my ears, although the rest of him was somewhere else. But good enough!

We got back in the car, followed the road down through a few switchbacks, pulled into a paved drive, and parked in Autumn's old spot. Bernie just sat there for a moment. Then he gave himself—yes!—a little shake, and we hopped out of the car. I was the only one actually hopping, but don't be fooled: We're a team, me and Bernie.

Thirteen

The house had a fancy wooden door, windowless, with a brass knocker in the shape of a snake head. I'd never seen one like that before and never wanted to see another. Bernie banged it a few times, and while he was doing that I heard water running somewhere outside. I started following the sound. It led me around the house, past a flower garden to the pool. I felt Bernie behind me, always our best line-up, side-by-side coming next. As for Bernie in front, I did what I could to make that not happen.

The pool house stood by the pool. It had an outdoor shower, screened off by a tangle of vines on a trellis. I could see running water from the showerhead, but the vines hid everything below that from sight. A man in the shower was humming, not in a way I found pleasant. Bernie singing in the shower is one of the highlights of my life.

The water stopped running. Then came toweling sounds, plus more humming. "Bada boom, bada boom," sang the man. He stepped out from behind the trellis, slipping on a terrycloth robe, and heading toward a table with a coffee pot and two mugs on top and a nice, wide-open view. There was also an ashtray with a half-smoked cigarette in it, one end lipstick red.

"What are you so happy about?" Bernie said.

The man whirled around, his hand to his chest.

"Walter Lessig?" Bernie said.

"Wha—wha?"

"I'm Bernie Little and this is Chet," Bernie said.

The man in the terrycloth robe was the middle-age type. Not as pudgy as some you see, but he did have one of those double chins where the lower part took up way more space than the upper part. Also he was a comb-over fan, but since he hadn't had a chance to do the actual combing over, the look was not yet in place. His eyes weren't particularly interesting—small, watchful, cold, a look you tend to see too much in our line of work. Maybe not interesting, but did they shift suddenly at the sound of our names? That would have been my take.

"What are you doing here?" he said. "This is private property."

Bernie walked over and handed him our card. He glanced at it.

"I—I don't understand. You're a private investigator?"

"That's what it says. Are you Walter Lessig?"

"I am. But this is private—"

"You already said that," Bernie said. "But I don't think you have a no-visitors policy."

Walter half turned his head, looking toward the house, or rather, it seemed to me, trying to look right through it and beyond. To where? And why? I had no idea. I was probably wrong about the whole thing.

"What is this about?" he said.

"Let's hear your best guess," said Bernie.

"I—I have no guess," Walter said. "No guess at all."

"Does the name Victor Klovsky ring a bell?"

Walter shook his head. A few drops flew from the long, thin strands hanging from the sides of his head.

"What about Lauritz Vogner?"

"Nor him," Walter said. "This must be some mistake."

Bernie nodded. "We're dealing with lots of that right now, but I think you can help us with the corrections. How about we sit down?" He gestured toward the table and chairs overlooking the drop-off.

"I'm already running late for an appointment," Walter said. "Perhaps we can reschedule."

Bernie didn't answer. Instead he walked over to the table, sat down, and poured himself a mug of coffee. I stayed where I was, close to Walter in case he . . . well, I had no idea. No way he was carrying, and dudes with chins like his stood zero chance against Bernie.

Bernie took a sip. "My, my," he said. "This is meant to be."

"Excuse me?" said Walter.

"We get our coffee from the same place, Walter. Isn't this Livia Moon's special dark roast? I'd recognize it anywhere."

"I—I have no idea," Walter said. "I grab whatever's on the shelf."

"Whose shelf?" said Bernie.

"Huh?" Walter said. "I don't understand you."

"Not even subconsciously?" Bernie said.

Walter blinked, always a good sign. We were starting to roll. I felt it.

Bernie filled the other mug and motioned Walter over. Walter moved toward the table slowly, like he was wading through deep water. I followed. He sat down, opposite Bernie. I sat in between.

Bernie took another sip. He really seemed to be enjoying the coffee! Maybe too much? Wasn't this an interview of some sort? Whoa! How bad of me to even come close to doubting Bernie! I glanced at Walter's ankles, bare and swollen, considered a plan or two, and decided to put it off for now.

"Were you ever a priest, Walter?" Bernie said.

"No."

Blushing you see from some kids and some women. From men? Hardly ever. But now a blush appeared on Walter's face. He sat back.

"Why would you ask a question like that? And you must be working for someone. Before we go any further, I have a right to know who." He held up his finger, perhaps even shook it a bit. At Bernie, if you can imagine that! Would biting it off be appropriate, on my part? There are lots of tough calls in our business.

"We never divulge the name of the client," Bernie said.

"How convenient! But let me guess. It's Livia Moon."

"Oh?" said Bernie. "Why her?"

"So you know the bitch?"

"Why do you call her that?"

"Because she's a bitch. A controlling bitch. She can't stand when any of her . . . her employees develop a . . . a relationship on the . . . an independent relationship. Ergo she hired a leg breaker."

A leg breaker? That sounded awful. Was Walter saying Livia Moon had a leg breaker working for her? I knew Livia—a very nice-smelling middle-aged woman and a big fan of me and Bernie—and found it hard to believe.

"So you have an independent relationship with one of Livia's employees?" Bernie said.

"That's between me and the young lady." Walter felt his head, then quickly swept the longish hairs over the top.

"Sure thing," Bernie said. "Instead why don't we talk about the Priory of the Valley? I understand you were their last business manager."

Walter glanced around, as though looking for help. No help was nearby. I'd have been the first to know.

Walter turned back to Bernie, his head lowered a bit like a bull, a look you sometimes get from a certain type. "What's this about?"

"Victor Klovsky. Lauritz Vogner."

"I already told you—those names mean nothing to me."

"What about the Friends of Merisi?" Bernie said. "Heard of them?"

Walter raised his head, gave Bernie a long look. I could feel him thinking hard and fast. Like he was going to out-think Bernie! This job can be a lot of fun.

"Of course I've heard of them," Walter said. "They were on the other side of a transaction."

"With the priory?"

"Correct."

"The sale of Nuestra Señora de los Saguaros?"

"Correct again."

"Who negotiated for the Friends?" Bernie said.

"They were represented by a local law firm."

"Which one?"

"Dale and Hoar."

"And who was in charge of your team?"

"Team?" said Walter. "I was the team."

"Then we're in luck," Bernie said. "You're just the man to take us through it."

"Take you through what?"

"The whole deal—the sale of Nuestra Señora from the priory to the Friends."

Walter shrugged. "The site had been deconsecrated and the buyer's only intent was to preserve and study it. After that it was nothing more than a routine real estate purchase and sale."

Bernie took another sip of coffee, gave Walter a look over the rim of the mug, not a look I wanted coming at me, and of course it never would. He lowered the mug and, oh my goodness! There was a slight smile on his lips. For a moment my Bernie was almost scary.

"Let's begin," he said, "with how you became the priory's business manager."

"Why?"

Bernie pushed the ashtray with the red-tipped cigarette butt slightly closer to Walter. "Humor me."

Walter gave Bernie a quick up-from-under glance. For some reason he didn't seem fond of Bernie. "I'm an accountant by profession. I did some work for the previous business manager. When he retired I took over."

"What's his name?"

"Father Henry."

"A priest?"

"Yes."

"Which you never were."

"I already told you that." Walter's gaze went to the cigarette.

"How did you get the job with Father Henry?"

"He was one of my teachers in school."

"High school?"

Walter looked down. "Seminary."

"So you wanted to be a priest?"

"I thought so for a time," Walter said. "I don't have the calling."

"Better to find out early," Bernie said.

Walter nodded. He had a new look in his eyes now, one you sometimes see in the eyes of the eventual loser of a fistfight, which made no sense because no fistfight was going down on this terrace, so quiet and peaceful.

Bernie swirled his coffee around but didn't drink. "Why did the priory dissolve?"

"The usual reason," Walter said. "The monks died off or got too old to work and no replacements were in the pipeline. There was no choice."

"What was the sale price?"

"Nine hundred seventy-five thousand dollars."

"If the Priory was dissolved, what happened to the money?"

"It went to various charitable organizations, twenty-three in all."

"What was your cut?"

Walter sat back. "Is that a serious question?"

Bernie gazed at him and said nothing.

"There was no cut, as you put it," Walter said. One of those strange greenish tubes humans have under their skins—this one in his neck—started throbbing. "It was part of my job."

"What was your salary?"

"None of your business. I don't even know why I'm talking to you."

Bernie reached out, moved the ashtray a little farther across the table. Walter tried not to look at it. That's an interesting human thing you see sometimes.

"This is why," Bernie said. "Victor Klovsky is a friend of mine. I may have steered him into trouble. We're going to chase down every lead until we find him. You're a lead."

"But I told you," Walter said. "I never heard of him."

"I'll take your word for it," Bernie said.

I felt Walter starting to relax inside. He reached for the second mug, raised it to his lips.

"But," Bernie went on, "you can still help us."

Walter lowered the mug. "How?"

"Let's start with the Friends of Merisi. Who are they?"

"A nonprofit dedicated to historic preservation."

"Where are their headquarters?"

"I don't know."

"They must have a board, a chairman, some sort of executive."

"I assume so," Walter said. "But I don't know the names. I dealt only with Dale and Hoar."

"But someone must have signed for the Friends, signed documents that you saw. What was the name?"

Walter went a bit pale, like he was afraid of something. "I probably did but . . . but I didn't take note."

Bernie gazed at him and said nothing.

"Maybe . . . maybe some foreign name," Walter said at last.

"Why do you say that?"

"It was just an impression. I can't tell you any more and no amount of"—his voice rose—"badgering will change that."

Badgers were in the picture? I'd run into badgers on an occasion or two. Walter had no idea.

Bernie stood up, went to the edge of the patio, looked into the distance. I could make out the downtown towers, the color of brass in that strange downtown light. He turned back toward Walter.

"You don't seem very curious about the Friends of Merisi."

"That wasn't my job," Walter said. "My job was to make a clean sale happen at the best possible price."

"A clean sale," Bernie said. He scanned Walter's house from one end to the other. "You've got a real nice place here, Walter."

Walter's mouth opened like he was about to say something, but no words came. Bernie made the little click click sound that meant we were out of there.

Fourteen

"When you come to a fork in the road, as Yogi Berra said, take it."

Uh-oh. Yogi Berra—a perp, no doubt, right now staying as far from us as possible if he knew what was good for him—had come up before, along with the fork in the road thing. Here was the problem. We weren't even on the road! Instead we'd driven a short way up from Walter's place and pulled over at the same lookout where we'd stopped before our little visit. Was Bernie okay? I studied him carefully. What a fine face he had! But that wasn't why I was studying him. Keep your eye on the ball, he often says. Which I don't need to do, by the way. I can catch a ball just by keeping my nose on it.

But we're way off course. I was studying his face because . . . because . . . right! Because I was worried he might be mixed up about something or other. He didn't look mixed up, had all his attention focused on the screen on his phone. *Tap tap, tap tap.* "One way leads to Father Henry, the other to Autumn. The sacred and the profane, big guy."

He'd lost me completely. *Tap tap, tap tap.* The light of the screen got reflected in his eyes. Sometimes I thought that humans—although not Bernie—were a bit too machine-like themselves. Not Bernie, but still I looked away, turning my gaze to the road. Watching traffic go by can be relaxing. In this case, there was no traffic. I gazed at empty road. Wouldn't it be fun if a roadrunner happened by? Not likely here in town, but possible. Roadrunners were not easy to catch, yet it could be done. At least by me. I was trying to remember a cartoon Charlie and I had watched that maybe touched on this subject when Bernie said, "Here we go—Father Henry, home address." He wrote something in the dashboard dust.

*   *   *

The sun comes up on one side of the Valley and goes down on the other. Don't think I haven't noticed that. I've even wondered about it a few times, getting nowhere, and then one day Bernie explained the whole thing to Charlie, drawing pictures in the dirt with a stick. I came oh-so-close to understanding! It felt great. Also I ended up with the stick, maybe goes without mentioning. Who's got it better than me?

Right now we were headed toward the side of the Valley where the sun sets. After you pass the very last subdivision the trailer parks begin. Some are quite fancy, some are all worn-out, and some are in between. They all have palm trees lining the sides of the little streets. In the fancy trailer parks the palm trees are tall and leafy; in the in-between ones they're short and dusty; in the worn-out ones they're dead. We pulled into a trailer park with dusty palm trees.

Bernie checked the writing on the dashboard. "We're looking for 41 Hickok Drive." We headed down a narrow street, turned onto another, and another, Bernie reading out the names. "Bat Masterson Way . . . Doc Holliday Circle . . . Earp Highway. Good grief." We came to the last road in the trailer park, bordering a treeless ravine, and stopped in front of the last trailer.

A small trailer, white with black trim, the whole thing maybe a little crooked, leaning away from the trailer next door. In the center of the tiny yard lay a tiny flowerbed with a few yellow flowers in it. Those yellow flowers seemed to be in good shape, better shape, in fact, than anything else around. Was any of that important to what Bernie sometimes calls the trained eye? Maybe not. To the trained eye, the important thing was probably that the door to the trailer was wide open.

"Hello?" Bernie called through the doorway. "Anyone home?"

No answer, but someone was home all right. Easy to tell from the grunting sounds, the kind of grunting sounds you hear when a struggle is going on.

We hurried inside, me first, went through a small kitchen that had not the slightest smell of food, and into a small living room. A living room with no couch? That was new. There were just two chairs, one the card table type, the other an easy chair, but with not much padding. An open book lay on the easy chair, and books were stacked against the walls. None of that had anything to do with the struggle, which was taking place on the floor and seemed to be about a man and a Christmas tree. The Christmas tree, with no decorations, lay on top. The man, his face obscured by the branches, was trapped underneath, grunting and struggling away but getting nowhere even though the Christmas tree wasn't particularly big. Sometimes you see funny sights in our line of work. Was this one of them? I glanced over at Bernie. He wasn't laughing, wasn't even close to smiling, in fact looked kind of horrified, an expression you hardly ever see on his face, but once you do, you don't forget it. Was that look on account of the man's leg, sticking out from under the tree? It was bare, kind of purplish, and ended in a stump where the foot should have been. A shoe with a plastic foot in it—plastic smell being unmissable—lay nearby. Bernie stepped forward, reached down, grabbed the trunk of the tree with one hand, whipped it off the man, and stood it in the corner.

The man lay on the floor, blinking up at us. He wore nothing but baggy cargo shorts and was old and very skinny, with wispy white hair, all of him kind of colorless except for his eyes, large and very dark, and of course that purplish leg. The man gasped for breath, gasps that wheezed in and out of his throat. The dark eyes gazed up at us, showing no fear. I decided on the spot that this old guy was not a perp.

"Are you all right?" Bernie said.

The man nodded a tiny nod.

"Think you can get up?"

The man raised his head, but not very much, and lowered it to the floor with a soft bump.

"I'll get you some water," Bernie said.

"V—v . . ." The man licked his lips—tongue and lips all so dry—and tried again. "Kind," he said in a whispery little voice that was mostly just air—somewhat boozy air, by the way. "Very kind."

Bernie went into the kitchen. I heard water running. I moved a little closer to the man, specifically to his stump. Was licking it a good idea? I was going back and forth on that when he looked at me and said, "Saving grace." Then he raised a hand and reached out as though to pet me. For that to happen I would have had to move closer still, but I hesitated a bit because his palm was bleeding. Not much, nothing like one of those terrible gushers I've seen a few times, never with a good result. This was only a trickle, coming from a small roundish cut in the middle of his palm. Still, I hesitated, for unknown reasons, and an instant later Bernie was back with a glass of water.

He knelt down, got one arm under the man's back, raised him up a little, held the glass to his lips. The man drank. A bit of color returned to his face.

"Thank you, sir," he said.

"You're welcome," said Bernie. "I'm Bernie and this is Chet. Are you Father Henry?"

"Just Henry," he said.

Bernie tilted the glass. Henry drank some more and then, making an effort—I could hear his quiet throat gulps—he downed half the glass.

"Want to try getting up?" Bernie said.

Henry nodded.

"Easy now," Bernie said.

Henry tried to sit up. He grunted and cords stood out on his neck, but all he could do was barely lift his head off the floor. Bernie sat him up, raised him to a standing position, although he couldn't actually stand properly, what with the stump, and sort of carried him with one hand over to the easy chair, the glass of water still in his other hand. Not a drop spilled. There are quiet little things about Bernie that make you think sometimes. Then, with no hand at all, he somehow moved the book aside, sat Henry on the chair, and placed the glass on the armrest. Bernie topping Bernie! You don't see that every day. What a world that would be!

Henry heaved a deep sigh. He licked his lips, his tongue a little damper now.

"Sorry . . ." He took a breath. ". . . to be such a nuisance."

"That's all right," Bernie said.

"So . . . so stupid," Henry said. "All I was trying to . . . to do was get the tree in the stand. But then—" He got a look in his eyes that a laugh was on the way, although the laugh didn't quite come. "—my foot came out from under me." He glanced at the shoe with the plastic foot inside.

"Do you want to put it back on?" Bernie said.

"In a bit," said Henry. His eyes shifted. "What I wouldn't mind right now would be a little . . . drop of something."

There was the tiniest pause. You'd have to know Bernie very well to spot it, and of course I do. "Where do I look?" he said.

"In the cupboard over the kitchen sink," said Henry. Or was it Father Henry? Had I missed something? Anyone can make a mistake, even Bernie. Once he'd thought I'd enjoy an escalator ride in one of the downtown towers! But only once.

Bernie went into the kitchen. I stayed where I was, keeping an eye on Henry even though he wasn't a perp. When you're a pro you don't stop being a pro, end of story.

Bernie returned with a bottle. He held it up so Henry could see.

"Just the thing," Henry said.

"Say when."

Bernie tilted the bottle over the empty water glass. Bourbon: an aroma I knew well.

"When," said Henry, although not as soon as you might have expected. He reached for the glass. That was when Bernie noticed the little round cut on the palm of his hand, still bleeding slightly.

"What happened there?"

Henry gazed at his palm. "It must have been when the tree fell. I tried to get hold of the trunk, but . . . ."

"Let's get it cleaned up," Bernie said. He left the living room, again returning quickly, this time with a wet towel and a box of bandages.

"I'm fine," Henry said. "You're very kind but please don't—"

"Hold out your hand," Bernie said.

Henry held out his hand. With his other hand, he reached for the bourbon. That was when we—meaning me and Bernie—noticed there was a little round cut on the palm of that hand, too.

"Whoa," said Bernie.

Henry took a look at it and shrugged. "My skin's not what it used to be." He reached for the bourbon, took a hefty drink, leaving a small bloody smear on the glass. Then his dark eyes went to Bernie, to me, back to Bernie. "You must be here for a reason," he said.

"We'll get to that," Bernie said. "First this." He tore off a length of bandage.

"Walter has a house in Horseback Hills?" Henry said. "That can't be right. Isn't it very pricey up there?"

Bernie nodded. There'd been quite a lot of back and forth by now but I hadn't been paying much attention. Why not? I'd actually been thinking about Lola, a member of the nation within I'd gotten to know one night down Mexico way. Funny how the mind works.

Meanwhile we had Bernie sitting on the card table chair, the bottle on the floor beside him, and Henry still in the easy chair but looking much better now. He had on a sweater, for one thing, covering up his scrawny torso, and Bernie had gotten his hands bandaged and his shoe attached, with the plastic foot inside. Also Henry was on his second glass of bourbon. He'd told Bernie to pour some for himself, and more than once, but Bernie hadn't. What was up with that? Bernie liked bourbon, liked it a lot.

"That's funny," Henry said. "Walter never had much money."

"He's an accountant by training?" Bernie said.

"Well, not an actual accountant. Did he tell you that?"

"He did."

"Walter's more like a bookkeeper. But when I taught him at the seminary, I noticed he had a bit of an aptitude for numbers. Later, when he dropped out, I sent him small jobs from time to time."

"So how did he become the business manager?"

"I was retired by then. In any case, all hiring decisions were made by our last abbot."

"Where's he now?"

"With God, I'm sure."

"Meaning he died?"

Henry gazed into his glass and thought about that. "Yes. You can be with Him here on earth, of course, but how can it be the same?"

"I have no idea," Bernie said. "Did he die of natural causes?"

Henry looked up quickly. "He did. Why do you ask that?"

"Something's going on," Bernie said. "I'm getting a bad feeling."

"In your professional capacity?"

"Yes. What do you know about the sale of Nuestra Señora?"

"Nothing firsthand."

"What's your take on it?"

"My take?"

"On the purchase price, for example."

"A shade under a million, I believe?"

"According to Walter," Bernie said.

Henry reached for the glass, paused, left it alone. "I would have waited."

"Because the price was too low?"

Henry shook his head. "Not so much that. And the charities on the receiving end need the money so badly these days, which argues against delay. But I would have preferred a buyer with local roots."

"The Friends of Merisi aren't local?" Bernie said.

"I don't believe so," said Henry.

"Where are they from?"

"I don't know," Henry said. He reached for the glass again, and this time drank not too much more than a sip. His dark eyes were starting to get a little bloodshot, never a good look in humans, in my opinion. He put down the glass. "I suspect Naples."

"Naples, Florida?"

"Oh no. The original and ancient Naples."

"The Friends of Merisi are Italian?" Bernie said.

"I can't say with any certainty. But I have an acquaintance with local roots who was trying to raise money for the purchase himself. Not for himself personally, you understand—his purpose was preservationist."

"Like the Friends?"

"Perhaps," Henry said. "But he was the one who suspected a Neapolitan connection. I have no evidence myself."

"Does he?" Bernie said. "I'd like to talk to him."

"That shouldn't be hard," said Henry. "He's a professor at the college."

"Oh?" said Bernie. Just a quiet, simple little oh like you often hear from humans, but this one made the whole room go still.

"In the art department," Henry said. "His name's Marco Folonari."

"He's on sabbatical," Bernie said.

"Ah. Sho—so you're way ahead of me," said Henry.

"I don't think so," Bernie said. His face darkened. "What the hell's going on with Nuestra Señora?"

For a moment Henry looked shocked. Why would that be? I didn't get it.

"That's an odd way of putting it." Henry picked up his glass and polished off what was left. He put the glass down on the armrest, his bandaged hand shaking just a bit, and then raised his eyes toward Bernie in a way that reminded me of . . . of begging. How strange! Didn't he know begging was a big no-no?

Bernie picked up the bottle and poured Henry more bourbon, a pretty hefty pour, more than you'd get at the Dry Gulch Steakhouse and Saloon, where the pours are known to be big. Sometimes begging works. That's what makes the no-no part so tricky.

Henry picked up the glass in a very delicate way and took the tiniest sip, his dark eyes on Bernie the whole time.

"*Falso penitente*," he said.

"Excuse me?"

"It means false penitent."

"I'm no wiser," said Bernie.

Henry gave him a long look. "You said you're a private investigator?"

"I am. Chet and I. We're a team."

"You speak like an educated man," Henry said.

"I am like an educated man, in some ways," Bernie told him. "What's this false penitent shit?"

Henry's eyebrows—thinned-out and gray—rose and he even shrank back, as though suddenly afraid of Bernie. Hard to believe, what with how nicely Bernie was treating him, getting his plastic foot back on, for example. But things often work better for us when people are a bit afraid, and not just of Bernie, but of me, too. You may not buy this but I can be pretty scary at times.

"I apologize for mystifying," Henry said. "Comes with the territory. We can live with mystery, men like me. In fact—" He paused and took another weensy sip. "—it's at the core of what we are. The twin of faith. Even conjoined, you might say."

Sometimes—although hardly ever—Bernie's eyes get this real flat expression that means you're not getting in. He never directs it at me, of course, goes without mentioning. His eyes had that look now.

"I suspect you're not the type who likes living with mystery," Henry said.

"I'm a private eye," said Bernie. "As we just discussed."

"My apologies." Henry glanced down at his hands, seemed a bit surprised by the bandages. He took a deep breath. It wheezed going in and coming out. "How much do you know about Nuestra Señora de los Saguaros?"

"Not a whole lot," Bernie said.

"Did you ever think about the name itself?"

"Not really."

"Don't you find it odd?" Henry said.

"In what way?"

"Saguaros are native only to the Sonoran desert, meaning they are only found naturally here and in Sonora, plus isolated parts of San Bernardino and Imperial counties in California. But far, far from the lands that Mary trod, mainly Judea, although there was also the Flight into Egypt. In other words, half a world away from our whimsical-looking cactus, which sometimes appears in cruciform shape, as you may have noticed."

"I haven't," Bernie said.

"Sorry," Henry said. "I was just musing." He reached for the glass. Bernie reached, too, and took his wrist, not hard but hard enough. Their eyes met.

"A man's life is at stake," Bernie said. "Save the musing for later."
He let go. The drink stayed where it was.

"Who is this man?" Henry said.

"Victor Klovsky. I already told you. You said you hadn't heard of him."

Henry's mouth open, closed, opened again. No words came.

"It's okay," Bernie said. His voice softened. "It's a complicated case." Then he did something that surprised me. He picked up the glass and took a drink himself, not a gulp, but not a sip either.

Henry smiled. He was missing a tooth or two and the rest of them were brown and yellow, but it was a sweet smile. He made his hand into a fist and fist-bumped Bernie, his weak, bandaged hand touching Bernie's mighty fist.

"You're a patient man," Henry said. "I'm a trier of patience, especially to someone like you, so present. I myself have spent so much time in the past—comes with the job. I won't say calling. I'm not referring only to the biblical past. There's also the past of Nuestra Señora. That was the original name, by the way. The saguaros part was added later, a few decades or more. Hard to say—the records from the early period are almost nonexistent. That's how faith and superstition get mixed up."

"Not quite following you," Bernie said, meaning, as so often happened, that our minds were running on the same track.

If Henry had heard what Bernie said, he gave no sign. His eyes seemed filmed over. "And that opens the door to plagues of strange ideas, curses, for example." Henry blinked. His eyes cleared and his voice strengthened. "Do you believe in curses, Bernie?"

"How do you mean?" said Bernie.

"That a person or place can be cursed," Henry said.

"No."

"Neither do I." Henry glanced at the glass and left it alone. "But Nuestra Señora de los Saguaros is cursed."

Fifteen

"Cursed how?" Bernie said.

Henry's eyes got filmy again and then closed. His breath began wheezing in and out, quite softly. Perhaps too softly for Bernie. "Uh-oh," he said, and leaned in close to Henry. "Still breathing."

Well, yes, although not the powerful way Bernie breathed. Bernie's breathing let the air know who was in charge, and in no uncertain terms. Also Henry's heart was beating rather quickly but with almost no force. Meanwhile my heart and Bernie's heart were pounding away, much more slowly than Henry's. Bernie's was a little slower than mine—actually just the right amount to be very interesting. How well they went together, those two hearts, a sort of music! Bernie and I carried heart music with us wherever we went. Whoa! What a strange thought! Did it make any sense at all? Probably not.

"Henry?" Bernie said. "Wake up. We need to talk."

Henry did not wake up.

"Henry! For god's sake!"

Henry moaned a bit, but slept on.

Bernie straightened up, looked around. "Let's check things out."

What a great idea! But that was Bernie. This wouldn't be the first time we've reconned a place with the perp passed out right in front of us. Except hadn't I decided that Henry was not a perp? Why had I done that? In my mind I went over the . . . what would you call it? Decision? Something like that. And found absolutely nothing behind it.

I followed Bernie through Henry's trailer, first from behind, then side by side, and as soon as possible from in front, our usual setup for moving together. We did a quick scan of the books lining the walls, me scanning with my nose. Books have a wonderful smell—sometimes reminding me quite a lot of trees! How do you explain something like that? An outdoor thing being indoors? The world is full of questions, perhaps best ignored. One thing about books: older ones smell better than newer ones, and a lot of Henry's books smelled old. Bernie pulled a very old-smelling one off a shelf and leafed through.

"Does he speak all these languages?"

I couldn't help him there, couldn't even begin.

Next we headed into a bedroom, small and narrow, with a small and narrow bed, neatly made, and a portable-type closet with hardly any clothes inside. After that the tiny bathroom, where Bernie examined a bunch of medicine bottles, all empty, and the kitchen, where the fridge had some milk and some oranges, and the cupboards, empty except for a box of animal crackers and a single Slim Jim. I'd come across animal crackers before—you see some bothersome stuff in this business—and had no interest in them, but Slim Jims are another matter. I looked at Bernie, not at all in a begging way, far from it, merely a very normal hey buddy what's up how's it goin' kind of look.

"Can't give you his last one, big guy," Bernie said. "Moment we're out of here we'll pick up one of those six packs. First thing. I promise. Chet? Don't look at me like that."

Like what? Like hey buddy what's up how's it goin'? I turned and headed back to the living room on my lonesome, tail up stiff and high, sending a message. Henry was still asleep. Bernie came in moments later, took a quick look at Henry, and then the Christmas tree, leaning against the wall. A cardboard box sat on the floor nearby, with tinsel sprouting out the top.

"Never actually done this on my own in my whole life, always just following orders," he said. "But I don't see why not."

Bernie got to work, setting the tree up in the stand, cutting off a branch or two with a breadknife from the kitchen, hanging a red ball here and a green ball there, and tossing on some tinsel.

"Too much tinsel, Chet? Don't want to over-egg the pudding."

Impossible of course, since we'd already established there

were no eggs on the premises. All the same, Bernie plucked off a single tinsel string and put it in his pocket. Then he took the last decoration from the box. Ah! I'd forgotten about this one, and wished it had stayed forgotten: a tiny sort of doll in human shape, only with wings. In other words, a bird-human combo. Why top this lovely smelling Christmas tree with something scary? But that was what Bernie did, standing on his tiptoes, tongue between lips. Angel? Was that the name? One Christmas when I'd been alone, just the tree, angel, and me in the house, I'd—

But before I could get to that memory—a mixed one, you might say—Henry's eyes fluttered open. They fixed on the tree first thing.

"A miracle," he said softly.

"Nope," said Bernie.

Henry blinked. He looked at Bernie, then at me, blinked again. His gaze returned to Bernie. He sat up—not easily—a little straighter. "Not all miracles turn out to have divine agency, when you look deeper. They're still miracles, in my opinion. Bernie? And Chet?"

"That's right," Bernie said.

"You're the helpful kind. It's a blessing. Thank you."

Bernie nodded. He has a number of nods that mean this and that or nothing at all. This one was close to nothing at all, but also maybe the slightest bit impatient.

Did Henry get that part? I didn't think so. It's not like Bernie to be impatient—Henry was right about that—but the rare time he gets impatient, I do, too. Henry sat up straighter still. "How can I help?"

Had I growled a bit? I wouldn't rule it out.

"Let's go back to the curse," Bernie said.

Henry nodded. "You have to understand I don't necessarily mean a curse that comes down from above. We can take actions here that curse the rest of our lives, or the lives of innocent others. I wonder, Bernie, if . . . if you've seen that in your work?"

Bernie nodded, a brief one-two. Brief, with very little movement at all, but that was a big yes.

"The effects can sound through generations," Henry said, "or even centuries, as is the case, I believe, with Nuestra Señora."

"What's the curse?" Bernie said. "What are the effects?"

"How much do you know about Nuestra Señora?"

Had Henry asked that already? Bernie's eyes shifted very slightly. If this was the second time through, he didn't mention it. "Just that it's very old but had nothing to do with De Niza," he said.

"True and probably true," said Henry. "So much of the history is undocumented." He motioned to the card table chair.

Bernie sat. I sat beside him. My gaze went immediately to that tiny winged human at the top of the tree. Not the tallest Christmas tree I'd ever seen, by the way, far from it. I felt an idea getting ready to happen in my mind.

"But if De Niza himself never appeared, there were other Spaniards coming up from Mexico not much later. We think of all this from an American Southwest point of view, but picture how it looked from Madrid."

"I don't understand," Bernie said.

"The Spanish empire was huge," said Henry. "So right here was the very edge of the unknown, the frontier, the Wild West. What kind of people are attracted to places like that?"

"Explorers?" Bernie said. "Missionaries? Soldiers? Prospectors?"

"All true," said Henry. "But you omitted outlaws, odd from someone in your profession. I'm talking about outlaws from Europe—and not just Spain, of course. Phillip III was also king of Portugal, as well as king of Sicily and Naples. European outlaws on the run passed this way—thieves and murderers. Would it be a stretch to imagine one or two seeking protection and even absolution from the church?"

"What are you telling me?" Bernie said.

Henry glanced at his empty glass, still on the armrest, a long and drawn-out type of glance, but Bernie seemed to miss it.

"I'm telling you," Henry said, now sounding a little impatient himself, "what I already tried to tell you."

"The false penitent?" Bernie said.

Henry smiled, the first smile I'd seen from him. Smiles usually make old people look younger, but not in his case. I suddenly saw the thinness of the skin on his face, barely holding together. "So you've been listening," he said.

Bernie didn't answer.

Henry nodded to himself and went on. "Nothing is written down. I'm not saying nothing was ever written, but there have been fires at Nuestra Señora—1692, 1741, 1770, 1802, and others. Parts of the structure have been built and rebuilt, and as for outbuildings that existed at one time—dormitory, school, kitchens—those are long gone, and the land where all that stood, mostly across the dirt road on the south side, has been sold off. But there's oral history, too—an old monk passes on a story to a young one who grows old himself, and, well, you can fill in the rest. One of these tales concerns the *falso penitente*. The date would be somewhere between 1590 and 1610, give or take. As the story goes, a wanted man, charismatic, handsome, possibly Italian, and a murderer, was granted refuge here. A very quarrelsome man. In the end he quarreled with one of the monks and stabbed him in the heart. With a dagger—that's the kind of little detail that argues for authenticity, at least in my book."

"So that's the curse?" Bernie said.

"Half of it," Henry said. "The false penitent fled, disappearing forever from these parts, but he left something behind, as an act of penance. According to the story he buried it by the light of the moon."

"What kind of something?"

"When I first came to Nuestra Señora—I was a young man, twenty-three, can you imagine that?—a very old monk told me it was an Egyptian ring. He'd even gone over the place with a metal detector!" Henry shook his head. "But if something was left behind, I believe it was the murder weapon. Then, you see, the curse could not be lifted until the weapon is found and removed."

Bernie said nothing. He gave Henry that flat-eyed look that

was so un-Bernie-like. It made Henry nervous. He licked his thin, dry lips.

"Superstition?" he said. "Probably. But sometimes at night, walking around the church, I felt an evil presence. Now there is no church, so all this is moot. Although the presence somehow lingers."

"What do you mean?" Bernie said.

Henry's eyes closed. He was quiet for a bit and then when he spoke his voice had become whispery. "Did I mention the stone from the crypt?"

"No," Bernie said.

Henry opened his eyes. His voice strengthened. "The crypt was destroyed a long time ago, but it was up front, to the left of the altar, where you can still find a few of the oldest stones, going back to the earliest days. A word was cut into one of those stones. Can you guess what it was?"

"I'm not a good guesser," Bernie said.

Henry smiled a quick smile, his teeth worn and yellow, although somehow it was a nicer smile than a lot of the huge white ones you see. "I doubt that," he said. "But I'll tell you anyway. The word was Merisi."

"Merisi?" Bernie said. "As in Friends of Merisi?"

"That struck me, too," said Henry. "I'll tell you a secret. Long ago, back when I heard the story of the Egyptian ring, I removed that stone and looked behind it. Searching for the murder weapon, if you're following along. I really think I was under a spell. There was no murder weapon, of course, nothing at all."

"I'd like to see the stone," Bernie said.

"You don't believe me?" said Henry.

"I do. But I still want to see it."

Henry raised his bandaged hands, let them fall into his lap.

Bernie sat motionless for what seemed like a long time. It was almost as though he'd gone somewhere else. Then he gave his head a tiny shake and said, "How about we take you to the hospital, get those hands looked at?"

"Thank you no," said Henry. He smiled again, that old, old man smile. "What I would like is a little sip of something."

Bernie picked up the bottle, checked the level inside, paused. Henry's eyes were now closed. He began to snore, soft and low, not at all an unpleasant sound. Bernie set the bottle on the armrest beside the empty glass.

"So much for the sacred," Bernie said, as we drove up to Livia's Friendly Coffee and More. "All set for the profane?"

That one blew right by me, but it didn't matter. I was all set for anything. That comes with the job, and it also comes with me, if you see what I'm getting at. If not, no problem. I'm not sure what I meant myself. We walked under the huge coffee cup that hung over Livia's door and entered the shop.

A nice, quiet coffee shop with coffee smells and blueberry muffin smells—Livia's blueberry muffins being the best in town if you're interested in blueberry muffins, which I can be in a pinch. We went to the counter. A kid with a number of rings in his nose, lips, and eyebrows said, "What'll it be?"

Here's a very strange thing. My teeth were struck by a sudden urge to bite him, not because he was a bad kid or a threat in any way, but just to kind of get in on the act. I kept my mouth closed tight, letting my teeth know who was boss.

"Is Autumn in?" Bernie said.

The kid shook his head. "Um, Autumn? She doesn't . . . uh, isn't in."

"Then we'd like to see Livia," Bernie said.

"Livia the owner?"

"Is there another Livia here?"

"I don't think she's in either."

"Make sure," Bernie said.

The kid's eyebrows rose, not very high, weighed down with all that metal. Bernie handed him our card. He took it and disappeared through a doorway behind the counter. Moments later he was back, and in a much brisker mood.

"Sorry to make you wait, sir. Please step around the counter and follow me. Would you like anything for . . . for while you walk? Muffin, latte, chai?"

"I think we'll be able to make it without," Bernie said. We followed the kid through the doorway behind the counter, into a storage space with sacks of coffee beans, and then through another door and into a nice sort of living room with a soft rug, some puffy-looking sofas and chairs, and a small bar, a room I remembered from a visit some time ago, mostly due to the heavy perfume smell. A woman, somewhat older than Bernie and wearing a dark pantsuit and a string of pearls, sat at a desk in front of a laptop. This was Livia Moon. She saw us and jumped up—or maybe not jumped on account of her being a big woman, big and curvy—and hurried to us.

"Bernie, Bernie, Bernie! My favorite Bernie in the whole wide world!" She gripped Bernie's upper arms, gave them a squeeze, and kept on squeezing. At the same time she glanced at the kid, who was watching with wide-open eyes.

"That will be all, Sean."

"Um, sure, but it's Simon, ma'am."

"Suit yourself," Livia said. "And where's your Santa hat?"

"I . . . I forgot to put it on," said Simon.

"In this shop we wear our Santa hats every day from Thanksgiving to New Year's Day. Are you a grinch, Sean, Simon, whatever?"

"No, ma'am."

"Then don't let me catch you without your Santa hat. That's a firing offense. Scram."

Simon hurried away. Meanwhile Livia hadn't let go of Bernie's arms. "You look great."

"Uh, no but you . . . do. Look great, that is."

"Shush," Livia said. "You also feel great. I've felt the arms of a lot of men in my day—comes with the territory—and I've never felt arms like yours."

That was enough. I squeezed in between in them.

Livia laughed. She had a real big laugh, maybe the biggest

I'd ever heard from a woman. "And this beautiful specimen. He takes the cake, he really does." She reached out and gave my neck a quick stroke or two, very very quick but somehow pure bliss. I've always been a bit afraid of Livia Moon, no shame in admitting it. And as for cake, I've eaten my share—maybe even more—but it's a take it or leave it thing, although in take it or leave it situations I tend to slip up on the leaving part.

"Is it true, Bernie?" she went on. "You want to see Autumn?"

"Yup."

"That's a surprise."

"Why do you say that?"

"Well, you've had an open invitation here for years—everything on the menu compliments of the house—which you've never once accepted. I wouldn't have figured Autumn for your first-time choice."

"Why not?" Bernie said.

"Call me sappy, but I always thought you were drawn to the more mature type."

For a moment, Bernie looked a bit confused. "Whoa! We've gotten off course. This isn't about . . . that."

"'That' being . . . ?"

"Yeah. Exactly."

Now I was confused myself. I wandered over to a wastebasket. And what do you know? The remains of a BLT. Have you noticed life has ups and downs? More ups than downs for me, and whenever there is a down an up seems to shoulder in pronto and shove it aside.

"Autumn's come up in a case we're working on," Bernie said. "I'd like to talk to her."

"Oh, brother," said Livia. "What's she done?"

"Nothing that I know of. She's a witness—a potential witness—at this point."

"A witness to what?"

"Livia? This works better if I ask and you answer."

"Damn it. I knew. I just knew."

"You knew what?"

"She's in danger, isn't she?"

"Not to my knowledge. Why would you think so?"

Livia sat down on one of the puffy little sofas. Bernie sat beside her on one of the puffy little chairs. I polished off the BLT.

"Autumn no longer works here," Livia said. "I fired her."

"Why?" said Bernie.

"She was freelancing on the side. That's forbidden. It's not about the money. Even if they kept paying the usual percentage it would still be forbidden. Worker safety is my number one priority. I can guarantee it here. I have no control if they start working on the outside, and that's not acceptable."

"I get that," Bernie said. "But it's not like you have security here."

"You don't know me better than that?" Livia reached behind a puffy pillow and pulled out a sawed-off shotgun with a pink wooden stock. "At one time I hired a muscle head or two. This is better—no three-hour dinner breaks, no attitude, no roid rage. The same type—if you mix in a nice big dollop of mean—who's caused all this trouble."

"What trouble?" Bernie said.

"With Autumn." Livia tucked the sawed-off back behind the pillow. "She's got this new boyfriend named Ricky Poole. A professional gambler—the kind who always wins just enough to lose big in the end."

"So he's pimping her out?" Bernie said.

"Not in so many words," Livia said. She took a pad of paper from a side table, wrote with a gold pen. "Autumn's real name is Becky Schwartz. Here's the address."

"The economy must be picking up," Bernie said, as we drove into the treeless foothills above the Rio Vista shopping plaza, "if they're building here again." We passed a few unfinished houses and pulled into the driveway of a finished one with what smelled like a brand-new grassy lawn—a smell they start losing on day one—parking behind a huge pickup with gold wheel rims. As we walked to the front door, sprinklers went on, spraying water to all corners of the new lawn, and making tiny rainbows. Bernie shot those rainbows a quick glance, not friendly. Did you know that all our water comes from the aquifer and when it's gone it's gone? That's a fact that never leaves Bernie's mind.

So he wasn't in his best mood to begin with. And then, as he raised his hand to knock, we heard a commotion going on inside. First, a woman said, "Don't, Ricky, please!" Then came a sound I knew well from my work, but did not like hearing at this moment, not one little bit, a hard-edged sound between a smack and a thud: the sound of a punch in the face.

The woman cried out in pain.

"Ease up on the waterworks," the man said. "It wasn't that hard."

Bernie tried the doorknob, then pounded on the door. "Open up!"

Things went silent in the house.

"Ricky," the woman whispered. "Someone's here."

"Bullshit," said Ricky.

"Open up," Bernie shouted.

A little pause, and then, "Get the hell off my property."

There's a force in Bernie that's sort of asleep most of the time, or maybe resting, but when it wakes up, you can't miss it. Now he raised his leg—his poor wounded leg—and kicked the door, a tremendous kick but quick more than hard, if you see what I mean, landing the heel of his sneaker right where it needs to land in a situation like this, namely beside the handle, where all those locking parts are hidden.

CRACK!

The door splintered, not just around the handle but also down the middle. Some of the construction here in the Valley isn't quite what you might want. We've run across some contracting dudes, me and Bernie.

But no time for that now. We charged, we burst, we stormed into that house side by side with me in the lead, and ended up in a huge room—tile floor, sparkling chandelier, big fireplace with a rack of fireplace tools, nothing else.

Can't leave out the two people, of course, which was the whole point. One we knew. That was Autumn, wearing shorts and a bra, half sprawled on the floor, half raised up on the fireplace hearth. She was bleeding from the mouth. There are some things you just don't want to see.

The other person was a stranger, but he had to be Ricky, unless I was missing something. Ricky was a pretty enormous dude, bare-chested, but wearing tight black pants and red cowboy boots. He turned toward us and didn't seem to like the view. I'd seen that kind of look before, so I wasn't in the least surprised when he grabbed the poker from the fireplace tool rack. In fact I was way ahead of him. By the time he raised the poker and started his swing I was already in midair.

One little . . . I don't want to call it a problem. Let's call it a thing. One little thing about being in midair: it's not so easy to change direction. For example, if you wanted to get your head out of the way of something, say the heavy, pointed head of a poker. I might even have been on the verge of thinking *Uh-oh,* when Bernie, also in midair, went streaking right by me, thumping shoulder-first into Ricky's chest. The poker went flying, they hit the floor, sprang up—Ricky springing up pretty fast for a dude his size—and closed in on each other, fists raised.

Ricky's lips were curled in a snarl—never a good look on a human, or on a member of the nation within for that matter—while Bernie's face showed nothing. Except for his eyes. Had I ever seen them so angry? It scared me.

Ricky wound up and threw an enormous punch. Bernie stepped inside and then came the sweet uppercut. Only, for the very first time, there was something not sweet about it, and it didn't land click on the chin like normal, but a bit off-center, knocking Ricky's lower jaw sideways in the strangest way. A tooth or two popped into the air and Ricky fell to the floor, eyes not rolling up but very glassy.

Then came a big surprise, something brand-new I'd never seen from Bernie. He reached down, grabbed Ricky by the hair and jerked him to his feet. Holding him up like that, Bernie reared back, his fist so hard and mighty and—

I have this bark for when something really surprises me, a short sort of bark that sharpens at the end. It just comes out of me. And it came out of me now. Bernie froze, then turned my way. Our eyes met. He let go of Ricky. Ricky slumped to the floor and lay still.

Sixteen

Bernie just stood there for a second or two. He shook his head like he wasn't happy about something, and then turned to Autumn.

"You all right?"

Autumn gazed up at him. Her eyes were wide and terrified and her lips were bloody, although the blood was no longer flowing much. She nodded.

Bernie took her hand, helped get her up and sitting on the raised hearth. He glanced at Ricky, on his back on the floor, eyes closed.

"Chet," he said. "Stay here. Keep an eye on things."

He moved off, went down a hall and out of sight. I changed positions slightly, stood over Ricky.

"Chet," Autumn said.

She touched her mouth gently with her hand, looked down at the blood on her palm. Right away I thought of Father Henry.

"Haven't see you in a while," she said. "Too long."

Water ran somewhere in the house. Also I heard a bird land on the roof, a big one, probably a buzzard. But not important. I went on keeping an eye on things.

"Oh, Chet," Autumn said. "I've messed up my whole goddamn life."

That didn't sound good. Autumn had a very nice wide-open desert smell, reminding me of Weatherly's, but toned down. Could things be completely bad if you smelled like that?

Bernie returned with a glass of water and a towel, dampened at one end. He set the glass down on the hearth, then dabbed the damp end of the towel gently on Autumn's lips.

"Just hold it like that," Bernie said. "I don't think you need stitches."

"Thanks, Bernie," she said, her voice muffled by the towel. "But what are you doing here?"

"Livia's worried about you."

"She sent you?"

"No," Bernie said. "We came for another reason."

"What's that?" Autumn's eyes: still scared, and now confused as well. Maybe because of the towel hiding the lower part of her face, those eyes looked very young.

"Drink some water," Bernie said.

Autumn picked up the glass and drank. Bernie's gaze went to her throat, a lovely throat, in my opinion, so beautiful in a way I could never describe. She put down the glass and was about to say something when a voice called from the front door.

"Uh, hello? Anybody home?"

We all turned to the door, except for Ricky, who kept on doing what he was doing, namely lying on the floor, out cold. Two long-haired dudes in Santa hats stood in the doorway, one carrying a cardboard box, the other holding up a tree.

"Merry Christmas!" they called. "Got your . . ." At that point they took in the little scene we had going on in this big empty house. From the looks on their faces I could tell they thought it was a bit on the unusual side, and knew right away they weren't in our business, mine and Bernie's.

"Um, Christmas tree," the dude finished up in a more . . . subdued? Would that be it? Close enough. In a more subdued sort of the voice.

"Plus the decorations you rented," said the dude with the cardboard box.

"You can rent Christmas decorations?" Bernie said.

"Sure thing," said the first dude. "For a small extra charge we'll do the decorating too, top to bottom."

"No need," Bernie said. "Just set it all down there."

They laid the tree down, the box beside it.

"That'll be three fifty."

"Three hundred and fifty dollars?" Bernie said.

"You lucked out. Rush pricing clicks in tomorrow."

Bernie glanced at Autumn. She shook her head. He rose, went through the pockets of Ricky's tight black pants, found a jewel-encrusted money clip.

"Is he okay?" said one of the dudes.

"All wassailed out," Bernie said. He handed over a wad of cash. "But in his dreams he wishes you season's greetings."

"Uh, thanks, mister."

"Don't thank me." Bernie closed the door on their open-mouthed faces. He turned to Autumn. "Not a bad-looking tree."

"A three-hundred-and-fifty-dollar tree?" she said.

"Includes the rental," said Bernie.

"But we're four months behind on the payments. Supposedly."

Bernie opened the cardboard box, found the stand, got going on setting up the tree. "What payments?" he said.

"The mortgage," Autumn said.

Bernie didn't answer. He took a candy cane from the box and hung it on a branch. He seemed to study it. After a while he took it off that branch and hung it on another one. Then came some more studying, followed by a crisp little nod. He fished around in the box, examined a tiny house with a tiny Santa climbing into the chimney, laid it down, fished around some more, came up with a bunch of shiny balls, red and green, and sorted through them, one by one. I began to worry about him.

Autumn drank some more water. Her lip had stopped bleeding and she was looking better. "Which is weird," she said. "The mortgage in the first place, I mean, since Ricky won the house in a poker game."

"How big is the mortgage?" Bernie said, stringing lights from branch to branch, the tip of his tongue sticking out. I had a terrible thought: Was Bernie, my Bernie, not behaving like a total pro? I refused to believe it.

"I don't know," Autumn said. "But I caught a glimpse of the last bill—before he . . . he took it away from me. Thirteen thousand and some dollars. Could that be the monthly payment?"

Bernie plugged the light cord into the wall and all the lights flashed on. "Ah," he said, looking very pleased with himself. He began braiding tinsel strands. "No point in trying to puzzle it all out, since I assume you're done with Ricky."

Autumn's eyes went to Ricky, still out cold, where he looked his best, in my opinion. "He's not as bad as you think."

"No?" said Bernie, concentrating on the twisted-up tinsel strands which he'd—whoa! Formed into the shape of a reindeer?

"He had a rotten childhood," Autumn said.

"Uh-huh," said Bernie.

"Plus he's very passionate. Full of life, maybe too full, but without much . . . what's the word?"

"Decency," Bernie said, now searching for a good spot for the tinsel reindeer, his back to Autumn, so missing the look on her face, like he'd slapped her. Impossible, of course. Bernie had never laid a finger on a woman and never would.

"Ricky's not like you," Autumn said. "Icy, way way deep down at the core."

"Him, you mean?" said Bernie.

"No," Autumn said.

Bernie, about to place the tinsel reindeer on the tip of a branch lost his grip and the reindeer spiraled slowly to the floor.

"You're not icy in a bad way," Autumn said quickly. "It's just there, maybe a good thing, with the kind of work you do."

Bernie stooped, picked up the reindeer.

"I may be wrong and if I am, I'm very sorry. But if I know anything for my sins . . ." There was a long pause and then Autumn went on very softly. "I know men."

Bernie turned and walked over to the hearth and sat down beside her. "Sins aren't my department." He handed her the tinsel reindeer.

"What's this?" she said.

"An attempt at a reindeer," Bernie said.

"I know that. And he's beautiful. But what am I supposed to do with him?"

"Whatever you like. Merry Christmas."

"Thank you, Bernie." She gestured with her chin at Ricky. "And thanks for—"

Bernie waved all that thanking away with his hand. "Like you, I also work with men."

Autumn smiled. Her teeth were unbroken but the front ones were smeared with blood. "But not quite in the same way."

Bernie laughed. "So maybe, coming from different places, we can put our heads together about one specific man."

"Who?"

"Walter Lessig."

Charlie has a face for when he tastes something he doesn't like. Autumn made a face just like that now.

"What?" Bernie said.

"Nothing," she said. "What do you want to know about him?"

"Anything at all. Anything unusual that caught your eye."

She sniffed. "Just the usual unusuals."

"What about other things?"

"Other things?"

"Not, um, in the bedroom," Bernie said.

Autumn shot him a quick look, one I'd seen before, namely the look of someone seeing Bernie in a new way.

"You're funny, Bernie."

"Yeah?"

"I take back what I said."

"About what?"

"Icy."

"That's all right," he said. "You're probably . . ." Whatever it was, he left it right there.

Autumn looked down at the tinsel reindeer, now in her lap. "There was this one thing Walter told me—he should have gone into the priesthood except sex was too important to him. But the thing is, he's terrible at it, Bernie! How does that add up?"

Bernie opened out his hands, human for when they have no clue. "What about money?"

"He pays, no problem. Plus tip."

"I didn't mean that, exactly," Bernie said. "Would you say money's new to him?"

"Oh, for sure. He's so proud of his house. He gave me the

complete tour on my very first visit. The kitchen countertops cost seventy-five grand."

"Did he say anything about where the money came from?" Bernie said.

"Kind of. Once when he was paying me, he said he never prayed for money because God would never grant a prayer like that. The money finally came because he didn't pray."

"So his god keeps track of the prayers and the unspoken prayers?" Bernie said.

"That's what the other man said, word for word!"

"Other man?" said Bernie.

"Lauri," Autumn said. "This was back before . . . before Livia and I went sideways. Walter was a client of mine there. And I suppose you could say I poached him away. That's what got Livia so angry."

"Who's Lauri?"

"This other man who was asking about Walter."

"A, uh, client?"

"One time only."

"And in that one time Walter came up?"

Autumn nodded.

"How did that work?" Bernie said.

"Like, when did he ask?" Autumn said. "It was at the end, after what Livia calls the oil change is over."

"The oil change?"

"They're the car and we're the mechanics."

"Only the bill comes first," Bernie said. "When the jalopy rolls into the shop."

"Oh yeah," Autumn said. "But at the very end there's sometimes a tip, and that was when Lauri asked about Walter. I was very surprised—nothing like that had ever happened before. He said he knew Walter was a client and that Walter might be just the person to help him in a business deal. But he needed to find out if Walter was the right person before approaching him, and there'd be money in it for me if I did some digging."

"Some digging?" Bernie said.

"His exact words. Of course I refused—that's a complete no-no in our business. That was where you came in."

"Me?" said Bernie. "I don't understand."

"Lauri asked if I knew any good private eyes. I gave him your name—hope that was all right. I guess he never got in touch with you."

"No problem—recommendations always welcome." Bernie sounded relaxed and casual, but I could feel a change inside him. He'd ramped up to high alert, although his tone didn't change at all. "Can you describe Lauri?"

"Sure. A very distinctive guy, Bernie. He's got an accent, for one thing, might be Swedish or German or something. On the small side," she went on, exchanging a quick glance with Bernie, the meaning of which I missed, "but with real big liquidy eyes and a real big ruby on his pinky."

"How were you supposed to get in touch with him?" Bernie said.

"We didn't get that far in the proposal, or whatever it was."

"And you haven't seen him since?"

"No."

"If you do, or if you hear from him, please let me know."

"Sure, Bernie. What's this about?"

Before Bernie could answer, Ricky began to stir. His eyes opened. They were real blurry. His blurry gaze found Autumn right away. I got the feeling he wasn't seeing me and Bernie at all.

"Oh god," he said in a croaky voice. He seemed to choke on something, coughed, spat out a tooth. I had a crazy urge to hustle over and snap it up, but perhaps this wasn't the time, especially not for a total pro such as I.

Ricky raised his head, tried to sit up, sagged back down. "Babe," he said. "What'd I do?"

Autumn didn't answer.

Ricky seemed to tear up a bit. "Babe. I'm so so so sorry. It'll never happen again."

Autumn rose.

"Autumn?" Bernie said.

Autumn didn't appear to hear him. She picked up the water glass, went over to Ricky, knelt beside him. Once on a case, all the other details now gone, I'd seen a human sleepwalking. That was how Autumn seemed to be moving now.

"You can't treat me like that," she said.

"I know," Ricky said. "I know like I've never known anything in my life. Cross my heart." His voice got all whispery. "I love you to death."

Autumn helped him raise his head, held the glass to his lips. Bernie rose. He picked up the poker, a bit of a surprise. We walked over to the little twosome in the middle of this big, empty room.

Now Ricky saw us for sure. He flinched at the sight.

"First, Autumn," Bernie said. "Stop freelancing. Go back to Livia, for your health if nothing else."

Autumn frowned, but said nothing.

"Second, Ricky," Bernie said. "If Autumn walks out of here right now, or soon, or never, it makes no difference. Anything happens to her and that will be your last day on earth. That's the soft option." Bernie lowered the poker and stuck the pointed end in one of Ricky's nostrils. Ricky hissed in fear, his eyes crossed, focused on the poker. "The hard option is to get rid of any uncertainty here and now."

"Don't!" said Autumn. "Oh, please don't!"

Bernie ignored her. "Ricky? Nod if you understand."

Ricky nodded, a very tiny movement, but that was understandable. Bernie withdrew the poker. We walked on out of there, Bernie pausing to adjust one of the tree lights on the way. He kept the poker. I knew one thing for sure. He wasn't sold on Ricky.

The sky was darkening by the time we pulled up outside Livia's Friendly Coffee and More. This day seemed kind of short to me, but there's only so much you can understand. Livia came out the front door wearing a white fur jacket. Fur's a big interest of mine. There's a lot to like about Livia.

Bernie got out of the car. "Livia?"

She turned to him. "Bernie? And so soon? Are you taking me out to dinner?"

"I'm sure you have plans already. In fact, I need a favor. I'm looking for a client of yours. Well, of Autumn's while she was still here. His name's Lauritz Vogner and—"

"Nope, Bernie. Out of the question. We don't hand that kind of information out to anybody, not even you. You're smart. You'd do the same in my position."

"True," said Bernie. "But not in this case. At least one life is at stake, maybe more. And don't say that's what they always say."

"Don't push me, Bernie. If you do we won't be friends."

Livia stepped over to a big white convertible, the leather seats of which had that tip-top of the high-end smell, climbed in behind the wheel, and drove off.

We went home. On the way, Bernie finally remembered the Slim Jim six pack he promised me. I'd almost given up hope, although not totally. I don't do totally when it comes to giving up hope. His phone buzzed when we were in the convenience store parking lot, chowing down.

"He was staying at the Desert Dunes," Livia said.

"Thanks," Bernie said. "Are we still friends?"

"Depends how you do on our dinner date," said Livia. "At the Ritz. Table eleven."

Seventeen

Fully night now, and we drove for a long way, although never leaving the Valley, easy to tell from the dark pink night Valley sky, spreading in all directions as far as I could see. There were also the night Valley smells, of course, much different than the daytime smells. Humans, for example, have a nighttime smell, funkier than in the daytime and also—

But before I could get to that, Bernie said, "Icy at the core? Is it true?"

Icy? Ice was on his mind? I know ice cubes, and once in a while someone fixing drinks drops one on the floor and I snap it up. It starts to turn to water in my mouth right away, cold cold water, lovely on a hot summer day. Was Bernie hankering for a drink? That was as far as I could take it on my own. We pulled up in front of a hotel with palm trees and a fountain out front—hotels always easy to spot from the doormen and the bell boys—and parked in the lot.

"The Desert Dunes," Bernie said as we walked to the entrance, "financed by gangsters in the forties. There actually were some dunes in the area but they bulldozed them to build the place."

One of the doormen, dressed in a red shirt and white pants, turned to Bernie as we went inside. "You talking to me, sir?"

"No," said Bernie.

The doorman glanced around, looking a bit confused. I didn't get it.

We crossed the lobby, decorated with a big silver and gold Christmas tree strung with flashing red lights. Bernie gave it a close look as we went by, not to the bar which I could see at the back and where I thought we were heading, but to the welcome desk at the side.

"Is Freddy Perez in?" he said to the clerk.

The clerk nodded. Bernie handed her our card. She disappeared into a back room, and returned almost right away with a skinny guy in a light-colored suit and a red tie featuring a laughing Santas pattern. He had one of those rubbery faces you sometimes see on skinny dudes. Now it stretched itself out in a huge smile that seemed to make the rest of his face vanish. That reminded me of something I'd seen on a cartoon show Charlie liked and I got a bit uneasy. Uneasiness is one of the strange things in life. Action makes it go away. Perhaps a perp would show up soon, all set to be taken down. You can always hope and I always do.

"Well, well, well," said the man in the Santa tie. He hurried over to our side of the desk, threw his arms around Bernie and pounded him on the back. "Bernie! Been way too long."

"Hey, Freddy," said Bernie, patting Freddy's back. Bernie had a small smile on his face, kind of shy.

Meanwhile the clerk was watching with big eyes.

"Emmy?" Freddy said. "Meet Bernie Little, genuine war hero."

"It's Amy," said the clerk.

Freddy didn't appear to hear her. "Saved my life and I wasn't the only one." He did some more pounding on Bernie's back. I could see Bernie trying to wriggle free, but Freddy turned out to be surprisingly strong. Finally he backed away, although not quite letting go of Bernie's shoulders.

"How's the leg?" he said.

"Fine," said Bernie.

He glanced over at Amy or Emmy—there seemed to be some dispute about the name. "Last time I saw this character that leg was hanging . . . wasn't lookin' too good."

"Oh my god," said Amy or Emmy, turning to Bernie. "Were you in an accident?"

"Accident?" said Freddy. "Dint I just tell you he's a genuine war hero?"

"Well, you could call it an accident of sorts," Bernie said. "And the last time we saw each other was back stateside, and I was all patched up. Remember, Freddy? You played guitar at that party with the, uh, dancing girls?"

"You play guitar?" said Amy or Emmy.

"Ba dada dada bomba," sang Freddy. "And this good lookin' hombre must be the famous Chet. Can he have a little T-R-E-A-T? Happen to have one in my pocket."

The fact that he had a little T-R-E-A-T in his pocket was old news, of course. Moments later Freddy was reaching into his jacket pocket and pulling out a revolver. "Oops," he said, trying the other pocket and this time getting it right. Not long after that, we were in a comfy dark corner in the bar, Bernie and Freddy with glasses of bourbon and me with a second T-R-E-A-T that Freddy had also happened to have in an inside jacket pocket. Why was I just meeting him now?

"Nice room," Bernie said.

"It's not a bad gig," Freddy said. "Pays better than what I was making at Valley PD and there's no bullshit politics. There's politics—no getting around that—but it's not the bullshit kind. It's out there, if you know what I mean, out there big time. How about you? Makin' any money?"

"No complaints," Bernie said.

"That bad, huh?" said Freddy.

Bernie laughed. Freddy laughed, too. They clinked glasses and laughed some more. What was funny? Were we making money? Yes? No? Could we just hustle up the answer?

But no answer seemed to be coming. Bernie kept laughing. Freddy, too, but his eyes were no longer into it. He took a breath, set down his glass.

"You still pissed at me?" he said.

Bernie's laughter stopped dead, just like it had been run over by a truck. Whoa! What a strange idea! With any the luck the last of its kind for a good long time.

"Hey," he said. "What are you talking about?"

Here's a complication that only someone who'd listened to Bernie in many many interviews—even though this little get-together might not be an actual interview, making things still more complicated—could pass along to you. Bernie has two ways of saying *what are you talking about*. With the first one he really doesn't know the answer. With second one he does. This was the second kind. He knew.

"Aw, Bernie," Freddy said. "We been in the same town here for years, pretty much since we mustered out. But this is the first time . . ." He spread his hands.

Bernie shrugged. "You know how it is, Freddy. We get to running in our own little channels and . . ." And he too spread his hands. Then they both looked down, both noticed their drinks, both drank.

"I was just a kid," Freddy said. "But it's no excuse. Of course the gas station guy was setting us up, so obvious now except—"

"Don't," Bernie said.

"But I was intel, Bernie, and it was up to—"

"Stop."

Their eyes met. Bernie rose. Freddy rose, too. Bernie embraced him. This time there was no backslapping. Tears rose up in Freddy's eyes and rolled down his cheeks. "How's the leg? Really now, my brother."

"Like new," Bernie said.

There were tears on his face, too. What was going on? First, Bernie's leg was not like new. It bothered him when he ran, bothered him on long hikes, and even on some short ones. Second, Bernie had no brother. If he did I wouldn't be finding out now. That's not how we roll, me and Bernie.

They sat down, wiped their faces on their sleeves with quick rough gestures, knocked back their drinks, suddenly looked hard and dangerous. The waitress came over.

"Another round, Freddy?"

Whatever was going on with Bernie and Freddy, they both snapped out of it.

"Please, darlin'," Freddy said.

The drinks came. They clinked glasses again. "Looking for a guy," Bernie said. "Possibly one of your guests."

Freddy took out his phone. "Name?"

"Lauritz Vogner."

"Popular fellow," said Freddy. "Well, not popular, but you're not the first."

"Someone else was asking about him?" Bernie said.

"That's what I'm trying to tell you. Naturally I gave him nothing. Finally a rule of the house but always my own personal . . . what's the word?"

"Credo," Bernie said.

"Asshole tried to bribe me," said Freddy. "First a C-note and then a handful of 'em. But what kind of credo would it be if the amount mattered?"

Bernie smiled.

"Snuck a photo if you want to see it," Freddy said.

"The guy who tried to bribe you?"

Freddy nodded. "Made an impression on me." He tapped at the phone, turned it so we could see. "Know him?"

"I don't actually know him," Bernie said, "but . . ." I knew where he was going with this. We'd seen this dude before, the fattish customer with the Santa beard and the Panama hat from the art museum gift shop video. Whoa! Who'd also shown up when Johanna was guiding us around Nuestra Señora. I'd watched through a crack in the wall as a big black SUV drove up outside and the fattish dude and his driver, a huge guy with a handlebar mustache, got out. They'd been headed toward the church until they spotted the Porsche. After that they'd booked. Did Bernie know that part? I barked.

"Chet?" Bernie.

"Ten to one he wants another T-R-E-A-T," said Freddy.

No! That wasn't it at all! I have a bark for straightening things out, and barked it now, straightening things out in no uncertain terms.

"Oh my god," cried the waitress from behind the bar.

"Darlin'," Freddy said. "Any of those Rover and Company biscuits on the bottom shelf?"

The waitress bent down, disappeared from view. "Don't see 'em."

Something was wrong with her eyes? Those Rover and Company biscuits were there, all right.

"Try behind the juicer," Freddy said.

The waitress—whose name was Darlin', unless I was missing something—popped up, the goods in her hand. I thought exactly what you would have thought: we needed more of Freddy in our lives. The next thing I knew the Rover and Company biscuit was mine and I was trying my hardest to make it last, failing completely.

"Doesn't he look kind of jolly in the picture?" Freddy was saying. "Not the same in real life."

"Where did this happen?" Bernie said.

"In the parking lot, when I drove in for work. They were waiting by my space, the bearded guy and his driver. The bearded guy has a bit of an accent. If I had to guess I'd say Italian, but don't hold me to it—we don't get a lot of Italians here, so my experience is pretty much the *Godfather* movies. The driver—six six, at least two forty—didn't speak. Their problem was our security protocols—like I said, we don't give out guest room numbers. We'll tell you if someone's registered and connect you, take a package, anything you like but no number."

"Good idea."

"Mine, actually. An easy sell to the powers that be. CYA, Bernie. That's their motto."

"Did you get a promotion?"

"Nope. But I didn't get canned and everyone else did."

"Everyone in security?"

"Everyone, period. We got taken over by some drama queens." "Yeah?"

"They're a hedge fund, but that's just an excuse. The point is, no room numbers and the bearded guy wanted a room number. We got six hundred seventy-three doors here, so you see his problem."

"He must have had a story."

"Surprise birthday party. I checked the registration later on and he had the date right, but I didn't give him the room number."

"All the more reason not to," Bernie said.

Freddy smiled. "Nail on the head." That sounded pretty horrible, but before any more scariness went down, Freddy's phone beeped. He glanced at the screen, rose, and handed Bernie a small black plastic card on his way out. "This should work. Four sixty-three. Don't be a stranger."

When it comes to going through doorways, I like to be first. Except when it comes to elevators. In an elevator situation, I don't like to be first. Or second, or any of the other possibilities on down to last. And last is no good either. All of this would maybe help you understand a little scene we had going by the elevator bank in the Desert Dunes lobby with Bernie inside an elevator, holding the door open, and me outside, pawing at the marble floor.

"Chet? Come on, buddy, you can do it."

I can do it, I thought. *I can do it, I can do it, I can do it!* I pawed harder and harder. I snorted. Somehow I went backward and forward at the same time. I shook my head. I growled. I pawed.

"Um," said a man standing at the back of the elevator.

We took the stairs. Here's a tip. Hotels always have stairs. You pick up a lot of useful information in a job like mine.

After a nice refreshing stair climb that actually reminded me of some hikes we'd been on, minus the getting lost part, Bernie and I stood outside a door at the end of a long hallway.

"Four sixty-three," he said. He knocked. No answer. He took out the little plastic card. Moments later we were inside.

It was nice and tidy in this room—Lauritz Vogner's, if I was following things right. The bed was made and there was no sign that anyone was actually staying here. Bernie opened the closet, and we gazed at the usual hotel room closet sights: iron, ironing board, white bathrobe on a hanger. But all the other hangers were bare. No clothes, no shoes, no luggage.

"Did he check out?" Bernie said.

We went down a very short hall and into the bathroom. No toothbrush in the holder, no combs or brushes, no Dopp kit, all towels clean, dry, and neatly folded. The shower wasn't the stall type but one of those shower and bath combos. The curtain was closed. Sometimes those curtains are see-through and sometimes, like now, they aren't. Bernie drew back the curtain.

The bathtub was filled with water, almost to the top. A naked man lay facedown at the bottom, actually more like he was floating just under the surface.

"Oh no," Bernie said. "Victor."

A very faint perfumey smell made me not so sure about that. Bernie bent down and turned him over, kind of urgently, as though there was still time for something good to happen. But there wasn't. The man's eyes were open—big dark liquidy eyes, dull and seeing nothing. Not Victor. An easy mistake for Bernie to make. In fact, you couldn't even call it a mistake. There are no mistakes when it's just between the two of us.

As for the dead man, it was Lauritz Vogner.

Eighteen

Bernie knelt by the bathtub. I stood right beside him. I wasn't at all thirsty although usually in a situation like this—meaning finding myself near an unexpected pool of water—I'd stick my tongue in and slurp up a sample anyway, just to check it out. But now I left it alone.

We gazed at the body of Lauritz Vogner. "I don't see any blood," Bernie said. "Smell any, Chet?"

I did not.

Bernie ran his eyes over the body, from head to toe and back. Then he turned Lauritz over again, using just enough force to get it done and no more.

"Water's cold, Chet. Below room temp. What does that tell us?"

It would probably taste good, the colder the better when it comes to water. That's what it told me. But still I left it alone.

Bernie took out his phone, aimed it at Lauritz, tapped the button. "What we need to find out," he began, but stopped himself, then leaned over the tub so his face was close to Lauritz's. Bernie's eyes weren't on Lauritz's face, instead peering slightly lower, at the base of his neck.

"Bruising?" he said. "Bruising that didn't have time to fully . . ." He put his hand on the little metal lever under the spout. "Suppose," he said, and then pushed the lever. A whiny sort of gurgle started up and the surface of the water went slowly down and down, Lauritz finally coming to rest on the bottom of the tub. Bernie pointed at Lauritz's neck, the tip of his finger almost touching a small light blue patch on the skin, and then another, smaller and harder to see.

"Accidental death by drowning?" Bernie said. That sounded like a tough one, way over my head. "Hard to prove when all you have is the body," Bernie he went on. "And it means a long delay no matter what. Can we afford delays? Or is it rough-and-ready time?"

Rough-and-ready time? What luck! Rough-and-ready time is when the Little Detective Agency steps to the front. Bernie leaned forward, flipped Lauritz over on his front, then took him by the ankles and tilted him up.

At first nothing happened. Then water seeped out from between Lauritz's lips, seeped some more and finally bubbled out, bubble bubble bubble. Bernie lowered Lauritz back down, so slowly and gently that the body meeting the tub bottom made no sound, not even to my ears. As for the look on Bernie's face: it scared me. He was real angry, a very pale anger I'd never seen before, but at what? Then I realized I had seen it, only once, the night of the terrible broom closet case—which we'd solved, except too late to save Gail Blandino, the little girl with blood in the twists of her braid. Later that night—in fact, just as dawn was breaking, the reddest dawn I'd ever seen—we'd taken care of justice on our own, me and Bernie. "Never think about this again," Bernie said when that was over, but we couldn't help it. Me and Bernie.

He rose. "Someone wanted something from him, Chet. Did he give it up?" Bernie gazed down at the back of Lauritz's head. "I don't think so." He turned to the toilet, took the lid off the tank. Sometimes you find interesting things in toilet tanks, such as a ticking bomb, but this tank turned out to be empty, except for the water inside. Bernie replaced the lid. "How about we turn this place upside down?"

What a fabulous idea! Who could have seen that coming down the pike? I sank my teeth into a fluffy bath towel and snapped it off the towel rack. Next—moving quickly now, as anyone in the grip of a fabulous idea would, I got my paw on the toilet paper roll and—

"Chet?"

How difficult to pause at such a moment! I couldn't have done it for you, for example. No offense. But Bernie is always another story. I paused, one paw raised in the air, and became aware that the toilet paper roll hadn't gotten the pausing message, taking off on its own. Nothing to do with me. I was being a good, good boy.

"We're going to turn it upside down mentally, big guy," Bernie went on.

Mentally? Mentally meant what, exactly? While I was trying to figure that out, getting nowhere, Bernie bent down and started rolling back up the toilet paper, by now pretty much totally unrolled. What a good, patient worker Bernie is! It was a pleasure to watch him, rolling and rolling that toilet paper up nice and tight, then searching for the metal thingy the roll goes on, finally finding it behind the waste basket. Those metal toilet paper thingies can be tricky and this one was, the pieces springing out of Bernie's hand and sailing all over the place. And as they did, a tiny folded baggy that had been hidden inside fluttered down to the floor.

Bernie went still for an instant, then picked up the baggy. There was a key inside. Bernie took it out, an ordinary sort of key but with a thin strip of tape on the top part, and on that tape some writing in black. Bernie read it aloud: "B twenty-seven." He stared at the key. His voice went quiet. "He didn't give it up. But what did he do to get it?"

I had no idea, didn't understand the question. Before I could get going on all that—which I may or may not actually have ended up doing—Bernie turned to me and said, "You're the best."

Well, well, well! How nice! Had I done anything special recently? Nothing that came to mind. All the better. Didn't it mean Bernie loved me no matter what? And I loved him the same way. How happy I was at that moment, perhaps a little odd, what with Lauritz's body in the tub, and all. If he hadn't been there I might have pranced around a little, maybe even slurped some water from the toilet. Instead I just sat still, gazing at the key in Bernie's hand.

Freddy took a deep breath, let it out slowly. He pointed at the body in the tub.

"What are those bruises?"

"They waterboarded him," Bernie said. "In cold water, although I'm not sure what difference that makes."

"It sends a message," Freddy said. "Like a sadistic cherry on top."

Bernie's eyes shifted toward Freddy. He nodded. Bernie has many nods, some meaning things I don't know, some meaning nothing, and some, like this one, meaning something, specifically that he liked Freddy.

"You're makin' the bearded guy for this?" Freddy said.

"For now," said Bernie.

"What's it about?"

"We're working on that, Freddy. It's an odd case."

"How so?"

"It feels old."

"What does that mean?" Freddy said.

Bernie shrugged. "Like it's based on something from long ago."

"It's the season for that," Freddy said. They both gazed down at Lauritz. There was a long silence and then Freddy said, "Any idea what they wanted from him?"

Bernie showed Freddy the key.

"You found it?" Freddy said.

"Not exactly," said Bernie.

Freddy glanced at me and laughed. "What would you do without him?"

"I hate to think about it," Bernie said.

Who were they talking about? I was kind of lost. Bernie says when you're lost step back and look at the big picture, so I moved back a bit. But the bathroom was small and most of the picture was about the body in the tub. Then it hit me: bodies in tubs are what we do! All at once I was no longer lost, far from it, this whole big-picture thing being just another example of Bernie's brilliance. The case was going well.

Meanwhile Bernie was handing Freddy the key. "Any ideas?"

Freddy examined the key, turning it over a couple times,

hefting it in his hand. "Not an airport or bus station item, if that's what you're thinking. Numbers are always stamped, never taped." He tossed the key back to Bernie, who caught it the way he catches things, his hand silently folding it in. "If I had to guess," Freddy said, "I'd say it came from the locker room of a gym."

"Thanks, Freddy."

"Don't mention it," Freddy said. He gestured with his chin at the body. "I have to call this in. You wanna be around for that?"

Bernie shook his head.

"Meaning I discovered the body?" Freddy said.

"Not if it bothers you."

"I'd do it for you even if it did, but it don't. And I get it—you don't want your name on the news about this."

"True," said Bernie.

"On account of you're the shy type or because the bearded guy might spot it?"

"The second."

"You carrying?"

"Not at the moment."

"Do me a favor till this—whatever the hell it is—is over," Freddy said. "Carry."

Bernie smiled.

"What does that mean?" Freddy said. "Yes or no?"

"I'll think about it," Bernie said.

"You know your problem?" Freddy said. "You're a lone wolf."

Whoa! Up until now, I'd been liking Freddy. Remember the Rover and Company biscuit incident from not so long ago, for example? But all at once—and this can happen with humans—he'd gone off the rails. Where to even begin? How about with lone? Impossible! We're a team, me and Bernie, so he's never alone, and neither am I. And somehow Freddy had missed that? Just as bad or maybe even worse was wolf. We have wolves here in our part of the world, not many but enough so I've run across a wolf once or twice. The time I remember best we were working a case—something about a stolen Ferris wheel, a case about which I understood nothing from beginning to end, the least understandable part coming when Bernie said he was too scared of Ferris wheels to ever actually go on one, which I must have misheard even though I never mishear—that took us into the high desert, where from over the next rise I heard the bleating of a sheep. What can I tell you about sheep? You can get them to go where you want them to go pretty easily, but when they're just standing around chewing away, their eyes a total blank, you can't help thinking, *Wake up! Snap to it! Show a little life!*

Back to this particular sheep, bleating over the next rise. I glanced around, saw Bernie quite some way behind, possibly huffing and puffing a bit, meaning there was plenty of time for me to check out the bleating, which came to a sudden halt. From the top of the rise I saw why. Not a pleasant sight and I won't describe it, but the point is a wolf was involved. He smelled me right away, looked up from what he was doing, and sized me up. I smelled him, too, of course, his scent quite like mine in some ways and in others even more so. As for size, I liked my chances. The truth is, even if he'd been bigger, I'd have liked my chances. But maybe that's just how I roll, no matter what. I ambled on down. This wolf came to a quick decision. He did not like his chances, and trotted away, an odd, low-slung trot that covered a lot of ground with surprising quickness, a desert-colored wolf who soon vanished from sight, although not from smell.

By now I'm sure you know why I brought all this up. Bernie was not a wolf, lone or any other kind. First, he never ran from a fight. Second, can you imagine him with sheep's blood dripping off his chin? Case closed.

When I tuned back into the discussion in this somewhat cramped hotel bathroom, wolves had been left behind.

"I can check registration from my phone," Freddy was saying. "In case there's anything useful."

"Thanks," Bernie said.

Freddy got busy on his phone. "Well, well," he said. "One of us."

"Oh?" said Bernie.

"Except for he's dead and we're not." Freddy held his phone so Bernie could see.

"Check this out."

Bernie peered at the phone. "He was a PI?"

Freddy pointed at the little screen. "Company name—Investigaciones Vogner, with a Madrid address. I'll text you the phone number."

"I owe you," Bernie said.

"Merry Christmas," said Freddy. "Also Happy Hannukah."

"You're Jewish?"

"Who knows? Perez was a very common name among the Marranos. Close to Peretz, if you see what I mean."

"I don't," Bernie said. "Who were the Marranos?"

"Look it up," said Freddy.

Nineteen

"Know how many gyms there are in the Valley?" Bernie said the next morning. "A shitload."

He'd lost me completely. Once we'd been held up by a wreck that began when a Porta John flatbed sideswiped a Johnny on the Spot flatbed, but had there been any gyms on those trucks? Not that I remembered, and kind of impossible given how tightly all those narrow cabins were crammed together—prior to when they got loose, of course—and also, although the air suddenly grew rich with powerful aromas they had nothing to do with gym aromas, which were all about human sweat and sanitizing spray, with the exception of the locker rooms where the air was more complex. In case you're wondering whether the sanitizing spray smell gets rid of the sweat smell, let me assure you that it does not. They kind of swirl around together in an interesting way until the sweat wins out.

Possibly we've gotten off track. I gazed at Bernie, hoping I'd do better on whatever was coming next.

"How about we start with LeSean?" he said.

Whoa! What a great idea! I'd never have thought of it myself. LeSean Stiller owned Stiller's Gym, or maybe he had owned it or was going to own it. Not the point, which was that gyms seemed to be a problem for us at the moment and we had experts for certain problems, Nixon Panero for car problems, say, or Prof for money problems, with the exception of how to get some. What made more sense than roping in LeSean for gym problems? But that was Bernie every time.

"Stick, stick, move," said LeSean Stiller. "Move, move, stick."

Stiller's Gym was mostly about free weights and the kind of guys and gals who liked lifting heavy, but the big attraction for boxing fans like me and Bernie is the ring in the center of the room. We've got a whole collection of great fights for when we're in a certain kind of mood, like after we've had Charlie for a weekend and now it's over. The Thrilla in Manila! No Mas! Ward-Gatti 1!

Nothing like that was happening in LeSean's ring, but what we had was still pretty good. LeSean was working with a strong-looking woman maybe a head taller than him, both wearing gloves, but only the woman with headgear and mouthpiece.

"Stick," he said, and she sent a real quick and nasty jab directly at his nose, which LeSean avoided completely without seeming to do anything at all. "Stick," he said again, and she threw another one, even quicker and nastier than the first. It made a faint whistling sound in the air. You don't hear that every day. In fact, you yourself have probably never heard it, no offense. Meanwhile this one missed, too, again with LeSean—a lean little guy with graying hair, by the way—doing nothing. Well, except for the fact that he'd begun to hum a little tune. Hey! Didn't I know this tune? Yes, "It Came Upon A Midnight Clear," for sure. A lovely tune, and there was a lovely sweetness to LeSean's humming. He stuck the big woman a real good one on the side of the head, thumping her headgear and making her grunt.

"Move," said LeSean, and they circled each other. He hadn't looked our way at all, but he said, "Shanice, say hi to my friends Bernie and Chet. Chet's the good-looking one."

Shanice's eyes shifted to us. "Hi," she said, her eyes shifting back fast, but not fast enough to avoid getting popped again, this time on the other side of the head.

"What we got here, Bernie," said LeSean, "is the future female heavyweight champ of the entire planet. Wanna strap on the gloves, go a round or two with her?"

"I was planning on a concussion-free day," Bernie said.

Shanice laughed. LeSean popped her again. This time she popped him right back, a hard hook aimed square at his ear, although it ended up glancing off his shoulder.

"Better," he said. "Move. Move."

They did some more circling.

"Got a gym key," Bernie said.

"Uh-huh," said LeSean, and then, "left foot, left foot, come on."

"Sorry, boss," said Shanice, breathing harder now and bleeding just a bit from her nose.

"Hell with that," said LeSean. "Get that left foot under you and stick stick stick."

Shanice grunted and threw that hook, missing LeSean's head again, but hitting his shoulder with a sharp smack.

"Ha ha, almost cookin'," said LeSean, dancing away. "Catch that hook, Bernie?"

"A thing of beauty," Bernie said. He held up the key. "Now all we need is the locker."

LeSean turned our way. Shanice came up from under with a tremendous punch, I believe called a roundhouse right. LeSean, still peering at the key, shifted his head slightly but oh, so quick, slipping the punch, one of the loveliest human moves out there and a pleasure to see. "Black tape like that?" he said. "Old school. Try the Downtown Health Club."

"Behind Valley College?"

"That's the one," LeSean said.

Without even looking, he popped Shanice a good one on the side of the head. But she was sending one his way at the same moment and she caught him on the chin, not square, more like a graze, but still.

"Ha!" LeSean said. "Now we cook."

Shanice faked a punch, circled LeSean, and got a real dangerous look in her eyes. She started humming the Midnight Clear song.

"We're closed," said the dude behind the desk at the Downtown Health Club. "Sprucing things up." He had a tiny Santa pinned to his jacket, flashing on and off, very distracting. Don't count on me for getting all the details of what happened next.

"How long's that been going on?" Bernie said.

"Three days. We open tomorrow."

"Mind if we take a quick look around?"

"Thinking of joining?"

Bernie nodded.

"The both of you?" said the guy.

Bernie laughed and laughed. Laughter is the best sound humans make—whining probably being the worst—and Bernie's laugh is the best of the best. But not this time. It almost sounded like . . . like he was making himself do it. Why would he do that? I had no idea. But the desk guy seemed pleased. He laughed too, waved his hand toward the big space beyond, full of gym equipment, and said, "Knock yourselves out."

Like that was going to happen? This visit was getting more and more puzzling. I was ready for it to be over. Instead I followed Bernie through the gym, down a hallway with some paint cans on the floor and a paint-spattered ladder standing by the wall, and into a locker room. If you're really into smells a locker room is the place to be. Take poop, just as an example. Usually when poop smells are in the picture you tend to find them low down, close to ground level. But in a locker room—especially a locker room with a sauna or steam bath—your poop smells will be found much higher, almost as though invisible poop was misting down on you. The locker room here at the Downtown Health Club had both sauna and steam, as anyone, although possibly not you, could tell without looking.

Lockers lined the walls and also stood in clusters in the middle of the room. We walked slowly through the clusters, Bernie scanning the lockers and muttering to himself. "D nineteen, C twenty-one, B eight . . . here we go. B twenty-seven."

He came to a stop. We gazed at a locker like all the others, yellow with a bit of green writing above the keyhole. Bernie took out the key and was about to stick it into the lock when he paused and turned to me.

"Anything iffy inside?" he said.

Iffy was what, again?

"Like a bomb, for instance?"

So iffy meant bombs? You learn so much in this business. A

lovely breeze started up nearby, clearing the air of just about everything, even the poop smells. It didn't take me long to realize it was my tail, getting into the mix as it sometimes did. Bernie stuck the key in the lock and opened the door.

What were we expecting? Once we'd opened up a musty old trunk and found a whole mound of gold dust that later turned out to be golden-colored dust, which in the end made a big difference I never quite understood. We had nothing like that in locker B-27. Instead there was a towel hanging on a hook, a racket wrapped in clear plastic leaning against the wall, and an unusual ball right at the front, black with two yellow dots, about the size of a golf ball, but rubbery smelling.

"Squash, big guy," Bernie said. "A kind of claustrophobic tennis."

You may have thought I missed that one completely, but you'd be wrong, since I already knew squash, in fact had sampled some on Thanksgiving. Not my kind of thing, but at least I was following along nicely.

Bernie removed the racket, still wrapped in plastic. The head seemed smaller than the head of a normal tennis racket and the handle was narrower. A kid's racket, maybe? Wow! Who was figuring things out all on his lonesome today?

Some kind of note was taped to the plastic wrapping. Bernie stripped it off and held it to the light.

"'Hey, Marco, here's your new strings, hope you like them. Took it down to twenty-five pounds for more pop. Have fun! Fifty-five dollars charged to your account. Thanks and Merry Christmas, Bob at The Racket Racket.'"

"Marco?" Bernie said quietly. His eyes had a faraway look. I could feel his thoughts, heavy and slow, thoughts that didn't seem to be getting a move on. He put the note in his pocket, stuck the racket back in, and began to close the locker door. Perhaps not a good move. I hate to go there, Bernie being Bernie, but I was against closing the door. Something was still in that locker, not visible, but very smellable, the smell a fascinating mix of real old leather and real old paper aromas, plus a hint of dusty dry clay. I barked my low rumbly bark.

Bernie glanced at me, his hand still on the locker door, but no longer closing it. He bent forward, removed the racket again, peered inside, patted around, and gave me a questioning look. I barked my low rumbly bark. That was my answer. Bernie did some more peering. I squeezed in beside him and helped out.

Nothing to see. But those smells? Unmissable.

"Gotcha," Bernie said. He took out a coin, reached inside the locker, and unscrewed the screws holding the metal rear panel in place. And would you look at that! Behind the panel lay a dark space, just big enough to hold a small gym bag.

Sometimes when important things happen there's lots of action, cars shooting off cliffs, for example. Sometimes there's no action at all, only silence and stillness. Right now we were in one of those still silences. Bernie pulled out the gym bag. Just an ordinary gym bag, the kind you see all the time. He unzipped it, reached in, and took out a small and worn stone block, slightly reddish. Something was carved into its side. Bernie read aloud: "'Merisi.'"

That wasn't all. Bernie reached into the gym bag again, this time finding a leather-bound book. Slowly he turned the yellowed pages of the book, some of them brown at the edges, but the turning of the pages made no sound, not even to my ears. When Bernie finally spoke, even though he kept his voice low, almost a whisper, the sound seemed huge to me, like a powerful storm.

"It's . . . it's a ship's log, Chet, from . . ." He turned another page. ". . . way way back. Probably belongs in a museum, unless . . ."

A card stuck out of the top of the book. We have some cards like that in the office. They make very nice paper planes for throwing out the window, a game Charlie loves. But in this case the card was clearly doing something else. Like . . . like marking the page? Was there something called a bookmark? Wow! I was on fire. It was actually a bit scary.

Bernie opened the book to the bookmarked page, glanced at the card, which was blank, and began reading the writing on the page. His eyes went back and forth, back and forth.

"Why is my Spanish so damn pitiful?" he said.

Which made no sense. Whatever Spanish was, exactly—perhaps something about amigos and cerveza—Bernie's had to be the best.

"Handwritten in an old-fashioned style with an old-fashioned pen on old-fashioned parchment, not so easy to . . . what do you suppose 'majestad' is? Majesty? The ship of his clemente whatever that is majesty Felipe III, something something . . . wait. What's this?" Bernie squinted at the writing. "Whoa! *Falso penitente*'!" He turned the page. "Veracruz? I just don't . . ." His eyes went back and forth, back and forth, almost . . . almost desperately. I didn't like to see that. Bernie started to say something but at that moment I heard footsteps in the hall. I went still, ears and tail up. Bernie stuck the stone block and the book in the gym bag, slinging it over his shoulder. Then he closed the locker and pocketed the key. Now we were just two friendly dudes doing nothing special.

A painter in white overalls came in. He was gazing at his phone and didn't seem to see us at all.

"Where are the squash courts?" Bernie said.

The painter looked up, startled. He pointed down the hall. We headed that way, turned a corner, came to a small open door. On the other side was a narrow, high-ceilinged room, all white except for some red lines here and there. After that came a few more rooms just like it. On the wall outside the last one hung photos of little groups of smiling people, all of them holding rackets like the one we'd found in the locker.

Bernie examined the photos one by one. They all had a line or two of writing at the bottom. Bernie ran his finger over those lines, reading to himself. On the very last photo his finger came to a stop.

"Folonari," he said. "Marco Folonari." He pointed to a man at the end of the top row. "That's him."

Marco Folonari. The name seemed familiar, but why? With my mind being on fire the way it was today, you might have thought the answer would come to me at once. I sure did! But no. While I waited I took a good look at Marco Folonari, a smiling type with longish dark hair, graying in places, and a greenish pendant around his neck, possibly called turquoise, a sort of jewel you see a lot in these parts. Bernie, too, took a good look at Marco Folonari, a long, long look. If I was Marco I wouldn't want Bernie looking at me like that.

We were out on the street when Bernie paused and said, "Hey, Chet, what you got there?"

Oh, nothing really, with the exception of this fascinating black ball with the two yellow dots, the second reason—you'll remember I had two, the other being the hidden presence of the logbook, whatever that was, exactly—why I'd wanted Bernie to leave the locker open a little longer.

"First encounter with a squash ball?" he said. "How do you like it?"

Oh, very very much. Fabulous mouthfeel, hardness, springiness, taste. So nice of Bernie to ask. We got in the car, both of us in very good moods, me on account of this ball—life keeps coming up with wonderful surprises if you only stick around—and Bernie for reasons of his own.

Sometimes in the afternoon we swing by Charlie's school and drive him home, not our place on Mesquite Road but where he lives with Leda and Malcolm in High Chaparral Estates. This turned out to be one of those afternoons. We pulled up opposite the school buses, and there was Charlie at the back of the line, talking to a girl with her hair twisted in a big knot on top of her head, although to be more accurate he was listening, not talking, and picking his nose a bit at the same time, although not deeply. Bernie moved his hand toward the horn, but before he could honk it, Charlie turned, saw us, and came running over.

"Hey, Chet! Hey, Dad!"

He squeezed past me and plunked himself down on the little shelf in back. What a kid! I turned around, leaned over the backrest of my seat—the shotgun seat, in case anyone needs reminding—and gave his face a quick, friendly lick. He laughed and said, "Dad?"

"Yeah?"

"Esmé says Christmas didn't happen."

"That was Esmé you were just talking to?"

"Uh-huh. She's the smartest kid in the class."

"Well," Bernie says, "Christmas seems to be happening right now, all over the place. See the wreaths on all the buses? And the bus drivers with their Santa hats?"

"Dad! She doesn't mean that. She means the baby Jesus and the manger and the three wise guys, all that shapeel."

"Spiel?" said Bernie.

"That's what Esmé said. It means stuff."

"Thanks."

Bernie sat there for a bit. Normally I'd be thinking, *Bernie! On the stick!* But for some reason I wasn't. Just sitting here doing nothing was okay.

"Dad?" Charlie said at last. "So? What about it?"

"What about what?"

"The whole Christmas shapeel."

"Don't rule it out," Bernie said. One of Charlie's feet—he wore blue sneakers with yellow Velcro straps—was sticking into the front through the gap between the seats. Bernie gave it a squeeze. Then he reached for the key, and was about to turn it when a woman with a bunch of books under her arm passed in front of us and waved.

"Hi, Charlie!" she said.

"Hi," said Charlie.

The woman moved on.

"Who's that?" Bernie said.

"Ms. Feliz," said Charlie. "The Spanish teacher."

"Wait here." Bernie grabbed the gym bag and got out of the car. Could "wait here" possibly mean Charlie and me? Surely it had to mean just Charlie. But how could leaving him alone in the car make sense? He was a kid. I ended up kind of half in and half out of the car, not a bad solution at all, to my way of thinking.

Meanwhile Bernie and Ms. Feliz were talking beside a nearby drinking fountain. A quick talk, and then Bernie turned to us and called, "Charlie? Chet?" He waved us over.

Soon after that we were near the swings behind the school, Bernie and Ms. Feliz on a bench, Charlie on a swing, and me sniffing around in the dirt. Cats had been on this playground, more than two and not long ago. I followed their trails, strange trails that led from nowhere to nowhere, making no sense.

"Very nice of you," Bernie was saying. "Of course we'll pay for your time."

"Oh no, I couldn't," said Ms. Feliz. She looked pretty young, not much more than a kid herself, and had the kind of cheerful face you like to see on humans. "Happy to help. I read all about you on the case about aquifers. So exciting!"

"Um," said Bernie. "Ah."

After that came an awkward moment or two, and then Ms. Feliz said, "You have something you'd like me to translate?"

Bernie took the small leather-bound book from the gym bag and handed it to her. "I think it's a ship's log from back in the days of the Spanish empire, but I'm not sure."

Ms. Feliz opened the book. "Looks old," she said. "And smells old, too."

I paused in what I was doing—which seemed to have something to do with a surprisingly deep hole—and glanced over at Ms. Feliz. Some humans make a very good impression on you right from the get-go. She was one of those.

Ms. Feliz went through the book, taking her time. After a while and without looking up, she said, "I know nothing about ship's logs but that would fit. It's like a diary of a voyage, two voyages, actually."

"Oh?" said Bernie.

Ms. Feliz nodded. "The first one began in Naples, stopped in Bilbao, and continued onto Veracruz, Mexico. The second one was from Veracruz back to Bilbao and then to Naples."

"Does it say when?"

"Oh, yes, there's a date for every entry," Ms. Feliz said. "It goes from October of 1609 to May of 1610. Mostly it's about the weather and things they saw, like islands and other ships, and whales."

Bernie leaned closer, turned a page or two. "What's this here?"

"*Falso penitente*? Kind of a strange term. I've never seen it. In English it would be false penitent, but whether that's because whoever it was didn't really repent or the person was the wrong penitent, I couldn't say."

Bernie gave her a quick glance. Ms. Feliz was making a good first impression on him, too.

"Is there any more about him?" Bernie said.

"Not much," said Ms. Feliz. "But whoever was writing this already knew him from the first voyage. He was a passenger from Naples. On the return trip he seems to have picked up the penitente apodo."

"Apodo?" Bernie said.

"Nickname," said Ms. Feliz. "Maybe closer to sobriquet."

"I'm not sure of the difference," Bernie said.

"Nickname has a positive spin that sobriquet—" Ms. Feliz stopped herself. "Sorry, I get pedantic sometimes. It makes my boyfriend so annoyed."

"At you?"

Ms. Feliz nodded.

"Tell him he's out of his mind," Bernie said.

Ms. Feliz blushed. What was going on? Hard to tell, especially peering over the crest of this hole, deepening fast.

"In any case," Ms. Feliz said, "there's no mention of falso penitente on the outward-bound trip. The passenger is just referred to by his real name."

"Which was?"

Ms. Feliz ran her finger down a page. "Michelangelo," she said. "Michelangelo Merisi."

Bernie rose. "Merisi?"

Twenty

When we drop Charlie off at Leda and Malcolm's house we always walk him right to the door, which is how Leda wants it. Once Bernie pointed out that there hadn't been a crime in High Chaparral Estates in fifteen years, but he never pointed it out again.

We knocked on the huge wooden door, the kind you might see in a movie with castles. The house didn't have the high walls with openings for shooting arrows through at the top, but it was enormous, and so were the flowers in the flower beds, and the wreath on the door, the biggest wreath I'd ever seen, giving off a lovely scent like we were deep in a forest, a forest full of pine cones, candy canes, red berries, and silver bells. All the silver bells tinkled when Leda opened the door. She wore yoga pants and carried a tiny pink dumbbell in each hand.

"Hi, Charlie," she said. "Hey, Bernie."

Some humans always say hi to me, too, and some, like Leda, don't. No biggie. My tail started wagging. I must have been happy to see her.

"Hi, Mom," Charlie said. "What do you think of the whole Christmas shapeel?"

"Excuse me?" said Leda.

"If it happened," Charlie said. "For real."

Leda's eyes shifted toward Bernie.

"Esmé," he said.

"Ah," said Leda. "Did you ask your dad?"

"My dad Bernie?"

"Yes," said Leda. "Your dad. Standing right here."

Bernie and Leda exchanged a real quick look. You had to be the alert type to catch it, and I am. As for what the look was about, I can't help you.

"Yeah, I asked him," Charlie said.

"And what did he say?"

"Don't rule it out," Charlie said.

"Well there you go," Leda said, and shot Bernie another look, but he wasn't paying attention. Instead he'd turned to the enormous wreath, and was changing the position of a candy cane or two. Leda's eyebrows rose. She opened her mouth to say something, but at that moment Malcolm appeared down the block. He was walking Shooter. That was one way to put it. What anyone actually watching would have seen was Shooter—on one of those extendable leashes—pulling Malcolm along the sidewalk, Shooter head down and straining crazily hard, every muscle bulging, his eyes burning with determination. You might call that puppyish behavior, Shooter still a puppy, perhaps, but an extremely large one. All at once I was struck by one of those—oh, what was the word? Bernie had used it just the other day. Revelation? Something like that. I was struck by a revelation. Shooter went perfectly with this huge house.

May have to back up here a little bit. Does anyone have a life with no problems? Now that I think of it, I come pretty close—who's got it better than me? But that wasn't where I was going with this, which was about Shooter, if not a problem then at least a troublesome character in my life. Summing up, Shooter has something to do with events that followed the sound of some very insistent she-barking from across the canyon on a long-ago night. Let's call that fact one, as Bernie would say. Fact two is "spit and image," something I've heard way too much, as in "He's the spit and image of Chet!"

No time for any more facts, even if they exist, because Malcolm, holding onto the leash with both hands, let go with one of them to give us a wave. A big mistake, as I knew right away. Malcolm was a tall dude, taller than Bernie, but very skinny and sort of bendable, like a giant weed, with long narrow toes sticking out over the fronts of his flip-flops.

That last part, about the flip-flops, was changing rapidly. One hand—at least one of Malcolm's hands—was not enough.

He lurched forward, right out of his flip-flops, and flew through the air, both arms straight out like that movie guy in a tight blue outfit who can actually fly. Malcolm cannot actually fly, of course, and landed hard on the neighbor's lawn, a soft, thick, putting-green type lawn of the kind Bernie and I don't like. In a normal situation I would have made a mental note to pee on that lawn at my earliest convenience, but there was no time for that. Malcolm lost hold of the leash, as I'm sure you've already imagined, and Shooter took off across the street, the leash trailing behind and soon twisting around a small bush that erupted out of the ground and followed him around a garage and out of sight.

And I haven't even come to the worst part, which was that as he ran, Shooter made lovely silvery-bell tinkling sounds. Why? Because he wore a new collar, red with silver bells. In short, a Christmas collar. Shooter had a Christmas collar. I did not. So when Bernie said, "Chet, go get him," I was already gone.

By the time we drove off, Shooter no longer wore the Christmas collar. Neither did I, although that had been my goal, namely to take over the wearing of that collar—I admit it—but that lovely collar with the silver bells had been . . . what was the term? Lost in action? Something like that. And I'd wanted it so badly. My gator skin collar was very nice in its way, but how fine to be sporting—

"Chet, for god's sake—snap out of it. How could you possibly wear bells in a job like ours?"

Bernie was right. Any—I wouldn't call it moaning, more like very quiet unhappy cheeping—came to a stop at once. I sat up in the shotgun seat, silent and alert, a total pro.

Bernie was silent, too, but not alert, at least not alert to the outside world. He'd gone deep inside his head, his hands—those beautiful hands of his—taking care of the driving. We ended up in the parking lot at the Sonoran Museum of Art. Bernie glanced at the building—gleaming white stone, mostly blocky but with rounded parts here and there, and one of those nice Valley views—and gave his head a little shake, as though surprised by something. That his hands had brought us here? Were his hands a bit like . . . like my tail? Kind of having a life of their own? Why did I have to have thoughts like that?

I watched Bernie carefully, just in case . . . well, just in case. Does there always have to be a reason in life? That wouldn't be how I'd roll if I was on my own. Which I didn't want to be, as must be clear by now. I wanted to be with Bernie.

He felt my gaze and turned to me. "The more you know the less you know," he said. "Ever think of that?"

The answer was no, and I never would. Also, it sounded like the kind of thought no one should be thinking. The problem is the mind has a way of thinking on its own. I considered ways to . . . to put my mind on a leash! Yes! That was it exactly. My mind was like Shooter and it was my job to—I stopped right there, actually felt a bit dizzy, which hardly ever happens.

"Maybe that's just another way of saying we're in over our heads," Bernie went on. "According to Father Henry, the falso penitente was a murderer. Was the crime unsolved?" He took a deep breath, let it out slow. "A cold cold case, big guy, but what can we do? It's ours."

It turned out that what we could do was have another talk with Katherine Cornwall, not in her office this time, but on the patio of the museum restaurant. A tiny Christmas tree stood on every table. Bernie made a few slight adjustments to ours before he'd even finished sitting down.

They drank coffee, black for both of them, and I had water, nice and icy, from a clean metal bowl, clean being my preference although it's not a deal breaker. More men than women drink their coffee black, in my experience, but why? Maybe Bernie would bring that up. I decided to pay close attention.

"Any progress on your missing person case?" Katherine said. A woman of the no-nonsense kind as I may have mentioned before, except now she looked a little less no-nonsensey, possibly because of a headband she wore, a headband featuring a red-nosed reindeer.

"Movement, yes," Bernie said. "Too soon to tell if it's progress." He handed her the old leather-bound book, a ship's log, if I was following things right, although I had no idea what a ship's log was. I understood leather very well. "Ever seen one of these?"

Katherine put down her cup and went through the ship's log. A gecko, brown with white spots, popped up beside a plant bordering the patio and did a few quick push-ups. They love doing push-ups, although no bulking up ever seems to happen. You can chase after geckos but they're not easy to catch, and what would be the point?

"My goodness," Katherine said. "A seventeenth-century ship's log?" She looked up at Bernie. "Is it authentic?"

"Not for me to say," Bernie said. "What do you think?"

"We have nothing like it," Katherine said. "It's not really in our wheelhouse."

"No?"

"Everything in our collection has some relationship to the Sonoran region—artistic, historical, ethnographic." She tapped the book with her finger. "This doesn't seem to qualify." Katherine turned a page. "But as for authenticity, my initial, unscientific take is that it passes the smell test."

Ah. I'd already been liking Katherine. Now I liked her a whole lot more. That often happens when two folks have something in common.

"But," she went on, "what's its provenance?"

"Provenance means where it came from?" Bernie said.

"Correct, meaning the whole chronology, starting when it was written and ending when it came into your hands."

"I only know the last part," Bernie said. "We found it today in a gym locker."

Katherine took a sip of coffee, watching Bernie over the rim of the cup. "You lead an interesting life."

"I don't know about that," Bernie said, one of those rare times he came close to not telling the kind of whole truth and nothing but we hear about occasionally in our line of work, the fact being that no one had more interesting lives than us. "I'm also not sure you're right that the log has no connection to Sonora. Didn't you tell us there was lots of back and forth between here and Mexico in the early days?'"

"True," Katherine said. She gestured toward the book. "But if there's something like that in here I missed it."

Bernie reached for the book. "I'm not so sure." He turned a few pages. "There's an entry or two that are suggestive at least."

"Suggestive of a Sonoran connection?" Katherine said.

Bernie nodded. He moved around the table and sat beside her so they could examine the book together. For an odd moment, her gaze seemed glued to his hand as he paged through. I got that, the beauty of Bernie's hands being what it is. The same thing has happened to me, and more than once.

"This guy, Michelangelo Merisi," Bernie said, "is an outgoing passenger landing in Veracruz in the fall of 1609. Then in the spring of 1610 he's on the ship, headed back. There's nothing about where he was or what he did in the meantime."

Katherine had glasses perched up on her head. She pulled them down and looked more closely. Her head and Bernie's came close to touching. For an instant I thought she was going to move a little bit more and make that happen, but she did not. Did Bernie notice any of this? Not that I saw. I smelled certain changes in Katherine, although none in him. Those changes, by the way, happen in some older women like her just as strongly as in younger women like Weatherly. Based on my own experience in the nation within, I had an idea or two about what was going on, but no time for that now.

"So you're saying—" Katherine cleared her throat and started over. "You're saying that this man came as far as Sonora? I suppose it's possible. There was already traffic on the Fed Highway 15 corridor for a few decades before this voyage, and the settling of northern Sonora had begun. But why is it important?"

"Well," said Bernie, "you can see right here that he picked up a nickname along the way."

Katherine peered at the page. "Falso penitente?"

Bernie nodded. "There's a good chance he got it here."

"Here in the Valley?"

"Specifically at Nuestra Señora. The presence of a falso penitente is part of their . . . what would you call it?"

"Oral tradition?"

"Exactly."

"My goodness." Katherine sat back, pushed up her glasses, turned to Bernie. "What a story! Are you saying all this is related to the missing man you're looking for?"

"Maybe. Right now we're just following the leads."

Katherine tapped the corner of the page. "There's something about this name that bothers me." *Tap tap, tap tap.* "Michelangelo Merisi. Maybe it's just the Michelangelo part, but it rings a faint bell. I took a lot of art courses in college, too many in retrospect—balance sheets and statistics would have been better—so you'd think—" She cut herself off and shot Bernie a sharp glance. "I assume you googled it?"

"Um," said Bernie.

One of Katherine's eyebrows rose in a way that said a lot, although I couldn't have told you what. But how interesting! Like Bernie's, Katherine's eyebrows had a language of their own. There's always something new in this line of work. I wouldn't trade it for any other job, certainly not herding sheep, for example.

Katherine got busy on her phone, not talking into it but doing other things humans do with their phones. I'm a big fan of humans—even most of the perps and gangbangers, now in orange jumpsuits and breaking rocks in the hot sun—but there's something a bit machinelike and disturbing in all of them. With the exception of Bernie! Whoa! I was just realizing that now? There's no machine in Bernie! He's the most human human I know. My luck is off the charts.

Katherine went still, then looked up from the phone. "My, my, I knew it was something." She moved the phone so Bernie could see.

Bernie peered at the screen. "I don't get it."

Katherine pointed. "What's that word right there?"

Bernie took a long look. "Caravaggio." His head rose and he seemed to gaze at something far away, although from where he sat there was nothing to see except the glassed-in museum restaurant, with a waiter coming through the door carrying a tray loaded with eggnog drinks, the smell unmistakable. "But I'm not sure I—"

Katherine interrupted. "Caravaggio's a town not far from Milan. It's where the Merisi family came from, so in full he was Michelangelo Merisi da Caravaggio. Caravaggio is how he's known today, one of the greatest of the old masters and his reputation keeps on going up and up. Are you familiar with his work?"

"Hadn't even heard of him until recently." Bernie dug in his pocket, took out a folded and somewhat wrinkled sheet of paper. He unfolded it. Uh-oh. I'd forgotten all about the picture of the dude holding up the cut-off head of another dude. Why couldn't some things stay forgotten? "Apparently Goliath is a self-portrait," Bernie said.

Katherine peered at the picture. "I didn't know that." Her voice got a little husky. "His power is overwhelming, even on a printout like this." She looked up. "How come you have it? Are you telling me that Caravaggio was actually here in the Valley? What's going on? And please don't say you're just following the leads."

"I'm asking the same questions," Bernie said, his voice sharpening a bit. He softened it and added, "When I have answers I'll let you know."

Bernie rose. I rose, too. And so did the gecko, who'd been napping in the sun. Could he possibly imagine he was coming with us? This case was unusual and getting more so.

Their eyes met, Bernie's and Katherine's. For a moment, Katherine lost her no-nonsense look completely. Then she got it back. Bernie's eyes shifted slightly.

"You've been a huge help," he said.

"I haven't done a thing," Katherine said. "What you need is a Caravaggio expert. And Valley College happens to have one."

"Oh?" said Bernie.

"In fact, he gave a talk here several years ago—on the Mexican Baroque. His name is Marco Folonari."

There was a long pause. Bernie just stood where he was, very still. Did Katherine think he was confused and needed a little prodding? I was pretty sure that wasn't it at all, but she prodded anyway, "Do you want me to get in touch with him? Make an introduction?"

Bernie shook his head. "We'll handle it," he said.

Twenty-one

"Does Christmas have some undermining affect on the rational mind?" Bernie said. "Not necessarily a bad thing, maybe even a rebalancing."

He fumbled under his seat, perhaps forgetting that he'd fumbled in the very same way quite recently, coming up with nada, cigarette-wise, not even a half-crushed stub, which was exactly what went down now. As for what he was talking about, I was hoping it was over, although I'd never allow myself to have a thought like that. Bernie could talk about whatever he wanted, and anyone who tried to stop him, including me, would have to deal with me! And in no uncertain terms!

Bernie glanced my way. "What's up?"

Nothing. Nothing was up.

"That was one strange bark," he said.

Bark? I'd heard no bark. I looked around. We were on the Crosstown, traffic heavy, no members of the nation within sight. There are mysteries in this life. Solving mysteries is what we do, me and Bernie, but how can we solve every single one? We need our sleep, for one thing, plus there's mealtime, fetch, and learning to turn doorknobs, all of which cut into the working day.

"Maybe," Bernie said, "we should hire Esmé."

Whoa! What a surprising idea! In a way I could see that Bernie and I had been thinking along the same lines, which happens more than you might imagine. But how could Esmé be the answer? I pictured her in the bus line, a little taller than Charlie, but only because of her enormous topknot. For one thing, didn't she have to go to school?

"She wouldn't have gotten blown off so easily on the sabbatical bullshit," Bernie went on. "Give me an F on that one, big guy."

No problem. I'd give Bernie whatever he wanted, and the second I knew the meaning of F it was his.

We took an exit and soon came to the big green quad across from the college. Some college kids had a game going involving beer kegs, 'shrooms, and Frisbees. A complicated game and before I could figure it out, including some possible role for me, we were parking in front of the reddish stone building where Prof had his office. Bernie was just reaching for the key when the phone buzzed. A voice I knew came over the speakers.

"Bernie? Freddy here. Got a heads-up for you. Did you try that number in Madrid, by the way?"

"It's on my list," Bernie said.

"Don't bother," said Freddy. "I did and it's disconnected."

"Thanks, Freddy."

"Don't mention it. And something more helpful turned up."

"What's that?"

"It's a who. Namely Lauritz's boyfriend. He's come to take the body home. The flight's tonight."

"So soon?"

"Autopsy was last night. Report's coming but word is it's heart problems exacerbated by a dangerous alcohol medication mix."

"Doc Hayes said that?"

"Hayes retired. This is the new guy—nephew of the governor."

"My god," Bernie said.

"No worries, he's board-certified," said Freddy. "Only took him six tries."

"Bernie Little," said Freddy. "Say hi to Gerd Erhardt from Madrid, Spain."

Bernie shook hands with Gerd Erhardt. Gerd's hands were soft compared to Bernie's, so very soft and white, like they never saw the sun, only coming out at night. He wore a big purple ring that looked just like Lauritz's.

"Sorry for your loss," Bernie said.

"Thank you, sir," said Gerd. He was on the youngish

side—somewhere between the college kids out on the quad and men like Bernie and Freddy—a small man with long blond hair and tears in his eyes. We were in a loading dock on the back side of the Desert Dunes. The steel door was rolled up and we could see the golf course. A golfer took a mighty swing, and I heard the thwack loud and clear, although the ball was invisible at this distance. From the way the golfer kicked at the turf, I guessed it hadn't gone far but might have gotten lost anyway, part of the fun of golf if I understood the game right. What else? Uh-oh. I'd left out the most important thing. Was Christmas getting to my mind, too?

The most important thing was the coffin, resting on a dolly near the door. I could smell what was in there, of course, meaning the smells of everything they use to hide smells, as well as the smell they were trying to hide.

"Bernie here is the best private investigator in the Valley," Freddy said. "Gerd's a—what did you say it was, Gerd?"

"Docent," said Gerd.

"Docent," Freddy said. He waved goodbye. "I'll leave you to it. Call if you need me." He lowered himself off the edge of the loading dock, stepped into a golf cart, and drove away.

Bernie turned to Gerd, gave him a little smile. Gerd looked down. "Where do you do your docenting?" Bernie said.

"Is that a word?" Gerd said. "My English is poor."

"Probably not a word," Bernie said. "And your English sounds better than mine."

What a nice man Bernie is! His English, whatever that is exactly, had to be the best there was.

Gerd glanced at the coffin. "Lauritz . . ." He choked up a bit and started over. "Lauritz spoke seven languages. He could learn a new one in a few days."

"Yeah?" Bernie said. "He told us eleven."

Gerd's head went back, almost like Bernie had slapped him. That could never happen, of course, Bernie slapping such a weak, little dude.

"I . . . I don't really understand your role in . . . in . . ." Gerd gestured toward the coffin.

"I'm a private investigator, just like him," Bernie said.

Gerd's brow, very smooth until then, furrowed up, as though he didn't like the sound of that. Was it because he knew there was no way Lauritz or anyone else could come close to Bernie when it came to private investigating? That was my take.

Gerd turned to me for the first time. He seemed surprised about something, although I couldn't think what. At first his scent had been mostly about tears. Now the scent of fear started getting into the mix. Gerd had nothing to fear from me, of course, unless he stepped out of line. And then? Good night.

Bernie walked over to the coffin. For a moment I thought he was going to touch it, but instead he simply gazed at the wreath on top. Just a plain wreath; I preferred the Christmas kind.

"And how about you?" Bernie said. "Did you help out with his work?"

"I told you," said Gerd. "I'm a docent."

"Where?"

"Mostly the Prado."

"A museum?"

Gerd's lips curled in an unpleasant way. "Currently number eight on the *Forbes* list of top museums."

Bernie turned to him. "Does it have any Caravaggios?"

Gerd's eyes shifted, then shifted again, a sight you don't see every day. Was grabbing him by the pant leg then and there the right play? I moved in a bit, got myself nicely within leaping distance. Gerd backed up a step or two, bumped into the coffin. We were all set.

"The Prado's collection of old masters is unsurpassed," he said.

"And Caravaggio qualifies?" said Bernie.

"I don't understand your question."

"As an old master."

"Certainly."

"So therefore," Bernie went on, "the Prado has at least one Caravaggio."

Have I mentioned that Bernie handles the so-therefores, while

I bring other things to the table? I'd heard many so-therefores in my career, but none better than this. It shook the truth out of Gerd in no time flat. He licked his lips, one of the most nervous lip licks I'd ever seen, and said, "Correct."

Correct! Baboom! We had Gerd where we wanted him. Nothing was clearer than that. I actually came close to thinking that nothing else was clear at all. But I didn't quite get there. Why not? Because my mind didn't want to worry me. What a great feeling! My mind and I were working as a team today. When that happens, look out!

Meanwhile Bernie was taking a slow walk around the coffin. Gerd eyed him the whole way. Bernie didn't notice. No problem. I was handling the noticing of Gerd for now.

"Lauritz tried to hire us," Bernie said. "Did you know that?"

"Who is us?" said Gerd.

"Chet and I," Bernie said. "When's the flight?"

"Eight thirty."

"Then we'll have to keep this short if you want to be on that plane. From here on in, how about I do the asking and you do the answering?"

"Are you suggesting you will physically prevent me from boarding the plane?"

"More like hinting," Bernie said.

Gerd gave Bernie the kind of look that comes before a certain type—for sure not him—takes a swing at somebody. "This country is despicable."

"But welcomes all opinions, yours included," Bernie said. He glanced at the coffin. "How come they released the body so soon?"

"The examination is concluded."

"Oh?" said Bernie. "And what was the cause of death?"

"The report will be ready by next week," Gerd said. "But . . ." A tear ran down Gerd's cheek. ". . . but poor Lauritz is no longer needed."

"Any ideas on the cause of death?" Bernie said.

"I'm not a doctor," said Gerd, wiping his cheek on the back of his hand.

"What if you had to guess?"

"I don't guess."

"Then let's deal in facts. Who were Lauritz's enemies?"

"He had no enemies. Everyone loved him."

Bernie took a deep breath. "I don't know you, Gerd. Maybe you really believe what you just said. Maybe you're not involved in . . . what should we call it? Lauritz's business dealings? Maybe the cause of death will shock you."

Gerd gazed at Bernie. His mind was working hard and fast. I could feel thoughts scrambling around, like they were trapped in a cave-in, cave-ins being something I knew from experience and wished I didn't.

"Why would I be shocked?" Gerd said at last. "I'm sure it was his heart."

"How come?"

"Lauritz had terrible heart problems. And I'm afraid he had trouble managing all the medications, especially . . ."

"Especially what?" Bernie said.

"Those that cannot be mixed with alcohol," Gerd said. "And he loved to take long, hot baths. Mr. Perez says he was found in the tub." Gerd spread his hands, a human gesture that meant there you go, or what can you do, or maybe something else entirely.

"A nice story," Bernie said. "But it's wrong. We found the body, Chet and I."

"That's not true!" said Gerd. "It was Mr. Perez."

Bernie shook his head, just a slight motion, but it seemed to mean no in a very big way. Gerd's mouth opened and closed. He looked past us, beyond the loading dock, as though help might come, but there were only golfers.

"I can't rule out heart involvement in the end," Bernie said, "but Lauritz was waterboarded. Do you know what that is?"

Gerd's face turned the color of a bone you might find out in the desert. He nodded slightly, hardly any movement at all.

"He was waterboarded to death," Bernie said, his voice quite soft. "He had enemies. We need the names."

Gerd began to shake, but not for long. Somehow he put a stop to it. He was much stronger than I'd thought. Now, for the first time, he met Bernie's gaze. Uh-oh. He hated Bernie. There was no missing that.

"Nothing to say?" said Bernie. "Don't you at least want justice?"

"What a typically American question," Gerd said.

"Justice is American?"

"Far from it. I meant the immature nature of the question. And now, please have the kindness to leave me alone. I have nothing further to say."

Bernie gazed down at Gerd. Did he hate him back? Hating someone back is a human thing we run across a lot, me and Bernie. I've sensed hate in Bernie once or twice, but not now. He nodded in a pleasant sort of way, like wrapping things up and hitting the road was fine with us. And here I'd been thinking that we were well on our way to a pant-leg grab. I kept my hopes up, not a tough job, since my hopes love being high all on their own.

"One more thing," Bernie said. "Unless we're dealing with sickos, waterboarders always want something. What did they want from Lauritz?"

Gerd folded his skinny arms over his narrow chest and just stood there, the coffin at his back. "We are finished," he said.

Bernie nodded and turned to go. That was a bit of a surprise. We didn't feel finished to me, but if Bernie goes I go. And I was just starting to turn away from the loading dock when a big black SUV drove slowly by. The driver looked our way. Hey! The huge dude with the handlebar mustache! Where had I seen him before? At Nuestra Señora, along with the fattish guy in the Panama hat? I thought so. And somewhere else? Would Bernie want to know about this? The handlebar mustached dude's gaze met mine. His eyes were cruel. You hardly ever see cruel eyes as someone's go-to expression. Bernie would want to see that for sure.

I barked. Bernie, at the door leading back into the hotel, glanced over his shoulder.

"Come on, Chet."

I considered barking again, but the big black SUV was gone.

We were out front of the Desert Dunes, walking through the parking lot, when Bernie's phone buzzed.

"Hey," said Freddy. "How'd it go?"

"Could've been better," Bernie said.

"Maybe it's not over. Lauritz's little German buddy just called me. He wants to go up to the room and take a quick look-see. Something about closure. Yes or no?"

"Yes," Bernie said. "But let us in first." He sounded excited. I love when that happens and get immediately excited myself.

"Easy, big guy. We've got to be quiet as mice."

How do some ideas start up, like mice being quiet, for example? They're actually quite noisy, busily scratching and chewing away behind the walls and under the floorboards of just about every house I've ever been in, including ours. With the exception, I guess I should point out, of houses with cats. Houses with cats have no mouse problems. I know what you're thinking: They have cat problems instead! I hear you.

Lauritz's old room at the Desert Dunes had one of those hotel-type closets with slatted doors. Once a meth-head with a meat cleaver and a bad temper had come bursting out of a closet just like it, screaming an awful scream and charging right at us. Poor guy. But not the point, which was that at this moment we were the ones in the closet, me and Bernie. Did that mean a meth-head with a meat cleaver was out there in the room? Not that I could smell or hear or see. Would he be showing up anytime soon? That was my hope. No complaints, but it was a bit crowded here in the closet, what with the suitcase stands, the ironing board, the fluffy robes on their hangers, and the two of us, much quieter than any mice of my acquaintance. Then the door to the room opened, making a faint swishing sound over the rug.

A man entered, if a meth-head then the quietest I'd ever come across. Through the gaps in the slats, I could see narrow parts of him, such as a soft, white hand with a purple ring on one finger. He went right past our closet, then turned and headed down the little hall to the bathroom.

Bernie put a finger crosswise on his lips. That meant not a peep. He pressed down on the door handle, real slow, and opened the door. We moved into the room. No one in sight. We walked silently down the little hall, me actually silent and Bernie silent for a human. The bathroom door stood open. We stepped in.

Gerd was crouched beside the toilet, his back to us and his hands on the toilet paper roll. He took it out of the small space in the wall, removed the metal tube, and was pulling it apart when Bernie said, "Let's start over."

Metal parts went springing all over the place.

Twenty-two

Gerd rose and looked around wildly. There was nowhere to go. Had he been a leaper like me, he could have soared right over our heads and gotten away clean, but Gerd was not a leaper like me, actually not like me in any way I could think of.

"Those tube things are impossible," Bernie said. "I assume there are better ones where you come from."

He bent down and began picking up all the parts. That opened a lane between Gerd and the doorway. I shifted over and closed it.

Bernie held the tube parts on the palm of his hand. I gave them my first close look. There weren't as many as I'd thought. Two tube pieces and the spring from inside, making . . . making three! My goodness! I'd gotten past two! Had that happened before? First I thought yes. Then I thought no. But what did it matter? I stood on the mountain of three! Chet the Jet! All at once I felt so kindly to the whole wide world. I even gave Gerd a kindly look, which he didn't seem to notice.

Bernie took the two tube parts and gave them a shake. Nothing fell out.

"Empty," he said. "What were you looking for, Gerd?"

Gerd didn't answer. He just stood before us, not at all a big guy and now even smaller.

"Come on, Gerd," Bernie said. "You've been caught with your pants down. That's a game changer."

Oh boy. Bernie is never wrong, and we have caught a surprising number of perps with their pants down, usually guys and also a gal or two, but Gerd was wearing pants. I had no doubt about that whatsoever. Black pants in the narrow-fitting style that Bernie hated. Whoa! Back up. Had Bernie just mentioned a game?

Perhaps a game where Gerd would soon be pantless? Things started making sense.

Gerd closed his eyes. "Oh, Lauri," he said, and then went silent.

"Go on," said Bernie.

Gerd's eyes opened. There's a defeated look men sometimes get, women, too, maybe not as much. Gerd didn't have it. "Why should I?" he said.

"It's in your best interests," Bernie said. "Especially if you want to be on that plane."

"You're taking me prisoner?" said Gerd. "Is brute force all you know?"

"I'm not sure I even know that," Bernie said. "But it's irrelevant because we'll have nothing to do with it, other than informing the medical examiner that you'll be needed as a witness."

Now came the first little sign of the defeated look. "I warned him," he said.

"Who are you talking about?"

"Lauri. I warned him about you. Not because he got your name from some whore—what did he imagine he was proving to anybody?—but because when I looked you up I saw immediately you were wrong for the job."

Bernie took a step toward Gerd. He was suddenly very angry, a vein in the side of his neck that I'd hardly ever seen now visible. Something terrible was about to happen, but before it did Bernie went still, a rigid sort of still that I could feel.

"First," he said, his voice much quieter than I'd expected, "don't call her that."

"Don't call her a whore? But—" At last Gerd sensed what had almost just happened and still might. He shut his mouth.

"In fact," Bernie said, "take it back."

"Take it back?" said Gerd. "Is that an American thing? How is it done?"

"Like this. You say, 'I didn't mean that and I'm sorry.'"

Gerd glared at Bernie. Bernie didn't glare back, just met that glare with an expression that almost seemed peaceable, but not quite.

Gerd looked down. "I didn't mean that and I'm sorry," he said.

Bernie nodded. He took a long breath, let a long breath out. "And now back to square one. What was the job? What did Lauritz want us to do?"

Gerd took a long time to answer. We waited, still and silent, just another one of our techniques at the Little Detective Agency. "He needed time," Gerd said at last. "That required a decoy. You were the wrong choice." One of Gerd's eyes narrowed a bit, the eyelid trembling. "But why did you decline?"

Bernie waved that question away with the back of his hand, one of his very many cool moves. "A decoy is supposed to draw someone away," he said. "Who was it?"

Gerd's hands began to tremble. "I don't know."

"Speculate," Bernie said.

Gerd's voice rose, high and thin. "Speculate? I can't speculate. I was in Madrid. And I wish to god I'd never gone there either. I'd never have heard about—"

"Heard about what?" Bernie said.

"Nothing," said Gerd. He started to cry. "Nothing, nothing, nothing. Why did he have to be so clever? We'd have gotten a share. And now it's all ruined!"

"Who is he?" Bernie said. "A share of what?"

"The profits, for god's sake! How can you be so stupid? Even the idiot you sent is smarter."

"Are you talking about Victor Klovsky?" Bernie said.

Gerd's mouth closed, nice and tight.

"Where is he?" Bernie said.

"I don't know who you're talking about," Gerd said.

Bernie didn't like that answer. I could see it in his eyes. When Bernie doesn't like an answer neither do I, which was why I moved closer, and why my lips drew back, giving Gerd a better look at my teeth. Have I described my teeth yet? We are talking about weapons, my friends. I have weapons in my mouth. You do not, no offense.

Gerd backed up until there was nowhere to go except in the toilet. I've seen perps fall into toilets on a surprising number of occasions, but that didn't happen now.

"Your dog is attacking me! This is barbaric!"

"Chet likes straight answers," Bernie said.

"What nonsense! It's a dog."

"He," said Bernie.

"I beg your pardon?"

I moved closer still.

"All right, all right! Just call it—he—off."

"Answer first."

"Klovsky is safe and unharmed," Gerd said.

"Where?"

"I don't know, I swear to you. Only Lauri knew."

"Then how do you know he's safe? The remains of his bike tell a different story."

"No, no—I did that."

"You crashed the bike?"

Gerd shook his head. "I merely damaged it."

"Why?"

"To—to schlammig das Wasser, as Lauri said. To muddy the waters."

"What did Victor think about that?"

"He didn't know. This was after the fact."

"The fact of what?"

"Stop this," Gerd said. "What does it matter now?"

Bernie's voice rose. "Where is he?"

"I told you—I don't know."

"I don't believe you. When did you get here?"

"It's of no importance. What matters is that Lauri kept me in the dark about many things. For my protection—that's how much he loved me."

"How's that working out?" Bernie said.

The color drained out of Gerd's face. For a moment I expected him to faint, which perps do once in a while. But then came a big surprise. He wound up and threw a punch at Bernie. Bernie caught Gerd's fist in midair. It made a smacking sound, quite pleasing to the ear.

Bernie let him go. You might have thought that was the end of any rough ideas from Gerd, but you'd have been wrong. Crying now, he grabbed Bernie by the shirt front, tried to shake him. I'd never seen that happen in my whole career. "Just let me go!" Gerd screamed. "Let me go!"

I was waiting for Bernie to push Gerd away or do much more than that, but Bernie did not. Instead he just gazed down and watched Gerd shaking him. To no effect, I should point out, since Bernie's body remained perfectly still. Maybe Gerd noticed that, because he sobbed, twisted away, and threw open the window, like he planned to jump out. The window was big enough but perhaps Gerd had forgotten that we weren't on the first floor, rather at the level of the tops of the palm trees, as anyone could see. You couldn't miss those palm trees, all strung with Christmas lights, bright even in the daytime.

But Gerd must have missed all that. Why? Because he was so terrified? Terrified of us? That didn't make sense. Why couldn't he see that we were basically the very nicest types, deep down. No time to figure that out. Before we could stop him, Gerd had grabbed the window sill, yanked himself up, and—

And then came confusion. Bernie reached out and grabbed Gerd by the collar. At the same moment, I heard a crack from somewhere outside, not very loud but a sound I knew right away without even thinking. Gerd went limp and fell back into Bernie's arms.

"Gerd?"

No response. There was a round red hole in the middle of Gerd's forehead. His eyes were open. For the briefest instant they still looked terrified. Then nothing. Bernie let go of him, then quickly turned and threw himself on top of me.

"Stay down, Chet. Stay down."

I felt Bernie's heart beating against my back. I stayed down.

I have lots of buddies on the SWAT team. When they were done searching all around the Desert Dunes, they packed up their stuff in the parking lot and drove away, but not before each and every one gave me a nice pat. There's lots to be said for being a law enforcement professional.

That left me, Bernie, and Freddy alone by a palm tree in a corner of the lot, except for a guy on a ladder busy with Santa, a bunch of reindeer, and a sleigh. Reindeer are a kind of deer. A sleigh seems to be a kind of cart, except on skis. I've had experience with deer. You could never get them to pull a cart. Christmas has its mysterious side.

For some reason, Bernie was keeping a close eye on the ladder guy. He even seemed to be about to say something to him, when Freddy spoke up.

"I never knew how exciting your life was."

Bernie turned to him. "Sorry, Freddy."

"Nothing to be sorry about," Freddy said. "The guests like the action, makes for a memorable vacation. And management's sending a fruit basket to every room, so it's a win-win. Except for the little German guy."

"I'm not even sure he was German," said Bernie.

"Born in Hamburg," Freddy said. "Spanish passport, which I happen to have." He handed Bernie a purple booklet.

Bernie opened it up. "My god. He was only twenty-six." He handed back the passport.

"I saw that," said Freddy. "Looked much older. Lauritz was fifty-eight but looked much younger."

"You've got his passport, too?"

Freddy pulled out another purple booklet. Bernie went through it.

"Born in Naples," he said. "Did you know the king of Spain used to be the king of Naples as well?"

"News to me," said Freddy. "Is it relevant to anything?"

"I think so," Bernie said.

"Go on," said Freddy, but at that moment a Valley PD cruiser pulled into the lot and parked nearby.

Two guys got out, one in uniform and one in a tan suit.

"Know 'em?" Freddy said.

"The uniform's Oxley from Missing Persons," said Bernie. "Don't know the other one."

"Spratt," said Freddy. "Homicide. They sent the Z team."

The Z team, whatever that was exactly, ambled over. Lots of the Valley PD guys and gals looked pretty good in their uniforms, but Oxley was more the bulgy type that did not. Also he walked like a duck, always an interesting sight, even when a duck was doing it. And what was this? The dude in the suit— not quite as bulgy but with one of those big moon faces—also walked like a duck? I was starting not to like the Desert Dunes.

"Well, well," said Spratt. He had a high voice that somehow went with the moon face, although the effect was not pleasant. "Fearless Freddy Perez, still in there pitching."

Freddy looked right at Spratt and said nothing. Spratt turned to Oxley.

"Introduce me to your friend."

"Hey, Bernie, this here's Detective Spratt from homicide," Oxley said. "He caught the case."

"What case?" said Bernie. "And how come you're here?"

Oxley waved his hand toward the hotel. "This shooting or whatever. And I'm with Missing Persons. I thought you knew that, Bernie."

"Who's missing?" Bernie said.

"Well, now," Oxley began, and glanced at Spratt.

"Victor Klovsky," said Spratt.

"Sergeant Wauneka's handling that," Bernie said.

Spratt smiled one of those complicated smiles that Bernie says are happy for the smiler but not the guy getting smiled at. "Ox? Bring him up to speed."

"Sergeant Wauneka's off the case," Oxley said.

"Why?" said Bernie.

"You don't know?" Oxley said.

"That's the implication of why," said Bernie.

Oxley blinked. Freddy laughed softly. Spratt's face reddened. Once when we had Charlie, Bernie got us all up at night to watch the moon turn red. Spratt's face reminded me of that night, although the beauty part was missing.

"Run along, Freddy," he said. "We won't be needing you."

"You're working on a homicide at this hotel and you don't need the house dick?" Freddy said. He waved goodbye, actually with one of those purple booklets, and walked away.

"Now we can get down to business," Spratt said. "What are you doing here?"

"Excuse me?" said Bernie.

"You're the—what's the word?" said Oxley, turning to Spratt. "Means connection."

"Connection means connection," Spratt said. "And I'll handle this." He pointed at Bernie. "You're the connection between the homicide of—" He flipped through a notebook. "This Gerd character, and the missing man, Victor, um . . ."

"Klovsky," Oxley said. "Another PI, by the way. Makes three in one case—Klovsky, Vogner, and you, Bernie."

"Crissake, it's not one case," said Spratt. "Not yet. That's the working theory."

"Gotcha," said Oxley.

Spratt's pointing finger had gone limp. He stiffened it back up. "So, bud," he said to Bernie. "What's your story?"

"Chet?" Bernie said. And he made the little click click sound, meaning we were out of there. Was he going to say goodbye to Spratt and Oxley? Goodbyes usually happened when humans left each other, but not this time. We simply walked away.

"What the hell?" Spratt called after us. "Where do you think you're going?"

Almost certainly to the Porsche was my take, but Bernie didn't let him in on that. Instead, not looking back, he waved goodbye with the other purple booklet.

Twenty-three

"Weatherly? Come on, pick up. We need to talk. It's me."

Weatherly did not pick up. Bernie smacked the dashboard, smacked it hard. That was the scariest thing that had happened on this whole case, the unseen snakes lurking under Nuestra Señora coming second. I retreated across the shotgun seat, squeezing against the door, and kept my eyes on Bernie. Does he worry? Yes, sometimes, and I can always snap him out of it. But once in a while he goes beyond worry to where some force seems to take hold of him, even bending him out of shape, like now, the way he was hunched over the wheel. Then there's nothing I can do. I tried anyway, putting a paw on the gear shift. Bernie always gets a kick out of that, says things like, *Want to change places, big guy?* Which had actually happened once on a night down in Mexico involving tequila, which Bernie hasn't touched since, and a very friendly young lady to whom Bernie had sung a very long song, I believe called "El Paso," while accompanying himself on the ukulele, all this before the surprising appearance of a gentleman with an AK who turned out to be the head of the local cartel and the boyfriend of the young lady. None of that important now, in fact, getting in the way of where I was going, namely that Bernie did not even notice my paw on the gear shift. He didn't seem to notice our speed, either, which was way faster than that of anyone else. But that didn't bother me, Bernie being the best wheelman in the Valley.

We slowed down, pulled up in front of the small lemon-colored house with the lemon tree in the yard and the nice shady porch, namely Weatherly's house. I realized that it was my second favorite house in the whole world, although I had no idea why. I'm sure you don't need my help figuring out which house is number one. We hopped out of the car—Bernie actually hopping, although hopping is usually a cheerful sort of movement and this was not.

Bernie knocked on the door. No answer. He knocked harder, called out, "Weatherly! Open up!" I'm pretty good at knowing if someone's home, especially when a member of the nation within is part of the household. No one was home.

Bernie turned to me. "Has something happened to her?"

Something like what? I had no idea. All I knew was that Weatherly wasn't in, and neither was Trixie.

Bernie turned back to the door and knocked again, a knocking you might actually call pounding. The wreath—I forgot to mention the wreath on the door, decorated with red flowers and pine cones—fell off and rolled across the porch, a bit like tumbleweed. Bernie grabbed it and stuck it back on the door. A pine cone dropped off. Bernie picked it up and tried to fix it back in place, but it wouldn't stay. He shoved it in his pocket.

"Come on!"

We ran to the car, jumped in, barreled downtown, double-parked in front of PD HQ, ran inside, down the hall, up some stairs, into Rick Torres's office, where we barged in without knocking.

Rick sat behind his desk, drinking coffee and nodding at whatever the person in the visitor's chair, also drinking coffee, had just said. That person was Weatherly.

They both turned to look at us, both seemed real surprised.

"Bernie?" said Rick. "Something up?"

Bernie didn't answer. Instead he strode over to Weatherly, picked her right up and out of the chair and held her tight.

"Whoa!" she said, and pushed him away.

Weatherly's tall and strong, although not like Bernie, so she couldn't push him away like that unless he was letting her. His hands fell to his sides. There was a very strange look on his face, as though he was just waking up.

Rick rose and picked up some papers. "I'll let you two talk," he said.

"I—" Bernie said.

Weatherly backed away.

"I—I'm sorry," he said.

"What are you even doing here?" said Weatherly.

"I was . . . concerned about you."

"Yeah? Imagine if you'd been really upset."

Bernie's head went back, like . . . like he'd just been . . . I didn't even want to go there. I'd never seen this before. Let's leave it at that.

"Is that a joke?" he said.

"Partly," said Weatherly. "What's going on?"

"You don't pick up when I call," Bernie said. "I thought you were just . . . um, whatever, but then Oxley got all mysterious about—"

"Oxley? That cretin?"

"—you being off the case, and I . . . I was afraid something bad, uh, which was clearly not the reality, although I still . . ." He looked down at this feet. I hadn't seen Bernie like this in a long time, or possibly never.

Weatherly shook her head, then smiled a small smile, not particularly happy. "What am I going to do?"

"About what?" Bernie said.

Weatherly sat on a corner of Rick's desk, the gun on her belt knocking over a trophy, I believe for bowling, judging from the tiny golden human with the tiny golden ball. I was actually once inside a bowling alley, although not for long. Weatherly set the trophy upright.

"You," she said. She glanced at the tiny golden bowler. He seemed to displease her in some way. She knocked him back down again with the back of her hand.

"What did I do?" Bernie said.

"It's not so much that," said Weatherly. "It's what you are."

"People can change."

"Full-grown adult people? You believe that?"

"It's worth a try," Bernie said.

"Not in your case," said Weatherly. "Don't change a thing."

"You're confusing me," Bernie said.

I couldn't have been more with him on that. Start with why she'd take such a dislike to the tiny bowler and go from there.

"I took myself off the Klovsky case, Bernie."

"But why?"

"Because—and don't misinterpret this, that would be a deal breaker—I didn't want to compete with you."

There was a silence. Then Bernie said, "My god! You already knew who the client was."

"Elise Klovsky," said Weatherly. "It's not rocket science."

Lots of things turn out not to be rocket science, if you listen to what people say, which I sometimes do. But it's too bad because Bernie's brilliant at rocket science. Not too long ago he and Charlie built a rocket called *Charlie I*, which blasted off from our patio and would have gone all the way to Mars, wherever that may be, if it hadn't shredded some overhead wires, which no rocket scientist could ever have expected, resulting in a flash, a boom, a power outage in our neighborhood and possibly several or many others, and a visit from Valley FD, where we have lots of buddies, so no harm no foul.

"So therefore?" Bernie said.

Whoa! Bernie was handing a so-therefore over to Weatherly? He handles the so-therefores. That's why he's Bernie. Well, let's not go that far. There are so many things that make Bernie Bernie, way more than two or even . . . or even the number that comes after two. What was it again? I had it totally under control, and very recently. I came close to feeling frustrated, but then it hit me. The number would come back to me on its own. Wow! What a life!

"So therefore, Bernie," Weatherly said, "in my opinion competition makes for a bad marriage. Which I realized too late, but at least I got there."

"Marriage?" Bernie said softly.

"Marriage—woo woo," said Weatherly in a sort of monster voice, raising her hands and making scary motions with them. This is maybe where to mention that Weatherly looked nothing like a monster. Everything about her face makes you want to take a longer look. Let's just leave it with her eyes for now, full of life, like Suzie's, although not quite as dark, yet with this mysterious add-on, like they could fire up at any moment. But why bring in Suzie? I had no idea. She just somehow gets brought in.

Bernie laughed, like the Weatherly monster was funny. Then, kind of cautiously, like the footing might be slippery, he moved toward her. Weatherly didn't go anywhere, not forward or back, just stood her ground, her face no longer scary, just hard to read. How carefully she was watching him!

"The point is I'm the one who needs to apologize," Weatherly said. "We all have our demons."

"What are yours?" Bernie said.

Weatherly shook her head. "Not now," she said. "What I'm trying to say is that I planned to tell you in person."

"Tell me what?"

"That I love you, Bernie. Just bear with me."

Bernie's mouth opened, but no words came.

"You don't have to say anything," Weatherly said.

Bernie nodded. He rocked back and forth a bit, then reached in his pocket, took out the pine cone, and handed it to her.

"What's this?" she said.

"It fell off your wreath," Bernie said.

Weatherly gazed at the pine cone, just an ordinary pine cone, with a tiny bit of tinsel caught in one of its little scaly things. Her eyes dampened. She held the pine cone to her chest.

Bernie took her in his arms, although not like the first time. I knew this was better but couldn't tell you how.

"No pressure," she said.

"Ha," said Bernie.

And then they kissed. I broke it up.

* * *

Weatherly checked her watch. "I've got five minutes. Take me through it."

We were in the lot behind PD HQ, standing by Weatherly's cruiser. Bernie patted his pockets, finally found what he wanted, which turned out to be a folded-up sheet of paper. He unfolded it and smoothed it out on the hood.

"It's about this guy," Bernie said, pointing with his finger.

"I don't get it," said Weatherly.

"It's an old painting—David with the head of Goliath."

Weatherly took a close look. "So we're not dealing with a who-dunit."

Bernie laughed. "This Goliath turns out to be a self-portrait of Caravaggio, the artist."

"Never heard of him."

"Neither had I," Bernie said. A breeze sprang up, lifted the sheet of paper off the hood. Bernie snagged it out of the air. "He's an elusive character, but his paintings are worth a fortune and—"

His phone beeped. He glanced at it. "Damn. Some problem with Mr. Parsons."

Weatherly folded the sheet of paper, handed it to Bernie. "To be continued." She gave his shoulder a punch, not particularly gentle.

Bernie called Mr. Parsons from the car. "Got your text," he said. "Are you all right?"

"Sorry to bother you." Mr. Parsons's voice sounded weak and scratchy. "It's just this car parked out front. Well, not so much the car, but the woman inside. She's just sitting there, Bernie. It's making Edna uneasy and I'm uneasy, too." And so was Iggy. His yip-yip-yipping made Mr. Parsons hard to hear.

"We're on our way," Bernie said.

"Thank you," said Mr. Parsons. "She's actually more parked in front of your place than ours, but . . . well, we're uneasy."

"Don't go outside," Bernie said. "Lock the house."

"I did," said Mr. Parsons. "I'm sure I did. I'm very careful when it comes to . . . but I'll double check."

※ ※ ※

We drove down Mesquite Road, the nicest street in the Valley, and pulled into our driveway. A dusty sedan was parked out front and Iggy was standing on his hind legs in the tall window in the Parsonses' front hall, yip-yip-yipping himself into a frenzy. We got out of the car. At the same time, the driver's side door of the dusty sedan opened and a woman got out. For a moment I almost didn't recognize her. She was wearing a dress for one thing, instead of denim, a red dress, kind of short, and she'd added lots of perfume to her natural smell. But it was Johanna Borden. By now Mr. Parsons had appeared in the window. Bernie gave him a thumbs up. Mr. Parsons sort of drew Iggy back from the window and Iggy sort of amped down the yip-yip-yipping.

Johanna smiled. She wore lipstick today and a little of it was smeared on one of her front teeth. "Hi, there. That little fella's quite the neighborhood protector."

Did she mean Iggy? Johanna was off to a bad start. Iggy was not the neighborhood protector. I believe you know the big fella who is.

Bernie didn't get into any of that. All he said was, "What's up?"

"Is there somewhere we can talk?" Johanna said.

Bernie is the friendliest guy you'll ever meet so naturally he was going to say, *C'mon in. Put your feet up.* But he didn't for what seemed like a long time, and he changed *c'mon in* to "Come inside," and left out the *put your feet up* part completely.

"Thanks," said Johanna. "Oh, and I've brought you a present."

"That's not necessary," Bernie said.

But Johanna ran back to the car—she was a good runner for a human—grabbed a present wrapped in silver-bells paper, and came with us into the house.

"What a nice place!" she said, as we sat in the kitchen, the two of them facing each other at the table and me on the floor in between.

Bernie nodded and said nothing.

"Merry Christmas," Johanna said. She slid the present across the table. "I think it's the kind you like."

"The kind of what?"

"Open it and see. I won't tell Santa."

"Who will you tell?" Bernie said.

"Huh?" said Johanna. "I just meant you don't have to wait for Christmas Day."

"What if I like waiting for Christmas Day?"

"Then by all means."

So—we were opening the present? Not opening? I had no idea, but Bernie ended up opening, which was what I'd have done if I'd been Bernie. Whoa! What a thought! I wasn't sure I was comfortable with it. What if I was Bernie and . . . and he was Chet! I knew one thing for sure. I'd give him a treat this very second.

Meanwhile Bernie was stripping away the wrapping, revealing a bottle of bourbon, the kind he liked, with the red flowers.

"How did you know?" he said.

"Now, Bernie," she said. "Let's not look a gift horse in the mouth."

Stop right there. Did Johanna think Bernie wanted to look for gifts inside the mouths of horses? We know horses, me and Bernie, prima donnas each and every one. He's a very good rider, as I'm sure you would have guessed, and who could ever forget Mingo, the look in his eyes reminding me quite a lot of the look in Iggy's, although there were many differences as well, starting with the fact that the ground trembled when Mingo ran and with Iggy it remains perfectly still. Johanna did not know horses. I shifted closer to her end of the table.

Meanwhile Bernie didn't say, *How about we crack 'er open,* which was what he always said when someone brought a bottle. He didn't even say thanks, or touch the thing.

"I don't know why you're here," he said, "but since you are, how about we clear up a little discrepancy?"

"I'll try to help any way I can," said Johanna.

He gave her a look he might give to a perp. Why? Just because she didn't know horses? Wasn't she a scientist of some sort? Or possibly a janitor? But a perp? I couldn't see it. I tried to imagine her breaking rocks in the hot sun, and—and found I could see that! She was big and strong and good at digging, as I already knew. Wow! I'd changed my mind, or it had changed on me. Neither one happened every day.

"Yeah?" said Bernie.

"Of course," Johanna said. "What's the discrepancy?"

"You told us you were in Marco Folonari's office to get some files he wanted."

"Correct."

"But Marco Folonari tried to block the sale of the priory to the new owners. Don't you work for them?"

"On contract to People For Preservation," Johanna said.

When we're not working and Bernie isn't buying something—say Charlie telling us there's no homework—you can see it on his face. When we are working you can't, so I had no idea whether or not he believed her, and had also lost the thread of the whole shebang.

"The point is Marco opposed your group," Bernie said. "Why would he come to you for a favor?"

That sounded complicated, but complicated in the way that rattles folks on the receiving end, so it was a bit of a disappointment when Johanna didn't look rattled at all. Instead her face brightened and she said, "I think you should ask him."

"So do I," Bernie said. "But according to you he's on sabbatical and unreachable."

"True," said Johanna. "Which is why I'm here. You have a reputation for finding people. I want to hire you to find Marco."

"Why?" Bernie said.

Now Johanna did look—maybe not rattled, but a little surprised. "I just told you—your repu—"

Bernie interrupted. Was this an interview? Maybe not. Interrupting isn't one of Bernie's techniques in interviewing situations. He just lets them talk and talk. Sometimes I nod off and when I wake up they're still talking! And by then I'm fresh, alert, all set for anything. They haven't got a chance.

"I meant," Bernie said, "why do you want to find him?"

"We're worried."

"Who is 'we'?"

"Me," said Johanna. "And my boss. Marco loves solo expeditions—art hunting, he calls it—but he's not getting any younger. What if he's way off in some—"

Bernie interrupted again. "Who's your boss?"

"At the moment I'm not authorized to say."

"Authorized by who?"

"Him," said Johanna. "He's very protective of his privacy, like many wealthy people these days, as I'm sure you've noticed. But if you're worried about payment, please don't." She reached into her purse, green leather, so nice and Christmasy with her red dress. Also, not visible but smellable, there was a gun in that purse, a gun that hadn't been fired in a very long time or even cleaned, which was maybe why I'd missed it off the top. Sniffing out guns is part of my job at the Little Detective Agency, but I don't bark every time one shows up. If I did, here in the Valley, I'd be barking from dawn to dusk and then even more from dusk to dawn, kind of like Iggy. Whoa! Was it possible Iggy—my mind refused to go there.

Meanwhile Johanna had taken out an envelope. "We'll pay double your usual fee," she said. "Here's a nonrefundable retainer of ten thousand dollars."

Bernie took the envelope and glanced inside. "Cash?"

"I assumed that would be your preference."

Bernie laid the envelope on the table. Was ten thousand a lot? That would have been my guess. And we were fine with cash, in my experience, as long as Bernie didn't stick it in the chest pocket of his shirt, which has led to long and bothersome searches in the past, some unsuccessful.

"Would you prefer Bitcoin?" said Johanna.

A look flashed in his eyes, as though Bitcoin, whatever that may be, somehow pleased him, but it was gone right away. You really had to know Bernie to spot it, and I do.

"We can figure that out later," Bernie said. "Right now I need to know how Marco contacted you."

"About what?"

"About needing those files."

There was a pause. I could feel Johanna thinking, light and fast. I could also feel Bernie's thoughts, fast as well, but much heavier. I couldn't feel a thought of my own at all, and suddenly got a very happy feeling.

"He asked me in person," Johanna said.

"How was that possible?"

"This was last month, before he left. He said there was no rush."

"And where were you supposed to send the files?"

"To his house."

"But he wasn't there."

"I assumed someone would forward them."

"Someone like who?"

"I don't know."

"Is he married? Does he live with someone?"

"No to the first. I don't know to the second. I'm not sure where you're going with this."

"No?" Bernie gave her a direct look. She gave him a direct look back. But those looks weren't the same. Johanna was afraid of Bernie. He had no fear of her.

"No," she said. "But I'm sure you know what you're doing."

"We'll see," said Bernie, instead of *Hell yeah,* which was the truth. "Where does Marco live?"

"Down in Immler Springs," Johanna said.

"We'll start there," Bernie said.

"It's hard to find," said Johanna. "I can take you."

For a moment, I thought Bernie was about to smile, but he did not. That made sense. If anything funny was going down, I hadn't spotted it either. He rose. "We'll follow you."

Before we left, Bernie locked the gym bag in the office safe, behind the waterfall painting. He left the ten grand on the kitchen table.

Twenty-four

"If you can tell whether someone's talking just from looking at the back of her head at this distance," Bernie said, "then I'd say she's talking. The question is who's on the other end?"

Up until that moment, this drive had been rather enjoyable, traffic light, the countryside hilly, and even a roadrunner sighting—"Amp it down, big guy"—but now came this very tough and complicated question. Think of bubbles, for example. When Charlie was little, we'd often blow bubbles for him, Bernie handling the blowing of the bubbles and me on the chasing end. If there's only one bubble, you can catch it easy-peasy, and the same for two or . . . or that horrible pesky number that comes after it. But a whole cloud of bubbles is another story. That's how I felt about Bernie's question.

Bernie gestured with his chin. "Check her out, Chet. On a call for sure."

Up ahead, but not particularly close, was Johanna's dusty sedan, which we'd been following the whole way. I could kind of see the back of her head, but if she was talking I saw no sign of it. That didn't worry me in the slightest. You don't worry a whole lot when Bernie's in your life.

We went over a hill—topped, by the way, with another two-armed saguaro with the arms outstretched, like the one near Nuestra Señora but not as big—and wound our way down to Immler Springs. Some of these hill-country towns are old mining towns, some are old hippie towns, and some are old outlaw towns. Immler Springs is all of them, but on our only other visit we'd been dealing with the outlaw part, specifically a biker gang called the Frenzies who highjacked an eighteen-wheeler they thought was carrying a shipment of sniper rifles but turned out to be umbrellas, all of that leading to bad tempers and an umbrella bonfire. Our client was the umbrella owner and she wanted the Frenzies to pay for them, which we persuaded them to do. They even threw in a little extra for what Bernie called "aggravating circumstances," a term that took some explaining, although possibly because the head honchos of the Frenzies were a bit distracted at the time, what with being tied to railroad tracks and all.

But today's trip took us to the hippie part of town, where the houses were painted in all sorts of colors and the sound of wind chimes never ended. Johanna parked in front of the last house on a street with not many houses. We parked behind her and all of us walked toward the house. I can't remember what it looked like, but I'll never forget what stood in the front yard, namely an enormous cat made of rusty car parts. I tried not to look but failed. Then I looked but tried to see car parts and not a cat— for example, those sneering eyes weren't eyes at all, but hubcaps. That didn't work either.

"Marco used to be a bit of an artist," Johanna said. "This one's called 'Burning Bright.'"

Bernie paused for a moment as though he'd had a thought. Then he glanced my way. "Chet?"

I watched him closely. Was he about to say, "Let's bag this, big guy. Back in the car"? I was certain he was and my spirits rose inside me. Instead he shook his head, possibly sending me a message and possibly not, and then walked to the door. I marked the cat very speedily and followed.

The door had a metal cat's head knocker. As Johanna reached for it, I thought: *Can't we go up against the Frenzies instead?*

Johanna banged the knocker a couple of times.

"I don't get it," Bernie said. "Is Marco here? Hasn't he disappeared?"

I wasn't sure what that was all about, but inside someone was on his way: a man, heavy, wearing soft shoes, possibly slippers.

Johanna smiled a bright smile. "I thought this would be an opportunity to meet someone helpful."

"Helpful with what?" Bernie said.

Meanwhile Johanna didn't seem to be paying attention. She was watching the door in a way that reminded me of the audience at a rock concert we once went to, just before the star came on.

The rock star, our client at the time, was a real skinny guy with all sorts of problems, although paying us hadn't been one of them. "Should be sufficient green under that pillow, mate," he'd said, pointing to his bed, in which several people seemed to be napping, the pillow still the most amazing pillow I'd ever smelled.

The man who opened the door looked nothing like our rock star. He was fully clothed for one thing, wearing a suit, and yes, slippers, plus a Panama hat—a fattish type with a short, curly whitish beard, and the sort of face meant to be jolly, like Santa's. The only slight hitch was that his eyes, somehow dark and bright at the same time, were not jolly.

"Bernie Little," Johanna said. "Meet my boss, Signor Francesco di Scarpa."

Signor Francesco di Scarpa was not quite new to me. I'd seen him before, although I hadn't smelled him, so my memory wasn't the sharpest. My smell memory is off the charts, if you don't mind me mentioning it myself. But I'd glimpsed him from inside Nuestra Señora through a crack in the wall, and wasn't he also in a video we'd watched at the museum gift shop? Could there have been yet another time? And had Bernie been in on all these sightings of the signor, or some, or any? Questions like those are far beyond my comfort zone. But if Bernie had seen him before, he gave no sign. Should I bark? Not bark? I went back and forth on that. My tail drooped. I hoisted it back up in no uncertain terms. That was all I could bring to the table at the moment.

Signor—the rest of his complicated name escaping me even though I'd just had it—held out his hand, soft and pudgy. Bernie held out his hand, big, strong, perfect. They shook.

"A pleasure to meet you, Bernie, if we may call you Bernie. And for the love of god please call me simply Francesco. Skip all that—what would you say? La-di-da?"

Johanna laughed. Francesco seemed to like that. He smiled, reached out for Johanna, pulled her close, sort of sideways, and gave her a kiss on the cheek, which lasted longer than any other cheek kisses I'd seen.

"So no la-di-da," he said at the end of it, turning back to Bernie. Johanna slipped past him and entered the house. "This is America, after all," Francesco continued. "Please come in. And bring this formidable fellow we hear so much about."

"Thanks," Bernie said. "But this isn't your house, unless I'm missing something."

Which never happens, missing things are more in my line. For example, right now I was missing the part about the formidable fellow. There was no one else around, just me and Bernie.

"How right you are about that," Francesco said. "But Marco is a dear friend and wouldn't mind in the least. And now that he's gone astray and you've so kindly agreed to find him, we thought you might want a look inside his . . ." He twisted around and called over his shoulder. "Bambolina? What please is the word?"

"House," Johanna called back from somewhere inside.

"No, no, something more . . . more . . ." Francesco raised a pudgy hand, thumb tip touching fingertips, and gave it a little shake.

"Abode," Johanna said.

"Grazie," said Francesco. "Abode, Bernie. We thought you might take an interest in Marco's abode."

"Who is 'we'?" Bernie said.

Francesco's eyebrows—white like Santa's but not as bushy—rose in surprise. "I, of course! We is I, Francesco di Scarpa."

"Is that Italian grammar, we is I?" Bernie said.

"Ha ha ha." Francesco threw back his head and laughed. "Yes and no," he said. "Ha ha ha. Come, Bernie, come." Francesco took Bernie by the hand and drew him inside, his eyes finally joining in with all the jolliness on his face.

Inside reminded me of Jada's art gallery, the name not coming, if I'd ever known it. Paintings hung all over the walls and sculptures stood on the floor. The good news was that none had anything to do with cats, except for one single painting, hanging over the fireplace. The bad news? Everyone's attention was on that single painting. In it a somewhat familiar looking man with long dark hair, wearing a beaded headband and with a green stone pendant hanging around his neck, sat on a chair and held a cat on his lap, a cat who seemed to be staring right at me in a way I didn't like one bit.

"Have you ever met Marco?" Francesco said.

"No," said Bernie.

"Or seen a photo of him, perhaps?"

"No."

No? That was interesting. I thought back to our little squash court visit, a snap to remember on account of the squash ball, now lying by my water bowl in the kitchen back home. Some things in life are unforgettable. But not the point, which was about the photo of squash-playing dudes hanging outside the court. Hadn't Marco been in that photo? In my mind I could see Bernie's finger, pointing him out. Never mind. If Bernie says no then it's no.

Francesco gestured to the painting. "There's your man," he said. "As seen through his own eyes."

"It's a self-portrait?" Bernie said.

"Marco is not without skill, for an amateur," said Francesco. He smiled at Bernie. "There is nothing of the amateur about you, my friend. May I ask the reason for your interest in Marco?"

"You first," said Bernie.

Francesco laughed again, but skipped the throwing back the head part this time. "Very fair," he said. "But what would be more fair?"

"Tell me," Bernie said.

"Ammazza! What a character! But more fair? Why, to throw a coin, yes?"

Bernie has a laugh for when he's not in a laughing mood but can't help it. He laughed it now.

"Johanna, darling?" said Francesco.

Johanna turned a little pink. "I'm so sorry. I never carry change anymore."

Francesco wasn't happy to hear that. All resemblance to Santa vanished at once. He glanced at Bernie. Bernie shrugged. Was this about coins? Bernie had some in his pocket. They'd jangled as we'd entered the house. But he kept that fact to himself. I suddenly realized we had a lot going on in this not particularly large room, including the presence of a snake somewhere under the floor.

Francesco fished around in the pockets of his suit, finally found a coin, a rather interesting coin, very big and made of gold, gold being an easy smell to pick up, and always exciting, which is probably on account of human excitement rubbing off on me, and gold gets humans excited.

"I throw, I call?" said Francesco.

"Well," Bernie began, but by then the coin was in the air.

"Tail," said Francesco.

I'd seen coin flips before. Sometimes the flipper lets the coin hit the ground. Other times he catches it and smacks it on the back of his other hand. This was that kind of coin flip, Francesco catching the coin with an easy motion that surprised me. He smacked it on the back of his other hand.

"Ecco," he said. "Tail."

And showed it to Bernie.

"Is there a head on the other side?" Bernie said.

Francesco laughed again. "You are the right man, Bernie." He turned the coin over so Bernie could see. "Umberto the first, survivor of several assassination attempts, with the exception of the last. Here, with my compliments."

"No thanks," Bernie said.

Francesco tossed it anyway. Bernie made no attempt to catch it. The coin fell to the floor. Francesco and Johanna stared at it, Johanna looking kind of shocked and Francesco . . . well, hard to tell. But his eyes, so bright and dark at the same time, were now somehow more of both. Meanwhile Bernie's eyes were on Francesco and the gold coin was just lying there. Once I'd found a gold nugget deep in a mine, just before a cave-in that became a bit of a problem. But—this was later, when we were rather dusty, sucking in deep breaths, and downing lots of water—I'd dropped the nugget at Bernie's feet and he'd just beamed. In short, I snatched up the gold coin and was about to drop it at his feet when I realized the coin had been at his feet when I picked it up. I went still.

The room, too, went still. Then Francesco clapped his pudgy hands. "What a clever animal!"

Right back atcha! That was my immediate thought, but it came and went so fast I didn't really catch it. Maybe it wasn't my thought at all but . . . but a Bernie thought? Somehow passing through my mind? I'd need a lot of time to sort that out even if I wanted to, which I didn't.

Meanwhile Francesco had reached down and begun patting my neck. He had no clue, the clumsiest patter I'd ever met. I was going on and on to myself about Francesco's clumsiness when I realized he'd slipped the gold coin out of my mouth and pocketed the thing. And Bernie had turned toward the painting for another look and hadn't even noticed!

"And now, Bernie," Francesco said, "to your interest in Marco. Would you like some refreshment while we talk?"

"Not necessary," said Bernie.

"Johanna?" Francesco said. "Refreshment, please."

Johanna gave Francesco a sharp glance, maybe like refreshment was somehow a bad idea. He didn't seem to notice her glance, but he watched her the whole way as she left the room and disappeared down a shadowy hall.

"Marco was her mentor?" Bernie said. "Have I got that right?"

Those un-Santa-like eyebrows rose again. "Certainly not. Marco was her professor. I am the mentor."

"Oh?" said Bernie. "I thought you were the boyfriend."

Francesco gave Bernie an odd sort of smile where the mouth did the smiling and the eyes wiped it out. "I am no boy," he said, and took a seat on a couch, gesturing for Bernie to sit at the other end. Bernie sat on an old wooden chair instead.

"Does Marco know about you and Johanna?" Bernie said.

Francesco's head went back a bit. "You ask a lot of questions."

"What did you expect?" Bernie said.

For a moment Francesco didn't like that one little bit. Then he changed his mind and laughed. "My relations with Johanna are complicated. I'm sure Marco is aware of that. And now, your interest in Marco, if you please."

Bernie shrugged. "His name came up in a case we're working on."

"Continue."

"It's a missing person case."

"The name of the person?"

"Victor Klovsky."

Bernie was watching Francesco's face real close as he spoke Victor's name. The expression on it didn't change at all.

"Any chance you know him?" Bernie said.

Francesco shook his head.

"Or have heard the name?" Bernie went on.

"No," said Francesco. "Who is your client?"

"That's something we keep to ourselves."

"Ha!" said Francesco. "And this 'we' is 'I'? You are like me!"

"Nope," Bernie said. "It's me and Chet."

"And who is this Chet?"

Bernie pointed me out. I must have been easy to spot, sitting on the floor halfway between the two of them, tall, alert, ready, but Francesco frowned like he was confused. Although I like just about every human I've ever met, I began to think slightly less of him.

"You are a character, Bernie," Francesco said. "Perhaps Chet is all about marketing?"

"Nope."

Francesco nodded to himself and then went on. "Is there anything else you are willing to say about your interest in Marco?"

"There isn't anything else, not that's relevant," Bernie said. "Over to you."

"So direct, you Americans," Francesco said.

"That's what they say," said Bernie.

"Do you know many Europeans?"

"No."

"Are you interested in art?"

"I know very little about it."

Francesco pointed to the painting over the fireplace. "What do you think of Marco's effort?"

Bernie gazed at the painting. "I like the cat."

Francesco pounded the arm of the couch, surprisingly hard. "Barilotto!"

At that moment, Johanna entered with a bottle of champagne and glasses on a tray.

"What is barilotto?" Francesco said to her.

"Bullseye," said Johanna.

"Bullseye, yes. Bernie here likes only Marco's cat."

"I didn't say only," Bernie said.

"But only is correct," said Francesco. "The cat lives. The rest? Dead."

Had I ever heard anything scarier? I moved farther away from the painting. Meanwhile Johanna was pouring champagne.

"A toast, Bernie?" said Francesco.

"To bullseyes," said Bernie.

Interesting. I knew bulls, of course, not exactly buddies of mine, but far preferable to cats. You can count on Bernie.

Francesco and Johanna didn't seem quite as pleased with the toast as I was, but everybody clinked glasses and drank, Johanna sitting on the couch near Marco, but not touching.

"It is our turn," Francesco said. "Explain me to Bernie."

"You're an art collector," Johanna said.

Francesco shook his head. He had a real slow way of doing that, brand-new to me.

"I am an art lover," he said. "That is what I am, not what I do. What I do is collect art."

"I don't see the difference," Johanna said.

"How disappointing," Francesco said.

Johanna put down her glass.

"Explain to her the difference, Bernie," Francesco said.

"I can't," said Bernie. "Do you want your ten grand back?"

A muscle bulged at the side of Francesco's face, almost like he was working on a wad of tobacco, which he most certainly was not. He took a big sip of champagne.

"You amaze me, Bernie. This is a lucky day."

Francesco downed what was left in his glass. Johanna leaned close and poured more. He gazed very closely at the side of her face as she did that. Then he raised his glass.

"Here is what you need to know. I specialize in the Italian masters of the sixteenth century, the masters of the masters. I own, for example, a pretty little Raphael. Of the Venetians particularly, I own two Titians, one early, one late. A Giorgione I would ki—I would love to have but there are so few, none ever coming on the market. But Tintoretto? Yes. Three, in fact, including a 'Flight Into Egypt.' Do you know that subject, Bernie?"

"Tell me about it."

Francesco took another drink. "The 'Flight Into Egypt' is a Christmas story, familiar to you, I would have thought, from the way Americans are so enthusiastic about Christmas."

"He didn't say he didn't know the story," Johanna said.

Francesco turned slowly toward her. "Some prosciutto would be nice."

Johanna gave him a look that showed nothing, at least to me, and left the room.

"The drama of the situation," Francesco said, "the little family on the run through a harsh land, danger at their backs—what a subject, I'm sure you would agree."

Bernie nodded.

"It is a subject not to Marco's taste, by the way. He says he despises melodrama. But his very favorite painter—and mine as well—was a master of melodrama. He raised it to the highest level of art. Marco refuses to see the melodrama. Do I hold it against him? Never! Did you know I support his research?"

"No."

"Marco is an excellent researcher." Francesco drained his glass, reached for the bottle, poured himself some more. Except for the toast, Bernie hadn't taken a sip. "He knows his way around all the dusty museum basements of old Europe, has uncovered a secret or two in his time," Francesco went on. "His problem—like so many academics—is ignorance of how the real world works.

That can lead to actions that look like rogue behavior although they are not."

"Has Marco gone rogue?" Bernie said.

"Oh no. No, no, no. Perhaps you are not listening. Marco has given the appearance of going rogue. All I want is to see him back, safe and sound. Will you do that for me, Bernie?"

"There are no promises in this business," Bernie said.

"No, of course not. Scusi, scusi." Francesco took another swallow, gazed at Bernie over the rim of his glass. "You have not asked the name of the old master, our favorite painter, mine and Marco's."

Bernie shrugged.

"It is Caravaggio," Francesco said. "The divine and satanic Caravaggio."

"A new one on me," said Bernie.

That was strange. Caravaggio wasn't even a new one on me.

"To possess privately a Caravaggio," Francesco went on, "to hang—" He noticed Bernie watching him, blinked, then gave Bernie a sharp look. "You don't like champagne?"

"I do."

"You don't like this champagne?"

"I do."

"Then why are you not drinking?"

"I'm building up a thirst," Bernie said.

There are moments in this job where some dude realizes what he's dealing with in Bernie. We had one now. The darkness in Francesco's eyes got darker and the brightness dimmed.

"Does the name Lauritz Vogner mean anything to you, Bernie?"

"Another old master?" Bernie said.

"Far from it," Francesco said. "An associate of mine, also with rogue tendencies."

"Do you want us to look for him, too?" Bernie said.

"Thank you, no."

By now I was completely lost. The name Lauritz Vogner meant something to me, and what would be the point of looking for him? I wandered off in the direction Johanna had gone, for no particular reason other than a ham-like aroma that was suddenly in the air.

I followed the hammy scent down a hall. There was a kitchen at the end, and in that kitchen I could see Johanna slicing something that looked very interesting. I was about to pick up the pace as I passed an open doorway on one side, and happened to glance through.

And what was this? A man was sitting on a bed, and not just any man but the huge dude with the handlebar mustache and the cruel eyes. He was busy loading a rifle, a long one with complicated add-ons.

I barked a savage bark.

The dude jumped right off the bed. Maybe frightened, but only at first. His mood turned to anger real quick. He came toward me, getting the rifle into firing position. Did he think I was scared of him? I barked again, more savagely than before.

Johanna burst past me.

"Vito," she whispered, a furious whisper unlike any I'd ever heard. "Moron!" She made a furious motion toward the closet. Vito looked pretty furious himself, but he didn't say a word, just hurried over to the closet and shut himself inside, taking the rifle with him.

Johanna turned to me. "Here you go, Chet. The best prosciutto in town." She held up a hammy slice that gave off a smell like no other. I would have followed it to the ends of the earth, but in this case I merely had to step outside the room. And then it was mine! Johanna closed the door.

Bernie was coming down the hall.

"Oh, Bernie," Johanna said. "Hope you don't mind—I gave Chet a slice of prosciutto. He seemed to want it pretty badly, as you might have heard."

Bernie looked around but there was nothing to see except for Johanna with a plate of—what was the name? Prosciutto? I would never ever forget it—and one happy camper. The next thing I remember clearly we were back in the car and I was polishing off another slice, this one for the road.

Twenty-five

"Here's one thing for sure, big guy," Bernie said, as we rode out of Immler Springs. "He's not buying what we're selling."

Uh-oh. What was this? We didn't have the job? But what about the ten grand, safely in an envelope on the kitchen table at home? There were certainly cases where we'd done the job and not been paid—don't ask me to even start with the list—but I couldn't come up with any where we'd been paid and hadn't done the job. Ms. Pernick, our accountant, had suggested several times that we tweak our business plan, "tweak" being a mystery to me. As for business plans, Bernie has never mentioned one. But forget all that. Maybe this was the tweak—$10K yes, work no. Good? Bad? Probably worth a try. I was tempted to give Bernie a nice big kiss, but we were taking a hairpin turn at high speed on the two-laner leading up and over a mountain, so perhaps it could wait.

"My own fault," he said a little later, as we hit the freeway, the tops of the downtown towers just visible in the distance, like they were floating in the evening sky. And even higher there appeared to be a sleigh, all lit up and headed across the Valley. A sleigh? I took another look and—whew—the sleigh turned out to be a helo, maybe the traffic-reporting kind. First I said to myself: *Chet! Get it together.* But then Chet said to me—and this may be getting hard to follow—*Why not a sleigh?*

"The mistake," Bernie was saying, "and how many times does it go down like this?—happened way earlier." He shook his head, an inward-looking kind of head shake he has for when he's not pleased with himself. "Remember when Johanna first mentioned finding Marco? And I said—no, blurted—something like, 'Why would you want to do that? Don't you work for the new owners? Didn't Marco oppose the sale?' Blah blah blah. So right then she knew, and Francesco would soon know, too—she probably told him on the road to Immler Springs—that we were way deeper into this than I was making out." Bernie glanced my way. "Lesson number one—never think aloud in front of others."

Lesson number one? That sounded important. Never think aloud in front of others. It seemed right in my wheelhouse. I was good to go.

"So we've got two missing man cases, maybe running parallel," Bernie said as we left the freeway on the ramp that led home. "Don't want to get your skis crossed in a parallel situation," he added, that one zipping right by me. Meanwhile we had a backup, and a guy with a cardboard sign and a paper cup was going from car to car, no windows rolling down for him. But our windows were already down, and the metal roof was in the garage at home.

"Wish I had that gold coin," Bernie said. "Perfect for moments like this." He fished some bills out of the cup holder and handed them to the guy just as he was opening his mouth, a mouth with only one tooth I could see, twisted sideways.

"Bless you, sir," the man said. "Merry Christmas."

"And to you," said Bernie. Traffic started moving and we drove on. Behind us another guy with a cardboard sign came up to our cardboard sign guy and yelled at him. An argument started up and then I lost sight of them.

"Speaking of the coin," Bernie said as we turned onto Mesquite Road, "Francesco was pretty smooth, the way he got it back—like a close-up magician." Bernie laughed. I saw nothing funny about it.

We pulled into the driveway. The neighborhood was quiet. Over the rooftops a wall of dark clouds had formed in the distant reddening sky.

The phone buzzed first thing in the morning, Bernie making coffee and me chowing down.

"Bernie? Jada Brooks. Over at Celare Artem?"

"Hey," Bernie said.

"I wondered if you had any news about Victor? I suppose I would have heard if you found him and all, but . . ."

"No news," Bernie said. "Do the names Lauritz Vogner or Gerd Erhardt mean anything to you?"

"No. Do they have something to do with Victor?"

"Yes."

"Are they friends of his?"

"No."

"I didn't think so. Victor didn't have a lot of friends."

"Any?" Bernie said.

"Not that I knew of," said Jada. "There was a cousin he saw sometimes but he moved to Dubai."

"Did Victor ever go there to visit?"

"Not to my knowledge. Even if he'd wanted to, Victor hates flying. Plus Elise—that's his mom—would probably have found out."

"I don't understand," Bernie said.

"Oh, sorry," said Jada. "Elise didn't approve of Jeremy—that's the cousin."

"Why not?"

"I don't have firsthand knowledge, but apparently Jeremy had a production company at one time. He sold it and now does something with green energy, but Elise doesn't forget easily."

"Forget what?" Bernie said.

"Well, the production company. They made porn movies."

"Ah."

"I'm not saying Elise is a prude," Jada said. "Her objection would come from a feminist angle."

"Was Victor involved with the production company?"

"Never! He's Elise's son. Maybe too much. A little separation would have been nice. I suppose, looking back, that's what the cabin was all about."

"Cabin?" Bernie said. He'd been pouring coffee in a mug, but now he switched over to a thermos and filled it instead.

"It belongs to Jeremy, actually, but he hardly ever used it and not at all now that he's overseas," Jada said. "Victor has a key.

Elise doesn't know. We sometimes went on weekends. He's like a different person up there."

I felt Bernie's heartbeat, always mighty, and now picking up speed. But you wouldn't know it from his voice.

"Where's this cabin?" he said, still sounding perfectly every-day.

"Do you know Redhawk Mountain?" Jada said.

"I've been there."

"There's a campground not far from Rosetta—that's the town. The cabin's a few miles past that, where the road's chained off in winter. There's an avalanche warning sign. Are you thinking of checking it out?"

Bernie said nothing, just gazed straight ahead.

"Bernie? Still there?"

"Don't mention the cabin to anyone else," he said.

"Like who?" Jada said.

"Anyone," said Bernie.

Bernie opened the garage. You get to see the insides of a lot of ga-rages in this business. Some are neat and tidy. Most are like ours.

"Chilly up on Redhawk," he said. "Gonna need the hardtop."

Oh no, please not the hardtop. Not because I prefer the open air flowing over me like a wonderful dry river—which I do—but because I didn't want to see what was about to go down. Putting on the hardtop shouldn't be too difficult, you might think, espe-cially if the person doing it has done it before, but the strange thing is it gets more so every time. Once, back before Mrs. Parsons got so sick, she was rearranging some stones in her garden while Bernie and the hardtop were out in the driveway, having a sort of fight. She'd snapped off her gardening gloves and come over.

"Mind if I lend a hand?" she said.

"Well, I don't think you'll be—"

But by that time Mrs. Parsons had the hardtop securely in place and was putting her gardening gloves back on. "Love this car," she said.

"Yeah?" said Bernie.

"Owned one, this exact same model."

Bernie tilted his head as though getting a new angle on Mrs. Parsons. We do the same thing in the nation within.

"Brand-new—that's how long ago it was," said Mrs. Parsons. "Drove it down to Acapulco the day I graduated high school."

"By yourself?"

"Me and my boyfriend."

"Mr. Parsons?"

"This was before Daniel. The gentleman in question was a gypsy guitarist who'd turned me upside down." She'd patted the hood of the car with her twisted old hand. "Ride safe, Bernie." And she'd headed back to her garden.

Somewhat later we were on the road, hardtop secured, traffic thinning, high country ahead, and those distant clouds from last night growing and growing. Windows down, Bernie's foot heavy on the gas, the Porsche purring its rumbly purr, city smells getting lost in country smells, and me in the shotgun seat: what more could anyone want?

"How about we try a theory of the case?" Bernie said.

A theory of the case! Of course! That was the more than anyone could want! Why hadn't I thought of it? Because . . . because I didn't have to! I could count on Bernie for things like that. Just to show him how much I loved him I placed my paw on his leg. The Porsche's purr rose to a roar, Bernie steering us back to our side of the road in nothing flat.

He gave me a look. "Everything all right, big guy?"

Never better, as I was sure he already knew, but sometimes Bernie just likes to make friendly conversation. I made some friendly conversation back, barking a bark that sounded surprisingly loud, although that might have been on account of the hardtop.

"Hungry?"

No, far from it. But the next moment I was a lot closer to it, and then I was ravenous. Bernie fished around in his door compartment and came up with a peanut butter cookie treat that had been there so long I almost couldn't smell it. Bernie tossed it over. I snapped it out of the air and downed the crummy old thing in a single bite. Hey! Delish!

"It's clear Marco and Francesco knew each other," Bernie said. "Marco's an expert on Caravaggio paintings and Francesco wants one badly—fair to say he's obsessed. Johanna was a student of Marco's but at some time got into a relationship with Francesco. Does she do some spying for him? Didn't we catch her in the act?"

Caught in the act? We'd witnessed that more than once, for example during the Teitelbaum divorce, our most bothersome case. Had we seen Johanna involved in that kind of thing? Not that I recalled, but if Bernie said we had, then that was that.

"That brings us to Gerd, docent at the Prado Museum and boyfriend of Lauritz Vogner, a private investigator who possibly already had a relationship with Francesco, but if not, soon would. Gerd notices Marco digging away in some Prado archive. Marco discovers the ship's log. Gerd does some snooping and gets at least some idea of what Marco found. Then one day the log is gone, and so is Marco. Gerd passes all this to Lauritz, who gets in touch with Francesco. Does he already have Lauritz on retainer? Or do they now partner up? Or does he just hire Lauritz for the job? In any case, Francesco can't be too happy with Marco, whose research he supports, going rogue, as he put it. And then Lauritz, too, starts having thoughts of his own. He planned to use us as decoys of some kind, but ended up with Victor. Lauritz gets waterboarded to death, Gerd comes to claim the body and gets killed by someone who's real good with a rifle, and Marco and Victor are both in the wind. And all this for something that may not exist, although there may be clues in the ship's log that we missed. Unless . . ."

Bernie didn't say another word until we came to a quiet town, not big, with a few office buildings, some bars and restaurants with no action happening, and what looked like a small hospital.

"Rosetta, big guy, a ski town with the lift company in chapter eleven. Redhawk's all about steeps for experts only, but the snow's been iffy so they're not coming."

I missed just about all of that. As we left Rosetta, the road got twistier, the country rougher and steeper. The air had been cooling for a while and now it was cold and we had the windows closed. Also the dark clouds now sat directly overhead, heavy and sagging. The pavement ended and the road narrowed. We drove on, past a huge red rock, around a sharp bend, and then up and up. On one side the campground appeared—a few picnic tables, a couple of sun-faded RVs, a shack, all behind a padlocked gate. On the other side a red rock, but much smaller than the first, went tumbling by, or more like bounding. It looked kind of dangerous. Bernie saw it, no question, but he showed nothing. I did the same.

Up ahead some tall, dark green trees unlike any we had in the Valley blocked the view, but then it opened up and I could see all the way to the top, white with snow that petered out not far above us. We took a switchback, and another, and came to a simple roadblock, just a chain between two trees, with a sign hanging from it. "'Danger Avalanche Area,'" Bernie read. "'Road closed.'" He stopped the car.

An unpainted wooden cabin stood in the woods, not far away, and a rutted lane led to it, but we didn't drive down that lane. Instead we walked—walking when we could drive, just one of our techniques—Bernie first flipping open the glove box, taking out the .38 Special, and tucking it into his belt. I hadn't seen the .38 Special in way too long. We headed for the cabin, side by side, my paws silent on the dirt, Bernie's feet almost so. Hey! I could see our breath. That had happened only once before, on the case where I'd first seen snow. Somewhere above I heard another bounding rock.

The cabin was small and had a stone chimney, blackened at the top, although no smoke rose from it. Not a sound came from inside—no movement sounds, no fridge sounds, no running water sounds. As for smell, that was a different story.

We circled the cabin, peered into the windows, of which there weren't many, all of them strangely frosted on the inside, and through the frost nothing to see but shadows. The only door was the one in front. Bernie raised his hand to knock, then changed his mind and tried the handle instead.

The door was locked. Bernie took the .38 Special from his belt, raised one leg, landed another one of his perfect kicks, not especially hard but right on the button, although there was no actual button. No time to worry over that one, because right away came splintering, and the door swung slowly open.

It was cold inside this cabin, colder than outside. I could see my breath and Bernie's breath and the breath of one of the two men already in the room. That man was Victor Klovsky. He was duct-taped to a wooden chair, slumped forward, head down, and maybe not even aware of me and Bernie. His glasses lay on the floor. The other man, with no visible breath, also duct-taped to a wooden chair, was slumped forward the same way, head down. I hadn't ever seen him before, but I was pretty sure I recognized him from the painting of the man with the cat. In between the two men stood a big black woodstove with a window for watching the fire inside, of which there was none, not even an ember. I felt a sort of power surge in Bernie, although on the outside there was no sign of it.

"Stay, Chet," he said, striding between the two men and into a small dark hall, the .38 Special raised. There was a tiny kitchen, a tiny bathroom, and a somewhat larger room with bunk beds, but no one in any of them. Bernie stuck the .38 Special in his belt, grabbed a knife from the dish drying rack in the kitchen, and returned to the main room. Around then it hit me that perhaps I hadn't stayed as Bernie had suggested, but he didn't seem to notice. He knelt before Victor's chair.

"Victor? Victor?"

No answer. Bernie placed a finger on the side of Victor's neck. "Victor? Victor?"

No answer. Bernie took the knife and sliced through the duct tape in short strokes that seemed careful and angry at the same time.

"So damn cold," he said in the voice he uses for talking just to himself.

But Victor, eyes still closed, responded. Just a whisper, faint and weak, but what he said sounded like, "Wood stove."

Bernie rubbed the backs of Victor's hands, which looked a bit bluish. "Victor? You all right?"

Victor's eyes opened. They were so dim! "Bernie," he whispered. "My salvation."

"Cut it out," Bernie said. He picked Victor up like he was a child, carried him over to the only couch in the room, laid him gently on his back, covered him with an Indian blanket. Then he hurried to the other man and knelt before him.

"Marco? Marco?"

No answer.

"Marco?" Bernie placed a finger on Marco's neck. There was a long, long pause and then Bernie let out a long, long breath. I heard a heavy bird landing on the roof.

Bernie rose and went to the stove, flung open the door, tossed in kindling and split logs from the pile, found matches, lit one, and a fire sprang up in no time. He looked at it in . . . in fury, coming close to giving me a fright. But when he turned to me, the expression on his face was all about being glad that I was there.

"Stay, Chet? For real?"

He hurried out the front door. I stayed for real. Well, not exactly where I was. Instead I drifted over to Victor, eyes now closed again. I licked the side of his face. So cold, hardly like human skin at all. I licked it again. This time it felt a little better. Victor's eyes fluttered open. He gazed at me.

"So you got my letter after all," he said, his voice very weak, but even if he'd been bellowing I wouldn't have understood what he was talking about.

Bernie returned with water bottles from the car, closing the cabin door with his heel as he entered. With one hand he sat Victor up, and with the other tilted a water bottle to his mouth. Victor's lips didn't seem to know what to do, but Bernie got a little water into him, a little more on the next try, and a decent

mouthful on the try after that. Bernie tucked some pillows behind Victor and pulled the Indian blanket higher. Victor drank
and drank. The wood stove started to crackle.

Not too much later, it was nice and toasty in the cabin, and Victor had his glasses on and was sitting up, the blanket around his
shoulders and his bare feet in a tub of warm water. Bernie had
heated up some soup and Victor was slowly spooning it up, able
to hold the bowl all by himself.

Warm and toasty, but Marco lay on the floor, covered by a
sheet, head to toe. Victor glanced at him and began to shake so
hard he shook the bowl and the spoon right out of his hands.

"Oh god, Bernie, we've got to get out of here."

"No rush," Bernie said. "Let's get you warmed up and hy-
drated."

"But he's dangerous!" Victor glanced around wildly. "Where's
my gun?" He tried to stand and could not, collapsing back on the
couch.

"Who are you talking about?" Bernie said.

"Lauritz," Victor said. "The client." Victor's eyes, no longer so
dim, took on a look that seemed a bit unpleasant to me. He actually pointed at Bernie. "The client you sent me."

I got a bit uncomfortable. Was Victor turning out to be a bad
guy? If so, I'd have to grab him by the pant leg. His pants were
rolled up to the knee. I was pretty sure I could handle that, but
how could I do it without hurting him? I really had no desire to
hurt Victor, not even a little bit. I gazed at Bernie and waited.

Bernie nodded. "I'm sorry about that," he said.

Victor looked down. "I take it back."

"No, you're right," Bernie said. "There were signs, but I missed
them. How about you take us through it?"

"The case?" said Victor.

"Starting with what Lauritz wanted you to do."

"He's awful, Bernie." Victor shot a quick look at the door. "You
should have seen what he . . ." Victor took a deep breath. "I'll start

where you said, in an organized fashion. The assignment was to set up a meeting with . . ." His eyes shifted to the covered-up body. ". . . with Marco Folonari. He's—he was—an expert on a painter named Caravaggio. That turns out to be important. I went to Marco's house—he lives in Immler Springs—and I got lost on the way and he was a bit miffed, but his mood changed fast when I told him what my client wanted to talk about."

"Which was?"

"He knew where to dig. That was all it took. Lauritz had asked if there was some quiet place where we could meet, and I told him about the cabin. He loved the idea, in fact, gave me a five-hundred-dollar bonus on the spot."

"How did you get here?"

"Lauritz drove me."

"What about your bike?"

"My bike? He had a big car. It fit in the back."

"Why did you bring it?"

"It was Lauritz's suggestion. He said I should take advantage of the setting, have a nice mountain ride. He was very charming, Bernie, at first. But why are you asking? Isn't my bike outside?"

Bernie shook his head. "How did Marco get here?"

"He drove himself up."

"What kind of car?"

"I didn't see the car. It was night." Victor thought for a moment. "I should have noted the car."

"It doesn't matter," Bernie said. "What happened that night?"

"Lauritz brought food. He made a nice dinner—steaks, shrimp, wine. He's a very good cook. They talked about Caravaggio. Marco had made some sort of amazing discovery about provenance—I wasn't clear on that part—and Lauritz knew about it. Marco didn't understand how Lauritz knew. Lauritz thought that was funny and started into an explanation, mostly in Italian, which I don't know. That's the last I remember of that night."

"I don't understand," Bernie said. "Were you drunk?"

"I don't think so. A second bottle got opened but it wasn't finished before . . . before whatever happened happened. What I'm trying to tell you is that when I woke up the next morning, it was like when you came in."

"You and Marco were duct-taped to the chairs?"

Victor nodded. "Do you think he drugged us, Bernie?"

"Go on with the story," Bernie said.

"Lauritz's mood had changed. He said Marco had stolen some book and he'd be going to prison unless he cooperated. Cooperating meant handing over the book. Marco denied that he had the book, even though I'm pretty sure he admitted it the night before. That got Lauritz mad. It was horrible. He took the corkscrew from the table and with no warning—" Victor went silent. We waited. He took a deep breath, let it out with a shudder. "Then Lauritz leaned over him and whispered in the other ear. I couldn't hear what he said, but Marco caved right away. Who wouldn't?"

Victor watched Bernie, maybe waiting for an answer. None came.

"Marco told Lauritz the book was in his gym locker and the key was in the glove box of his car. Lauritz said if Marco was telling the truth then everything was jim-dandy—verbatim, Bernie—and he'd be back by nightfall to let us go. The fire went out that afternoon. What day is it?"

"Tuesday."

"Jesus." Victor wiped away a tear. "Four days! He knew the fire could never burn that long."

Bernie seemed about to say something, but did not.

Victor's gaze went to the sheet on the floor, covering Marco's body. "How come I'm alive and he's not?"

"You were stronger," Bernie said.

Victor looked very surprised, like someone had given him a gift out of the blue. He turned to Bernie. "He got incoherent at the end—slurring his words, mostly just the one phrase."

"Which was?" Bernie said.

"Flight into Egypt," said Victor.

"What did he mean by that?"

"I don't know. I'd been meaning to look it up. He asked me if I'd heard of it the first time we met."

Bernie rose, went to a window, wet now from the melting frost. "Lauritz never said where to dig?"

Victor shook his head. "Marco thought it was all a bluff, too late, of course. Lauritz just wanted the book. Marco did steal it, by the way. He was kind of proud of it. 'I had to have it.' That's what he said. Do you know anything about the book, Bernie?"

Bernie shook his head. Had he forgotten it was in the safe at home, behind the lovely waterfall painting? Nobody's perfect. Except Bernie. So he must have forgotten for a very good reason! That's him every time.

"Come on, Victor," he said. "There's a hospital in Rosetta. Let's get you checked out."

"No hospital. I'm fine." Victor rose. Or tried to. But he couldn't stand on his own.

It was night, dark and starless, by the time we got Victor admitted to the hospital.

"Gonna call your mom?" Bernie said.

Victor, in a wheelchair, looked down. "It'll just confirm what she thinks of me."

Bernie knelt so they were eye to eye. "You know better, Victor. She'll be nothing but happy."

"Are you sure?"

Bernie nodded. "But no details about the case."

"It's not over, is it?"

"No."

Victor squared his shoulders, tried to look strong. "You hear one crime leads to another like dominos," he said. "But I'm starting to think it's more like a mutating virus."

"Get some rest," Bernie said.

Twenty-six

"Everyone's missing the same piece, big guy," Bernie said. "The whole gang—and that's what they are, torn apart by greed—has got provenance nailed down, but the rest—the payoff—is all about faith. What happens when faith gets completely detached from fact?"

I had no idea. And hadn't we missed a meal somewhere along the way? Whoa! Meals were a fact—maybe the biggest fact out there—and here we were, detached from them! All at once I understood Bernie completely.

"It's like a balloon floating free," he said. "They drift higher and higher but they always burst in the end."

Meaning we were going to chow down, and real soon, or not?

"Meaning," Bernie went on, "that we're as informed as any of them—maybe more—so why not take a swing at it ourselves?"

That was the meaning? Nothing about chowing down? I curled up on the shotgun seat and tried not to think about food. That went on for some time, and then the motion of the Porsche took over and rocked me to sleep.

The motion came to an end. I opened my eyes, rose to a sitting position. We were back down in warm country, a beautiful night with a soft breeze and a full moon. Once Bernie had said to Charlie, "Imagine if we had two moons," and Charlie had said, "Do I have to?" I missed Charlie, but I knew this wouldn't have been a good time to have him along. First, it felt pretty late. Second, looming before us stood the church of Nuestra Señora de los Saguaros, not really a huge building, although its moon shadow was much bigger, stretching far across the fields in a way that made me uneasy. In short, not the time or place for kids.

We got out of the car, neither of us actually hopping, Bernie because he hardly ever did, and me on account of the powerful snaky scent in the air, kind of discouraging, although I never sink all the way down to discouragement. Bernie opened the trunk and took out our folding spade and the headlamp, which he strapped to his head but didn't switch on. We moved toward the door of the church. The wind rose slightly, whining in the bell tower high above.

The scarred old wooden door was padlocked, not a surprise. Bernie tugged at the lock. It didn't give. We walked around the church, past the wheelbarrows, the picks and shovels, the sand pile, the roped-off pits.

"There's something frantic about all this digging," Bernie said. "Missed that the first time." We came to the trailer. No lights shone inside, and I smelled and heard no one. Bernie didn't knock or even try the knob. He just put his shoulder to the door, one of our trailer park techniques. The door opened with a loud crack that got my tail going, big-time. Bernie switched on the headlamp. There wasn't much to see, and we didn't spend time looking. As soon as Bernie found the heavy rusted key hanging on a wall hook we were out of there.

Back at Nuestra Señora's door, Bernie stuck the key in the padlock and turned it. Moments later the door was creaking open. We stepped inside. Shadows pressed down from the roof and inward from the sides, squeezing out all light except for the headlamp. We followed its beam toward the roped-off pits.

"According to Father Henry, the crypt must have been here," Bernie said. "Meaning the stone with 'Merisi' carved on it must have been somewhere on that wall." We both gazed at the wall, where some rows of stones were missing, replaced by two-by-fours. Stone blocks were scattered around the pit. Bernie climbed down, unfolded the spade, and began digging.

I love digging. And I'm good at it. Normally I'd have been down there digging side by side with Bernie, but how could I do that and guard him against snakes at the same time? I stayed up top, pacing back and forth along the edge, waiting for the appearance of the first snaky head.

At first Bernie dug at a nice pace, tossing out spadeful after spadeful, but after a while he slowed down. "This is too easy," he said. "It feels already dug, like she—"

The headlamp went out. For a moment we had total darkness, and during that moment a ray of moonlight poked into Nuestra Señora through a tiny hole in the roof high above. It shone down on a nearby bench seat, turning it silver.

Bernie spoke, not loudly, but his voice filled the church. "The false penitent buried it by the light of the moon. By the light of the moon, Chet."

He scrambled out of the pit, trying and failing to get the headlamp working, hurried through the darkness to the bench seat, kicked it aside, pried up the worn floor tiles that lay in the circle of moonlight, and began digging. Who could hold back at a time like this? I pushed right in and got to work, first with just my front paws and then, as we got deeper, with all of them, dirt and little stones and dust flying and whirling and dancing in the moonlight. We were going to be rich, although what we were digging for escaped my mind. Did that matter? Why would it? We dug and dug and—*clang*.

Bernie went still. "Bedrock?" He tried another spot and then another. *Clang* and *clang*. "Bedrock."

Bedrock turned out to be bad. We climbed out of the hole—the rim now above my head—and just stood there breathing.

"We're missing something, big guy," Bernie said.

We walked out of the church. The moon still shone brightly but a line of clouds, foamy-colored at the lead edge but otherwise very dark, was sliding across the sky, putting out the stars. We headed around Nuestra Señora, Bernie deep in thought and me not. When we reached the back, I took a little detour across the dirt road and over to the broken old building stones beside the giant saguaro. I decided to mark those stones, for no reason, really, just to make myself useful. And then I picked up that faint linen aroma I'd noticed before, an aroma that reminded me of Bernie's only suit, as I may have mentioned. I pawed at the hard desert ground, not because I expected to find the suit, most likely hanging in the closet back home, but . . . but you never knew! Wow! What a thought! You never knew! Imagine that!

I began digging for real. Yes, getting into it! How much fun to stir things up! I dug and dug, dug like it was a competition and I was the champ—Chet, champ of the digging world! Wow! Didn't that sound totally right? I ramped it up, if you can believe it, clawing and pawing and clawing and pawing and—and thwack. Thwack? A woody sort of thwack, kind of strange, but I ignored it and went back to work—or was this play?—digging and—

"Chet? What are you doing?"

I looked up. Whoa! Way up. And on the rim of this deepish pit we now seemed to have, stood Bernie, gazing down.

What was I doing? Well, digging. Digging on my own time, if that made any—

"Chet?" Bernie pointed down to the floor of the pit. "What's that?"

I looked down. It appeared to be—

But before I could get any further, Bernie was beside me. He got down, scratched and dug with his bare hands, then grunted and raised something out of the earth, namely a thin wooden box, longer than it was wide. Very old wood, I should add, cracked and whitened. We climbed out of the hole and Bernie laid the box down in the moonlight, carefully, like it was made of glass.

Bernie knelt beside the box. I knelt beside Bernie. He took the spade and gently wedged the tip into a corner of the box, where two sides met. Wriggle, wriggle, wriggle, and all at once the whole box sort of fell apart. Inside was some sort of package wrapped in an unusual thick and yellowed wrapping.

"Smell that?" Bernie said, his voice quiet but with a deep throb of excitement at its core. "Linen, Chet. It's old sailcloth."

That was a first, Bernie explaining a smell to me. I got the wonderful feeling that the Little Detective Agency was just getting started.

Were Bernie's hands shaking a bit as he unwrapped the package? I didn't believe it, but a lot of time seemed to pass before he'd removed the sailcloth and laid it aside.

And there on the stony desert ground lay a painting, not particularly big, and framed with a simple wooden frame, the wood whitened but not cracked. There were three people in the painting, walking from one side to the other. In the lead was a woman with a baby in her arms. She leaned forward a bit, maybe because they were going uphill, the ground rough, in fact a lot like the ground we were on right now, me and Bernie. Behind her came a man. He was looking back and there was fear on his face, like something bad was coming. But here's something odd I noticed, maybe on account of faces being important in our line of work. The face of this man looked pretty much the same as the face of Goliath, except maybe a little older, and of course alive and not dead. What else? There was a big moon up above, casting silvery moonlight here and there, although most of the picture was darkness. Hey! Kind of like right now, out here behind Nuestra Señora. And I shouldn't leave out one last thing. Rising behind the woman and the baby and the man stood a saguaro, the two-armed kind with both arms out to the side, just like the one we had right here with us.

"It's like we're in it," Bernie said. "Or they're out here." He glanced around, but it was just us. Bernie took my head in his hands. "Flight into Egypt with a saguaro, big guy. Who's a good good boy?"

That would be me.

"And see this?" Bernie pointed to a corner of the painting. "He signed it." Bernie sat back on his heels, took a long long look at the painting lying there in the moonlight but also making moonlight of its own, and very softly began to sing: "It came upon a midnight clear."

Twenty-seven

We wrapped the painting back in sailcloth, Bernie handling the actual wrapping and me watching how carefully he did it. Then he tucked the painting under one arm, gathered up the pieces of the broken box, returned to the car, set the painting on the little shelf in back and the wooden pieces on the floor. After that he padlocked the door of Nuestra Señora, but didn't return the big, rusty key, instead throwing it into the night. The whining of the wind in the bell tower was getting louder. My ears weren't happy about that, although the rest of me was pretty close to tip-top. We hit the road.

"Are we in the driver's seat?" Bernie said. "Sure feels that way."

Well, of course it felt like that to him. I myself, as Bernie had to know, was in the shotgun seat. I waited for him to clear up the confusion, but before he could the phone buzzed.

"Bernie? It's me. Victor."

"Why are you whispering?"

"Shh. Keep your voice down."

"Victor? Something wrong?"

"Just practicing due diligence."

"I can't hear you."

"Due diligence. I ducked into the bathroom but it doesn't lock, some sort of hospital protocol."

"Speak up."

"Shh. I don't want her to hear. Not until I know it's kosher."

"Who are you talking about?"

"Your assistant."

Bernie pressed harder on the gas. We shot forward on the old De Niza highway, long and straight in the night.

"Describe her," Bernie said.

"You want me to describe your assistant? Tall, blond, good looking, nice tan. She says you sent her to drive me down to your place. I'm just being extra careful. It's all been a bit unnerving, if you want the truth."

"Victor. Do not leave the hospital."

"No?"

"Don't even leave the bathroom."

"Don't leave the bathroom?"

"Is there a button to push?"

"Button?"

"Or a string to pull? For the nurse."

"There's a string."

"Pull it."

"Now?"

"Now."

Silence. We merged onto a freeway, pedal to the metal. Over the phone came sounds of movement, a door opening, a footstep or two.

"Mr. Klovsky?" a woman said. "Are you all right?"

"Bernie? The nurse is here."

"Mr. Klovsky?"

"Victor," Bernie said. "Is the other woman out there?"

"Your assistant?"

"We don't have an assistant. Answer the question."

"Um. Looks like she's gone. What's going on?"

"Go back to bed. Do not leave the hospital. We're on our way."

"Good thing I called, huh?" said Victor.

Bernie clicked off.

The clouds, like an enormous roof, slid across the sky, finally covering it completely and shutting off the moonlight. The air grew colder and colder and soon some sort of black ashes were flying at us through the headlight beams. I didn't like the look of that, not one little bit.

"No worries, Chet. It's just snow."

Snow? Snow could be black ashes in the air? I'd only seen snow white and lying peacefully on the ground. I turned sideways and looked through the window. The black ashes turned to white flakes in front of my eyes, and snow was covering everything in sight— the red rocks, the trees branches, even the road itself—covering the whole world, fast and deep. We were climbing now, climbing Redhawk Mountain, the back end of the car kind of developing a mind of its own, like it wanted to go somewhere else. Bernie had both hands on the wheel. You didn't see that every day.

We came into Rosetta, no members of the nation within in sight, no humans, not a light showing.

"Power failure," Bernie said. "But the hospital'll have a generator."

The hospital appeared on the far edge of town, a small, low brick building, with snow piling up on the roof, lights glowing faintly in some of the windows, and the reddish bar light over the entrance flickering. Snow whipped and swirled around us, and even going their fastest the wipers couldn't keep the windshield clear. The hospital parking lot, small, unlit, tucked into the woods, was empty. Bernie pulled in, the tires going crunch crunch, and parked.

He twisted around to the little shelf in back. "Better not leave the painting," he said. "Wouldn't it be crazy after all this . . ."

I missed whatever would or wouldn't be crazy because a movement in the woods on the other side of the parking lot caught my attention. A shadowy movement and not easy to make out with no lights and all the blowing snow. The air was full of smells, all mixed up, but was I picking up a trace of one certain smell, very important in our line of work? First I thought so. Then I didn't. I pressed my nose to the side window, rolled up, of course, which didn't help. I sniffed and sniffed and yes, picked up that smell, almost for sure. At the same time a dark form appeared at the edge of the woods.

I barked a bark that couldn't be missed.

Bernie whirled around to look. Right then the dark form moved. What little light there was glinted on a rifle barrel.

"Down!" Bernie yelled, and he put his hand behind my head and pushed me onto the floor, with astonishing power and none too gently. Then he leaned over and covered me with his body, just as—

BLAM!

Blam of the rifle, followed immediately by the windshield shattering, glass flying everywhere.

BLAM!

The whole car shuddered, like a wounded creature. And yes, the Porsche was a sort of creature, a creature that meant a lot to me and Bernie. I started to get mad and tried to wriggle my way out from under Bernie and get busy with what needed to be done.

"No, Chet! Stop!"

BLAM! Now my window shattered, little pellets of it stinging through my fur. I don't mean stinging. Little glass pellets could never hurt me. But the poor old Porsche shook again.

Bernie grunted, fumbled around, trying to free the .38 Special. I squeezed against the door, tried to make myself small. The .38 Special slid out from between us. Without raising his head Bernie poked the barrel out the window and laid down a real quick POW POW POW, like a whole army! POW POW! The roar of the .38 Special filled the night.

"Stay down," Bernie said, his voice right in my ear. He rolled off me, ducked behind the wheel, cranked 'er up, roared us out of the parking lot and—

But oh no. Not out of the parking lot, because a big black SUV blocked the way.

"Chet! Didn't I say down?"

If true, that was a complicating factor. We had no time for complicating factors because all kinds of things were happening fast, like Bernie jerking the wheel hard to one side, bouncing us off a fire hydrant, which spun us across snow and ice, whirling and whirling, right around the SUV and onto the street. The face of the SUV driver was green in the glow of the dashboard light: Johanna. Francesco was sitting beside her. He pointed a gun out the window. *CRACK CRACK*. Our rear window blew out. Bernie tried to get us facing down the road, but the car fishtailed around, and we ended up pointing the other way, up the mountain. Johanna closed in, the SUV like a tower right behind us. Bernie stomped on the gas and we shot up the road, sliding from one side to the other and back. Johanna throttled down, but it was only for the rifleman, sprinting out of the parking lot. As he threw open the rear door of the SUV to jump in, the interior lights flashed on and lit him up. It was Vito, with his handlebar mustache, thick with snow, and his cruel eyes.

"You all right?" Bernie said as we flew out of town, the Porsche really feeling airborne, the air itself snowy and icy and blowing freely through openings where windows used to be.

What was the question? Was I all right? Never better was the answer.

Not that there weren't problems. For one thing, we no longer seemed to have a rearview mirror. Bernie glanced back over his shoulder. And so did I, hardly needs mentioning. A pair of headlights shone behind us, but nicely dim and distant. When we hit the switchbacks above Rosetta the headlights disappeared completely. I began to think about food.

Bernie glanced at me and smiled. "Two small problems. One, we took the bait. That's in the past. Two, we're going up, not down. That's in the present and can still be fixed."

Bait? Like worms wriggling in a can? I remembered no such thing in this case. But if Bernie said worms were involved, then that was that. The good news? I was picking up not the slightest wormy scent. We were cookin'. Imagine our situation if we had a whole mess of worms wriggling around in the car!

Meanwhile we were switchbacking up and up, snowy wind howling through the car, Bernie hunched over the wheel, squinting ahead into the wild scene in the headlight beams, the engine shrieking, and—this was the scary part, well, not actually scary, maybe just a bit worrying—the tires fighting and fighting to keep us on the road, now deepening with snow. How fast the snow was piling up! The air was thick with it, like I was breathing snow air. As for speed, although it felt like we were zooming, when you looked to the side the forest was passing by quite slowly. I tried not to look to the side.

"Here's what we'll try," Bernie said. "On the next—"

I very much wanted to hear this plan, sure to be brilliant, but before Bernie could get to it, light flooded in from behind. We both glanced back. And there was the black SUV, so huge and almost on top of us.

"They've got chains," Bernie said, eyes front, hands and feet nonstop busy with the pedals, the wheel, the gear shift, doing his best to keep us on the road. We'd come across chain-wielding types before—a nasty weapon, for sure—but right now I was more concerned with the rifle poking out of one of the SUV's rear windows.

BLAM!

Not a very loud blam this time, almost smothered by the storm, howling now, but I heard the round buzz over our heads, so near, and then came a smack and a crack and a huge branch fell from above, landing with an enormous thud practically across the whole road. Bernie spun the wheel and my side of the Porsche rose right up, only the wheels on Bernie's side touching now, and—yes! We were going to squeeze through the tiny gap, make it clear to the other side and—

But no.

There was a thwack, not very loud but it made the Porsche shiver, and then we really were airborne, me, Bernie, and the car, all of us spinning high above the road and into the woods and darkness. Then came horrible sounds as the Porsche went crashing through the trees—I caught a shadowy glimpse of it, upside down and slicing off a treetop high above, headlights out, dashboard still glowing—but I myself landed quite softly in deep snow, so deep I had to dig my way out, which I did in no time at all, what with my digging skills and all. I gave myself a quick shake and . . . *Bernie? Bernie? Bernie!*

Whew! There he was, practically within touching distance, also digging himself out. I bounded over and helped. He rose and raised a finger—easy to see, the night not quite so dark here in the trees—and put it crosswise across his lips, meaning not a peep. Snow kept falling, less sideways now that we weren't in the open, whitening Bernie's hair and clinging to his clothes, maybe not quite the right clothes for this kind of night—jeans, sneakers, Hawaiian shirt. He took the .38 Special from his belt, checked the part that spins, the name escaping me at the moment. I could see for myself we had only one round left. We started walking, side by side, Bernie sinking to his knees on almost every step. Pieces of the Porsche lay here and there. And what was this? The painting, still wrapped, at least partly, in the sailcloth wrapper? How lucky was that? Bernie picked it up and tucked it under his arm. We kept going, higher and higher. Hadn't Bernie mentioned something about heading back down? I was fine either way. We moved on, leaning into the mountain, me in the lead, Bernie following with the painting.

He began to huff and puff a little bit. I turned to him and he gave me a quick grin, but on the very next step he sank to his waist. I was helping him dig out when a beam of yellow light passed right over our heads. A man yelled, Francesco for sure. I don't forget a voice, especially not a perp voice, and Francesco turned out to be as perpy as they come. Bernie wriggled himself free just as a second beam of light passed over us, followed by another, which hovered and came down and down and down, finally shining in our eyes.

BLAM!

The bullet tore through branches right by our heads. Then more yelling: Francesco again, Vito, Johanna. Bernie and I scrambled out of the light and deeper into the woods. We came to a big, snow-covered rock and crouched behind it.

Snick snick. Snick snick. What a strange sound, totally new to me! Whatever was making it closed in.

"Snowshoes," Bernie said, very softly. He peered around the rock. I squeezed in next to him and did the same.

A light appeared, coming our way. Then a second, but from another angle. And one more. Then I heard Francesco, very near.

"Idiots! He's got a gun."

All the lights went out.

Snick snick. Snick snick. Closer and closer. This was maybe not a good situation, but then all at once I understood Bernie's plan. We were going to let them pass right by us in the darkness and after that we'd mosey our way back down the mountain. Oh, the brilliance of the man!

Snick snick. Snick snick.

Around then I noticed that the night didn't actually seem so dark anymore. A kind of milky light was filtering down through trees. Also, a strange rumbling seemed to be happening deep down somewhere. We huddled behind the rock.

Snick snick. Snick snick. Louder and louder, and then Vito came in sight. He wore what looked like tennis rackets strapped to his boots, and moved easily on top of the snow, the rifle in his hands. He passed by our rock, so close I could hear his heart beating very fast, way faster than Bernie's. The plan was working. Vito was going to keep going, on and on into the woods. I felt pretty excited inside.

Can someone feel your excitement, even if you're keeping it inside? I didn't know, but for whatever reason Vito stopped abruptly. He turned, kind of slowly, and saw us.

Everything sped up, got going so fast it was hard to keep up. Vito smiled at us, his teeth very dark in this milky light, but his cruel eyes shining. Bernie rolled out from behind the rock. I sprang the other way, spreading out how we did at times like this. Now, out in the open I could make out Francesco approaching, a gun in his hand, and Johanna, some distance away. Vito swung around toward Bernie, raising the rifle. Bernie whipped the .38 from his belt and fired his last round.

It must have hit Vito, although I couldn't see where. He sank to his knees but still had the rifle. The look on his face was horrible, all about loving bad things. He pointed the rifle at Bernie, so close he could almost have touched him with the muzzle, then put his finger on the trigger and—

And I sprang, a tremendous spring out of the snow, one of

my very longest, hitting Vito hard, yet maybe not as solidly as I'd hoped.

BLAM!

No, not as solidly as I'd hoped. I heard the sound of a bullet smashing through flesh and bone. Oh no! Too late! Too late! Too late!

But . . . but there was Bernie, rising to his feet, unharmed. I turned and saw a small red eruption still blooming from the side of Francesco's head. He toppled over. Johanna screamed, pivoted, and started snick-snicking away as fast as she could go. In the distance I could see the clear white mountain through the trees, very steep. Then came another deep-down shiver.

"Stop!" Bernie called.

But Johanna did not.

Vito lay flat on his back now, eyes no longer cruel, just glassy. The snow beneath him grew redder and redder. I went over, picked up the rifle, and carried it to Bernie. He rose, took it, and heaved it away with all his strength. Vito watched our every move. And then he didn't.

Bernie said nothing. I made no sound. There was more than enough sound already, the storm somehow louder than ever. We went after Johanna. She was far ahead and moving much faster than us. We were almost at the edge of the woods when we spotted her, out on the steep, treeless slope and snick-snicking fast toward more trees on the other side.

"No!" Bernie called. "Stop!"

Johanna glanced around to look at us but didn't stop. I felt another rumble, not as deep down as before. Johanna turned her head slightly to gaze up the mountain. The expression on her face changed into one you'd never want to see on anybody. Bernie stepped past the last tree and so did I. We peered up the mountain. The whole huge snowy top was coming down.

"Johanna!"

She didn't move.

But we did, and fast. Bernie grabbed my collar and pulled me into the trees. Actually it was me pulling him, pulling my hardest.

Still, we hadn't gotten very far before a tremendous roar started up, like the whole earth was roaring and roaring, and the white mountain top came flooding down, snapping off all the trees between us and the steep slope.

And then: complete silence. Nothing moved, except for one tiny snowball, rolling and tumbling the mountain. We stood alone in the bare, still, smooth whiteness, me and Bernie. There was no sign of Johanna at all.

The wind died down. The snow let up but didn't stop completely. All was calm and peaceful, although not bright. It was a dark morning. We found our way to the road and walked down Redhawk Mountain, me first, Bernie following with the painting. Didn't it have a name? "Flight Into Egypt," maybe? I wondered what it was about. Then I tried rolling in the snow. It felt great. I threw in some wriggling. That felt even greater.

Twenty-eight

We propped up the painting against the toaster in our kitchen and left the front door open so friends and neighbors could come in and take a look. Iggy, both a friend and a neighbor, was one of the very first, although his visit was brief. Of all the visitors, the one who got the most pleasure out of "Flight Into Egypt" was Rui, Nixon Panero's paint guy. He parked himself on a kitchen stool and stayed the whole time. With a shotgun across his knees, I should mention. Rui had worries about security, kind of crazy, what with me in the house.

I shouldn't leave out the booze. Or all the gifts people brought. Father Henry was too sick to come, but he sent a beautiful tree, all decorated. In between getting hugged and kissed and patted on the back, Bernie stripped off all the decorations and put them on again, but in the way he liked. At one point I heard Weatherly, Suzie, and Leda discussing that. "I don't understand him at all these days," Leda said. "He seems to be changing a bit," said Suzie. Weatherly just smiled.

Suzie got the scoop, of course, and it turned out to be big news in the art world, which was maybe not huge, and in the money world, which was—you don't need me to tell you that. She didn't stay long because she had work to do on her party, the one with some sort of snow under a dome. I'll try to get to what happened there a little later.

Meanwhile Nixon managed to haul most of the Porsche down off Redhawk Mountain, but there was nothing he could do.

"Can you find us another one?" Bernie said. "Maybe a little older?"

"What the hell are you talking about?" Nixon said. "I'll build you the best car on the planet from scratch."

"Sounds expensive."

"What do you care?" Nixon jerked his thumb at the painting. "They say that thing's worth a hundred mill, at least."

"We're not keeping it."

"Course not. Take a picture off your phone. You can look at it anytime you like. When you need a break from counting the money."

"Experts still need to examine it."

"Here's to experts," Nixon said. He clinked glasses with Bernie. "Here's a tip. They say what they think will advance their careers. Merry Christmas."

Around then was when Bernie noticed the envelope with the $10K inside, no longer on the kitchen table but for some reason lying by my water bowl. He took out the cash, riffled through it, and said, "Here's what we're gonna do."

What we did with the $10K was throw the biggest Christmas party you ever saw. Did you know, for example, that Esmé's dad was a jazz trumpeter, her mom turning out to be an actual rocket scientist? At one point, Bernie found out that Esmé's dad could play the Roy Eldridge solo from "If You Were Mine." How many times did we end up hearing him play that? Bernie took the Billie Holiday part, handled it extremely well in my opinion.

Experts did come, by the way, from all over. Experts were new to me. They loved champagne, and also Weatherly's pecan and pinon tarts which she baked nonstop in our oven. They peered at "Flight Into Egypt" every which way, examined it through magnifying glasses, drank more champagne, got wasted, sang Christmas songs in many languages. The hora, which I'd witnessed at the Muertos party the night we ran into Victor, got danced in our kitchen, in fact, throughout the house. I hadn't realized the hora was such an important part of Christmas. You're always learning things in our line of work.

Some of the Muertos guys and gals showed up. Bernie explained about no motorcycles in the house. I could tell from their faces they didn't get it, but none of them made a fuss. They brought a number of cases—way more than two—of the bourbon

Bernie likes. Some of the cases looked a bit battered, like they'd had a fall of some sort, off a truck, for example, but the bottles themselves—at least all the ones that got opened at the party— were in good shape.

Victor and Elise dropped by. "I don't know what to say," Victor said.

"That's enough right there," said Bernie.

"We can never repay you," said Elise. "But at least here's your fee."

Bernie held up his hand in the stop sign. "Consider me repaid."

"Victor insists," Elise said.

"Mom," Victor said. "I can say it myself. I insist."

Bernie took the check. "Uh, mazel toff," he said.

"It's pronounced *tov*," said Elise.

"Ah," said Bernie, sticking the check in his shirt pocket. I wasn't happy to see that. We'd had problems with checks and shirt pockets in the past.

When Katherine Cornwall came over, we took her down the hall to the office.

"Here's the ship's log," Bernie said.

"Right," said Katherine. "You've shown it to me."

"Take it."

"Thank you, Bernie," she said, "but my understanding is it should go back to the Prado. I'm sure there'll be a reward."

"Um," said Bernie. "Uh. What about the painting?"

"What about it?"

"You can take the painting, can't you? Isn't it part of Sonoran history?"

"Bernie. It's worth tens of millions, a hundred million, maybe more. There isn't a museum in the country that could afford it."

"Oh," Bernie said. "But the thing is, I meant, ah, sorry, I wasn't clear. You know. A gift."

"A gift?"

Bernie leaned across the desk. "On one condition. It hangs somewhere in the museum where people don't have to pay to see it."

Katherine Cornwall, a no-nonsense type of woman if there ever was one, burst into tears right there in our office.

Not long after that, some of us paid a visit to Suzie's party, the one with snow blowing machines under a dome. Les Erlanger, the new senator, or perhaps soon to be the new senator, possibly on account of us and a ferret name of Griffie, way too complicated to go into now, was at Suzie's party and real happy to meet us. Bernie wasn't as happy to meet him, but you'd have to know Bernie real well to spot that, and of course I do.

"Heard what you did for Katherine's museum," he said. "Isn't she great?"

Bernie nodded.

"In case you're worried about any litigation regarding ownership," Erlanger said, "put your mind at ease. That lot across from Nuestra Señora was repossessed for nonpayment of taxes a few years ago. I guarantee there won't be any problems. What else can I do for you?"

"Merry Christmas," Bernie said.

Have I mentioned that Trixie and Shooter were also at Suzie's party? They'd never seen snow before, although this snow didn't feel quite right under my paws. But never mind that, the point being I had to show them how to roll in snow, how to wriggle in it, how to roll and wriggle at the same time, how to roll and wriggle and then race around crazily, followed by more rolling and wriggling and shaking off the snow from our coats every which way, and then doing the whole routine over and over again. We were just getting started, in my opinion, when we had to leave quite suddenly.

Back at our party, Bernie gave Charlie what he wanted for Christmas, namely a driving lesson. Since we had no car at the moment, Bernie borrowed a golf cart from one of the neighbors and taught Charlie out on the street, all blocked off by that time, thanks to some PD buddies. Charlie couldn't steer and reach the pedals at the same time, so Bernie got down on the floor and did the pedal part with his hands.

"Faster, Charlie!" Esmé screamed. Did I mention she was in the shotgun seat while I had to manage on the rear-facing seat in back? "Pedal to the metal, Bernie! Pedal to the metal!" We careened up and down Mesquite Road. I barked my head off.

By the time Christmas dinner rolled around, things had quieted down some. The air was loaded with wonderful smells, the best ones coming off the enormous deep-fried turkey waiting to be carved, a deep frying that Bernie had managed beautifully until almost the very end. Weatherly sat next to him at the head of the table.

"Haven't had a chance to get you a present yet," Bernie said.

"What are you talking about?" Weatherly undid the top few buttons of her shirt. The pine cone hung around her neck.

"I could do a Fabergé thing with that," said Rui from the other end of the table. "While you wait."

"Thank you, Rui," Weatherly said. "I like it just the way it is." Then she took what looked like a big Christmas card from her bag, a Christmas card with a photo and a red border. "This is for you, Bernie. Freddy did most of the work—"

"But it was her idea," Freddy called from somewhere down the table, where he'd just said something that made Mrs. Parsons laugh and laugh.

Bernie looked at the card. So did I. In the photo stood a bunch of young men, all in uniform. Whoa! Was that Bernie in the middle? Looking almost like a kid? He turned the card over. There was writing on the back.

"They all signed," Weatherly said. "All the . . . survivors."

Uh-oh. Was Bernie about to cry? I felt huge forces in him. He ended up not crying but I think it was close. He laid his hand on Weatherly's.

Rover and Company had baked me a special Christmas biscuit,

so big it was decorated with tiny red and green biscuits, a thing of beauty. The only problem was that they'd made the mistake of also baking special Christmas biscuits for Trixie and Shooter and I liked theirs just as much as mine, or possibly even more. That led to me taking five out onto the patio. Very soon after, something happened in the house, and Trixie and Shooter emerged to take five of their own.

Have I mentioned our back gate, a very very high gate? For a long time the belief in these parts was that no one—obviously not a human, but also no member of the nation within—could possibly jump that gate. But one certain someone had proved that it could be jumped—by that one certain someone. Among many other things, that's the reason Shooter's . . . well, Shooter. A story for another time, perhaps. Meanwhile, do I have to cough up the name of our wonderful leaper, or can you guess?

I gave Shooter and Trixie a look that said, *The party's over. Time for you dudes to split.* They didn't seem to notice my look. What does anyone think at a moment like this, when anyone is not even being noticed? Anyone thinks I'll show them! Which was why, without another thought, I turned and leaped over the gate, clearing the top by plenty, amigo.

After that, out in the canyon back of our place, I pranced around a bit. You'd have done the same. I was still prancing when something happened that was so outrageous I don't even want to mention it. Maybe I'll just keep it to myself.

But if you really want to know, here goes. I happened to glance at the gate and what did I see? Shooter and Trixie leaping over it, side by side. And the worst part? They had candy canes in their mouths! We in the nation within don't even like candy canes. They were out of their minds. I'll leave the part about how I set them straight and in no uncertain terms to your imagination.

ACKNOWLEDGMENTS

Many thanks to my very smart editor, Kristin Sevick, my excellent publicist, Libby Collins, and to Linda Quinton at Forge for her much appreciated support of Chet and Bernie. And also thanks to my father, Edward Abrahams, for some research help. Hope I got it right, Dad.

Turn the page for a sneak peek
at the next Chet & Bernie mystery

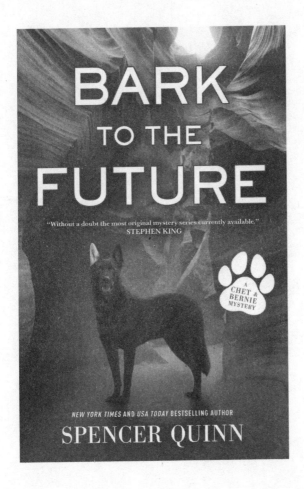

Available now from Forge Books

One

"Let's see what this baby can do," Bernie said.

And there you have it. Bernie's brilliance, lighting up the whole oil-stained yard at Nixon's Championship Autobody. *Let's see what this baby can do.* Can you imagine anyone else saying that? I sure can't. I wouldn't even try, and who knows Bernie better than me? Sometimes humans talk to themselves, as you may or may not know. Humans have a lot going on in their heads. Too much? I couldn't tell you. But I wouldn't trade places. Let's leave it at that. The point is that when they're talking to themselves they're trying to dig down through all the too-muchness and get to what's at the bottom, digging, as it happens, being one of my very best things. Maybe we'll get to that later. For now, the takeaway is that Bernie talks to himself in front of me. So I know what's at the bottom of Bernie, way down deep, case closed. Closing cases is what we do, by the way, me and Bernie. We're partners in the Little Detective Agency—Little on account of that's Bernie's last name. Call me Chet, pure and simple. Our cases usually get closed by me grabbing the perp by the pant leg. Although there were no perps around right now and we weren't even working a case, my teeth got a funny feeling.

Nixon Panero, owner of the shop and our good buddy, patted the hood of our new Porsche. We've had others—maybe more than I can count, since things get iffy when I try to go past two—but never one this old. Could I even remember them all? Perhaps not, although I have a very clear picture of the last one in my mind, upside down and soaring through snowy treetops, the windows all blasted out and me and Bernie also in midair, although slightly closer to the ground. I'd miss that Porsche—especially the martini glass decals on the fenders—but this one, with an interesting black and white pattern, as though a normal PD squad car was rippling its muscles, if that makes any sense, looked none too shabby. In fact, and in a strange dreamlike way, a thing of beauty. And to top it off, my seat—the shotgun seat, goes without mentioning—couldn't have been more comfortable, the leather soft and firm at the same time, and possibly quite tasty. A no-no, and I forgot that whole idea at once.

"One last thing," Nixon said.

Bernie, hands on the wheel, ready to go, glanced up at him.

"All parts guaranteed original and authentic," Nixon said. "Excepting certain aspects of the engine."

"No problem," Bernie said. "You're the expert."

"Thanks, Bernie. But what I'm saying is in horsepower terms authentic might be stretching it the teensiest bit. So my advice would be to take it on the easy side at first."

"Sure thing," Bernie said, sliding his foot over to the gas pedal.

"On account of what we've got here," Nixon began, "is kind of a—"

Beast? Was that what Nixon said? I couldn't be sure, because at that moment Bernie's foot—he was wearing flip flops, one new-looking, the other old and worn—touched the pedal, just the lightest touch to my way of thinking, but enough to get our new engine excited in no uncertain terms. It roared a tremendous roar and this new dreamlike ride of ours shot out of Nixon's yard and into the street. I felt like my head was getting left behind, meaning that shooting out doesn't really do the job here. Was it possible we were actually off the ground? I believed we were.

"Woo eee!" Bernie cried as he brought us safely down, all tires on the pavement. "Woo eee, baby!"

As for me, I got my head and body properly organized, sat up straight, and howled at the moon, although it was daytime and cloudy to boot. We had a beast on our side. No one could touch us now, although the truth was no one ever had before. I felt tip-top, or even better.

"My god," said Bernie as we came off a two-laner that had taken us deep into the desert and far from the Valley, where we live, and merged onto a freeway, the tops of the downtown towers visible in the distance, their lower parts lost in the brassy haze. "Can you believe what just happened?" We slowed down to what seemed like nothing, although we were zooming past everyone else. Bernie patted the dash and glanced my way. "Rough beast, big guy, its hour come round at last." That one zipped right by me, but Bernie laughed so it must have been funny. "Did we hit one forty? Next time I'll snap a picture of the speedometer. You'll have to take the wheel."

No problem. That had actually happened once, if very briefly, down Mexico way, where Bernie and I had had to leave a nice little cantina in somewhat of a hurry, following a misunderstanding between Bernie, a very friendly lady, and a late-arriving gentleman who turned out to be her husband and also the head of the local cartel. Bottom line: Bernie could count on me.

Not long after that we were winding slowly down the ramp at the Rio Vista Bridge, close to home. There's always a backup on the ramp, and at the bottom a few leathery-skinned men holding paper cups or sometimes cardboard signs are waiting. Today there was only one, a real skinny barefoot guy, wearing frayed cargo shorts and nothing else, his shoulders the boniest

I'd ever seen. He was mostly bald, but had a ponytail happening at the back, a gray ponytail with yellow-stained ends, the same yellow you see on the fingertips of smokers. Also—and maybe the first thing I noticed—a small but jagged scar across the bridge of his nose. A cigarette was hanging from the side of his mouth but its tiny fire had gone out. Traffic came to a stop when we were right beside him. He looked down at us, his eyes watery blue. I was pretty sure I hadn't seen him before, and certain I'd never smelled him. My nose is never wrong on things like that. In this case it wasn't even a close call. Had I ever picked up a human scent so . . . how would you put it? Complex? Rich? Over the top? You pick. As for me, I was starting to like this dude a lot. Meanwhile Bernie dug out a few bills from the cup holder and handed them over.

Except not quite. Yes, Bernie held out the money, but the dude made no move to grab it. Instead he shook his head and said, "Can't take your money, Bernie."

"Excuse me?" Bernie said.

The dude took the cigarette out of his mouth, plucked a little twist of something from between two chipped and yellowed teeth, and said it again.

Bernie gave him a close look. "Do I know you?" he said.

"Guess not," said the dude. He glanced down at the money, still in Bernie's outstretched hand, and his lips curled in a sort of sneer, like that money was way beneath him. "But I'll take a light," he said.

Bernie stuck the money back in the cup holder, fumbled around inside, found a book of matches and held them out. The guy took the matches, broke one off, but he couldn't get it lit, his hands suddenly very shaky. In front us traffic started moving. From behind came honking, not easy on my ears. Bernie pulled off the ramp, getting us mostly onto the narrow dirt strip next to the bridge supports. He opened the door, put one foot on the ground, and looked back at me.

"Better stay, Chet."

Too late. Meanwhile the traffic from behind was on the move, perhaps still slightly blocked by us, but hardly at all. A truck driver leaned out of his window, an unpleasant expression on his face. He opened his mouth to say something, saw me, and changed his mind.

"Here," said Bernie, holding out his hand.

"Here what?" said the dude.

"The matches."

The dude handed over the matches. Bernie lit one, cupped the flame. The dude leaned in, got his cigarette going. For a moment, his face—so weathered, wrinkled, with little blotches here and there—was almost touching Bernie's hand, so perfect. The dude straightened, took a deep drag, let it out slow, smoke streaming from his nostrils.

"Waiting for me to say thanks?" said the dude.

"No," said Bernie.

"Then get back in your super-duper car." He glanced over at me, turned away, then gave me another look. "The both of you."

"In a hurry to get rid of us?" Bernie said.

The dude was silent for what seemed like a long time. Then came a bit of a surprise. He smiled. Not a big smile, and lots of teeth were missing and the tip of his tongue was yellow-brown, but he no longer looked quite so messed up.

"You haven't changed," he said. "Always those goddamn questions."

"For example?"

The dude thought for a moment or two. Then he stiffened and shouted at Bernie, a shout with a sort of whispery, ragged edge, so not particularly loud, but real angry. "You makin' fun of me, Bernie? That's another question you just asked. Think I'm nothin' but . . . but . . ." Whatever it was, he couldn't come up with it.

"Sorry," Bernie said, "I didn't—"

The dude's eyes narrowed down to two watery slits. "You was always an asshole but not mean. What the hell happened?"

"Look," Bernie said, "I—"

"Aw, the hell with it," the dude said, his anger vanishing all at once. He waved his hand—fingers bent, nails thick and yellow—in a throwaway gesture. "You stood up for me. I don't forget things like that. Well, I do. I forget . . . you name it." He laughed a croaky laugh that got croakier until he finally spat out a brownish gob. It landed at the base of one of the bridge supports. I moved in that direction. At the same time, the dude took a very deep drag, blew out a thick smoke ball, peered through it at Bernie, then wagged his finger. "But I sure as shit remember that time with Raker."

"Coach Raker?" Bernie said.

"Who the hell else are we jawin' about?" said the dude. "He was gonna bench me for showin' up late to the game against Central Tech and you said hey coach bench me I forgot to pick him up on the way to school. Which wasn't even true. No way you don't remember that. You were on the mound and don't deny it. Two outs, bottom of the ninth, bases loaded, up one zip, and some dude hits a scorcher in the gap and who runs it down?" The dude tapped his skinny chest. "Game over. Took us to the state, uh, whatever it is."

Bernie has wonderful eyebrows, with a language all their own. Now they were saying a whole bunch, but amazement was a big part of it.

"Championship," he said softly.

"Yeah, state championship, what I said," said the dude. "Next year you guys won it but I was . . . was . . . like movin' on."

"Rocket?" Bernie said. "Rocket Saluka?"

The dude—Rocket Saluka, if I was following things right—nodded a slow, serious kind of nod, and stood very straight before us, there in the bridge shadows, his shoulders back, his scrawny bare chest rising and falling. He and Bernie had played on the same team? Had I gotten that right? Baseball, for sure, bottom of the ninth and bases loaded being baseball lingo, but how was it possible? Rocket was an old man.

Traffic on the ramp was now mostly stop and not much go, meaning folks had plenty of time to check us out. Rocket didn't seem to notice them, and neither did Bernie. He and Rocket were just standing there, Rocket smoking his cigarette, Bernie watching him. At last Bernie said, "I could use a burger."

Rocket nodded another slow, serious nod.

"How about you?" Bernie said.

Rocket took one last drag and tossed the butt away. Bernie ground it under his heel. I took a good close-range sniff of Rocket's brownish gob, lying in the dirt. Was actual tasting necessary? I was leaning in that direction when Bernie made the little chkk-chkk sound that meant we were out of there. Burgers or brownish gobs? Burgers! Burgers for sure! But that was Bernie, always the smartest human in the room. Just follow him—especially from in front, like I do—and you can't go wrong.

There are many Burger Heavens in the Valley—just one of the reasons it's the best place on earth—but our favorite is the one between Mama's Bowlerama and Mama's Kitchen, Bath and Fine Art, mostly because Mama owns it, too, and Bernie's a big fan of Mama, has told me more than once that she's what puts America over the top. Perhaps a bit confusing—I had a notion that Bernie and I were Americans and that was pretty much it—but it didn't matter. Mama's burgers were the best I'd ever tasted. I was enjoying one now just the way I liked it at a picnic table on one side of the Burger Heaven parking lot, on a paper plate, no bun, no nothing, and over in a jiff. Bernie sat on one side of the table, dipping fries into a ketchup cup. Rocket sat on the other side. He'd polished off his first burger real fast, taken a little more time with the second, and was now working his way through the next one, the number for what comes after two escaping me at the moment. Except for ordering, no one had said a thing. Now and then, Mama glanced our way from the kitchen window of the hut, her huge gold hoop earrings the brightest sight in view.

Rocket burped, sat back, searched the pockets of his cargo shorts, pulled out a switchblade knife, not an uncommon sight in my line of work, but it seemed to surprise him. He shoved the knife back in his pocket. The top of the handle, rounded off with a green-eyed human skull decoration, peeped out from inside his pocket.

"What you got there?" Bernie said.

"MVP," said Rocket.

"Most valuable player?"

"Close, real close," Rocket said. "Most valuable possession."

"What makes it valuable?" Bernie said.

Rocket shoved the knife deeper in his pocket, the green-eyed skull now disappearing from view. "Let's keep that between the two of us, me and me," he said. "Keep on keepin' it thataway." His hand was still in his pocket, rummaging around. It emerged with a bent cigarette. "Smoke?"

"Sure," said Bernie, meaning he was about to take one of those breaks from giving up smoking.

Now would be when most folks would be expecting Rocket to produce another cigarette, but that didn't happen. Instead he broke the bent one in two and handed half to Bernie.

"Thanks," said Bernie, striking a match.

They smoked in silence for a while, Rocket taking quick glances at Bernie, Bernie looking nowhere special. I got the feeling something might be going on in Bernie's mind, but whatever it was he was in no hurry. I was about to settle down under the table for a little shut-eye when the Burger Heaven back door opened and Mama stepped out with a package in her hand. She came over to the table. Rocket didn't seem to notice her until she was right there. Then he looked startled.

"What the hell?" he said. Rocket's hand went right to his cargo shorts pocket, the one with the flip knife inside.

About the Author

Lannan O'Brien

SPENCER QUINN is the pen name of Peter Abrahams, an Edgar Award winner and the author of the *New York Times* and *USA Today* bestselling Chet and Bernie mystery series, as well as the #1 *New York Times* bestselling Bowser and Birdie series for middle-grade readers. He lives on Cape Cod with his wife, Diana, and dog, Pearl.

spencequinn.com
chetthedog.com
Facebook.com/ChetTheDog
Twitter: @ChetTheDog